A
TALE OF LOVE
& DESTINY

The passionate life of a beautiful
heroine

Barry Shaw

Also by Barry Shaw

Israel Reclaiming the Narrative

Fighting Hamas, BDS, and Anti-Semitism

BDS for IDIOTS

1917. From Palestine to the Land of Israel

A
TALE OF LOVE
& DESTINY

A passionate affair. The loss of
a lover. A witness to genocide.
A tale of espionage and
courage.
For love of country.

Barry Shaw

SARAH

The sweep of the bay was always a magnificent sight.

Sarah sat on the damp sand. She looked up from the gentle rhythmic ebb and flow of the water around her naked feet to the distant horizon, a slim line drawn between the emerald blue of the sea and the lighter blue of a cloudless sky. A warm gentle breeze caressed her face.

She sat at the eastern most point of the Mediterranean Sea gazing west across the ocean, relaxed, marveling at the smooth calmness of the waters. Usually, there was motion. Today, the tide was having a day off. Sort of like her. She had done her morning chores and was relaxing in her favorite spot. On a beach that formed a bay of golden sand. There was nobody to be seen. This was as she liked it when she wanted to relax, to think, to contemplate her life. A life that had, so far, taken her from childhood, into her teen years and now into the early stirrings of womanhood. A life that was presenting her with purpose and opportunity.

Sarah was happy, content. She had helped her brother all morning to catalogue plants and seeds at the Agricultural Research Station where she worked with a passion. She was in awe of her talented brother. Now she was giving herself some quiet time before heading home.

The sea made a rhythmic soft lapping noise in a final failed attempt to produce a wave. A weak flow of water broke into a scurry of white foam that washed ashore bathing her bare feet before sinking reluctantly into the sand.

She gazed at the beauty of the scene. She was happy with her life. She considered herself a lucky girl. She felt peace and contentment. Fortunate to have a loving home and family. Happy to have someone special in her

1

life. Glad to be under the influence of such a talented older brother who taught her so much about the land that she loved and an ambition for the Future that added meaning to her life.

The day was pleasant. She drew a deep breath, breathing in the fleeting sea breeze that barely flustered the surface of the sea. Time to head home. Sarah rose, brushed herself down, put on her sandals, and strolled over to her handsome black stead that had been standing patiently, staring vacantly at the ground, seemingly oblivious to the heat of an early summer afternoon.

Sarah tenderly patted the neck of her horse. "Come on Samson, let's go home." The stallion nodded its head seemingly understanding that it was time to head home. She loved this bold, strong horse and had given it a name that suited his character and his imposing appearance. And she always felt that her favorite horse loved her back. She gathered the leather strap and began walking from the beach to the road that would take her home. The sun was about to set as she negotiated the sandy incline out of the wadi. She rode south toward the promontory and the remains of an ancient fortress. She detoured off the road along a path and approached the ruins. She dismounted and climbed up some square-shaped stones that had once been part of the ramparts. He wanted to watch the sky turn red as the sun descended toward the distant horizon.

The ruins on which she stood was a Crusader castle build to withstand attacks from powerful enemies, built to display the strength, power and prestige of a foreign civilization.

The ruins of Castle Pilgrim, or Chateau Pelerin as it was better known to students of Crusader history and architecture, commanded the small sweep of the bay. The promontory on which she stood had been cleverly selected by the Knights Templars as a sea facing fortress during the Fifth Crusade of the Holy Land.

Although it had been built to accommodate up to four thousand Christian soldiers in siege conditions, it had easily fallen to the attacking Mamelukes seventy years after its construction. The Mamelukes were an army of slave soldiers bought by an Egyptian lord who fed them, clothed them, housed them, trained them, and led them in conquests throughout the Middle East

A mutual respect was earned and the slave soldiers were loyal, to the point of death, to their master. Their glory spread and their victories were followed by architects and other slaves who built impressive structures at their places of conquest. They reached as far north as Acre, the Crusader fortress town on the Mediterranean Sea, twenty-five miles north of Castle Pilgrim where Sarah stood looking at the vision of the sun disappearing below the sea's horizon.

A few miles north of where she stood, along the road from the Crusader ruin, a large decorative wrought-iron sign impressively boasted in flowing script *"The Jewish Agricultural Experiment Station, Haifa, Palestine."* At the bottom of the sign appeared the name, *"Aaron Aaronsohn. Managing Director."* To emphasize the international importance of what lay beyond the metal sign appeared two lists of distinguished names. On the left under the heading *"Officers"* were listed *Julius Rosenwald, Chicago. President. Professor Morris Loeb. New York. Vice-President. Paul Warburg. New York. Treasurer. Miss Henrietta Szold. New York. Secretary.* The right of the large sign declared that *Cyrus Adler, Philadelphia, Samuel Pels, Philadelphia, Louis Marshall, New York, Judge Julius W. Black, Chicago* were the Board of Directors.

This stylish sign drew important visitors along an avenue decorated on either side by long rows of imposing tall palm trees that offered shade to those approaching the two wooden buildings that housed stored plants, documents, filing cabinets, research desks, tools, equipment, a kitchen, an office, the upper sleeping quarters, a large basement, and the staff that manned the station. The immediate surrounding fields displayed the orderly

3

progress of those who worked the land to test and prove the viability of plants to grow where nothing had grown for generations.

If Castle Pilgrim demonstrated the ghost of a past era, the research station showed the way to the future. It declared the genius and innovative talents of the young woman's older brother, Aaron.

But the story began before Sarah and Aaron were born.

THE BARON

Sarah shared a family heritage with much of the children of her village. It took a lot of guts and no small amount of commitment to abandon a family home, a lifetime of hard-earned possessions and personal connections, and to leave a country of birth for a distant land and an uncertain future, but this is what Sarah's parents, Ephraim and Malka, did in Romania. They joined a group of Romanians who were angry at being the scapegoats of neighbors so unhappy with their national lot that they blamed these simply, honest people with unjustified insults and physical attacks. They blamed them because they were Jews and easy, defenseless, targets. Some were so badly injured they required hospitalization. Some died. The rest, including Sarah's mother and father, collected their few belongings and made for a distant land that was once theirs.

They were the lucky ones that saw the signs early and got out just in time. That was just before the violence and the looting reached its peak and left many more innocent victims of a misplaced hate in its wake.

They made the long journey by land and sea to Palestine. There, they were sent by a central committee up to the Carmel mountain range. Here they collectively bought a tract of land from a wealthy Arab landowner. The sloping terrain was rocky. But they had come to reclaim the land by their hard work and a determination to build a new nation. To the west, their land offered the panoramic vista of a marshy coastal lowland and the blue Mediterranean Sea.

The area where the immigrant laborers dug their first shovels into the parched and brittle ground was called Zamarin. It was named after a hilltop huddle of grubby hovels occupied by fellahin and shepherds, according to the Arab who sniggered to himself at the ridiculous price offered to him by eager Jewish fools. Money in return for dead earth was always a good deal.

5

The Arab land seller, perhaps feeling a twinge of guilt at taking so much for a patch of earth that gave so little, told the local peasants that the barren land now belonged to the Jews.

He ordered them not to trespass on this plot. That was back in 1882.

The group called themselves *"Lovers of Zion,"* a name that expressed the lofty resolve that Jews would return to their ancient homeland and reclaim the land through honest purchase and hard physical work.

But dysentery plagued the poor community. Sick from impure water sources, poor from the frustrating efforts of their unproductive labor, and undernourished, some turned their backs on their miserable lives and headed to Jerusalem and Jaffa. Others packed their meager possessions and returned to an uncertain fate in Europe.

The remainder begged for help from Jewish charities and Zionist organizations. They never expected that their savior would be one of the richest men in Europe.

Agents of Baron Edmond Benjamin James de Rothschild, a member of the French banking dynasty, had heard of the efforts of a bunch of Romanian pioneers. The agents arrived one day to explore the possibility of turning the failed workers into productive farmers. They offered the settlers a deal that they, in their ravaged condition, could hardly refuse. The Baron was prepared to buy the land if they agreed to work together, collectively. The Baron was pioneering the ideal of community farming on large plots of land capable of establishing agricultural mass production. The Baron intended to create the agricultural foundation of an eventual Jewish homeland. The impoverished immigrants were in agreement. He insisted that they maintain an amicable relationship with the local Arabs in the spirit of good neighborliness.

The Baron's agents found the topography of the land perfect for the growing of grapes and the production of wine. A vineyard was established and a winery was built on the road just below the village. The grapes grown on the sunny slopes of the Carmel would go to the factory for the making of wine.

The Baron wanted Zamarin to follow the successful venture he had begun in Rishon leZion, some forty-five miles to the south, and up in the north at Rosh Pina where the waters of Mount Hermon flowed down into the Sea of Galilee.

The villagers, so thrilled to be the beneficiaries of the generosity of Baron de Rothschild, decided to rename their village. As a collective thanks to their Benefactor, they honored the memory of his late father, Jacob, by calling their community Zichron Yaakov, in memory of Jacob.

Baron Edmond James de Rothschild had taken it upon himself to help committed Jewish farmers who were prepared to engage in the physical hardship of renewing the land. The Benefactor paid for the construction of homes and farm buildings. He provided farming equipment, imported the seeds and supplies needed to create the success he demanded. The good lord was not naïve in his generosity. He sent planners to survey the land, design the village, and to allocate housing plots strictly to those who were there to offer their hard labor for the development of the community.

The villagers threw themselves on his mercy assuring him by written letter that they would put themselves into his generous hands. They offered him their lands and themselves, promising to do whatever he commanded them to do.

The good Baron sent them an agronomist to advise them how to nurture the land, an architect to help them plan and design the village, homes and public buildings, and an administrator to ensure the orderly running of the village. With these European visitors came farm equipment such as plows and threshing machines, and equipment needed in the new village winery.

The Benefactor, as he began to be called, provided the village with a doctor, a midwife, a rabbi, a school teacher, and even a *shochet*, a ritual slaughterer, to comply with their kosher meat requirements.

The Baron commissioned the construction of a synagogue that carried the name of his father to serve the spiritual needs of the community. The Baron also sent in a clerk to oversee the financial side of the enterprise. Elijah Shweid supervised the community's expenses. He allocated salaries to the resident farmers. They were expected to be productive, economically viable, and not to be dependent on their Benefactor's generosity forever. The topography was perfect for vineyards and the production of grapes and wine. After early failures that included a plague of grapevine-killing parasites, American seedlings, resistant to the plague of parasites, were introduced. Yet the little village, though attracting new residents, remained far from profitable.

The Baron made his first visit in 1887. He was accompanied by his wife. The journey by carriage from his private yacht moored off the shallow coast of Tantura up the road to Zichron Yaakov, perched on the heights of the Carmel hills, took almost an hour and a half. They were greeted by the villagers dressed in their best clothes, although it was hard to distinguish between work clothes and weekend best on some of the villagers.

The Baron and his wife remained in the village for four days. While the lord inspected all aspects of the farming, wine industry, and the overall planning of community construction, dispensing advice, and instructing his administrators on his methods of communal management, his lady examined the education, children's and women's welfare, and the medical needs of the community.

The day before the Baron's departure was a Saturday and the newly built synagogue was packed with villagers dressed in their Sabbath best. The men wore white shirts over back trousers. A few of the immigrant men still possessed suits, which they wore for the first occasion since arriving in Palestine. What good was a suit when toiling in the sun, or working in a wine factory? The women came in their Shabbat white dresses while others wore black. When empty, the village synagogue looked spacious but, with the presence of their important visitors, everyone wanted to be part of the occasion. The hall was so packed that many had to remain outside keenly trying to see and hear what was going on inside by peering through the open door or with heads pressed to the closed windows.

Pride of place was given to their Benefactor. His wife was given a center seat in the upper women's section so that she could look down on the traditional proceedings.

When the scrolls containing the Torah, the holy writings hand-written in decorative lettering by Hebrew scribes on parchment, were dressed and returned ceremoniously back into the sanctuary of the holy ark, the rabbi called upon Baron Edmond de Rothschild to address them.

The Baron rose and made his way to the center of the raised dais facing the congregation. The room hushed in anticipation.

Rothschild slowly looked around the expectant audience.

"Friends! I praise you for your dedication to our land and for your hard labor. Without this, the land will remain barren and unblessed as it has been since our people were driven out of our ancient homeland.

"Please be aware at all times that you are not doing this for me. We are all, you and me, masters of the destiny of this land. We are destined to do what we can, each of us in

our way, to develop the land and turn it into a nation. We are simply here to pave the way for the multitude that will surely follow."

The Baron paused. The room was hanging on to his every word.

"In your endeavors never forget to obey the instructions of your supervisors. They are here for your collective benefit. I urge you to deal graciously with your Arab neighbors. They will share the benefits of our enterprise and, treated fairly, they will be of service to our efforts. Treat them with the required good neighborliness.

"Keep faith with our ancient traditions so they become embedded into the fabric of the society we are developing, for what is the use of our labor upon the land if we forget that it is our heritage which, one day, we will bequeath, by loyalty and fealty, back into the possession of our people.

"And remember this, at all times, that what we are doing today will be received with grateful thanks by those who will follow in our footsteps.

"If you remain honest to these principles, you will have my undying support. God bless you, and God bless us, in this holy mission."

The congregation erupted in grateful applause for their patron. A few ungrateful souls muttered under their breath.

The next day, Sunday, the Baron and his wife departed. Before mounting into their carriage, they shook hands with the village leaders accepting their thanks for his generosity and listening to their assurances that they will do what they could to turn their village into a successful enterprise.

The Baron implored them to speedily complete the construction of the village school and to ensure the diligent presence of all the children.

"Education," he told them, *"is the only way for your children to lead the village and the nation into a better and more advanced future."*

The children presented the lady with a handsome bouquet of flowers.

As the Rothschild's carriage began the first leg in their long journey home, the villagers lined the street wearing their Sabbath clothes as a mark of respect for their Benefactor.

The carriage was escorted out of the village by a contingent of local Bedouin men. Dressed in their tribal fineries, and armed with old rifles, they acted as an honorary and ceremonial guard of honor. They too felt the importance of the Baron's visit. Although his patronage was directed for the benefit of the Jewish community they knew his visit would ultimately benefit them also. He was, after all, the Jewish Sultan.

It didn't take long for the initial enthusiasm to wane and dissatisfaction set in. Even though the Baron's agents showed goodwill by relieving their debt, returning to them the few precious articles they had hocked for loans gone bad, and paid each family an advance on salaries for their future labor, some showed a begrudging reluctance to the village benefactor. Why should they so easily hand over their land to a wealthy banker and landowner, they complained. What were they thinking? They were being treated as serfs under a feudal French lord, surely?

The Rothschilds barely had time to arrive back at their palatial French home when word was received of troubles in Zichron Yaakov. Relations were strained between the settlers and the Baron's administrators, particularly Elijah Shweid. This wasn't helped when Rothschild's man discovered wholesale pilfering of fruit and produce by some of the villagers. Not even pleas of poverty by those wanting to feed their family beyond what they received in their allocated allowance was accepted. No excuse was tolerated by the French lord's agents. It was fiefdom in a good cause, but fiefdom nevertheless.

The local Arab fellahin were stoic in their poverty. They had known nothing else. It was a condition handed down from generation to generation, but the previously bourgeois Jews found their relentless poverty emotionally draining.

Despite the arid beauty of their surroundings, the Jews lived between rocks in a harsh place. Subdued by the instructions of their benefactor to till the barren land, grumbling over their lot, suffering the strictures of their increasingly demanding Turkish overlords, bothered by the heat of long summers, they found it difficult to see something more substantial emerging from their sweat for future generations. They were, some complained, laboring for a lord who would inevitably get the honor and the glory for their manual toil.

In order to appease the discontented souls, the Baron's men took steps to improve their conditions. They filled the local library with hundreds of books and magazines. They introduced tourism with the construction of lodges and small inns to accommodate and feed the occasional visitors. This offered an alternative to the back-breaking agricultural and farming work that had been found temperamentally unsuitable to some of the villages, mainly for the women and girls. Musical instruments were bought. The villagers, including the children, were taught music and created a brass band. The villagers were even allowed to form a committee.

They met and collectively brought their complaints and requests to the administrators. All this was done under the distant but watchful eye of the Baron.

EPHRAIM

Sarah's father, Ephraim, was a rebel of sorts. Not for him the obedience to committees who dictated how to run the lives of others. Not for him to sit and order what others should bring to the collective, and how to divide it. He had seen and disapproved of wrong decisions made in his village. Not for him the conformity of Socialism. He was never happier than he was when tending his own vineyards on the slopping hills of the Carmel a few minutes' walk from his house. Ephraim attended synagogue, saying his morning prayers. Despite this, he never became subservient to the collective. He was a man of independent thought and character. He installed into his children the history and heritage of the land for his people. The driving force that had taken him from the place of his birth to this place had been grounded in historic memories and values. All were based on the land itself, the earth which muddied his boots in winter and dirtied his hands in summer.

Ephraim and Malka raised a bunch of intelligent and free-minded children. He bred a motivation into his growing sons and daughters of the importance of the cause. He instilled into them the reason for their existence in their land together with a stubborn determination to pave the way for those that would come.

For an aging man, Papa Ephraim loved talking about the future. What a wonderful country they would have when free of the Turkish yoke one day. That was the future, but Ephraim was also a traditionalist. Though not a strictly religious man he threw his family into enthusiastically celebrating the unfolding of the Jewish calendar through hearty participation in the seasonal festivals. Sarah shared his love of each passing festival. She enjoyed the variety and the unique significance that each one offered. Passover, 'Pesach' as they called it, was the season recalling her people's miraculous liberation from bondage and persecution in Egypt, just like her

13

Papa had escaped persecution in Romania, and arrival in their Promised Land, again just like her papa and mama had done, not too many years ago.

Sarah was an avid reader. She searched the library for anything she could read about her dispersed people. She was drawn to the period of the Spanish Inquisition in which her people suffered for their refusal to renounce their faith. They were cruelly tortured and executed as commanded by the Catholic Church under the edict of the Spanish king and queen. She shuddered as she read about the horrible tortures of men and women summarily arrested and put on the wrack to persuade them to adopt *"the one true faith."* Those that resisted the torture were forced to walk the humiliating gauntlet through mocking and spitting crowds to the town square and up the wooden steps to the gallows or, worse still, tied to a pole and forced to watch the church wardens set fire to the kindling wood which gradually roasted them alive.

Sarah often wondered if she would have the courage and conviction to resist the forces that hated her people so much that they would inflict such evils simply because they were Jewish. But, in Sarah's private reading, this heroism at the stake was not confined to Jews. She found a personal heroine in the form of Joan of Arc who, like her, was a simple farm girl. With no military experience the French heroine inspired and persuaded the crown prince to lead the French army and achieve a remarkable victory against the British. Joan was later captured, interrogated, sentenced and burnt at the stake on the false charges of witchcraft and heresy. Sarah read that Joan of Arc was elevated to sainthood after her death. Such faith. Such courage.

Sarah found similarities in history to the fate of the Children of Israel who, as slaves in Egypt were led to freedom and established their own land, to her dreams for her people's future. The young Sarah loved the biblical story of Miriam. In this story, Moses sister accompanied him out of Egypt and sang his praises as he led the Children of Israel on their long journey through the wilderness to their Promised Land. Promised, but not yet delivered.

She saw herself as Miriam to her father, Ephraim's, Moses. Like the biblical leader, her beloved papa, Ephraim, had made the crucial part of her family's journey from the hateful suffering of Romania, out of the European wilderness across another sea to the same Promised Land.

To Sarah, it was a destiny whose future depended on the courage and wisdom of its pioneers.

"But papa," Sarah asked her father as the family gathered to celebrate Passover together, "surely the Turks are doing to us as the Egyptians did to the Children of Israel?"

Ephraim gave his daughter a benign smile.

"They may be corrupt and dishonest," he answered, thinking of Romania, but they don't send their gangs to beat us and kill us." Then he added, "And, one day, God will return this land to us. You wait and see."

"No, papa." This was Aaron interjecting. "We will not wait and see. We will make it happen. Believe me. We will not wait for others. Our being here is only the opening act in a great new chapter in our history. It is we who will reform the land. It is us that will make it ready for those who will follow."

The young Aaron's comments showed a maturity beyond his years. They were met with approval and the raising of wine glasses.

Sarah smiled across the table at her elder brother. Aaron was well-named. He seemed to her to embody the biblical Aaron. He scouted the land seeking places where a people could thrive. He mapped out a potential land flowing with milk and honey.

Shavuot, the harvest festival marking the harvesting of the fruit, the wheat and the grapes. The Aaronsohn children loved this festival. It was all about

15

their connection to the land. The village came together to celebrate the gathering of the crops and the produce of the fields. They felt it to be their personal festival.

Her imposing father with this strong features and white beard turned his home into an educational environment for his children. He encouraged them to learn the history of the land and of the Jewish people. When Ephraim's dear wife, Malka, passed away, little Rivka dedicated herself to perform the household chores in her place. She did them so well that the family relied on her to keep the place clean. She turned into an excellent cook. They enjoyed her meals and complimented her on her ability to surprise and delight them with her tasty offerings. Sarah even whispered to her she was a better cook than mama was. The two girls giggled. Rivka was as in awe of her beautiful and strong-willed sister as she was with her impressive older brother. Sarah was happy that Rivka relieved her of having to fuss around the house. She was more excited to live the outdoor life, to understand how the world ticked and, under the spell of wonderful Aaron, discover how to make a difference to the world.

Before he became a teenager, Aaron would disappear into the fields and return with a handful of plants. He would scour his father's manuals searching for the Latin names of his botanical finds. When he couldn't find certain plants listed he pestered his father to buy books that would include details of the missing plants. His patient father tolerated his son's enquiring mind and taught Aaron how to organize and catalogue his growing collection.

As he became more knowledgeable, his enthusiasm left its impression on his brother and sisters, mainly on Sarah who was enthralled by his passionate hobby. Sarah implored Aaron to take them with him on one of his expeditionary trips. They were excited when, one evening over one of Rivka's amazing meals, the teenaged Aaron asked,

"Do you want to join me tomorrow? I'm heading south of Hadera and want you to come help me look for plants and box them for me."

"Can we, Aaron? Really?" Sarah gripped her knife and fork in great excitement.

"That's if papa will let you come with me."

"Will you, papa? Please," pleaded Sarah.

"Well, as it's during your spring break from school, why not. You may learn something from your brother. Make sure you take good care of them, Aaron, and bring them back safe."

"Of course, papa."

As the two boys and the two girls rode on horseback to the edge of Zichron Yaakov they stopped on the heights of the Carmel mountain range overlooking the coastal valley below and the blue sea beyond.

"Look," said Aaron, sweeping his arm across the panoramic view below them. "Nothing but barren landscape, a few sketchy fields being tilled by the Arabs as they have done for centuries, but mainly empty with spots of marshes and the sand dunes along the coast. But it needn't be like that."

"There," he said, pointing southward at the ruins of Caesarea, a once powerful Roman town with its grand amphitheater, it's hippodrome where they once held chariot races, a mighty port city that once was home to thousands. "And there," he said pointing to the north west," the Crusader fortress at Atlit." Sweeping his arm, he said, "and there, in the middle, Tantura, once the Phoenician port of Dor. All gone. But just think. To sustain such civilizations, this land once had timber, crops, the fruits and vegetables, the wheat and barley, to feed large populations. This was the

17

bread-basket of a thriving Judea before it was conquered by the Phoenicians, the Romans, the Crusaders. Now look at it under the Ottomans. It's gone. Desolate! Now we have come. This is our home, and it's up to us to make this land thrive and flourish again. And we will be followed by millions. They will come because this is their land. They will come to escape the hate and the persecution they suffer for simply being Jews, as mama and papa did."

Aaron spoke words beyond his years.

"Our parents experienced it and came here. Theodor Herzl witnessed it at the Dreyfus trial and wrote about the necessity of an Old New land here. They hate us over there in Europe, and our people will be drawn here like a magnet to rediscover their heritage. They will come in their masses, driven by a mission to reclaim their ancient land. This is why I believe it is up to us to us to prepare the land for their arrival. Where there is sand there will be fertile fields. Where there are dry wadi beds there will be springs and water. Where there are poisonous swamps there will be freshwater ponds. We can make that happen."

Sarah grew to love these trips with Aaron. She got to see the country, listened avidly as Aaron pointed out the secrets of the landscape, its features and its possibilities as he pointed out places from the Bible. Over a period, Rivka confined herself to the house. They gave her added work in the family herbarium. Alex enjoyed seeing their happiness but preferred to spend his spare time with his village friends. This left Sarah to accompany and learn from Aaron. It gave her life importance.

Occasionally, on these trips to new places, he would dip into his satchel and extract his Bible, knowingly flick through the pages of the good book to arrive at the verses where the location in which they stood was documented. Sarah's knowledge of the Bible was good and she enjoyed listening to Aaron explain to her the places where battles had taken place, or where biblical figures had passed.

They regularly returned home dusty, sweaty, their pack mules carrying boxes of flora for their growing collection. Sarah would help Aaron carry them into the rear house of their three house compound to catalogue their names and the locations in which they had found them. Aaron was nothing if not precise and scientific in his methods. The venture excited Sarah enormously.

One day, after they had returned to the house from another day of botanical foraging, Aaron and Sarah burst in on their father.

"Father. The plants have Latin names. Why don't they have Hebrew names?"

Ephraim smiled at his inquisitive children. He admired his constantly enquiring mind.

"Some do. They are mentioned in the Bible. Others have not been given Hebrew names. Perhaps you should start to do it for us."

They did. Armed with a copy of the Bible, Aaron, helped by Sarah, searched for biblical references to the plants, flora and fauna they had found and cross-checked each one with the samples in their records. They took pictures of the plants they found, cataloguing their Latin names, and referenced their biblical Hebrew names. When they couldn't find any, they invented Hebrew names, listing them next to their Latin titles. The precocious Aaron and Sarah even sent a list of the new plant names to the Jerusalem home of Eliezer Ben Yehuda, a man who was developing a global reputation as the father of Modern Hebrew. They received an acknowledgement from the famous linguist that he had accepted some of their names into official use. Aaron became a town celebrity after his school received confirmation that one of their village students had given birth to botanical Hebrew names.

Sarah basked in his local fame. She loved working with Aaron. She felt she was doing something new and vitally important. She felt it held a purpose to her life, and the work fascinated her. Her life fell under the spell of her charismatic and talented older brother. She adored him. She knew instinctively that he was on the road to his destiny. It was a road that she yearned to share with him, no matter where it led.

Sarah and Aaron lived in a different world to the other boys and girls of the village. As Sarah blossomed as a teenager, the boys in the village were attracted to her. She could see that by how they gathered in small groups, avidly staring at her and whispering behind their hands at school or as she passed them on her occasional shopping errands for Rivka. Her close friends among the village girls jokingly teased her by telling her which of the boys fancied her the most. An embarrassed and innocent Sarah dismissed their taunts as teenage pranks. Sarah noticed that some girls singled her out for abuse. She couldn't understand why until her more intimate girlfriends told her that they were jealous of her for attracting the attention of the boys they fancied. Sarah dismissed this with a giggle.

Sarah's busy life with Aaron and her activities with her brother kept her unaware of her emerging beauty, her striking posture, and her independent spirit. Not for her the small talk of the girls in school. She spent most of her spare time helping Aaron. Aaron noticed how receptive she was and how quickly she learned. He gave her the work of documenting and filing samples, and organizing the card system he had devised. Then, one day, their life changed, particularly for Aaron.

AARON

When Baron Edmond de Rothschild returned to Zichron six years later he was met by the village band playing *"Land of Our Forefather's Pride,"* but vexing rumors had reached the ear of the Benefactor. Despite his investments, the village debt had grown. His agents informed him that the once pioneering spirit had dissipated into bourgeois behavior by the settlers. Many had given up the hard graft of daily fieldwork. They used part of their monthly stipend to pay local fellahin to do their back-breaking labor for them. They comported themselves like low grade country squires, discussing matters over coffee, establishing committees, and bossing other people's lives. This behavior not only reached Rothschild's attention. The famous writer, Ahad Ha'am, had visited the settlement and reported that the Benefactor's unlimited financial support had produced little more than *'indolence, dishonesty, deceit, wastefulness, loss of self-respect, and other harmful traits."*

This was an embarrassment for the Baron who was doubly annoyed. Not only had the villagers betrayed his trust in them, their conduct was reaching public attention.

After inspecting his investments, he called a meeting of the village committee in the administration building opposite the town square at the end of Benefactor Street. The message was clear. He was having none of it. After hearing their complaints that the size of available land could not sustain the growing population of the village, he gave them an ultimatum to increase productivity, decrease their expenses, obey the instructions of his administrators, or face the consequences.

For the unhappy founder of Zichron Yaakov there were only two positive things he took from his visit. Some of the wines being produced at the winery were of excellent quality. He ordered a couple of crates to be packed for him to take back to France to show his influential friends that the Jews of Palestine could produce quality wine.

Rothschild also took a young and talented teenager back to France with him.

The Benefactor had an eye for talent and had heard, through his overseers, of the extraordinary ability of a young man who was obsessed with research about the land and who wanted to learn new farming methods and apply them to the barren soil of Palestine. The Baron asked to meet the young boy. An arrangement was made for the Baron to be invited to visit the Aaronsohn family home.

He was received by the Aaronsohn family, all dressed in their fineries to suit the high occasion. Sarah had bought material and, with the help of a Paris fashion magazine, sewed a couple of dresses for herself and for a grateful Rivka. They knew that young Aaron was to be the center of attention but each of them was introduced to the Baron and his lady. Little Rivka curtsied while shaking hands with Baron Edmond de Rothschild. Sarah simply bowed her head and returned her gaze into the white-bearded and dignified face of the French lord. Alex chatted informally.

During his tour of the Aaronsohn compound, which consisted of three buildings, the Baron was shown Aaron's botanical collection and his archives. Aaron explained in some detail his research and interest in botany. He spoke glowingly of Sarah to the Baron informing him of the many hours she had dedicated herself to the research and recording of his project. Over a reception of food and drink, the Baron probed Aaron about what he wanted to do with his life. Aaron's enthusiasm spilled over the dining table.

"Sir. The scientific approach to our agricultural development is far too limited. Land is often bought with little consideration to whether that land will be fertile or productive."

"Are you saying, young man, that the money I have spent on buying land has been wasted?"

The precocious Aaron leapt in with enthusiasm and little deference to rank.

"In certain cases, yes. Part of the land you bought on the western slopes is too steep and too rocky to produce anything of value or use. It was a waste of money that could have been spent elsewhere. In places where nothing will grow, why buy it? However, sometimes, sir, what looks like useless land can be the most fertile. For that we need the knowledge of what land to buy, what can be produced there, and the science to know how to convert it to productive use. Take the marsh land between us and the coast, for example. Today, it is a malarial swampland but, if the land is properly drained, it could be made fertile and productive."

"And how do you know it will ever be productive and fertile?"

"Because, sir, it was that way at the time of the Romans and the Phoenicians. Where there are malarial swamps today there were forests that were chopped down by these empires for their timber. The land became desolate and the winter rains gathered in the hollows and festered into poisonous pools. That is what we have today. It doesn't have to stay that way, sir, if we have the knowledge on how to change it."

The Benefactor turned to Ephraim.

"Mister Aaronsohn, you have an impressive family. They do you credit. Aaron is clearly a talented young man. Your son can be of great value not only to the town but to the country we hope to create one day. Palestine still lacks the institutions that can adequately develop talented young men like your son, Aaron. I would like to make you a proposal, Mister Aaronsohn. Allow me to take Aaron back with me to France. He will be under my safe protection and patronage. I will enroll him at the best agricultural college in Europe and pay for his education. It is located at Grignon. This is not too far from where I live. Your son should be given the opportunity of becoming the first European-trained agronomist in Palestine. Well, what do you say Mr. Aaronsohn? Can you spare your oldest son for the sake of our future nation?"

Ephraim's firm face broke into a smile.

"That depends entirely on the will of Aaron. If he accepts your kind offer I willingly give my paternal approval."

All heads turned to Aaron.

"Yes. Yes. I would be honored. Thank you!"

Aaron blushed as everyone broke into laughter and shouts of "Mazel Tov!" Sarah beamed proudly at her brother.

The Baron stood and shook hands with Ephraim.
"We have a deal, sir. I am sure he will be of immense benefit to our people. Your son is clearly a talented young man. Let's nurture that talent. Thank you."

Ephraim's emotions got the better of him. With a lump in his throat he could only mutter, "Thank you. Thank you, sir." He wiped his eyes and turned to his eldest son. "Well, my boy. It looks like you have to go and pack for your future."

Sarah and Rivka were crying with happiness and pride.

Aaron enjoyed his stay at the college. The gregarious young Palestinian made friends easily. He impressed them with his outgoing manner and his deep interest in whatever was taught to him. He shared lively conversations with his fellow students who were as deeply immersed in their studies as he was. He quickly made up the deficiency in his French. The Yiddish spoken in his village helped him enormously to improve his German at the school and enlarge his social group to include the students that came from Germany to study at Grignon. But the atmosphere in France was threatening. He studied during the period of the infamous Dreyfus trial. A Jewish military officer was on trial for treason. The trial whipped up a wave of anti-Semitism which frightened even the powerful French Jews such as the Rothschild family. Aaron wrote home of the disturbing political climate. It drove him to defiance. When a school registrar asked for his nationality, he boldly answered, *"Jewish!"*

On his return to Zichron Yaakov, Aaron threw himself into practicing what he had been taught and applying his newly found knowledge to the practical aspects of farming and agricultural production in Palestine where the climate and weather-affected terrain were far different from European conditions. He set out to cover as much of Palestine as he could, mapping the territory, studying the topography and the geology, gathering plant life and recording their locations. He studied why fertile land had eroded into wasteland over the centuries. He used his bible to chart where and how populations had sustained themselves on the land. He wrote theses on the subject and submitted his papers to leading European journals.

As Aaron matured into manhood, he made contact with agronomists abroad. Aaron travelled to Germany to meet with agricultural scientists. They showed him samples of *Triticum Dicoccoides.*

"This, Herr Aaronsohn," they told him, "is the holy grail of grain production. Find this, and you will have found the source of the wheat necessary to sustain mankind."

This wild wheat was thought to be the ancestor of the modern domesticated grain that was needed to be cultivated for large scale grain production.

"Finding the original sources of this wild emmer would be a breakthrough of global proportions."

Aaron took up the challenge. He told his family that he was going in search of what he called *"the mother of all wheat."*

He scoured the land searching for weeks for strains of the wild wheat that the European agronomists had told him held the future of mass cereal production. Using his knowledge of the Bible, and a history of crop production in Roman times, he searched the central and northern regions of Palestine. He trekked up arid hills and through valleys. He refused to be discouraged. This was a land where once mighty empires thrived, and they needed bread as a staple diet to survive. It had to out there, hiding somewhere. He knew it. Somewhere wheat and barley had been cultivated more than two millennia ago. There had to be strains of this hardy wheat hanging on to some sparse piece of ground. But where?

"Patience, Aaron. Patience! You will find it. It is out there waiting for you," he told himself after one of his many missions of failure.

His patience paid off. Aaron explored the foothills of Mount Hermon in the far north east region of Palestine. While checking the flora of the area as part of one of his research projects, he stumbled across a few ears of dry wheat on a hillside.

Aaron sank to his knees. Excitedly, he reached out gently to the yellowy tufts of a hardy emmer that danced invitingly in the gentle breeze. Aaron could not help himself. His eyes teared up as he stared excitedly at the spiky ears atop a dry but firm stem. Aaron was still unsure if he had indeed discovered the missing link that drove agronomists to distraction. But as he touched it, felt it, he knew for sure that here, between the springs that took the mountain rains down into the biblical Sea of Galilee, he now held in his hand *Triticum Dicoccoides.*

Aaronsohn broke into a loud celebration of laughter that bounced off the mountain side. He stood up and, with arms aloft, shouted to the world, *"I found it! I found it!"* He was almost in tears as he pondered how to extract the wheat from the land it had clung to, unnoticed, uncared for, for centuries, without damaging his precious find.

With rugged determination these few strands of hardy ears of wheat had clung to the mountainside for barren centuries despite the ravages of harsh climates and human neglect. *If it succeeded in surviving such desolation how productive could it be if nurtured, cross-pollinated, and developed for arable mass production,* Aaron thought. Despite, or maybe because of, a climate that swung from the snowy cold of winter through rainy spring into the dry heat of summer, through the windy Fall and back into another blanket of winter whiteness, it had survived unseen and unloved. *Something,* Aaron thought, *like his people,* surviving in this barren place, unseen and unloved but, with his expertise and determination they, like these few tufts of hardy wheat, would flourish, multiply and fill the land, living healthy and productive lives.

He smiled to himself. The German agronomists had challenged him to find the holy grail of wheat production. *Aaron,"* he said to himself, *"you have discovered the Holy Grain".* What would they say in Europe, and in America, when they learned that he had found what they had told him could be the harbinger of sustenance for a hungry world. As he carefully, delicately, removed the plants from the earth into which they had stubbornly sunk their roots, he knew that they could become the elixir of future life for so many people if he would be able to cajole it to flourish and multiply under his expertise and care back in Zichron Yaakov. This was his next task, perhaps a more challenging one than the long and often frustrating search

27

for their existence. These few tufts of hardy wild wheat, when grown in quantity, would give sustenance to many, industrial and productive work to others, and taxes to the demanding Turks that ruled his people's lives.

As he removed the precious plants from the earth to carefully placed them into his sample boxes on the backs of his pack mules, he considered what to do next. He would inform his fellow agronomists in Europe and America of his find. They would be thrilled by the news. He would photograph the plants on his return home and send them with his report to his overseas colleagues. There had to be a source of funding that would allow him to continue his agricultural research and development projects, particularly if they verified his find.

He smiled as he boxed the last tufts of wheat. *"Come on my beauties. You survived here for so very long. Surely you can survive the long ride home. Do that for me and I promise I will make you fertile again. "*

Aaron's discovery brought international attention. The scientific community in Europe, particularly the leading agronomists and researchers in Germany, applauded his success.

Aaron was invited to America. He was received by the top brass at the US Department of Agriculture.

"Mister Aaronsohn," David Fairchild said to him after their initial meeting, "No foreigner has ever been in my office with such a knowledge of the soils, the climate and the adaptability of plants to their environment as you. Are you sure you haven't been to California before?"

Aaron smiled. "No, Mr. Fairchild. This is my first visit but your climate is similar to large regions of Palestine."

"Well Aaron, I will help you any way I can your research can have an amazing affect in parts of America. How about accepting a senior position at Berkeley?"

"Thank you, that's very kind of you, but my ambition is to establish a research station in Palestine and continue my experimentation there."

"I'm impressed. Not many people turn down a professorship at Berkeley."

David Fairchild's calling card enabled Aaron to enter into the company of wealthy and influential supporters in New York and Chicago. Aaron pitched his case to run a network of agricultural research stations in Palestine. There was nothing they liked better than putting their money behind talented and charismatic pioneers like Aaron, particularly as he was making an impression on the American lecture circuit.

They were enchanted by Aaron. His powerful personality and his obvious scientific knowledge were persuasive. Here, he told them, was a rare opportunity for them to partner with him in developing agricultural projects in the Holy Land that would eventually feed the millions that would come to claim the land. Aaron returned to Palestine with the funding. The trustees came over from America and visited both Zichron Yaakov and Atlit. Aaron had the presence of mind to invite Turkish officials to attend the opening of the Atlit research station. Sarah was by his side as the American guests cut the ribbon under the impressed roadside sign.

SARAH

Sarah rode south along the flat coastal plain passing Tantura, a tiny low-water Arab fishing port which occasionally received small ships bearing important visitors from Europe to Caesarea and, occasionally, to Sarah's small town of Zichron Yaakov. One such guest was the generous Benefactor from France who had blessed her village and her brother with such good fortune.

When such guests arrived, their boats were moored offshore while they and their baggage were navigated down a ladder to waiting row boats that would ferry them through the gentle breakers to the fixed wooden walkway that led to Tantura beach and the waiting carriages.

When Sarah rode by that late afternoon, the shore was deserted. The Arab fishermen, having brought their daily catch ashore at early light, had retired home for a well-deserved wash, feed, and rest, waking before dawn to set out to sea with hope of better fishing the following day. Their fish had been sold and delivered to eager mouths before Sarah rode by the port that afternoon.

The ride was long. The journey usually took Sarah more than an hour but today she hurried urging Samson into a gallop until they reached the point where she needed to navigate her way through the marshes of the coastal plain. These neglected pools attracted wild boar and foxes that relieved their thirst in the brackish water. The indolent farmers refused to reclaim this wetland that had become a breeding ground for malarial-bearing mosquitoes that spread infection into the farms and villages of those who lived within range of the blood-searching bite of the insect that spawned within its poisoned waters causing constant illness and death. This was particular virulent during the hot summer months. The marsh mosquitoes shared their disease without discrimination. Arab, Jew, and Turk, suffered equally.

Sarah rode through the flatlands approaching the hills. Sweaty and swarthy fellahin would look up from their back-breaking labors at the swiftly passing apparition. A young woman riding alone in that landscape was a rare sight indeed.

She reached the narrow fertile strip between the swamps and the foothills. She headed toward the split in the Carmel range of hills. The split divided the Arab village of Faradis in the northern foothills from the rise up to Zichron to the south. Through the entrance to Wadi Milik, the gorge that split the Carmel hills and led to the huddled villages of Bat Shlomo and Shefiya to the Plains of Esdraelon and the Jezreel Valley.

The flanks of Sarah's steed reflected the late afternoon sunlight off its shiny black muscles. She stopped at a spring of fresh water that emerged out of the Carmel rocks forming a pool in the mountain side before returning underground through a rock crack that caught the pool's overflow. She allowed Samson to drink from the pool's cool waters.

As she splashed her face with the clear water she acknowledged a cry of recognition from a passing Arab. Ahmad sat at the front of his cart being drawn by a brown mule which bore its master toward his home in Faradis. She recognized him as he passed the roadside spring.

"Shalom, Ahmad!" she shouted as she passed him with a wave.

"Salaam, Sarah! The Arab responded with a friendly smile and a wave.
Faradis housed about three hundred Arab souls etching a living from the reluctant land. Most were shepherds and goat herders. Others were woodcutters, while a few tilled the land. Sarah knew some of them, the ones that provided labor or services to the Zichron villagers.

31

Sarah ascended the twisting road that took her into the Carmel hills. She passed the winery with its noise of clinking bottles and the labor of industry. The road rose and twisted more sharply. It offered a panoramic view to the north and to the Mediterranean in the west. It was known to the village as Wine Street. Instead of following Wine Street, Sarah cut off the road and followed a narrow path through the vineyards below the Davidson family home and toward the threshing floor. She glanced at Faradis spread out below her before urging Samson up to the rear of her home on the northern side of Founders Street. As Sarah rode into the yard of her Zichron Yaakov home she saw him, buried in the shadows of the house by the corner of the stable barn. Her horse strode obediently toward the barn and the handsome young man.

"Hello, Avsha. Waiting for me?"

As she dismounted from her sweaty horse he strode over to her and greeted her with an attempt at a kiss. Sarah took a half stride back. She held up an outstretched arm. Sarah's face was red from the exhilarating ride home and the embarrassment of the good looking man's open advance.

"Not here, Avsha." Sarah looked anxiously at the house.

"I couldn't stay away, Sarita. I had to see you again."

He called her by the family's pet name for her, ever since she had been a little child.

Sarah smiled. "Control yourself, young man."

She patted the neck of her horse and began to lead Samson into the barn. Avsha walked alongside her and felt for her hand. They smiled at each other. The barn had been one of the sheltered venues of their secret tryst.

Here, and at Atlit, where Avshalom was a regular worker at the research station.

Avshalom Feinberg was an impressive young man. He was known affectionately by the Aaronsohn family as *"Avsha."* He had been drawn to Zichron Yaakov by the magnetic fame of Aaron Aaronsohn. Since his arrival he had contributed greatly to her brother's pioneering agricultural project. Aaron had appointed the talented Avshalom to head the new agricultural sub-station at Hadera where the capable leader had recruited several keen young men. Like Aaron, he too had received an excellent agricultural education in France. Singularly intelligent, Avshalom was a man on a mission, a hard working young man with the ability to use his initiative. This was a quality much needed in a project that was breaking new ground in more ways than one. Avshalom was also a poet and a romantic, an excellent horseman, and a practiced sharpshooter with a spiritual soul and a burning desire to change the world. Sarah was in love with the handsome, romantic, adventurer.

From the kitchen window the diminutive figure of Rivka watched as her older sister and Avshalom disappeared into the barn together.

When they emerged from the stable and entered the main house. Sarah was no less flushed or disheveled. This was not solely due to her long ride home, nor was it from the labor of washing Samson's hot and dusty flanks. As they parted company, Sarah smiled and placed a warm hand on Avshalom's handsome face before walking into the kitchen.

"I'm here," she announced cheerily to her sister.

"Yes. I saw you arrive." Rivka was washing the vegetables in the sink.

"I'm just going to shower and change," said Sarah. "I'll be down to help you as soon as I can."

"That's alright. I've almost finished everything. Perhaps help me set the table. We have a lot of guests tonight, remember."

"Yes, I know. That's why I left Atlit early. It should be exciting, don't you think, Rivka?"

"It's always exciting to be an Aaronsohn, Sarita. So much coming and going. So much action. My work never stops."

Sarah reached over and gave her younger sister a peck on the cheek.

"What would we do without you, little one," she teased jokingly as she squeezed Rivka's cheek.

"Off with you and get that shower. You're hot and sweaty, and you smell," Rivka chided, shooing away her elder sister. "But hurry back and get the table set before our guests arrive."

"What do you think of Avsha, Rivka?" asked Sarah with a smile on her face.
"I love him," Rivka replied.

"Don't we all," said Sarah as she grabbed a freshly washed red tomato before Rivka could smack her hand away,

"Go already!" Rivka clearly commanded the kitchen of the Aaronsohn family.

The dining room seemed to shrink when the invited guests gathered around an extended dinner table that groaned with plates and dishes of steaming food. The chatter lulled into silence as Ephraim lifted a silver chalice and began to recite the blessing for the Sabbath wine.

"Blessed are Thou O Lord and God of the Universe, who gave us the fruit of the vine."

His blessing was received by a collective "Amen!" One wit said, "That prayer was written for Zichron Yaakov. What would we do without the fruit of the vine." Everyone laughed and began to dig into the food dishes. Conversation flowed around the table. The atmosphere was convivial. Most of the assembled guests were young men, though a couple of young women engaged Sarah in conversation. With Rivka shuttling between the kitchen and the dining room the guests enthusiastically complimenting her on the excellent presentation and taste of her cooking. One or two of the young men raised their glasses to her. Avshalom loudly told her, "Rivka. We love your cooking but, most of all, sweet Rivka, we love you." Rivka hastily retreated back into the kitchen to avoid showing him her blushes.

As the meal reached its conclusion, Aaron tapped his wineglass with his knife to draw everyone's attention. "Why don't we retire to my study. I have some interesting news to share with you all. Bring your drinks with you. I have a couple of spare bottles and we can keep you replenished in my study. Rivka! Join us please as soon as you finish here."

Ephraim rose. "Go about your business everyone. I'm heading for bed."

The dinner guests approached the Aaronsohn elder. Each respectfully shook his hand, thanking him for his gracious hospitality. Sarah gave him a kiss and a warm embrace. She whispered, "Good night, papa. Sleep well." Ephraim kissed her and tenderly patted her face. "What would we do without you, Sarita. I know that Aaron's job would be impossible without you."

"I love it, papa. I feel this is what I was born to do."

"Things are stirring, Sarita. You will do things that no other woman has done. Whatever you are doing now is preparing you for your destiny. Mark my words, Sarah." He shooed her away. "Go now! They're waiting for you. I'm heading for my bed. Good night, my lovely Sarita."

Sarah gave him a hug and followed the others out of the main house and across the courtyard through the white latticed portico and into Aaron's house.

The study was crammed with the assembled guests. Aaron sat behind his large desk. The visitors sat bunched together between the small window and the bookcase.

"I've brought you here to give you some good news. But first, in case you don't yet know everybody here let's do a quick introduction." Pointing to a good looking tall man, Aaron said, "this is my brother Alex, and the radiant beauty in the room is my sister, Sarah." This brought appreciative glances from all the young men present and smiles from the women who saw Sarah squirm with embarrassment. Aaron pointed to a tanned, dark haired man in his twenties. "This is Reuven. He is handy to us mainly because he only lives a few houses away from us along Founders Street." This brought gales of laughter. "No. That's not fair. His talents have been very helpful to us as have those of Avshalom. He has helped us greatly both here and at Atlit." Avshalom nodded to the assembled group. "I want to thank Naaman for coming up from Rishon leZion. As you know, like Zichron, Rishon was founded with the generous patronage of Baron Rothschild. Now Naaman has brought our science into that settlement and the south to good effect. Thank you Naaman."

Naaman raised his hand in acknowledgement.

"His brother, Eitan, has joined us. Where are you Eitan?"

Out of the crowd, a fair haired charming young man rose from his chair and was met with a round of polite clapping. "And we have another newcomer from the north. Please welcome Joseph, Joseph Lishansky." A study looking young man with wavy hair rose and nodded to the group. "Joseph used to be a member of the HaShomer self-defense group in the north. Now he is helping us at Atlit and bringing our knowledge to the northern settlements." Aaron continued, "From Hadera we have Nissan Rutman." A handsome young man of medium height stood, bowed his head, before returning to his chair. "And finally, we have Tova. Tova Gelber." A pretty young woman quickly rose and sat with a smile and a wave. "Tova lives here in Zichron. She helps Sarah with the documentation but we will be using Tova more in the future. Hopefully Rivka will join us when she finishes her chores. She has been helping Sarah in the cataloguing of our files."

Aaron paused and looked around the room. "Yesterday I was informed by our trustees that we have received a generous donation from a new donor in New York that will enable us to extend our work to other locations."

The room exploded in loud cheers. Smiling, Aaron raised his hands for quiet. "This means we can extend our reach and bring our work to the north and the south. I will be asking you to work with me in leading our agricultural development into places that I always wanted to reach but didn't have the resources or the manpower to achieve. You will be those leaders. You will recruit suitable intelligent and resourceful people to join us. Naaman, I want you to open a branch in Beer Sheba. I want you to work with me to investigate water sources and the ability to turn that desert area into a fruit basket again as it was in the past. Eitan, I want you to coordinate with us at Atlit to extend our research into the far north. Joseph. You have extensive contacts with farmers in the Galilee and around Tiberias. I want you to contact them and have them benefit from our methods and to send us data on climate and crop production. Our progress means that I will

37

increasingly need to be abroad. While I am away the project will be run by Avshalom and by Sarah. I want to take instructions from Sarah. I want you to take instructions from them. When I'm away I will be in regular communication with them. If you have any problems, they will either help you solve them or refer your problems to me. By the way, I am likely to put more strain on you in the way of requests from my European and American colleagues in agronomy, geology, and agriculture. So get ready to prove your leadership and reliability. Now, another other business?"

Reuven raised his hand. With a nod from Aaron, he rose out of his chair.

"I want to raise the problem of cattle thieves and the trespassers who ruin our crops. We have to do something about it. The problem is getting worse. I was woken in the middle of the night by Nahum Katz. Some of you may know him. He occasionally helps out in the Atlit fields. Gangs were stealing one of his cows. Not only are they stealing our animals, they let their herds of goats and cows drift into our fields and eat our crops, usually at night hoping not to be caught..."

"Wait a minute," Aaron interjected. "Who are *they*?"

"They are the surrounding Arab tribes. I rode with Nahum and a couple of other guys from the village. The fields to the south east and also those between Wadi Milik and the sea have been badly chewed up. It was the herdsmen from the neighboring villages. Baruch Shapiro is complaining he had his best milk cow stolen a few nights ago.

Aaron raised a hand. "We can't go accusing people of theft or trespass until we are sure of who is responsible. We have to maintain our good relationships with the local Arab and Bedouin. We cannot inflame things by making rash accusations."

38

"I agree," Avshalom said, adding, "but clearly we have a serious problem and we need to do something about it. We have suffered damage in our fields both at Atlit and Hadera. You know that, Aaron." Aaron nodded silently.

Avshalom continued. "It's a regular problem but as Reuven said, it's getting worse. We can't rely on the Turkish gendarmerie to deal with this. What are we supposed to do when we catch a thief? March him to the police chief and tell him to arrest him? If the damage was a force of nature I'm sure we'd come up with a plan to deal with it. We have to treat this nuisance the same way. Joseph put together a patrol that prevented a lot of the theft and damage in his area. Let him to talk to us about how he solved the problem in the north. Joseph, tell us how you operated."

The stocky man with wavy hair and a trim moustache stood. He glanced around the room, smiling at Sarah as he did so.

"We suffered a lot of theft and damage, always from Arabs brigands who ride in to steal what they can in the dead of night. We had no choice but to guard our property from people who think they can just ride in and take what's not theirs. That's how the HaShomer started. They now have a large squad of volunteers to go out on patrol every evening. They ride round the fields checking for signs of trespass. Sometimes, they prepare an ambush. We got to know which route took and followed their tracks. The HaShomer now have so many volunteers that they can rotate their volunteers so that they don't have to go out night after night as we used to do. They patrol both the private and collective lands. They act as sentries for everybody's property. They also built observation towers on the high ground to spot incoming trespassers."

Alex said, "We need to do the same here. I volunteer to recruit young men to patrol our properties." Reuven said, "I'll join you in recruiting the men and riding with them."

Joseph Lishansky raised his hand. "You cannot do it without being armed. Don't forget, you may be dealing with vicious thieves in the darkness of night. We have had a couple of our people killed. They were robbed and we found their bodies in the fields the following morning. We purchased rifles. We trained our volunteers in rifle shooting and target practice, including riding and shooting on horseback. Be armed, and do not go out on patrol with less than three men. Two to deal with any incident and a third to ride off for additional help if necessary. If there is deliberate theft by these gangs, you need to show force when you come across them."

Reuven looked over at Aaron. "You remember what happened here a month ago when Doctor Joffe was riding back to the village in his carriage with Rachel, his niece., one evening?" The out of town guest had heard rumors but didn't know the details. Reuven explained. "They were set upon by a gang who beat the doctor to a pulp before dragging the poor girl from the carriage. They raped her. This gang had been prowling round the outskirts of Zichron at night time. The doctor and his niece were on their own against a bunch of ruthless young Arab thugs out for a bit of vicious fun. They were defenseless."

Avshalom added, "I'm ready to do the same in Hadera. We have gotten to the stage where we need to defend our settlements and our people. The Turks aren't going to do it for us."

"All right. Alex. You take charge of putting together our group of defenders." Aaron warned, "Just make sure that whatever action is taken will not be reckless and endanger the cooperation we have with our neighbors. Before you take any precipitous action, make sure the trespassing was done deliberately and not negligently. I don't want to hear of any incident caused by a shepherd boy who fell asleep letting his flock stray into our fields by accident, or by someone who loses his way in the dark. We don't want to start a blood bath, or have the Turks on our necks. And I don't want any of us to get killed or arrested because of it."

Aaron looked around the room. "If we don't have any other business the meeting is over. Now get some sleep. We will meet again after breakfast tomorrow morning."

There was a buzz of excitement as the participants slowly left the room. There as much shaking of hands and back-patting as they engaged each other in informal friendly conversation.

In the courtyard, Avshalom briefly took Sarah aside and held her hand.

"It looks like I am going to be busy here. Thank you for this afternoon. Will I see you at breakfast?"

Sarah smiled up into his handsome face.

"Why not. I'll be here. I may even be the one preparing your breakfast for you. Sleep well Avsha. "

He squeezed her hand, not daring to kiss her in the presence of his project colleagues. Their affair was intimate and secret.

" Bless you, Sarita. Sleep well, my love."

In the meeting the next morning the group expanded on the proposal to form a patrol unit. Reuven reckoned he had an initial twelve volunteers ready to participate.

"We can do four patrols of three men every couple of nights. It's not possible to work a full day in the fields and go patrolling every evening to morning."

Joseph advised, "You have to build up your squad so that you can patrol every night. You can't possibly know which night they are going to come. Those committing these acts will be your local Arab tribes or Bedouin herdsmen. Aaron was right when he said yesterday there will be incidents that happen by accident or carelessness, but we found we have to respond firmly. If you don't show them that you are determined to protect what's yours they will take advantage of your inaction. You have to stop their free access to your fields, crops, and animals, otherwise they'll keep coming back and sneak off with whatever they can find. And, as I told you last night, you have to be armed. We lost a couple of farmers who weren't armed when they tried to tackle a bunch of cattle thieves. So either arm yourself, train yourself how to shoot, or don't go out on patrol."

Avshalom reminded the meeting, "Joseph's point is we don't go out at night only armed with our tongues. We never know what we are likely to encounter."

Aaron recommended, "Speaking of tongues. I recommend that Alex and Avshalom pay respectful visits to the local sheikhs and clan leaders to let them know we are no longer going to tolerate the destruction of our fields or the theft of our farm animals. Tell the sheikhs and the muktahs firmly but politely that they have to take responsibility for the actions of their clansmen and family members."

Turning to Joseph Lishansky, he said, "I want to thank you, Joseph, for taking the time and trouble to come down here and giving us the benefit of your experience, It's greatly appreciated."

Joseph replied, "Don't mention it. It gives me the opportunity of visiting you and learning firsthand about your great work at Atlit."

Aaron smiled. "We are always ready to bring our methods and knowledge to your communities up north. Our work leads the way to the future,

Joseph. We must all play our part in nurturing the earth that will feed the millions yet to come."

THE NIGHT PATROL

The recruiting, planning and training of the volunteers for the night patrol kept them busier than ever. Sarah and Avshalom had precious little time for more than the occasional covert embrace and a few discreet kisses. Avshalom frequently rushed in with information for the Atlit files before rushing off again on another mission. When he wasn't doing that he was coordinating with Alexander about the manpower and the schedule of the Atlit-Hadera joint patrol. Alexander decided to call their group *The Gideonites*.

"Remember Gideon. He was the Jewish warrior. With an army of just three hundred men he set out on the other side of the Carmel mountains to turn back the marauding Midianites from our land. Our patrol will be named after him."

The size of the Zichron Yaakov land stretched to nine thousand dunams with some isolated plots scattered around the Carmel range. The research project had more land bought in large patches that spread from north of Atlit, down the coastal valley. They included the area around Hadera, on the land that Avshalom's family owned but on which he farmed in conjunction with Aaron's projects. They also included cultivated parcels of land in Wadi Milik and approaching the Bat Shlomo village.

Avshalom and Alexander covertly purchased rifles for the members of the Gideonites. They found the most easily available weapons were second hand Mauser rifles and a number of short-barreled pistols. Their enforced absence from the agricultural projects made for an even heavier workload for Sarah which she accepted willingly. She even took time during the day to go into the fields of the Atlit station with Reuven for a spot of target practice. Sarah begged him to allow her to fire a few shots. Reuven was impressed how quickly she got the hang of it and how proficient she was with her accuracy.

"Very good! Perhaps they should add you to the Atlit patrol list, Sarah," he said jokingly.

"Of course, they must."

Reuven laughed, but Alexander and Avshalom didn't laugh when Sarah came out of the stables with her horse one evening as they prepared to go out on patrol with Reuven and Joseph. She was dressed in men's trousers, a long-sleeved shirt, and a jacket. She was ready to join their night patrol. Sarah didn't carry a rifle, but Reuven spotted a pistol in the holster on her leather belt.

"Where do you think you're going?" Alexander enquired.

"On patrol." Sarah had a determined face.

"I don't think we can allow a woman out with us."

"Don't worry. They won't recognize me as a woman in the dark." Sarah said, wrapping her bunched up hair beneath a gray and black keffiyah. "There," she said. "How do I look?" In the dimming light she could pass as a man as she mounted her tall horse. She tapped her pistol. "My extra gun may come in handy," she said to Reuven. "You told me I'm a good shot."

Reuven glanced embarrassingly at his two riding companions. Alex said with some reluctance. "Aaron is going to kill me for this but, it's your life, sister. Follow us in the rear. Let's go, boys."

He need not have worried. The night was uneventful. There was no sign of trespass, apart from the tracks of a wild boar that had passed through the lowland fields less than a mile from the swamps.

"Must have been drinking in the marshes before going back to its lair," Sarah suggested.

To break the monotony of the long night they met up with the boys at the foot of the Carmel hills by the spring. They dismounted and went to sit with them as they chatted by a small fire they made to heat the water for thick brown cups of Turkish coffee. It took a few minutes before the young men from the village realized that one of the Atlit patrol was Sarah.

When one of lads identified her after she joined the fireside chat everyone fell about in surprised laughter.

Sarah poked Alex in his side. "You see. They are our neighbors and they didn't recognize me. I told you, didn't I?"

Alexander complained, "Yes, but it will be all over the village in the morning and Aaron will kill me now for sure."

"Don't worry, Alex. If I can protect you from the marauders, I can protect you from Aaron."

Again, the young men fell about in uncontrolled mirth.

Sarah wanted to join them when Alexander, Reuven, and Avshalom discussed going to meet the local Arab village chiefs and the heads of the local Arab clans, but they convinced her that it would be disrespectful for a woman to be included in the visiting delegation.

The next day, the three men set out to sit with the tribal chiefs. They began with Sheikh Bashir of the el-Hamdun tribe. They were greeted with the traditional Arab hospitality of strong coffee and sweet sticky cakes, which were accompanied with dishes of fruit. As they sat in the chief's large tent the conversation eventually turned to the matter in hand but, when the sheikh refused to take responsibility for the actions of his tribesman led by his family members, voices became heated.

For a moment Reuven lost his cool. "Sheikh Bashir. We want good relations with you but if any of your men lay a finger on either our cattle or our crops we will demand justice from Ahmed Bek," he said, referring to the tough Turkish police chief who administered the area out of his headquarters based in Caesarea, the old Roman port built on the waters of the Mediterranean. "And he will take care of your family," he threatened.

The elderly sheikh gave a forced smile hoping it showed that he would not be intimidated. "And I will deny any knowledge of it, so save your bakshish to this corrupt Ottoman."

Reuven would not relent. "Sheikh. How can you allow your sons to steal from us? You know you got your best milk cows from us, and you bred them to produce more cows for you to feed your people."

"Yes, and I paid good money for them."

"You did indeed, Sheikh Bashir. I know that. But Ahmed Bek doesn't know that, does he? It's your word against ours, and our large bakshish added to our bottles of wine will be more persuasive than any word from you."

The sheikh was silent. The atmosphere in the tent was brooding. Then Avshalom spoke up. "Honorable Sheikh Bashir el-Hamdun," he said diplomatically, "why do we need to talk like this? We have enjoyed friendly, even prosperous relations with each other. Let us continue to respect each other. We do not come to steal from you or to cause you damage. We only come to ask for your help in stopping the theft and the damage to our property and crops. You are a wise man and a leader. Simply give us the same respect. Help us to stop the damage from the men and beast that invade our land."

The sheikh looked slowly at each of them. "You Jews are buying all the good grazing land. How do you expect us to exist with no pasture left for our goats and cattle?"

"Go east, Sheikh, not west. Instruct your herdsmen to head through the Wadi to the valleys of Megiddo and Jezreel. There is lush fertile land there between the Carmel and the mountains of Gilboa and Tabor."

"That is far."

"It's not all that far, Sheikh. Don't let lazy herdsmen and thieves damage the friendship we have between us."

"You are the law in your tribe," Alex interjected. "Show your authority and please tell the other tribes that we are determined to protect our property as you would protect yours."

1913

1913 flashed by in a blur of frenetic activity. With funding coming in from the American trustees, added to the investment for their research work from the US Department of Agriculture, the Aaronson's Agricultural Research Station spread its projects to other parts of Palestine. They recruited keen young talented men and a few women. It was a busy time for the team of dedicated workers. They began to employ local Arabs to help them in the Atlit fields and to maintain the station buildings under Sarah's supervision.

The fame of his work opened doors for Aaron. Aaron's influence reached into the highest levels of the Turkish government. He exploited his agronomic prominence by developing contacts with leading American and German diplomats in Beirut and in Damascus.

News reached them of a radical revolt in Turkey. The three Pashas, Djemal, Taalat, and Enver, led an uprising that deposed the ineffective Sultan. The Young Turks, as they called themselves, usurped power in Constantinople from the fading Ottomans. When the military joined their revolution, Mehmet, the 35th Sultan of the Ottoman Empire, was unable to withstand the popular demand for political change. The new leaders were gentle with him. They were smart enough not to bring the world down on their heads. They reduced the Sultan to an impotent figurehead, trotting him out on official occasions. The bearded and weak Sultan lived in splendid but solitary confinement in Topkapi Palace, but the rulers that replaced him were not only trouble makers at home, they went in search of conflicts beyond their borders. After losing a war to the Italians in Libya, they became embroiled in the Balkan Wars.

Palestine to them was little more than a backwater and a source of finance and sustenance through taxation. Its growing agricultural development, provided by the expanding Jewish agricultural settlements, brought them much needed food stocks and taxes. Increasingly, they raped the Palestine countryside of all it could surrender to them, though they had a vested interest in allowing the Atlit research and cultivation projects to develop.

It was a happy and active time for everyone connected with Atlit and the Aaronsohn household, though the community heads of Zichron Yaakov looked on their independence and success with deep suspicion and not a little jealousy, particularly when Aaron drove into the small town one day in a brand new Ford Motor car. It was rare to see such vehicles in the town. They usually brought wealthy foreign visitors and the rare industrialists and bankers. The car helped reduce the time required by Aaron to get to his appointments and meetings around Palestine though, truth be told, it stood for most of the time unused in the Aaronsohn compound during the lengthy absences of his European and American travels. At such times, Avshalom and Sarah ran the operations. They were greatly helped by an expanding and enthusiastic coterie of capable managers recruited from Jewish communities throughout the Turkish district of Palestine.

YOUNG LOVE

They went to the beach. Sarah and Avshalom.

"Let's go feel the sea breeze on our faces," Avshalom had suggested as Sarah put the finishing touches to her documentation and filing tasks in the office at the main Atlit building.

The day was already dimming. Reuven and Eitan still had an hours work to complete. Sarah suggested they wait for them, but Avshalom was insistent that they not waste a second of the remaining light. They grabbed a couple of towels and a large blanket.

Sarah was dressed in a loose cotton slip of a dress that flowed around her shapely legs as they walked along the avenue of palms toward to road. They chatted. Avshalom was waxing eloquent about the rumblings of war. Rumors spread like wildfire on the winds of European uncertainty.

"War is horrible," said Sarah.

"Not this war. This is where our future will be forged," Avshalom answered. "We must be ready to exploit the opportunity we will be given when the war arrives in Palestine, no matter the risk or the danger."

Sarah was excited by his firebrand rhetoric.

They crossed the road and reached the soft sandy descent to the beach. Avshalom reached for her hand which she took in the dimming light of the unlit path to the sea. He gave it a squeeze. In the growing dark she saw a warm smiling face looking into hers.

When they reached the water's edge Sarah unfurled the sheet and spread it on the dry sand. Avshalom immediately and shamelessly stripped off his trousers and shirt. He threw them on the sheet and, wearing only his white underwear, rushed into the breakers that washed ashore with the sound of the crashing waves. He dived into the surf and emerged with a hoot of celebratory excitement. "This is great! Come on, Sarita. Come in. It's wonderful!

Sarah kicked off her sandals and walked into the shallow water pulling her dress above her knees as she began to wade.

"That's my girl. Come on. Swim!"

"What! In this dress. No."

"Come on. You only live once."

She waded deeper, stopping as the waves crashed against her thighs, soaking the dress around her legs.

"Come on, Sarita. Dive in."

" No!"

Avshalom dived into the waves that sped toward the beach. They swept him ashore to the standing figure of Sarah. He grabbed her waist and pulled her into the breakers. She lost her balance and fell screaming into the water.

Avshalom laughed as she struggled back to her feet wiping the sea water from her eyes and face. Then he stared at her.

"Look at you. Just look at you. Aphrodite. Pure Venus. God, you are lovely."

Sarah was embarrassed. Her wet dress clung to her firm body. Her round breasts were emphasized by the protrusion of her nipples through the now opaque cotton fabric that contoured her slim waist before widening into her shapely hips. Avshalom was struck by the vision before him. He waded the two strides toward Sarah and put his arms around her waist. He stared into her eyes before moving his face toward hers and slowly planted a long kiss on her salty lips. She relaxed and absorbed the love he was giving her. His hands moved down her back and gently grasped her rounded buttocks. He pulled to her towards him so their bodies were bonded into one. A sudden strong wave made them stagger. Still holding each other they fell into the shallow tide as one.

The kiss remained but Avshalom's hands were following the curved shape of her hips and thighs. Sarah responded in kind. Her hands groped his back and wandered down to his firm bottom. Her heart was racing. She thought he could hear the beat as they explored each other. What was this ecstasy. This feeling. His feeling. Her feelings. She groaned at her confused thoughts. Should she fight it, resist it, or explore the exciting rhythm of love. He was trying to enter her but she groaned her refusal. The waves washed their bodies as he excitedly continued to explore her. He was kissing her breasts and nipples through her soggy dress. He groaned. She groaned. They began the dance of love as they swayed back and forth in the foam to the ebb and flow of the waves. Slowly at first but then increasing the rhythm as their passion and confidence grew. He held her close. She held him firm as she joined him in a dance of passion. The rarity of the moment, the uniqueness of the setting, added to the ecstasy of their love making. They were washed by the bubbling white foam that surged over them, providing a warm wet blanket over their heaving bodies. The sound of the waves drowned out their cries as both experienced the bliss of climax. Neither cared who was giving and who was taking. Drowning in the ecstasy. They groaned as the waves rocked them back and forth.

When they were spent they looked at each other and laughed. It was almost an embarrassed laugh. Or was it a laugh which let each other know how they felt for each other? Either way, not a word was spoken.

They emerged from the rushing waves and, clinging to each other, fell with laughter on to the sheet. They lay there kissing each other in waves of passion. As darkness fell, they shared a final kiss before grabbing the towels to wipe the water, sand, sweat, and love from their bodies. They rose. Avshalom wrapped the blanket around Sarah. Then he took her hand and walked her back into the shallow water.

"Sarita. Dance with me."

Sarah looked up at Avshalom.

"I thought we did just that. Dance. Without music."

He put her hand on his beating heart.

"Here, Sarita. Here is the music. Can you hear it beating in rhythm with yours?"

He put his hand beneath the blanket and onto her wet breast and kissed her salty lips. Avshalom pointed to the ocean.

"Listen to crashing of the waves bringing our waltz to a crescendo."

He grasped her in his arms, kissed her lips, and slowly they began to sway.

"Let the orchestra in your lovely soul play the music, Sarita. Dance with me."

She smiled. They embraced. Then, with one arm round her slim waist, they began to walk a three-step waltz in the shallow tide. They swung around in the foam as he shouted out the rhythm of a waltz with growing gusto. Sarah was laughing. She dizzied in his arms as they swirled around. They circled and spun, first one way, then the other. She swore she could hear music in her head and they splashed in the ebb and flow of the sea.
They kissed as they danced.

Avshalom gazed into her eyes as they danced.

"Smother me with your love, Sarita. I need someone special to surrender their life to me. Will you be that person, Sarita? Will you? "

"Maybe, Avsha, she teased. "Maybe."

"When, Sarita? When?"

"When our future is more certain."

"Now, Sarita," Avshalom insisted. "Now."

"Not now, my love. Not now."

"Why wait, Sarita? Who knows what the future will bring? Let's face it together. Let's go with our passion. Grab the moment. Will you be mine, Sarita? Will you dedicate yourself to me as I will to you? Will you, Sarita?"

"You're so impulsive, Avsha. You always go where your heart takes you."

"Doesn't yours, Sarita?"

They stopped dancing. They stopped their embrace. They held hands. They searched each other face. Both were searching for Sarah's soul. Sarah was a sea of confusion. A storm of emotion raged in her mind. She loved this man but the sudden proposal had caught her out. She struggled to find the words.

"Avsha. You always let your heart gallop ahead of you. I'm not ready for marriage. Not yet. I have so much yet to do. I feel like I am just starting out in life. I have been under Aaron's wing. Now he is giving me to move up in the world. I want to grab that chance. To prove to him, to me, that I can do it, that I can make a difference that will change our world. I can't let that opportunity slip by me."

"But you can do that with me, Sarita."

"I want to. I want to so much, but not in a marriage. Not now. No yet. I am not ready for it. There is so much more I need to discover about myself. I am not yet a complete person."

Avshalom squeezed her hands, "Let me make you that complete person, Sarita."

Sarah looked into her lover's eyes. "I am finding out who I am as a woman with you, Avsha, and I love that, but I need to find my path as a person for myself, with your help but by myself, and I cannot do that within a marriage. I know this flies against tradition but I need time to discover my potential, for myself, for our people. Can you understand that, Avsha?"

He opened his anguished mouth to answer her. She pressed a finger to his mouth to silence his lips.

"A marriage would mean a home and a family and that would leave me anchored, while you would be free to go out and change the world. I love you, Avsha, truly I do, but I am not ready for that. Not right now."

She touched his face tenderly and forced a smile to her lips. He was rooted, speechless, to the soggy sand beneath his cold wet feet.

"Don't ask me to make that sacrifice. Not at this time. Please Avsha."

They were standing in the water. Separated now. Two stiff figures. A divide between them that even love couldn't breach. A space where love lingered but couldn't find a mutual resting place. Time stood still in their silence. Avshalom's mind was a cauldron. He was confused, like the ebb and flow of the tide, going one way and then the other. As it swilled around his ankles, his brain swirled. The poet in him was lost for words. The man of ideas was bereft of an adequate response, unable to mouth a plea. He felt drained. Sarah was in shock at herself. *What have I done? This was my chance. To surrender to my lover and leave the world to sort itself out and me with it.*

As they began to walk silently away from the sea Sarah's mind continued to rage. *Why am I rejecting him, the man I want more than any other? Am I being selfish and stupid, too tied up in myself and my ambition? Am I better off forgetting about my life, my destiny, and just surrender into wedded bliss with Avsha?*

Darkness surrounded them as they groped their way off the sand and up to the road. Before crossing, Sarah turned to Avshalom and said, "I do love you, Avsha, but there are things I must do."

He looked at her and smiled a sad smile. "And I love you too, Sarita. I always will."

THE POEM

When they met the next morning Avshalom greeted Sarah with a kiss, but there was a sense of distance between them. In the following days Sarah would gaze at Avshalom as he left his frequent meetings with her. Part of her pined for a missed opportunity, but her heavy work load always dragged her back to the importance of her responsibilities.

It was a busy time for the crew at Atlit. New young recruits, both men and women, joined their staff. Local Arabs were employed to help in their field work. Frida and Adal were taken on to help around the building and the compound. Their work was appreciated and a bond soon developed between them and Sarah's team. The generous help of their American donors allowed them to grow. Sarah burnt the midnight oil writing up reports to send to the trustees. Their American trustees demanded nothing less than transparency and progress with the money they were dispatching to them. Atlit became a conduit of funding for the settlements that met the approval of their American donors. All this required meticulous book-keeping by Sarah. It was not exciting work but necessary in maintaining the faith and goodwill of distant supporters.

Draining the mosquito-filled swamps on the coastal plain required the importation of eucalyptus trees from Australia, a major project and ambitious work that would not have been possible without healthy American funding. Sarah occasionally joined Aaron and Avshalom in inspecting the efficiency of the eucalyptus trees. The roots of the Australian trees sucked up the brackish water greedily.

Aaron trained some of the staff in how to conduct and record meteorological studies throughout Palestine, Syria, and Lebanon. Aaron asked Naaman Belkind to accompany him down to Beer Sheba. There, he carried out a geological survey to find hidden sources of water. Once Beer

Sheba had been a flourishing oasis. Now it was a sad, dry hovel of a place but with growing importance to the Turks as a way station from the north to the south of Palestine. Aaron demanded a more scientific approach.

Based on advice he received from his Californian colleagues he searched specific areas around Beer Sheba and carried out preliminary surveys of rock formations. Together with Naaman, they dug and drilled and brought back samples of rocks and sand to record their physical properties, and to detect locations where hidden aquifers, buried for centuries under the desert sand and rock, could be hiding.

This hidden water project excited Aaron as much as his search for the special emmers that were beginning to flourish in the welcoming soil of Atlit. Water in that arid landscape would make the desert bloom again. They found salt crystals below the surface indicated locations where water could be found with a deep dig once the financing was found to excavate and sink shafts. Needless to say, when Aaron pleased with the Turkish authorities for funds to dig, the Turks pleaded poverty despite the fact that an increased water supply was essential for their growing needs in Beer Sheba. Using their usual indolent nature as an excuse, they informed Aaron that they had sufficient water from the existing wells. And so the desert remained a desert, apart from the sparse locations where the Jews were making the desert bloom.

A couple of months went by and Sarah's increasing responsibilities brought her to travel widely throughout Palestine, visiting the outlying satellite stations in the north and south that were part of the growing Atlit agricultural network. There she met and talked with the keen young farmers who went about their work with great enthusiasm and dedication. Travel was cumbersome and slow but she knew that Avshalom was managing the center in her absence. Aaron was, as usual, abroad for much of the time courting their donors and returning to them the knowledge and results of their experiments in agricultural development.

Sarah was often escorted from one farm to another on horseback or carriage by one or a couple of the pioneers who were armed in protection of the girl they adored. They refused to listen to the fearless Sarah's protests that their presence wasn't necessary. They would not let her ride alone. Any excuse would do. Just to spend that extra time with her was a good enough reason to ride alongside her on a wagon or on horseback engaging in conversation. While she travelled, Sarah spent some of her time visiting families of her team or interviewing potential new candidates to be employed in the Aaronsohn experiment.

She returned to Zichron in the early afternoon of a late fall, tired but satisfied with their growing influence on the land and in the communities. Sarah, respected her father's wishes to spend the holy days of the Jewish New Year and Yom Kippur, the Day of Atonement, with the family and, as the dutiful daughter that she was, she kept to that schedule. In addition to the traditional event the family also had an important visitor from Constantinople coming over for dinner a couple of days before the auspicious New Year. Aaron had also arrived back from his foreign travels. It promised to be a busy week at the Aaronsohn household. There would be much to discuss during the holiday period.

She found the house in bedlam as she carried her luggage with the help of one of the family workers to her bedroom. Servants rushing everywhere, cleaning, preparing linen, cooking food.

As she unpacked one of her trunks, Rivka burst into her room. She rushed up to Sarah excitedly and greeted her with a huge hug and a noisy kiss.

"Welcome back, sister. Have you heard my wonderful news? Have you heard, Sarita? Avsha and I are engaged!"

Sarah was stunned.

Rivka, with a big smile on her happy face, extended her left hand proudly displaying a silver ring.

"I'm engaged Sarita, to Avsha. Isn't that wonderful?"

Sarah struggled to find the words.

"When did this happen? So suddenly. What? When?" she stumbled.

Rivka happily bounced herself on Sarah's bed.
"It was quite sudden, actually. I've always had a crush on him. You know that, right, sister? Well, after you told him you didn't want him, about three weeks ago he sent me a love letter. Then he asked me to meet with him, privately," she said coquettishly, "and he told me how much he liked me. Well, one thing led to another, and before I knew it he sent me this…"

Out of her pocket she handed Sarah a couple of sheets of paper. The handwriting was clearly Avshalom's. She began to read a poem.

> 'A thousand kisses to you my love
> A thousand, a kiss, and a kiss.
> A thousand kisses to you my dear one
> So small, so sweet, so beautiful.
> And also to your ivory white innocent neck
> Flexible like the neck of a swan.
> I will cover in a chain of kisses
> Girl of pure water, my little one.
> And now I will put my head on your breast
> In order to find in it your heart
> And kisses for no reason too without lust or limit
> Like flowers thrown for a bride.
> A thousand kisses to you, my love
> A thousand, a kiss, and a kiss.

A thousand kisses to you, my dear one,
So small, so sweet, so beautiful.'

Sarah couldn't read any more. Weary from travel and now suddenly this. It was too much for her. She began to shake. Her face was ashen.

"What's the matter?"

Rivka noticed her sister quaking. Sarah summoned a smile from somewhere as she struggled with the news.

"It's nothing, my little sister. I'm exhausted, that's all. Congratulations, Rivka. I'm so happy for you. I know you'll make him very happy."

Rivka bent over and gave her older sister a hug.

"Thank you, Sarita. I know you two like each other. It will bring us even closer together. Avsha will become a part of our family now, won't he?"

This thought left Sarah more bereft than ever.

Sarah looked at her slim little sister. *So sweet, as Avsha had written.* And so naïve she thought as she struggled through her confusion. *Jealous?* Yes, she was. Yet Rivka's naivety would be perfect for Avshalom. She would be right for him. *Would I? Would I have been right for him? Would he have been right for me? Have I missed the one chance at a perfect paradise of love?* She knew she would never find another like Avsha.

They hugged. Rivka's hug was one of joy. Sarah's hug was one of sorrow.

"Now get out. I want to rest before dinner. Run off to the kitchen like a good little housewife."

Rivka giggled, gave Sarah a big kiss on her cheek and skipped out of the room.

Yes, Rivka would be there for him, steady as a rock. Nothing would suit her better than keeping his house in perfect condition, giving him children. She would be there, feeding him, laying out his clothes, fussing over him, caring for him, doing all his bidding, lovingly soaking in his overwhelming passion that would leave her head and her heart with little thought for anything other than providing him with her love, care, comfort, and the family he craved for. Lovingly soaking in his overwhelming passion…

Sarah lay on her bed and cried. Eventually, she crawled to the bathroom to wash her face. She stared at her reflection in the mirror. *Stupid girl! What have you done? You have given away the man of your life for a life unknown.* Sarah tugged the soft towel to her face burying herself in the turmoil of her thoughts. *Did I do the right thing by not accepting him above everything else? Have I made the biggest mistake of my life?*

She tormented herself with impossible questions. Questions she couldn't answer. She had made her decision. Now came the consequences. *Was it impulsive of me to reject the one I love?* Had she loved Avsha conditionally? Not willing to make a lifetime commitment?

Sarah returned to her bed not willing yet to join her family. She stared at the ceiling trying to think things through, but her mind was a whirl giving her no conclusions, no rest, until the sleep of physical and emotional exhaustion overtook her.

THE VISITOR

Sarah slept the sleep of the dead. Out to the world, until she was roughly disturbed by Alex, her brother.

"Wake up, sister. Wake up!"

Sarah stirred, recognizing his voice.

"What time is it?" she asked in the drugged voice of the semi-conscious.

"What a way to great your brother."

Alexander gave her another shove. "Come on, get up. You're late. Everyone's downstairs waiting for you."

She opened her eyes. "Hi Alex. How have you been?"

"I've been fine, Sarita. Now get out of bed and come downstairs. Immediately."

He gave her a kiss and a tickle in her ribs to revive her and to make sure she was sufficiently awake to get out of bed. Sarah threw a pillow at her departing brother, and then sprung from the bed to select a dress to wear for the evening. She hurriedly washed her face, pinned up her hair, dressed and made for the stairs. She could hear voices coming from the family dining room. She took a deep breath. As she entered the room she was greeted by cries of "Here she is!" Her brothers and Rivka broke out is a derisory round of clapping. "Her majesty has decided to grace us with her presence," Alex remarked.

Aaron rose and kissed her before placing his hands affectionately on her shoulders. "How are you, Sarah? How was your schedule? Did you achieve everything you set out to do?"

"Tiring but fine, thank you Aaron. I'll discuss it in detail with you tomorrow morning when I've pulled myself together, if that's all right with you? How was your trip?"

"I'll tell you about it after dinner."

Sarah nodded and went to her seated father. She planted a kiss on his forehead.

"How are you, papa? You look well."

"I am, my daughter. Good to see you again. May I introduce you to our special guest?"

He pointed to a distinguished looking man seated to his right.

"May I introduce you to Chaim Abraham. He joins us from Constantinople."

The visitor rose, received Sarah's extended arm, and politely kissed the back of her hand.

"Delighted to meet you, Miss Aaronsohn. I have heard so much about you."

Chaim Abraham was a well-dressed sturdy man who appeared to be at least a decade older than Sarah. "Welcome to our house, Mr. Abraham."

"No, please. Call me Chaim."

Sarah nodded politely at the guest and made her way to the vacant chair. She looked around the crowded table. Avshalom wasn't there.

"Where's Avsha?" she whispered to Rivka.

"He's not here. Isn't that a pity? He is spending the New Year with his family in the south," Rivka answered sadly. "Come on, Sarita, come to the kitchen and help me serve the food."

The girls rose to leave the dining room. Sarah nodded politely to their guest.

"Well? What do you think of our guest?" Rivka asked as they reached the kitchen and began taking the warm food out of the oven. "I hear he is very rich, very influential, and not married."

"Is he?" said a disinterested Sarah as she and her sister took the hot food from the oven and began to divide up the portions onto the serving plates and place them on a trolley. They worked quickly before pushing the food trolley into the dining room.

"What wonderful girls I have!" Ephraim beamed at them and the men applauded their arrival. The sisters placed the large bowls of steaming food on the table and returned to their places as the men began to take the food from the various dishes onto their own dining plates. Chaim solicitously passed the food dishes to Sarah before he took his own share. The conversation was about family and local matters. Chaim Abraham told his hosts that although he was born and raised in Germany and, indeed, still had a house there, he was now spending most of his time in Constantinople due to his business interests.

Alexander asked, "What brings you to Zichron Yaakov, Mr. Abraham?"

"I came to Palestine to explore some business possibilities. The Zionist enterprise is producing products that, because this place is under Turkish sovereignty, makes it potentially interesting to export items from here to Constantinople and then distribute them to Europe via Germany. I hope to open markets in Germany for your excellent wines. I came here from Rishon leZion where I visited the Baron's wineries and sampled some of their excellent wines. I intend to meet the management of your winery here immediately after Rosh HaShana," he said, referring to the Hebrew name of the Jewish New Year.

"I have heard so many excellent reports about your work, both in Germany and in Constantinople, Mr. Aaronsohn. I would very much like to hear more about it from you and to visit your famous research station.

Everyone in Germany is talking about it. The Turks even boast about it in official circles in Constantinople."

"They should," Alex retorted. "They take so much out of it without putting a stingy kurus into it," he said referring to the old Ottoman coin.

Aaron diplomatically silenced his younger brother.

"I will be delighted to show you what all the fuss is about, Mr. Abraham."

"No, please, as I said to Sarah, call me Chaim. Let's not stand on ceremony here. I feel I am among friends."

"Both my brothers are correct," Sarah interjected herself into the male conversion. "And Aaron is being too modest. Thanks to his genius, our project is one of the few bright spots in Palestine."

A smiling Chaim Abraham looked appreciatively at Sarah. "I understand that you play an important role in the organization, Sarah?"

"I do indeed, Mr. Abraham...Chaim...My brothers entrust me with the running of the venture together with Avsha, I mean Avshalom Feinberg. He's the one who directs the operation when Aaron is away."

"I'm impressed. I very much look forward to visiting Atlit, Aaron."

The evening passed with convivial conversation. Rivka, between serving courses, chatted with her brothers and Mr. Abraham about her engagement. Sarah listened but remained detached from the small talk.

In the general conversation Chaim Abraham explained that he had close contacts with the hierarchy of Turkish business, banking, and political life in Constantinople where he owned a house and a busy office.

As the evening drew to a close, the men retired to another room to smoke and to drink brandy. Sarah helped Rivka clear the dining table and wash the dishes and cutlery in the kitchen sink. As they chatted in the kitchen all Rivka could talk about was Avshalom. Sarah remained silent.

Ephraim escorted his guest out of the house through the graveled compound to the wrought iron entry gate. Chaim Abraham turned to him.

"Mr. Aaronsohn, I hope you don't think it presumptuous of me to enquire if your daughter, Sarah, is betrothed, or seeing anyone?"

"No Mr. Abraham. Why do you enquire?"

"She seems to me to be such an intelligent and capable young lady. It's a wonder that nobody has swept her off her feet."

"She's a strong minded girl, Mr. Abraham. Much too senior for her years to tolerate flighty young men. Sarah is too grounded and responsible in her habits for flippancy. I suspect, Mr. Abraham, she hasn't yet met a serious enough suitor."

Thoughtfully, Chaim Abraham shook his host's hand.

"I thank you, sir, for your generous hospitality. You have a delightful and interesting family. Allow me to call on you again before I leave Zichron Yaakov."

Sarah was in the kitchen the next morning when her father walked in.

"Can I get you anything, papa?"

"Just a cup of coffee, thank you, Sarah."

As Sarah poured the thick bitter Turkish coffee into a small glass, Ephraim sat at the kitchen table.

"You made an impression on Mr. Abraham last night, Sarah."

"Don't be silly, papa."

"Yes you did. He was smitten by you."

"Why would you say such a thing, father?"

"Oh, I don't know. It's just an impression I got. When he was taking his leave of me all he could talk about was you."

"Nonsense, papa. He was just being polite, I'm sure."

"Don't be so sure, daughter. Don't be so sure."

Sarah and Rivka accompanied their father to synagogue on the first Day of Awe to soak themselves in the solemn prayers of repentance where man pleads with God for forgiveness for his human weaknesses and sins. It is a period of contemplation and, this year, Sarah had a lot to contemplate. As they made their way down Founder's Street to the synagogue, they acknowledged the greetings of some of the villagers. Sarah walked in silence as Rivka chatted gaily with her father.

The girls entered the house of worship, kissed their father, and made their way to the women's section to listen to the inspiring ancient lyrics sung by the cantor in front of the open doors of the holy ark that contained the ornamentally decorated Torah, parchment scrolls containing the intricately hand-written Hebrew text of the five books of the Old Testament.

With the tremulous rise and fall of the tenor voice of the chazzan, Sarah was transported to her inner thoughts. They revolved around where her life had brought her, and where it was taking her. The spirit of the temple, on this auspicious day, was fused with the sounds of the congregation chanting in harmony with their prayer leader. As they sang their devotions, Sarah reviewed her life and her emotional turmoil over Avshalom. She tried to rationalize her fateful decision about him but the pain was still deep inside her. She looked at Rivka sitting next to her. She was wrapped in her concentration of following the Hebrew service. Sarah loved her sister. She had, she thought, unintentionally gifted her with her one true love. Here, in the sanctity of this place, at this awesome time, it seemed to cleanse her soul. She looked down into her prayer book and her eyes fell on the words of a psalm; *"As for me, may my prayer to You, my God, in Your abundant kindness, answer me with the truth of Your salvation."*

The intermediate days between Rosh HaShana and the Day of Atonement were a frantically busy time for the Atlit network. Sarah rode to Atlit with Aaron and Reuven Schwartz who lived up the road and was an eager recruit to the enterprise. Sarah noticed that Aaron was in ebullient mood.

70

They detoured to examine how the flourishing eucalyptus trees were draining the coastal swamps, before heading north along the coast to the station.

Reuven busied himself with checking with the loyal Arab field workers how things had progressed over the last few days and advising them on the work that needed to be done in the coming week. Aaron was everywhere, both in the orchards and fields, in the archives, and then in the office with Sarah. They sat with Abu-Farid, their loyal driver, trusted messenger, and reliable employee, and set him a schedule of visits to their Rehovot branch with money and instructions and then to do the same with Naaman Belkind in Rishon leZion. They dispatched him with detailed instructions of what they needed from them. Abu-Farid was to bring their reports and samples back to Atlit to be dealt with after Yom Kippur.

The workload meant that Aaron and Sarah slept at Atlit overnight. Reuven also remained there for another day. They spent the evening discussing developments. Aaron chatted about his meetings in America and how their efforts were being favorably received both by their trustees but also by a US Department of Agriculture that valued their contribution to their knowledge, particularly on desert agronomy and cultivation. He spoke about the vast arid landscape of America that made Palestine miniscule by comparison. The Department of Agriculture, Aaron explained, deeply appreciated the results of their experimentation and findings to the effect that the State Department had informed their embassies in Damascus and Constantinople to cooperate with him on any future issues relating to agronomic matters. In particular, Aaron had requested that their embassies in Syria and Constantinople emphasize to the Turkish rulers how important the efforts of the Atlit agricultural project was to the United States. Then Aaron surprised them.

"Sarah. I never thought I would succeed so quickly but, I have to tell you, I just received a telegram that no less a figure than Henry Morgenthau, the

American Ambassador to Turkey, will be visiting us sometime next month."

Sarah clapped her hands in excitement. "Well done, Aaron."

Aaron went on, "I want you to help with the arrangements of his visit. I'll give you the schedule when I have the exact date. When he comes it will be a timely reminder from Washington D.C. to the Pashas how much America appreciate our efforts."

Sarah loved her brother dearly. Now she saw how he had grown into an accomplished diplomat.

The next day, after helping Aisha and Amira to clean the rooms at Atlit, Sarah joined Aaron for the ride back to Zichron. Reuven needed more time to finish his work schedule and stayed on for another night.

As they rode into the compound, Avshalom was there waiting to greet them. As they dismounted he walked over and shook hands with Aaron. He gave Sarah a kiss on both cheeks. Without wanting to stare she saw how well he looked. Her heart skipped a beat. Clearly refreshed from the few days' break that the High Holidays had afforded him, he seemed full of his usual dynamic energy. Avshalom glanced at her. There was an embarrassed look on his face as he quickly engaged Aaron is conversation. Aaron was oblivious of this barely noticeable exchange. "Come, Avsha. There is something I need to discuss with you."

Sarah gathered the reins of her brother's horse and together with Samson, led them into the stables, as the two men walked towards Aaron's pink-stucco house.

After stabling the horses, Sarah headed to the kitchen of the main house to get herself a glass of water. Rivka was preparing dinner. She was happily humming. Sarah understood why. Avshalom's arrival lit up little Rivka's routine world. After the normal small talk, Sarah excused herself saying she was going to take a shower and get ready for dinner. She detoured into the study to kiss her father who was reading a newspaper. He gave her hand a squeeze and smiled before she headed for her room.

Later, when Sarah came out of her room, she found Avshalom hovering at the bottom of the stairs. He waited as she descended before approaching her.

"Sarah. I…"

"Avshalom! How are you my friend?" Alex emerged from the study and walked over to shake Avshalom's hand. "How are your people at home? Well, I hope?"

"Yes, Alex. Everyone is fine. Thanks."

He noticed Sarah walking rapidly away from him toward the kitchen. Avshalom had little choice but to engage Sarah's brother in work conversation.

After dinner, Sarah followed Aaron as he led Avshalom and Alex across the courtyard to his house for an informal business chat. As they sat in his book lined study, Aaron began discussing the upcoming visit of Henry Morgenthau to Zichron. He told Avshalom, Sarah, and Alexander that no one in the village should know about his visit until Aaron had received a definite date and that the schedule had been arranged by Morgenthau's embassy staff. When pressed, Aaron estimated that the Morgenthau visit would take place sometime toward the end of winter or early Spring of the next year, 1914.

"He will not be here on an official visit to the town. He will be here to learn more about our projects. Any community formalities must be kept to a minimum as his time here will be short. He can visit the winery and the soap factory, but we control the time and his schedule. Understood?"

They were treated to Aaron's anecdotal experiences in America, and how their influence had spread. Sarah had already heard his story. They talked about the money supply that had to be sent to Meir Dizengoff, an entrepreneur that was building a Jewish suburb just north of Jaffa. They chatted about this new modern community which was attracting much attention in America. It was to be called Tel Aviv.

Aaron offered the view that, "a Jewish Palestine will not be complete without its bustling cities. This doesn't conflict with our mission. It compliments it. These cities will attract more Jews to come live here, to give them housing, employment, education. All of them will need to be fed. Hence the growing importance of what we are doing. We have to buy more land, farm more fields, find the resources to grow more crops, develop methods for mass crop production."

He continued, "We need to plan for the industrialization of crop production. This will require a mechanized system of ploughing, planting, harvesting the crops. It's good to have thousands more to work the land but, eventually, manual labor will prove too inefficient for the essential mass production of food stocks in a country of millions."

Sarah was in awe of the far-sighted vision of her brother. She turned her head away whenever Avshalom glanced at her.

Sarah gave a report of her pre New Year tour of Palestine. She handed over a list of new names she had recruited during her trip and gave an anecdotal account of the qualities of each candidate.

74

Later that evening, as they left Aaron's house under the dark shadows cast by the tall palm trees, Avshalom caught up with Sarah as she made her escape following the meeting. He grabbed her arm.

"Sarah, please. I wanted to tell you about Rivka but you weren't here and I wasn't here when you returned from your trip."

It was 'Sarah,' now, not 'Sarita,' she noted.

"That's all right. You are free to do whatever you like."

"Don't be mad at me, please, Sarita." He always knew how to read her thoughts.

"I said, it's all right. I'm over it." But she wasn't. "I hope you two will be very happy. Rivka will take good care of you. I'm sure of that. She is happier than I have ever seen her. Don't break her heart." *As you broke mine,* she thought. *No. That's not fair. I was the one who chose to end it.*

"Let's not be enemies," Avshalom pleaded. His voice was sincere. From somewhere, Sarah forced a smile.

"We will never be enemies. How could we be?"

They smiled awkwardly at one another.

"I'm tired, Avsha. It's been a long day. Good night."

"Good night, Sarita. Sleep well."

Sarah allowed herself a hug from her former lover, now betrothed to be her sister's husband. Try as she might she couldn't come to terms with her anguish. It weighed on her mind and on her mood. She couldn't repress the feeling of longing for him. She was smitten. Whenever she glanced at him her heart throbbed.

Later in the week, the day before the auspicious Day of Atonement, Ephraim invited Sarah to sit with him. Despite their closeness it was rare for her father to talk with her privately. Generally, he gave his fatherly advice about life in family gatherings or while walking together, but he rarely offered his opinion on how they should deport themselves. He took pride in the mature and responsible demeanor of his offspring. They were, to him, a source of pride and joy.

As they sat in the armchairs of the family lounge, Sarah noticed he appeared edgy. Ephraim looked at his eldest daughter through his bushy grey eyebrows. His strong face a mask of seriousness.

"Sarah. Rivka has been pressing me to allow her to marry Avshalom. You know this, of course?" he enquired.

Sarah nodded. "I do, yes. Papa."

There was a silence. Ephraim clearly searching for the right words.

"Of course, I am ready to give her my blessing. I allowed them to become engaged, but she is pushing me to give her a date for her wedding."

Again, a pause.

"Sarah. According to our tradition I cannot give her permission to marry while her older sister is still a spinster."

The silence was held. Sarah tried to collect her thoughts.

"I don't understand, papa. What has this got to do with me?"

"Sarah. You know we follow our laws and traditions wherever we can. Rivka cannot marry until you have found a husband."

"Why not, papa? Let her be married and allow me to choice my own direction."

"It cannot be, Sarita. What will people think…"

"Who cares what people think? What business is it to them if Rivka marries before I do?"

"It is our faith's business, Sarah. It's our societies business. Can we be seen as the bad example in our community? Have we lapsed so far away from our customs? No, Sarah. I cannot allow this to happen. I wish you to take this seriously."

"But this is so old fashioned, papa. So out of date. What if I decided not to marry? Would that mean that Rivka could never marry? It's preposterous, papa."

"Old fashioned or not, that is how it must be, Sarita. Think on it."

Sarah was at the precipice, for the first time in her life, of defying her father. Her love and respect for him could not prevent her from standing her ground. How could he demand that she marry? To whom? Despite her affection for the handsome young men associated with her work there was no one she considered romantically. Neither was there anyone in the town who appealed to her, although many of them were clearly attracted to her. What was she to do with this dilemma? She felt the need to extract herself from this conversation.

Playing the dutiful daughter, she muttered, "I will, father." With a nod from her father, she got up and left the room.

They observed the family tradition of fasting and participating in the solemn synagogue ceremony that was Yom Kippur. From the opening incantation of *Kol Nidre,* a rabbinical plea on behalf of the congregation to God that each individual obligates to take upon themselves the vows demanded of their faith, and throughout the twenty five hours of collective and private prayer, confession and commitment, expressing the determination to shake off the jealousies and transgressions of the past and to go forward with a pure heart into the future, to the final *Kaddish* and the sounding of the shofar, the ram's horn that heralded the arrival of the Children of Israel into the land that God had promised them. Throughout it all Sarah brooded. She felt the familial pressure to allow her sister to marry the man they both adored. She had become the obstacle blocking the future of Rivka and Avsha, the only man she had truly loved.

"Sarah. The latest accounting to our trustees is wrong. You have included figures that make little sense to me and the final figure seems excessively high. You've also made several grammatical errors in our letter to them."

Sarah was standing in Aaron's study. He brother was seated at his desk studying the papers in front of him. He looked up at her.

"This is most unlike you, Sarita. What's wrong? What's troubling you?"

How could she tell him that she had become so distracted, her emotions so muddled, that the efficiency of her work was suffering? How could she tell her brother that she was stuck on the horns of a dilemma with no discernable solution? How could she burden her imposing elder brother with her private problem? For all the love of their kinship she couldn't bring herself to divulge her distress.

"I'm sorry, Aaron. Give them to me. I'll go over them immediately and give you them back within the hour."

As he handed the papers over to her he said, "I'm worried about you, Sarita. Let me know if I can help you with anything. I'm here for you. You know that, don't you?"

With a nod Sarah received the papers and hurriedly left the room. As she exited the house she burst into tears. Embarrassed, she took out a handkerchief to hurriedly wipe her eyes before anyone could see her as she crossed the compound.

As she entered the main house she heard murmured voices and giggles emanating from the kitchen. She identified them as the happy voices of Rivka and Avsha. She quietly but quickly rushed up the stairs to her room and closed the door quietly behind her before collapsing on her bed in a storm of tears.

It must have been an hour before she managed to compose herself. She rose from her bed, went over to the large mirror where she adjusted her rumbled dress. She walked to the bathroom sink and washed her face. As she toweled herself she stared into the mirror at the sad eyes that met her gaze. After combing and pinning up her hair she took a deep breath, left the room, and walked slowly down the stairs. She headed to the study of the main house and found her father reading a book in his favorite armchair.

"Papa," she said. "Please tell Mr. Abraham that I agree to marry him."

MARRIAGE

The wedding took place at the agricultural station in Atilt.

They rode along the palm-lined avenue and found the workers had decorated the building. Sarah had insisted on it. She didn't want a communal display with the whole of the town gawking at the bride and groom. She wanted, she said, a private family affair. Chaim Abraham readily agreed. It was a good sign, he thought, that his bride was a thrifty person, not easily taken to extravagancies. She wasn't, but that was not the reason for her resistance to a public affair. Sarah was concerned for her emotional state had Avsha been present with his arm around her sister's slim waist. How much more difficult would it have been with the town folk gossiping about an ill-matched couple being escorted to the synagogue for their marriage. As it turned out, Avshalom was not in attendance at the wedding. Rivka whispered to her that Avsha had a bad cold and had taken to his sick bed. *Perhaps he couldn't bring himself to see me marry someone else?* Sarah banished the thought as Ephraim walked her across the gravel to the wedding canopy.

Tables had been set up and acted as the reception for the food and drink after the traditional wedding ceremony. Although only a limited number of the team leaders had been invited including Abu-Farid and his wife, both Aisha and Ayala were on hand to serve the guests.

The marriage night was an embarrassment. Chaim's gentle endearments were awkward and formal. Sarah remembered Avsha's poetic passion. The groping under her nightgown was more fumbling than loving. Her husband lacked the knowledge or experience to bring a woman to climax. The removal of his clothes was more comic than stylish, and when he entered her it was painful and brutish. As he rammed to a climax she felt his body soaking in sweat. She gritted her teeth as he moaned her name. Thankfully, the suffering was brief. He kissed and thanked her, promising her to be a caring husband. She gave a fleeting obedient smile and made her way to the bathroom. The memory of Avsha was still too fresh. She closed the door, sat on the edge of the bath and quietly sobbed.

A couple of days later, the married couple left Zichron Yaakov.

In her anguish, she had to put a feeling of distance between the ones she loved, especially Avshalom. She needed space to calm her spirits and put her life into perspective, so the departure from Zichron Yaakov gave her a modicum of ease for her wounded soul. Chaim had promised that he would bring her to visit her family as frequently as he could. There had been the hint that, in the successful culmination of Chaim's business venture, they would retire to a house of their own in Zichron.

Abu-Farid drove the newlyweds to Haifa where they boarded a passenger ship to Constantinople. Sarah took a mild interest in the fellow passengers that they met as they strolled the deck or who dined at the same time of them for their meals. She dreaded the night ahead aboard ship but by keeping Chaim entertained late into the night either dining or in conversation over a bottle of wine or a few beers, her husband was tired by the time they withdrew to their cabin with its two single beds and was satisfied with a gentle kiss and an embrace before taking to his bed, quickly surrendering to sleep. His sleep was usually accompanied with a snoring noise that sounded like a grunt.

Sarah had expected to be taken to an impressive house in a prestige area of Turkish capital. Chaim had spoken about how well he was connected in the highest circles of government and commerce. It led her to believe that he lived in a lavish mansion. Instead, the carriage that took them and their luggage from the port went through the center of Constantinople and into a suburb that was clean but modest. When the carriage driver stopped outside the building that Chaim indicated was his, Sarah stared at a plain gray house little different to others on a busy street. They walked up three stone steps to the front door and Chaim inserted a key into the lock. When the door opened he pressed the key into the palm of her hand and said, "This is for you, my dear. Welcome to your new home."

Sarah half expected her husband to sweep her off her feet and carry her over the threshold. She had been told that this was the tradition between newly-weds. Instead, Chaim stepped aside and, with the wave of an arm, invited her to enter the house first. She walked through a narrow hallway with a stairwell against the wall on her right side. At Chaim's invitation she opened the door to a room on her left. As he followed her into the room he lit an electric light switch which barely lit up the darkened room. The heavily draped curtains hid a pair of wooden shutters that had been closed. Both blocked out the Turkish sunlight. The large room gave the appearance of being a study and a reception room according to the pieces of furniture spread around the carpeted floor. There was an empty fireplace along the facing wall. The room gave off a staid and musty smell. If it had any discerning character at all it was of a room of an untidy middle aged bachelor.

Chaim showed her around the house pointing out the chores that he expected her to do. "We do have an occasional cleaning lady," he explained, "and we have kitchen staff for the occasions we will have guests."

"But what of the food deliveries, the groceries?" Sarah began to see her future laid out for her as the obedient housewife of a successful businessman, a role she had foolishly rejected with Avshalom.

"We have the provisions delivered to the house. We can't have my wife be seen carrying shopping baskets through the streets of Constantinople, can we?" Chaim smiled. "That would never do. I will leave you sufficient money to pay the bills. We keep a ledger in which we record our household expenses."

He opened one of the drawers in his heavy wooden desk and pulled out a large ledger to show her where it was kept before returning it in its place.

Chaim spoke jovially, but Sarah did not find much humor in his words.

"Because we have been away so long I have instructed my cook to come this afternoon and prepare an evening meal for us. She is due here," he said, looking at his pocket watch, "in about an hour or so. I will introduce you to her."

This is how it will be, she realized, the regimental orderliness of her new life. And why did he not prefer to take her to a restaurant that night for a meal rather than invite his cook? Did he not consider it more interesting to show her the sights of Constantinople, the city he so readily boasted about to her family when they had so generously hosted him at her home in Zichron, and treat her to a romantic meal rather than order in a housemaid? Was it because he was not a romantic soul, like Avsha? Or was it because he could not see past his frugality? It was, she thought, a combination of both.

"Do you have any friends here in the town?" Sarah enquired.
"Oh, yes. I have some. I will arrange a soiree once you have settled in so that I can introduce you to them."

The gray house in the Kaisariou district of Constantinople was located a short walk from the Kontoskalion Harbor. A couple of weeks into her arrival and Chaim still had not arranged a reception to introduce her to his friends and associates. He claimed to be busy catching up with the backlog of work that had built up during his absence. Sarah asked if she could help him, at least with the paperwork. Chaim insisted that he would not ask his wife to be his secretary. Sarah reminded him of the money he could save by not employing a secretary, that she, Sarah, was willing to devote her spare time to his files. Chaim was sorely tempted but his social conscience and deportment would not allow him to agree.

Usually, Chaim left the house after breakfast promptly at eight in the morning to talk a brisk walk to his office in Galata, the bustling business district of Constantinople. He was usually home by five thirty in the afternoon, though he arrived after six if he had a day of meetings followed by late office work. Sarah one day asked to accompany him to work so that he could show her what he did. He was appalled at the suggestion. The formal Prussian upbringing he had adopted in Germany meant that a lady had no place in the master's working environment. Women, in his formal professional life, were suited to secretarial work, cooking and cleaning. It was unheard of for a wife to be seen in the management levels of commercial business places.

Sarah found the rules of social comportment stiflingly restricting. One day, by the mid-afternoon, after pacing the house and unsuccessfully pass the time by trying to read, she needed to escape the lonely confines of her silent house. She pinned a hat to her head and set out for a walk to the Bosporus River and along the pathway toward the harbor. At she arrived at the port she initially felt intimidated by the hustle and bustle of the crowds of workmen, laborers, sailors, and fishermen who stared at her with open mouths and leery grins. She had visited Haifa a number of times but this was overpowering. Taking a deep breath, she approached the harbor and sat on a wall watching the daily maritime life of Turkey. It was all so alien to her as she was gawked at by peasants bearing huge heavy sacks, or carrying loaded wicker baskets on their backs attached to their foreheads with thick leather straps. Navy sailors walked by wearing white cloth uniforms and black fez head coverings, while middle aged and elderly men in long coats clustered in talkative groups, most wearing red fez hats. Most looked poor and shoddily dressed. She gazed at the numerous miserable and dirty unemployable souls who sat dejectedly on the cobblestones. Their wretched condition added to the weight of depression that was gathering inside her. She felt so far from home. And lonely.

As she made her way sadly back to her new address her thoughts were about her family and what they must be doing. As she started to put the key in the lock the front door opened with force. Her husband stood there glaring at her.

"Where have you been?"

"You're home early, Chaim." Sarah attempted to enter the house, but Chaim Abraham blocked her way. He only moved when he noticed a pedestrian glance at them as he passed by. Not wanting to make a public fuss he moved aside to let her in and closed the door.

"I asked you where you have been?" He repeated angrily.

"I was bored. I needed some fresh air and walked along the harbor front."

"You walked to the harbor? Alone? Are you insane, woman! Do you not not deport herself among sailors and peasants. What has gotten into you, Sarah?"

"What do you expect of me? You drag me here and leave me to suffer the isolation of this dreary house. Do you think that I have no intellectual capacity? Do you think you have married a simple cook and cleaner? Is that all I am to you?"

"A wife's role is to serve her husband, to supervise the house, is it not? Soon I will introduce you into society. You will begin to meet people, important people, but it cannot be that the wife of a well-known businessman is seen wandering the streets on her own and around the docks, among the peasants. Do you not understand this, Sarah?"

Sarah was angry. She felt trapped and terribly alone. After a silence, Chaim softened. Putting his hands on her shoulders, he said, "It must be hard for you, Sarah, after living all your life in that little village to come to a cosmopolitan city like Constantinople, but give it time. Life can be pleasant here."

She nodded. "I will make your dinner for you." She walked away from him into the kitchen.

They ate their meal in silence. Chaim glanced up from his evening newspaper and stared at her with a worried look on his face.

"Sarah. Maybe I have been inconsiderate of your feelings. To you, this must seem such a contrast to your little town in Palestine. You must feel so lonely to be away from your beloved family. But this is the center of Turkish power." He smiled a sympathetic smile. "We will have a party next Sunday. What do you say, Sarah? You will meet some of the people I know. You will begin to find your place in our society. I will explain to you how one behaves in our world here. It is time that my acquaintances get to meet my beautiful young bride."

Later that night, in bed, Chaim tried to show Sarah his softer side. He caressed her with tenderness. She resisted at first but eventually allowed herself to feel the love he was trying to offer her. Her eyes were closed and she imagined a different man making love to her. That image shattered in the final frantic clumsy stages of his heavy passion. When he was wasted she got out of bed and made her way to the bathroom. She sat there numbly for several minutes before cleaning herself and returning to her bed. Chaim was in a deep slumber. All she could hear was his muffled snoring and her aimless thoughts.

The next day, Chaim surprised Sarah by again returning home slightly earlier than normal. His beard had gone, replaced by a cleanly trimmed moustache.

"Do you approve?"

She looked him over. He looked dapper, younger. Sarah smiled.

"I certainly do." She gave him a kiss.

"I decided that your husband needed a new image."

Sarah appreciated his effort to appeal to her. "It suits you, Chaim."

"I detoured from the office to the Seraskerat," a street with roadside barbers, "for a shave and haircut. Are you sure it suits me?"

"Absolutely," she said. "You look quite the handsome businessman."

"Sarah. I'm glad you think of me as your handsome husband."

Chaim was true to his word. Over breakfast the next morning Chaim leaned over to her. "Sarah. I want you to buy a nice dress for our soiree. This Friday we will go into town to find one for you."

They took a carriage into the center of the city as Chaim had promised. At first, he took her to one dress shop but the style and cut of the dress was not suitable for a lady to wear at a social function. Chaim was showing his inexperience at knowing where a lady would buy such apparel. Sarah decided to take over the shopping expedition. When they returned to the carriage Sarah asked the driver in fluent Turkish to take them to the area in town that sold quality ladies wear. She sat back and gazed at the people and the busy streets until the carriage arrived at their destination.

Eventually the driver entered a street with a number of stores that appealed to her female senses. As they dismounted from the carriage outside one promising looking shop window, Chaim told the driver to return in one hour.

"Oh. I think we will need longer than that, my dear," she said.

Chaim was surprised by Sarah. This was a side of her he hadn't seen since he had first met her at her home. Chaim smiled and told the driver to return to the other end of the busy street in two hours. He followed his young wife, listening to her ask the female shop assistant about the latest styles, watching her go into a cubicle to try on dresses, smiling as Sarah emerged to ask him what he thought of her selection. He enjoyed the intimacy of a husband treating his new wife to a set of fine clothes. Save for the price, it gave him pleasure that he had never experienced before.

They went from shop to shop. Sarah bought a couple of dresses and two pairs of shoes. They went in search of a bag shop. No woman is complete without a matching handbag, she explained to him. He nodded, gently sighed, and took the pain of the financial hit he knew would surely come. When they came to a large clothing store Sarah suggested that Chaim go sit in a café across the road and read a newspaper over a coffee and allow her to browse through the store. She asked him for some money telling him that she needed to buy fresh underwear and it would be unseemly if he followed her around a shop selling lady's intimate undergarments. After arranging that she would meet him at the café in half an hour, she gave her husband the large bags containing the results of her shopping, gently shoved him in the direction of the coffee shop, and walked into the emporium. She emerged, thirty minutes later, holding a number of bags. She joined Chaim at a table, called the waiter and ordered a cup of coffee.

Chaim eyed the bags containing Sarah's additional purchases. "I don't suppose you have any money left?"

"Not much."

It had been a costly day, but it was the first day that Chaim had seen his wife look content.

Sarah had to admit to herself that her husband threw an impressive party. A list of important guests crossed their threshold to view Mr. Abraham's new bride. It was clear from the nods and the surprised stares of the dignitaries that the men admitted their business colleague had found himself an exceptionally good catch. As they bowed to kiss Sarah's hand after they were introduced to her several could not take their eyes off her delicious face. Some smiled in admiration before releasing her hand. There were a number of Germans in the room. Chaim whispered that they were mainly diplomatic officials. A distinguished looking man who bowed deeply as he took her hand was introduced to her by Chaim as being the commercial attaché at the German embassy in Constantinople. He viewed her with obvious pleasure through his monocled eye. Try as she may, Sarah couldn't remember all the names of the mainly black-suited men that were introduced to her. She found a number of the Turkish names difficult to pronounce despite her fluency in the language.

As the invited guests mingled, waiters presented them with drinks. A table had been set up against the far wall of the large study by the window where waiters delivered trays of food prepared in the kitchen by a team of chefs. The appetizing dishes were served to a line of eager mouths by waitresses attired in black dresses covered with white aprons.

Small groups chatted. Initially the conversation was clearly about Sarah as people looked in her direction over sipped glasses of champagne and wine. She noticed how heads turned her way as they whispered to each other about her. Many of the guests complimented Chaim on finding such a fresh and single minded young lady after they had engaged her in brief conversation. At twenty-three-years-old, Sarah was the youngest person in the room, yet she grasped the significance of the conversations that buzzed around the room. The chatter centered on developing events that threatened war. Sarah discovered that the invited guests were firmly of the opinion that Turkey was about to strengthen its ties with Germany.

They all spoke enthusiastically about it. Sarah reckoned that this was beneficial for Chaim's business interests, but she found their enthusiasm disturbing. Turkey was engaging in military adventurism. They had lost heavily in a war in the Balkans and, according to the talk, it was in the throes of a major reorganization and military reconstruction effort as the two nations reached out to each other. Politics were working in her husband's favor and, watching Chaim's animated conversation, it confirmed what he had told her privately, that he was an ardent supporter of the two counties having even closer ties. A major war, however, was another matter entirely.

Among the guests were a few members of the Jewish community, and Sarah found herself gravitating toward these people as the evening wore on. She engaged them in happy conversation, hoping to find in them a sympathy and friendship. Nissim and Esther Russo lived close by. They owned a linen shop in the Galata district. Doctor Zvi Cohen and his wife, Rachel, lived in Galata. He worked at the hospital. Rachel helped run a charitable soup kitchen to help the poor of which, she said, there were many. Sarah leaped at the opportunity to offer to help her. Rachel gladly accepted. Sarah invited Rachel and Esther to visit her for coffee and a chat and both accepted. There was an age difference, but Sarah was oblivious of it. Her need for companionship outweighed any other consideration. Two latecomers entered the room and walked over to the Cohen's. Rachel called Sarah over to meet them. Both men wore dark suits. Both worse identical moustaches combed in the popular style of modern day Turkey. Both were clutching their tarboosh hats, the traditional, brimless, flat top, felt head gear. As Sarah joined them she was surprised to find she was shaking the hand of David Ben Gurion, a small man but with a dynamic presence, and his friend, Yitzhak Ben-Zvi. Both men were leaders of the Zionist

90

movement in Palestine. Chaim had told her that a few Palestinian Jews may attend the party but he hadn't mentioned names. Sarah was surprised to see them in her house. The Cohens explained that both men were lodging in their house while they completed their studies at the university. Ben-Gurion explained to her that they had travelled to Salonika in 1911 to learn Turkish before moving to Constantinople in 1912 to study law.

They apologized for their late arrival late explaining to Sarah that they had been studying before heading to the Cohen's house to wash and change before attending the celebration.

After Sarah was introduced to them, Ben-Gurion said to her, "Your family has made a great contribution to our people. I admire what you have done to improve the knowledge necessary to cultivate our land. Science is a wonderful thing when it is applied to agricultural development."

"But that is why I am so surprised to discover you are here studying law and not there, in Palestine, preparing the land with us for our future generations."

The small stub-nosed Zionist smiled up at Sarah.

"Yes, agriculture is very important, but we will only bring about the emergence of our country when we begin to speak the language of politics in *Eretz Israel*. We are living in political alienation. Just as our agronomic ignorance kept us weak, so does our political ignorance weaken our efforts to establish ourselves in our own land."

"And how will we establish our own nation when it remains under Turkish control?" Sarah probed.

"The day will come when Turkey will have a leader that appreciates our contribution to the land…" Ben-Gurion was distracted by a commotion as an impressive-looking uniformed figure entered the room.

"Ah! I think that man has just arrived." Both Ben-Gurion and Ben-Zvi excitedly rushed to join the guests who were eagerly shaking the hand of the new guest, or kissing both sides of his face.

Both the Cohens and the Russos held back as the rest of the guests gathered around the newcomer.

Who is that man?" Sarah asked Zvi.

"That," said Doctor Cohen, "is none other than Major Mustafa Kamal.

He is a hero. Although the Turks lost the Balkan War, he proved his military prowess by recapturing the lost province of Adrianople. He has now returned to Constantinople, but the leaders look on him as a potential political rival. He could become the future leader of the nation."

Nissim Russo grunted. "That's if he survives the coming war. The Pashas will shunt him off somewhere dangerous to remove him from the center of power. Just watch what happens to him."

The others nodded in silent agreement as Sarah stared at the gaggle of her distinguished guests who were still mobbing the major. Eventually, the elegant officer was shaking her husband's hand and mouthing compliments on his marriage. Chaim brought him over to Sarah's group saying, "and this, major, is my new wife, Sarah."

Mustafa Kamal's handsome face broke into a warm smile. "I am delighted to make your acquaintance, Mrs. Abraham. I hope you'll be happy in our country."

"Thank you, major. I have heard some impressive things about you."

"And I heard that you recently arrived from Palestine, and I admire the scientific approach that your brother has taken to the expansion of agriculture over there. This is very important. Like you I am a modernizer. We share the same approach to the future of our farming and crop production here."

Sarah stared into the piercing blue eyes of their special guest as others gathered around. Then she said, "I was raised with the appreciation of Ottoman history and the protection of my people."

"The Jews have contributed greatly to the well-being of our nation. I was born in Salonika and, growing up, many of my friends were Jewish. I am a secular Muslim, Mrs. Abraham, but if I may share a secret with you, I have at home an ancient Hebrew Bible from Venice."

He leaned into her ear and whispered, "Shema Israel, Adonai Elohenu Adonai Ehad. Is that correct, Sarah?"

Sarah was impressed. He had recited the words of an ancient Hebrew prayer. She whispered back the translation, "Hear O Israel, the lord our God, the Lord is One."

They smiled at each other. Then Kemal admitted, "I twice visited Jerusalem. Maybe you know Eliezer Ben-Yehuda, the one giving your people their modern Hebrew language, and his son, Itamar? What a fine achievement to revive an ancient language. I call them my friends." He spotted Ben-Gurion and Ben-Zvi, and added, "as are my friends, David and Yizhak."

Chaim was pleased with his bride's intelligent banter with Mustafa Kamal as she and the officer were surrounded by admirers listening eagerly to their conversation.

Major Kamal kissed Sarah's hand and moved on to greet other guests. When Sarah rejoined her new neighbors the diminutive Ben-Gurion had a broad smile on his pugnacious face.

"That man will lead his nation one day a look kindly on us. We have to build the platform of our future nation on his example, a thrusting, modern, secular society that is proud of its heritage and history, and that respects its minorities. That has to be the Zionist identity. Now you understand Mrs. Abraham why I admire this man so much."

"He will have to lead his soldiers in an impossible war soon," Nissim said.

"True," answered David Ben-Gurion, "We are on the brink of major historical events that will change the politics of Europe and our world. This is going to be our opportunity to change history if we make the right decisions and act decisively."

WAR

As spring turned to the warmth of a European summer the political climate was heating up.

On the twenty eighth of June, nineteen-year-old Gavrilo Princip, suffering from terminal tuberculosis, decided to shoot to death Austrian Archduke Franz Ferdinand and his wife, Sophie, as they rode through the streets of Sarajevo. They called it the shot that rang around the world. Gavrilo was an aggrieved Serb. He was upset that the Austrians were ruling his country.

Back in 1871, the Prussian statesman, Otto von Bismarck, had predicted that "one day, a great European war will come about due to some damned foolish thing in the Balkans." This was that "damned foolish thing."

The irony was that it wouldn't have happened had the Archduke's driver not taken a wrong turn at the junction of Appel quay and Franzjosefstraase. He did, driving straight into the path of a loitering and armed Gavrilo. As a member of a resentful political group, the sick young man recognized the vehicle. Instinctively, he took advantage of his opportunity by running to the open car and fired at the distinguished occupants at point blank range.

The Austrian-Hungarian government did not blame Gavrilo for the murder. They blamed the Serbian nation. They declared it must be punished, and punished severely. They declared war. Other countries quickly took sides. Russia rushed to defend the Serbs. Germany stood with their Austrian-Hungarian neighbors. Precisely a month later, Austria-Hungary declared war on Serbia and European peace collapsed as nations rallied to one side or the other. Belgium, France and Great Britain lined up against Austria-Hungary and Germany, and the Great War began.

The talk in every household in Constantinople was whether Turkey would enter the war. Sarah dreaded the thought. The one thing that kept her sane in her troubled confinement were the letters she received from her brothers and sisters. They wrote about their concerns. Despite not being in the war officially, they wrote that Turkish officials had come to Zichron and taken vital farm equipment, animals, and other essential items as part of their war effort requisitioning. As Alex wrote, the Turks were robbing them by day and the Arabs brigands were plundering their property by night. Alexander admitted in one letter that the Aaronsohn household, with their independent way of life supported by their American trustees, were not as badly affected as the poor Zichron farmers but, although Alex and his Gideonites night patrols were very active in catching some of the thieves, there was little they could do against the thievery of Turkish officials save for hiding whatever items they could, or the application of greasing palms with bakshish in a desperate effort to hold on to items that were essential for their agricultural survival.

Despite Sarah's weekly involvement in Rachel Cohen's charity work and the occasional forays into town with the doctor's wife and Esther Russo, she was bored to distraction. Through Esther, she had made contact with Batya and Shimon Ben Ezra. The Ben Ezra's traced their heritage back to their family's expulsion from Spain. This was a history that fascinated Sarah. Their families had escaped to Turkey and been protected and prospered under the Ottoman Sultans, though Shimon thought the emergence of the Young Turks to be a matter of dire concern. The benign relationship began to fracture, Shimon told her, the moment the Three Pasha's gained power. "There are troublemakers," he declared. "They are not good for Turkey. They are not good for us Jews. We must show our loyalty, but they are not to be trusted. Mark my words."

The Ben Ezra's had family in Haifa and contacts with the Zionist leaders in Palestine and Europe. So desperate was Sarah for any contact with home that she begged to meet with anyone who came to them from Palestine.

Sarah received a flurry of communications from home after Britain announced they were entering the war against Germany. Even Avshalom wrote to her. After writing of his concern for her, he asked if she had any news she could share with them. Avshalom wrote excitedly about how a British victory could mean the end of Turkish rule should they be persuaded to fight the Turks in Palestine. She was enticed by the thought.

It was in sharp contrast to everything she was hearing in the heart of Turkey, so far away from the people the people and the land she loved. Aaron's letters were always deeply personal. He also requested her to send him the latest news about the Turkish build up for war. He asked her to be careful and not to write anything that may put her at odds with the authorities or with her husband.

Sarah was already at odds with Chaim. He was an ardent supporter of the Germans. Over evening dinners, after spending the day with his German and Turkish business colleagues and clients, he lectured her on the German support for Austria, particularly over the issue of Serbia. The murderers of the Archduke were terrorists, not freedom fighters, he told her. He spoke with scorn against Britain's decision to enter the war against his beloved Germany.

"What right have the English to be on the Serbian side against Germany? he protested. "What a perfidious Albion! What traitors they are to betray their blood brethren. Victoria married Albert, did she not? Was he a Serb? No. He was a German. Kaiser Wilhelm is a blood relative of the English queen, and yet her nation now supports the Serbs? Bah!" he exploded. "Wilhelm was Victoria's grandson, for heaven's sake. He even attended her funeral. And, despite all this, England goes to war against Germany! Shame on them!"

Chaim could not be appeased. Sarah was more concerned for her family and the Jews should war descend on Palestine.

"Aaron tells me that our people in Palestine are beginning to suffer as a result of the war preparations. The authorities are not being reasonable with their requisitioning for the war effort."

Chaim advised, "They will be fine, as long as they remain loyal citizens."

"Chaim, you promised me you would take me to visit my family. I have asked you when will that be. When will you take me? I am desperate to see them again."

Chaim patted her hand. "My dear, you must understand how busy I am. It is my work that sustains us. You see that, surely?"

Sarah was frustrated, and angry. "I see that your work consumes you. I see that you have no considerations of my concerns."

Chaim objected. "That's not correct, Sarah. There are things going on that are keeping me frantically busy. When things settle down we will go visit your family. I promise you, my dear."

Sarah realized they were living in two different worlds.

Chaim's commercial interests continued to improve with the urgent needs of an impending war. This kept him busier than ever. Although he offered her the evening and weekend companionship of a boring but faithful husband, he was forced to apologize frequently to Sarah for his increasingly important business travels and trips to Germany. She accepted it with equanimity, but she was left alone for days on end with increasing frequency. His absences gave her the opportunity to defy his bidding and freely explore Constantinople. Frequently she took her friends, Esther and Rachel, into town where they shopped and enjoyed lunch together. Sometimes she took a taxi alone to one of the elite hotels where, hiding behind a copy of the *Sabah* newspaper, and nursing a cup of coffee in the elegant marble floored lobby, she eavesdropped on the conversations of men who, by their appearance, were professionally involved in commerce, the military, or government. She gathered that the Three Pashas, who controlled Turkey, were waiting for Germany to officially declare war before they would announce an alliance with the Kaiser. It was a done deal, she heard.

She had barely rushed off a letter to Aaron to this affect when Russia declared it was siding with Serbia. Germany responded by declaring war on Russia. Turkey ratified an alliance with Germany the next day.

On October 28, Turkey officially entered the war, and the next day the Turkish fleet entered the Black Sea and attacked the Russian ports of Theodosia, Odessa and Novorossiysk.

Turkey was at war while Chaim was away on his business travels. Sarah felt even more alone and in need of her family.

It was shortly after that Sarah received a startling letter in early November from a distressed Rivka. Avshalom had been arrested by the Turks on suspicion of espionage. She wrote that everyone was working to try and get him released but he was being held in a Turkish prison in Beer Sheba and was probably being beaten and interrogated.

Sarah's mind was in turmoil. She felt so helpless, so removed from what was important to her. Avshalom. *Avshalom! May God keep you alive. Oh, how I hate the Turks.*

October heralded the end of the neglectfully benign Ottoman reign and the beginning of a much darker period of brutal Young Turk power as Turkish war ships pounded Black Sea ports. Sarah didn't care about the fate of the Turkish navy. All she cared about was the fate of Avsha.

She feverishly wrote letters to Aaron, Alex, Rivka, even to Avshalom's sister, Tzila, who was studying in Berlin. She wrote to anyone who could give her news about Avshalom.

1915

1915 was a bad year. In truth, it was a disastrous year for Jew and Arab in Palestine.

Palestine had become a theater of war. Without there being conflicting sides battling with each other, war preparations were gathering strength. The repressive Turks inflicted a war tax on the population. They imposed it more heavily on the Jews, particularly on the farming settlers who had their properties and possessions confiscated by the authorities. People were being conscripted into the army. Sarah was told by Alex in a letter that those who didn't have a wazira, an exemption form, were summarily conscripted and taken away for military service. Fortunately, he wrote, because of the importance of their work for the Turks all the men in their agricultural project had been given a wazira.

Then came the dreaded expulsion order of "enemy nationals." Most of the Jewish Russian immigrants were in this category. This was implemented by Djemal Pasha's subordinate, Baha al-Din, the governor of Jaffa. Initially, five hundred Jews were dragged off the streets and taken to the police headquarters. From there, they were taken to the Jaffa port and put on boats to Egypt. They were quickly followed by a mass round-up of six thousand men, women and children who were marched to the port and kept there under guard without food and little water until they were put on boats to join the others in refugee camps in Alexandria.

Djemal Pasha came to Jerusalem and declared publicly that Zionism was an anti-Turkish revolutionary movement that had to be wiped out. He ordered all Jews to surrender their weapons and anyone found with a weapon would face criminal charges.

In late January, the Turkish foolishly decided to attack the British on the Suez Canal. Their attack was futile and they were driven back to Gaza.

In the spring of that year, under the order of Winston Churchill, the First Lord of the Admiralty, the British took on the Turks in the Dardanelles by mounting a massive amphibious landing on the beaches of Gallipoli. Joining them were thousands of Jews from the refugee camps of Alexandria. They had been recruited and trained by a Russian firebrand by the name of Ze'ev Jabotinsky. His persistence had persuaded the British War Cabinet to include them as an auxiliary force of mule pullers to provide support for the forward troops on the battlefields of Gallipoli.

In Palestine, another curse descended on the land. The man-made disasters of war coincided with a natural disaster of biblical proportions to create a crippling blow on the population. One of the ten biblical plagues that had been inflicted on the Egyptians emerged out of that country and turned its curse, dormant for three millennia, on the ancient land of Israel.

A huge grey cloud of low flying destroyers headed north out of the dry barren land of Egypt and Sinai. People reckoned there must have been a millions of them. Their numbers were endless as they blackened the sky and devoured everything that lay before them, every leaf and every plant, in a frenetic storm of destruction. Locusts in their tens of thousands fell from the skies on any sight of green. Rapidly, all crops were lost to the flying vermin. The countryside, the farmers, the shepherds, were defenseless against the ravaging winged insects. When the Zichron villagers tried attacking them in the vineyards, crushing many hundreds underfoot with their rushing boots, they employed useless methods to kill or dislodge them from the sprouting vines. The locusts stubbornly remained and multiplied, gradually flying off to waiting corn crops after there was nothing left of the green grapevines to devour. The locusts moved frenetically from field to field attracted by any sign of greenery or golden head of wheat. Controlled fires and anti-pesticide sprays had no effect.

It went on for days. Djemal Pasha came down from Damascus to inspect the disaster. In exasperation, The Turkish overlord summoned Aaron Aaronsohn to meet with him in Nazareth to discuss the locust plague. Aaron demanded and received *boyouroulton* travel permits for all his trained staff to enable them to travel throughout Palestine unhindered by Turkish police and military officials. He requested from Djemal Pasha large quantities of gasoline and for the Djemal Pasha to order all able-bodied men to work under Aaronsohn's teams to dig large pits into which his men would funnel the massed locusts before dousing them with gasoline and burning them before they laid their eggs. If they could not prevent the egg spawning, he warned the Turkish leader, they would have to deal with another generation of the plague in a relentless and losing battle.

"The female locusts are not flying," he explained to the Turk, "because they are heavy with eggs and are burying them into the ground. We have to prevent them from hatching."

Djemal Pasha ordered that every male from the age of fifteen to fifty must work under the supervision of Aaronsohn's team to collect and destroy locust eggs and anyone not contributing to the national effort would be punished by the accompanying local Turkish officials.

Alexander sent Sarah a detailed letter illustrating their efforts and frustrations.

"It was a plague from the Old Testament. Black clouds of locusts emerged out of the Egyptian desert. Their visitation came like a threat from God. They came fully grown, ripe for breeding. The ground was covered with females frantically digging in the sand to deposit their package of eggs. We knew when that happened we would be overwhelmed with the next generation of this plague for there was not a piece of ground where these eggs were not found.

"The menace is so great that the military authorities are obliged to deal with it as we all watch our trees and crops rapidly denuded of their greenery. Famine is staring us in the face.

"Djemal Pasha summoned Aaron and entrusted him and our organization with a campaign against the insects. Aaron wanted to recruit the Arabs but they are lazy and fatalistic. They call the locust plague, 'Djesh Allah,' God's Army, and cannot understand why man would fight against God's will.

"In addition, we are harassed with a lack of petroleum. Our plan was to have thousands of workers dig huge pits while we direct the army of locusts into the pits to hatch their eggs. We would then set fire to the locusts but this is failing because the Turks refuse to provide us with the fuel to destroy them. They claim they need this fuel for their army but they ignore the famine that must follow and this famine will prevent them from feeding their soldiers. Meanwhile, the Arabs sit on their haunches and watch our efforts. It has been hopeless. As the prophet, Joel, said, 'The field is wasted, the land mourns, the corn is wasted and the new vine is dried up. The land is as the garden of Eden before them, and behind them a desolate wilderness.'"

Sarah turned the page and was shocked to read, *"I have seen the wet faces of Arab babies being devoured by the locust plague before their mothers could respond to their child's cries. I have seen the carcass of dead goats heaving under the undulating, rustling, blanket of insects. The men of Zichron go to the synagogue wailing and praying for the Almighty to lift his anger."*

Sarah put down the letter and stared out at the bustling street. *What am I doing here?* she thought as she glanced at the scene of people she didn't know going about their daily business, and the lines of uniformed troops being marched to useless deaths on unknown battlefields in alien lands that had been neglected by Turkish leaders who now sent them to die for national honor. It was so frustratingly hypocritical. *I don't belong here. I belong with my people in the land that I love.* She was torn between longing and duty to her people and her isolation and purposeless duty to her absent husband.

The shocking news she was receiving from home was made infinitely worse when a letter arrived in June from her sister, Rivka. It had been mailed to her from Beirut. Rivka told her that Aaron had sent her out of

Palestine for her safety. She had gone under the cover of being a student at the American School in the Lebanese capital. Rivka wrote that the real reason was to wait for the arrival of Alex and that he had arrived and they were applying to take ship to America.

Sarah was puzzled. *Why Alex? Why was Avshalom not escorting Rivka to safety? Was Avsha still in prison? Was he alive?*

As Spring turned to summer, the letters reduced in volume. It was like someone turning off a tap. Letters failed to drop through her letter box. She couldn't understand why. The abrupt silence was unbearable. By August, the tortured Sarah wrote desperately to Tzila, the sister of Avshalom;

"I would like to tell you something interesting, but I have nothing that is likely to interest you. My life is monotonous. I am cut off from everything. I hardly visit any one. I find no pleasure in anything, and I am indifferent to everything, except home.

"I look forward to the happy day when I shall return home and settle down among those that are dear to me. If you think, my dear, that, from here, I am involved in the affairs of Eretz Israel and what is happening to our families, you are mistaken. They don't write to me and my nerves are racked. This life, so far from my family, has become intolerable. Meanwhile, I believe the family home has become empty, and poor father remains all alone. My heart aches for him.

"I cannot continue writing. My tears are streaming and my heart is breaking. Sarah."

Sarah thrived on little else but the regular contact with her local friends, Esther, Rachel, and Batya. They took occasional jaunts into town by taking a horse-drawn tram. The pace was leisurely and they could watch the bustle of daily life in Constantinople intensify as they reached the Grand Rue de Pera where they disembarked from the tram carriage and crossed the busy

105

road into the palatial Hotel Tokatlian. They walked through the shiny marble-tiled floor of the lobby to the tearoom, whispering admiringly at the elegance of their surroundings. Sarah told them she much preferred the window seat at the Grand Hotel Kroecker. It was less grand but gave a view that always enchanted her of the sea and the ships that were either entering the port or leaving for distant parts. She visualized herself on one of those ships sailing from Constantinople to the port of Haifa and home.

On one occasion, as they sat at lunch in her favorite Grand Hotel Kroecker, Sarah was distracted from gazing at the ships when Rachel asked, "Have you heard the news that the American Ambassador to Turkey had written a report accusing the Turks of carrying out what he described as *"a crime against humanity."*

Sarah stared at her in alarm. "Where? Here, or in Palestine?"

"Here," her friend answered, and in Syria. "

"Why? What happened and to whom?"

Rachel told her that America is accusing Turkey of carrying out massacres against the Armenians. "Have you heard anything," she asked Sarah.

"Chaim told me about some disturbances, some transfer of the population, but not massacres. There was news about troubles in the north by a few Armenians involved in the war, but nothing so dramatic as mass murders."

"The foreign newspapers talk about Armenian Christians being deported and killed in large numbers while other have been arrested and executed as saboteurs."

"Where did you hear that? It's hard to find any foreign newspapers here."

106

Rachel replied, "My husband heard about it from an Armenian doctor he works with at the hospital. Zvi told me this doctor had said that the American ambassador had complained to the government of systematically uprooting Armenians and raping and murdering them. Of course, the government is denying it. They call it anti-Turkish propaganda and lies, but why would the Americans lie about something like that?" Rachel asked.

"I heard reports on the radio of Armenians being involved in acts of sabotage. Maybe the Turks are right." Esther said.

Sarah said, "I heard these reports too. Chaim told me there had been some trouble in the north but it had been sorted out by the military."

When Chaim returned home from work that evening, and while Sarah was preparing dinner, she casually mentioned the rumor she had heard about an Armenian massacre.

"Where did you hear that nonsense?"

"I heard that Henry Morgenthau has complained to his government about what he calls a crime against humanity. Chaim, that is no small thing."

"Again, where did you hear this nonsense?"

"From my friends, Rachel and Esther. We had lunch together. It's all over the foreign press."

"My god!" Chaim snorted. "Why do you listen to such dangerous gossip?"

"Ambassador Morgenthau is an admirer of Aaron and our Atlit project. He visited us once. He is not the sort of person who makes up stories, Chaim. Is it true?"

"Turkey's enemies will stop at nothing to discredit Turkey. It's part of their war propaganda. You shouldn't listen to idle women's gossip, Sarah."

"Not Morgenthau. He's an honest and decent man. And America is neutral in this war, so what have they to gain by lying? What about the deportations, the murders?"

"This is ill informed slander. Yes, a number of Armenians have been relocated because of the war. The Armenians were being caught up in inter-ethnic violence. They have been moved away from the war zone for their own safety, and the migrants have been brought into Ottoman borders. This is normal in a war situation, and the government is recognizing them as citizens. Now tell me, what is wrong with that?"

"But what about the murders, the rapes?"

Chaim was bristling now. He held his body stiffly. His face beginning to flush. "Sarah, I insist. Do not go around speaking such dangerous talk. There have been one or two incidents of saboteurs being arrested and sentenced for crimes against the nation, but this exaggeration is not in order. I insist that you stop these defamatory remarks. This is serious, Sarah. You must not speak further on this matter, and certainly not in public. You put yourself in danger by spreading such slander against the state."

Sarah brooded for days over her husband's denial. With government censorship on the foreign press access to outside information was hard to come by. She tried unsuccessfully to tune in to the BBC on her radio. She felt so restricted. So cut off from the world. It was pleasant to luxuriate with her friends over coffee or lunch in fine surroundings but she knew they were cocooned from unfolding events, events that must be affecting her family and friends in Palestine.

One day, as she and her friends chatted while tasting the club sandwiches and pouring tea into their cups from the warm teapot, Sarah asked Rachel is she was related to Israel and Manya Shochat.

"Yes. Zvi is a cousin of Israel, her husband. Why do you ask?"

"I heard about them in a letter I received from my brothers earlier this year. I understand they are living here in Turkey?"

Rachel paused, looked around the room, and said in hushed tones, "Yes. They are here. You know why they are here, don't you?"

"I heard it had something to do with smuggled weapons, or belonging to a banned organization that the government did not approve of."

Rachel conspiratorially leaned over the table. "Yes. They were expelled as leaders of the HaShomer self-defense group."

The other women leaned in to better hear Rachel's whispered voice.

"Manya and Israel are remarkable people and she is an example to all women. She is no great beauty but she has certainly changed the way women think and behave in Eretz Israel."

She looked around the room to make sure nobody was eavesdropping into their conversation before continuing.

"She rides like a man. She shoots like a man. She even dressed differently than other women. She usually wore a black Arab abaya with a Bedouin cloth head-dress as she rode through Palestine and Syria looking for suitable land for cultivation. Then she went to the Zionist organizations to get money to buy the land and help set up collective farms. When she went to Rothschild's land in Hauran in southern Syria she found that the Jewish farmers had stopped working the land. They employed Arabs worker instead to do all the physical labor that Rothschild had paid them to do. She was livid. Do you know what she did then? She got on a boat and went to France to tell the Baron about it. She complained that she wanted to see the spirit of Zionism being carried out by Jewish pioneers and that meant them doing the hard physical work. But Rothschild sent her away, so she went to meet with Max Nordau, the man who founded the World Zionist Organization with Herzl, and he told her to go see a psychiatrist."

They all laughed but Sarah found this story intimately familiar. This was what the Baron had been angry about at Zichron.

"She had been asked by the HaShomer group to buy weapons so, while she was in Paris, she went back to Baron Rothschild and he actually gave her the funds to buy the weapons. Would you believe that? But it's true. She's crazy, but the Turks found out about it after she got to Palestine and sent her and her husband into exile here in Constantinople."

The authorities, Rachel told her, had wanted to put them in prison for the duration of the war but had come under tremendous pressure from top level people in the American Administration and, not willing to draw the United States into the war, the Germans had restrained the Pashas into letting them live quietly in exile in Anatolia. Israel Shochat, Rachel explained, was taking the same law degrees as David and Yizhak but Manya still had this thing against Ben-Gurion that kept them apart.

Sarah felt a kinship with this mad woman.

"Rachel, I have to meet her. Can you arrange it?"

"I don't see why not, Sarah. I will ask Zvi to speak with Israel."

Some time elapsed before Sarah asked Rachel if she had heard from Manya about a meeting. Her friend looked embarrassed.

"I don't know how to say this but Manya will not come to my house as long as Ben-Gurion is there. They had a sort of falling out before she was exiled here in Anatolya. She doesn't mind Ben-Zvi because he is married to her best friend, Rachel Yanait, but she doesn't want to bump into David. In any case, with the two men lodging with us we don't have a spare bedroom anymore."

"So why not invite them to my house. We can invite them to stay over when Chaim is away on business. I am so interested in meeting them. It's been so long since I spent time with people from Palestine who are dedicated to our land."

Sarah looked in her diary and gave her friend a couple of dates where they could come and stay over a weekend when Chaim would be in Germany.

She was thrilled when Rachel told her that they had agreed to come for a weekend at the end of August. The date couldn't come quick enough for Sarah but she kept her excitement in check, not even telling Chaim in advance about her weekend guests. She knew, with his ardent support for Turkey, that he would never approve of having people with the status of enemy aliens as guests in his house, but to Sarah they were the same passionate Palestinian Jews as she was.

Close to the date of Manya's visit, Rachel told Sarah, "You know that both Ben-Gurion and Ben-Zvi have returned to Palestine."

Sarah was shocked. "No. I hadn't heard. Why did they break off their studies? Because of the war?"

111

"Partially that, but mainly because David wanted to hone his political ambitions in Palestine by building an organization, and Yitzhak went with him." Rachel paused," I guess with them gone I can now receive Manya and Israel into my home."

"No!" Sarah protested. "I won't think of it. I want them as my house guests. Allow me to host them here. Please, Rachel."

When Sarah answered the knock on her front door she found a plain looking woman on her doorstep. Under a mess of black and grey hair was set a pair of round-lensed glasses. This was not the impressive figure Sarah expected. She was accompanied by a skinny man of medium height wearing a long black goatee beard the style of a Russian socialist intellectual. Rachel introduced them to Sarah and, after shaking hands, Sarah ushered them into her house. She asked them what they wanted to drink as she led them into the kitchen. Everyone went for tea with no milk. Israel asked if she had any sugar lumps. Sarah produced a small bowl of white sugar cubes. While they waited for the kettle to boil they engaged in ice-breaking platitudes about where they were living and how they found Constantinople. Their replies echoed Sarah's emotional state of not only missing their home but their inability to contribute to the preparation of a future homeland in which they could control their own destiny. They discussed people they knew who were still in Palestine and what they were doing. Sarah delivered a tray of cups, saucers, a teapot, and a plate of cakes to the kitchen table and poured their refreshments for them.

The ever direct Sarah asked Manya how well she knew David Ben-Gurion. This drew a frown, but the woman was equally direct in her reply.

"Israel and I lived and worked at Sejera. You know where it is, Sarah? It is in the Lower Galilee. David heard about our work and came to join us as a laborer. He loved his work and did his stint of guard duty. He liked our civil defense ideas, but he tried to inject his ideas into the committee of which he wasn't elected. That upset many of us who had established the settlement and wanted to run it according to our principles, not his. That was basically why David and I had a falling out. I was the one who had to tell him he wasn't accepted on to the kibbutz committee or as a member of Sejera. I guess it had to do with a clash of personalities. We are both uncompromising individuals. By that time Rachel and Yizhak came to work with us. Rachel Yanait was a very good looking girl and she was engaged to Yizhak Ben-Zvi. Ben-Zvi was David's friend even before they arrived at Sejera, but he was less pugnacious than David so they were accepted as members, but not David."

Sarah looked at Manya. "I guess you and I have one thing in common. The dream to see our land coming to life with Jews returning to our homeland and the hope of future self-determination."

Manya nodded. "That is true. I have no doubt that David will make a great leader one day, but he shouldn't look for conflicts with people who have a similar aim at the end of the day, and I question his judgment."

"What do you mean by that?"

"Pah!" Manya exploded. "Without completing his studies both David and Yitzhak got up and returned to Palestine leaving Israel and me to fend for ourselves. A fine set of lawyers they turned out to be, and with Yitzhak, in my family. Pah! All he does is follow David like a little puppy. You know what David Ben-Gurion did when he got back to Jerusalem? He volunteered dozens of our young men to serve in the Turkish army. He contacted Djemal Pasha to accept them. What a foolish mistake! Fortunately for us a miracle happened. Djemal rejected them. Can you imagine? The war is on. The Turks need men, yet they turned him down. Not only that, he deported Ben-Gurion and Ben-Zvi from Palestine along with thousands of other Jews. This, by the Turks that David loves so much. He wants the land to be ours yet he offers the bodies of our wonderful young men to fight and die in the wars of our oppressors. You see what I mean about his judgment?"

Sarah was shocked. "I hadn't heard about the deportations, but not about him volunteering our boys to fight for the Turks. It's bad enough about the conscriptions that are going on in Palestine. I know a few from Zichron that have been conscripted into the army. They did not go willingly. That's my problem here, Manya, I am so cut off from everything that is happening back home. I feel so isolated, so impotent."

Manya gave a sympathetic smile.

"I understand you perfectly, my dear."

Sarah asked, "Tell me your views on women in advancing our cause. I hear you didn't accept women having second status in anything."

Rachel laughed. "You should have seen her riding like the devil between the settlements dressed in her Arab clothes. She scared a lot of the men."

Manya glared at Rachel but didn't object to her description. "They think we are weak, and too many of us like to leave them with that impression. This is a big mistake. Men respect a strong and decisive woman. I insisted that the girls had to go out into the fields and work alongside the men. In Sejera I objected to the exclusion of women in the field work and guard duty. I will not surrender to a man's notion that our place is in the kitchen, the bedroom, and the kindergarten. Not if we really want to contribute or full share to our national home. If someone comes plundering at night to steal from us or to do us harm, a bullet fired by a woman will stop him as dead in his tracks as that of a man. In Kfar Giladi and Tel Hai, women are treated as equals in farming and in fighting. When we have our own country and our own army our women will serve as soldiers alongside the men. It's emancipating."

"Why were you expelled?" asked Sarah.

"I was one of the people who established the HaShomer defense network to defend what we had built from criminal robbers. What do you think we should do when they come in their gangs to rob and kill us? Go find a Turkish policeman? That's why they arrested me. Because we had the weapons to defend ourselves. Djemal wanted everybody to turn in their weapons and we didn't. That's why we are rotting here and not there helping to develop our settlements," Manya said angrily.

That story was familiar to Sarah. She remembered being a part of the Gideonites back home. Sarah was fascinated by this woman. Manya was a plain-looking woman, but she was anything but plain. She was determined and single-minded, a woman deserving of admiration. She was inspirational. Sarah saw herself in every word she said. She gave voice to what Sarah felt inside.

Israel spoke for the first time. "Now you see what attracted me to Manya. This is the new breed of Jew we are creating in Palestine. Compare her to the bourgeois European Jew. Ask your brother, Aaron, if I am right. He is an example of the new Jew we are creating in our land. I am sure he sees the difference when he goes to Europe and has to deal with them."

Sarah could not but think of Chaim. She began to compare him to Aaron and Avshalom. Chaim's focus was hard work dedicated to his personal financial gain. For Aaron and Avshalom money was simply a way to help them develop the land for others.

These thoughts reopened the never-ending home sickness in her repressed soul. To put it out of her mind she asked Manya, "Is it true you persuaded Baron de Rothschild to give you money for weapons?"

"Yes," she smiled. "You have to remember that many of our young pioneers have to deal with pogroms in Russia even as they are preparing to come and live with us. It was understood between us, between me and the Baron, that we would not use the weapons against the Turks or to cause an uprising against the Arabs. They were to be used strictly for defensive purposes only. He gave us the money. We bought rifles in Czechoslovakia and smuggled some of them to our young defenders in Russia. The rest we shipped and smuggled into Palestine and distributed them among our northern settlements. It was quite an operation."

"Were they used at all in Russia? Weren't you frightened about them being discovered by the authorities?"

"Oh, they were used. The Jew haters were shocked when our men defended themselves in the pogrom at Yekaterinoslav, but the authorities were in with the rioters so we had to smuggle the men and their weapons out of Russia to keep them alive. Most escaped and are in Palestine now."

"And you, Israel, what of you? It must be painful to be confined here."

The man stroked his beard with downward pulls as he framed his thoughts. "I still have a vision of a promised and purchased land being cultivated by Jewish labor without dispossessing a single Arab. The Negev, the Galilee, the coastal plain that you know so well, the Jezreel Valley, even in the harsh climate of the Jordan Valley. They are all empty, waiting centuries for our return to make them pregnant again with life and hope. It has to be a collective effort. It has to be done with the friendship and understanding of our Arab neighbors. It cannot be done without peaceful coexistence."

The conversation flowed for hours into the middle of the night. It filled Sarah with renewed yearning for a previous and future life. She was glad she had invited this couple to stay with her. She learned that efforts were being made to persuade the Turkish authorities to release them both from their Anatolian confinement and allow them to return to northern Palestine

116

after Israel had completed his law studies. If only, Sarah thought, she could join them.

As the summer heat began to recede, the letters from home dried up. Instead of receiving bunches of letters bursting with full pages of family and work gossip, intimate information and news, the flow had reduced to an occasional letter from Aaron.

Though it wasn't indicated in written words, Sarah reckoned that the increasing problems and pressure were taking their toll on the ones she loved. The problem was, for Sarah, that nobody told her what was really happening back home. In her brother's rare letters, she was constantly reassured that everyone was well, but she was sure they were keeping something from her. This set her mind ablaze guessing what it could be. The war had to have something to do with it. Although no fighting was going on in Palestine, both Alex and Aaron had written to her about the increasing visits of Turkish officials poking their noses into every farmyard looking for anything to take away for the war effort, and their conscription of any able bodied man they could find. The decimation of the land in the aftermath of the locust swarms would have obvious consequences for the Atlit project that would keep everybody busy. They must surely be short-handed, exhausted, and more than likely hungry and desperate. The trickle of letters was devoid of any mention of their condition, and this worried her.

Sarah's father was never the best of letter writers. His feelings were expressed through the letters sent to her by her brothers and sister. Now their flow of correspondence had inextricably ended. She wrote frantically, begging to be told what had happened. Surely they hadn't turned their backs of her? She instinctively knew this was not the case. But what could be the reason?
Sarah was conflicted by the portent caused by the sudden reduction of mail from home and the obtuse letters sent to her by Aaron. It was

insufficient for him to tell her that everyone was well when, clearly, something was not well at all. If something had happened back home she needed to be there. If they were so overloaded they had no time to write to her, then she needed to be there helping them. And what of the fate of Avshalom?

As she stared into the bottom of her drained breakfast cup she decided it was time to take a personal responsibility for herself and for her life. She got out of her chair and walked out of her empty kitchen along the empty hallway and into her empty living room. She drifted to the lace-curtained front window and stared out unseen at the bustle of a busy street. She realized she had become an empty, useless, ghost in a deserted house so far from home.

Have I rejected the love of Avshalom for this? Is this what I dreamed my life would mean? Here, in a loveless marriage? Trapped in an alien land? How stupid I have been. Sarah was reaching a decision that had been festering in her mind for some time. *I have to take my life back into my own two hands. I have to return and help my people. It's what I was searching for all the time, and it was there under my own roof. How stupid I was. It's time for action. I have to get back. For love of country.*

It was indeed time for action.

YEARNING

Chaim left early for his office. As he kissed her on her cheek at the front door he told her not to wait up for him as he would be home late that night. After she closed the door she went to the study and searched through the drawers where she kept her paperwork. She shuffled through her files before extracting a number of documents. She read through them before heading up the stairs to her bedroom. She changed into a dress that would make a good impression in the mission she was planning. She checked herself in the mirror, put on a suitable hat, and returned to the study to gather up the selected papers before heading out of the house to the edge of the pavement where she hailed a cab.

She told the driver where she wanted to be delivered and sat back as the cabby navigated his way through the morning traffic. They eventually stopped at the destination and the cab driver pointed to the entrance of a large dull looking building. She rustled through her bag and extracted money for her fare.

As she stepped out of the cab she took a deep breath and marched determinedly into the government building. She was stopped by a porter who asked what she was looking for. When she told him she had come to apply for a travel permit he directed her up a flight of marble stairs and then to go left to the office at the end of the corridor. She followed his instructions and found she had to wait in line behind eight other people who were queuing to speak to someone sitting behind a small window opening. She waited patiently as the queue slowly shrunk. She reckoned it took her at least half an hour to get to the head of the queue. A weasel-looking middle aged man with thinning hair that manned the open window. She told him that she needed a permit that would allow her to travel to see her family in Palestine. With a tired expression, lifted slightly by having a

119

strikingly attractive young lady in front of him, he reached down and passed her a couple of white forms.

"What do I do with these?" she asked politely.

"Fill in the forms at the desk along the corridor and taken them to the room at the other end of the corridor," he said pointing in the direction she had come.

Sarah walked over to the writing desk and had to wait as two men were busy reading through their forms and slowly filling in their details. When they finished and moved on, Sarah discovered there was no pen provided at this desk for the customers. She went through her bag but realized she didn't carry a pen with her. She couldn't remember ever needing a pen outside of her Turkish house. She realized that the clerk at the end of the long corridor must have a writing implement so she walked to the required office. There she found she was fifth in line. This queue, although shorter, took her longer to get to the front. Each person seemed to engage in lengthy conversations with the clerk. She reckoned it took her an hour to reach a mustachioed and again middle aged man. It occurred to her that all the young men had been conscripted to the war. She smiled and apologetically asking the clerk if he could help her complete the form as the government hadn't provided a pen and she didn't have one with her. The official, taken in by the beauty that stood before him, agreed. Sarah thanked him for his gallantry and patience which she knew derived from her appearance and not from any sense of bureaucratic courtesy. Playing the part of a vulnerable woman she asked him to fill in parts of the form for her, though she knew perfectly well how to complete them having travelled so many times to the local government office in Haifa on behalf of Aaron and her work at Atlit.

The conversation was about the form but it was clear to Sarah that he was beginning to flirt with her. She maintained her decorum but smiled at him to encourage him to complete his job without problem. He asked her where her destination was. When she told him that she would be travelling to visit her family in Palestine he told her that as she was an Ottoman citizen and would be travelling within Ottoman territory only the *boyouroultan* permit was required and not a full international passport. She nodded. He pointed to part of the form and asked her to sign her name. She did so with a flourish, offering him a big grin. He asked for the twenty piasters fee for the form. He countersigned the form, giving it a noisy bang with his official rubber stamp. Then he wrote out a receipt for the money.

Sarah expected him to give her the *boyouroultan* and was surprised when he told her she had to go up to the second floor and look for room 204.

"You will have to pay a hundred piasters when the form is ready. Just show them this receipt," he advised her.

She thanked him and made her way up the stairs to the next floor. She checked each door until she came to one marked 204. She opened the door and found herself in a waiting room with six people sitting in chairs. She took a seat and waited. After ten minutes, a couple emerged from an office. Their place was taken by a businessman who entered the office and closed the door after him. The atmosphere, she thought, was like being in a doctor's surgery. It must have been ten minutes before the man exited to be replaced by the next person.

Eventually, after almost an hour, it was her turn to enter the office. A senior official, who had vainly dyed his grey hair a dark black, invited her to sit. She handed over her receipt and he asked her for some personal identification. Sarah dipped into her bag and brought out her citizenship documents and marriage license.

"What is the purpose of your travel, Mrs. Abraham?"

"I will be visiting my family in Palestine who I have not seen for over a year."

"Will your husband be travelling with you?"

"No. He has to go to Germany on business. His work is part of the war effort. I will be visiting my family while he is away."

"How long will you be away? Do you have a date for your return?"

Sarah replied, "No. I don't have a return date. That will depend on when my husband will return from Germany. I intend to confirm my return date while I am over there."

He smiled. "Yes. It must be a strain what with the war and everything, but don't worry, Mrs. Abraham. With Germany's and Allah's help we will be victorious and stronger than ever."

Sarah tried to put a positive expression into her smile.

"When will I get my travel pass?"

"Oh, that will take some time. Mrs. Abraham. The wheels of bureaucracy during a war always turn more slowly," he said with a shrug of his shoulders. "You should get them in about a month."

A month! Sarah was stunned. She dipped into her bag and took out a couple of crisp bank notes and slid them across the table. "Is it not possible for you to speed up the process for me? I really miss my family and I would like to complete my visit while my husband is away so that I can return to take care of him," she said with an appealing look on her face.

The manager looked at her. The notes quickly disappeared into his inside jacket pocket.

"I can't promise anything, Mrs. Abraham, but I'll see what I can do."

He wrote a short note, filled out a form, and attached it to her receipt.

He smiled at her. "You will receive a notification with a voucher in the mail in due course. Please bring the voucher to my office."

"Do I have to go through the process again when I return, or come directly to you?"

The official gave a short laugh. "No, Mrs. Abraham. You come directly to me, and don't forget to bring the voucher with you. I will then be able to give you your permit.

"How long will that be?"

He looked appreciatively into her pretty face, smiled, and said, "For you, my dear, within a couple of weeks. No more."

Sarah produced a grateful smile, "Thank you, sir. You have been most kind."

"Not at all, Mrs. Abraham. Call me Sadik."

"Thank you, Sadik."

She rose and shook his hand. His grip lingered seconds longer than a normal handshake.

The large clock face hanging high on the wall of the atrium of the government building showed the time to be approaching one in the afternoon as Sarah emerged into the noisy street. She walked to the roadside of the pavement in search of transportation. She had one more important visit to make before she returned home.

A horse-drawn carriage pulled up. She would have preferred a motorized taxi for speed but gave the driver an address asking him if he knew where it was. He gave a nod and she stepped into the carriage.

The carriage drew up outside the residential address of Doctor Cohen. Rachel was surprised to find her friend on her doorstep when she answered the ring of the doorbell.

"Sarah! What a nice surprise! Come in. I was just having lunch. Don't tell me you have eaten. You must join me."

"No. I haven't eaten. I'm sorry. I didn't want to disturb you and Zvi but I have a favor to ask of you, if I can talk to you discreetly."

"Zvi isn't here now. He's working at the hospital today. Come in."

Despite all the excitement of the day Sarah eagerly shared Rachel's lunch. After initial small talk, Sarah came to the point.

"The other day, when you brought Manya and Israel to my house, you mentioned that the HaShomer was sending an emissary here to request they be allowed to return to Palestine."

Rachel nodded. "That's correct."

"Do you know when that will be?"

"We are not sure," Rachel replied. "We haven't been given an official date for the hearing yet, but we think it will be in a month or so. Why do you ask?"

Sarah hesitated before blurting out. "Rachel, please keep this a secret. I've decided to return home. I've just come from the documentation office. I have applied for a travel permit to go to Palestine. Oh, Rachel, I have to find out what is happening there. I am choking with worry not knowing what has happened to my family. I have to go to them, Rachel. I have to."

Rachel got out of her chair and gave Sarah a hug before resuming her seat. "I know what you have been going through, Sarah, but what has that to do with Manya's case?"

Sarah looked across at Rachel. She felt tears welling up but she fought for control of her emotions.

"I can't travel on my own. It's too dangerous what with the war and the unrest, and I can't ask Chaim to take me. He is far too busy with his business and he would never allow me travel with all the turmoil and disruption going on. He would certainly prevent me from making the journey but, if they are released to go home, I want to go back with them."

"But what if Manya and Israel are not released from exile? How would you travel without them?"

"I thought about that. This emissary, he would have to return to Palestine, wouldn't he, after the hearing, no matter the result? I will ask him to take me with him and act as my escort."

Rachel looked deep into Sarah's face. "You are determined about this, aren't you?"

125

"Yes, I am. You will tell me when he is to arrive, won't you, Rachel?"

Rachel nodded. Sarah leaned over and gave her friend a return hug.

"Introduce me to him and let me be the one asking for his help. I'll explain everything to him."

"For you, darling Sarah, anything."

She gave Rachel another hug. "Thank you, dear Rachel., I knew I could rely on you. I have to be there so badly. You know that, don't you? It's where I am needed right now. I feel it."

Rachel gave Sarah another embrace and a kiss.

"I feel so out of touch here, Rachel. So useless. Having Manya over for that weekend made me realize how wasted my life is here. I have to be there helping my family." She paused, then added, "helping my people."

A silence descended. "And one more favor, please Rachel."

"What is it?"

"Please don't tell Chaim. Leave that to me. And please tell Zvi not to mention it to Chaim."

Sarah tried to remain calm during the following two weeks. Her main obsession was the mail delivery. Every day she waited expectantly for the arrival of the postman. Despite the shortage of young men, the postal service in Constantinople remained remarkably efficient. Mail usually arrived at the Abraham house in mid to late morning when Chaim was at his office. Sometimes, if Sarah went with her friends or ventured out alone, she would return to find a pile of letters on her hallway floor just under the postal slit of her front door. In these waiting days, Sarah preferred no to go out until after the postman had arrived at her mailbox.

When Chaim told her that he was preparing for yet another extended trip to Germany she panicked. What if he went to apply for his travel pass from the same officials that had served her? Would they ask him if he was related to a Mrs. Abraham who had recently requested a travel pass to Palestine? Sarah's nerves were jangling close to breaking point. The period between the arrival of the government notification of her travel request until Chaim confirmed that he had received his passport were unbearably tense. She tried not to show it but she was scared that, one day, Chaim would burst into the house having discovered what she was planning.

She need not have worried. She was so fraught she had forgotten that her husband traveled on his German passport. Chaim happened to slip this into his conversation over their evening meal. He told her he had to show his German passport when booking his train ticket from Constantinople to Berlin.

"It's a difficult journey these days, my dear. I go via Sophia to Belgrade. Then to Budapest and from there to Vienna. I will have meetings in Vienna before taking a train via Munich to Berlin. With the war, there may be interruptions in the train schedules in either direction. I am unable to tell you exactly what date I will return but, be assured my dear, that I will send you a telegram as I book my ticket home."

"Will you be safe, my dear?" Sarah genuinely did not wish for Chaim to come to any harm.

"I'm sure I will be safe and protected, my dear. No reason to alarm yourself."

"What date you will be leaving?"

"I will know that in a day or so."

Sarah felt mixed emotions over what was about to happen. Although she had suffered, she understood, with a respect almost bordering on sympathy, of his single-minded dedication to his business interests. Now, at the moment she was preparing to leave him, she found herself identifying with his concentration on something that was the central and most important thing in his life. She identified with it because this was precisely what she was about to do herself. Chaim was leaving her to pursue his growing commercial interests. She was about to leave him to dedicate herself to a greater cause in bosom of her loved ones. But she did have a tinge of guilty conscience over the manner she had to escape. from here, despite the fact that he, unknowingly, had left her with no other option. In a perverse way, at the moment they were about to part, Chaim had made her aware of her own identity.

That night they made love with a passion they hadn't experienced before. It was, she thought, their final embrace?

The letter confirming her travel permit was waiting for her with Sadik dropped through the mailbox just a couple of days before Chaim gave her the date of his departure from Constantinople. Sarah rushed to the government office, her voucher clutched in her eager hand.

Chaim was to leave a week later. The emissary had already arrived and was busy meeting with Manya and Israel in preparation for their tribunal set, as Sarah discovered, for the day after Chaim was due to leave for Germany. She begged Rachel Cohen to take her to meet the emissary. Two days later, Rachel came round to tell her that he agreed to meet her the day after the tribunal had deliberated on the request to allow Manya and Israel to return to Palestine.

Sarah helped Chaim pack for his journey. They did not have much time to relax together before his departure. He was, as usual, busy wrapping up matters and having last minute meetings before he left on his lengthy business trip. He ordered a motorized taxi to take him to his train station. The Prussian in him demanded that he leave a good hour and a half before his train was set to depart. Orderliness and efficiency was everything even at a time of intimate parting. They were in the living room. Chaim's luggage lay in the hallway near the front door.

"Are you sure you will be all right, my dear."

"Yes. Don't worry about me, Chaim. I will be fine."

Sarah stood by the window as Chaim gathered a few papers from the drawer of his bureau, read them and put them into his attaché case.

"Here! I think this must be your taxi," she said, pointing to the street.

Chaim came over to the window. "Yes. That must be it."

They walked into the hallway stopping only for Chaim to gather his coat, hat, and umbrella from the hallstand. There was a knock on the door. Chaim answered it and ushered the cab driver into the house, instructing him to carry his cases to the vehicle. He turned to Sarah and embraced her.

"Please take care of yourself, my dear."

Sarah gave him an affectionate kiss that surprised him. He looked into her eyes. She responded. "And please stay safe, my dear, dear, Chaim."

They held each other until Chaim noticed the driver was waiting for him.

"Goodbye, Sarah."

"Goodbye, Chaim."

And then he was gone, his black vehicle mingling with the flow of traffic and disappearing from view.

Sarah paused a moment longer. There was little to do except to wait for the outcome of the Ben-Zvis hearing. It came soon enough. Rachel came round to tell her that the authorities had rejected the request to allow the Ben-Zvis to return to Palestine. As promised, a meeting was arranged between Sarah and the emissary and, as discretion was vital, Sarah invited Rachel to bring the emissary to meet at her house in the late morning and to have lunch together.

Rachel arrived with a handsome, tanned, man. Sarah assessed him to be in his late thirties or early forties. He had the air of authority about him though he professed to be a kibbutz settler. He gave his name as Joshua Haus. As he drank tea and ate her cakes in Sarah's kitchen, Haus spoke scathingly about the harsh arrogance of the Young Turks. True, there was a war going on but, in his opinion, they seemed hell-bent on making enemies with everyone.

"You cannot believe what they are doing to us in Palestine. They are stripping us of everything we need to maintain ourselves and still they demand taxes from us. Look at the horrors they are bringing on the poor, desperate Armenians, just because they are Christians."

He told them that the stubborn judges at the tribunal had little patience to hear what contributions Manya and Israel had made to the development of agriculture throughout northern Palestine.

"They looked on them as enemy aliens, telling them they are lucky to be allowed to spend their time at liberty in Constantinople rather than in jail. One judge actually told them he could send them to jail."

Sarah asked Haus how long he expected to stay in town.

"I have a few people I need to see. I plan to go back in a week."

Sarah looked into his blue eyes.

"Take me with you."

This demanded an explanation.

"Let me put our lunch in the oven and I'll explain."

Over lunch, Sarah told the emissary about her life and the mistake she had made that now left her feeling like Manya, angry and frustrated by a wasted life.

"Unlike Manya," she explained, "I am in a self-induced exile. I have to get back to my people. To make myself useful again. You, Joshua, are my only lifeline. Without you, I cannot rejoin our efforts. You have no choice. You have to take me back with you."

Joshua stopped eating his meal. He looked at Sarah long and hard with a serious expression on his face. Her told her directly, "I guess I have no choice. I came here to take Manya back with me. I failed in that mission. I may as well return with you."

Sarah wanted to hug him but restrained herself. "Thank you. Thank you so much. When can we leave?"

"We can go next week. How about we leave next Tuesday? Rachel can you find out the train times. We can get the Baghdad Express to Aleppo and from there to Beirut, and from Beirut to Haifa. It's a long journey, Sarah."

"Yes. I came by boat from Haifa via Beirut. I appreciate that the train is slower."

Joshua paused. "Sarah. I have to warn you. The journey will not be pleasant. In fact, parts of it will be very unpleasant."

Sarah looked startled. "You mean dangerous?"

"Not dangerous, but very distressing."

"What do you mean? Why?"

"We have to pass through the places where they are mistreating the Armenians. You are going to see some horrible things. I just want to warn you about it. That's all."

Sarah and Rachel wanted to hear more, but all that the reticent emissary would say is, "these Turks are committing an international outrage. One day, they will be brought to justice for the crimes they are committing."

Sarah and Rachel looked at each other. Sarah was shame-faced. Could Chaim have lied to her? Did he know about what this Joshua Haus had seen but denied it was happening? Or did he genuinely not know? Sarah guessed she may never know the answer to that enigma.

On the Monday night, after Sarah had packed two cases, she sat at Chaim's desk and composed a letter to her husband.

"My dearest Chaim,

"I am aware you may be shocked when you return home and find the house empty and I am so sorry that I couldn't kiss you one more time before I left, but I have been bereft with uncertainty about the fate of my beloved family. You know they stopped writing to

me and, being all alone here, I have been tearing my soul apart with worry. "You were right that it would not be wise to travel alone but I had the opportunity to have a reliable person to escort me back to Palestine during these troubling times. He is an emissary for the HaShomer group. His name is Joshua Haus and is known to Rachel and Doctor Zvi Cohen, so I am not travelling with a total stranger.

"Be assured that I mulled over my decision to go back to Palestine long and hard, and you were, of course, a strong part of that consideration. I hope, if all is well and we have better times, I will return to you next Spring to spend Passover together.

"I know you will miss me as I will miss you, but I am sure that your intense business interests will take away some of the vacuum of my absence. Please know I love you and will be thinking of you.

"Goodbye, my love.

"Your affectionate,

Sarah."

THE JOURNEY

The Haydarpasa train terminus was an impressive tall building built in neo-classical style by German architects, Otto Ritter and Helmuth Cuno. It stood proudly on the Asian side of the Bosporus. It was built as a gift from Kaiser Wilhelm to Sultan Abdul Hamil the Second. It was also part of the Kaiser's grand strategy to extend the German Empire deep into the Middle East. It was to be an important terminal in the Berlin-Baghdad rail line.

Sarah and Joshua descended from their carriage and entrusted their luggage to a couple of porters. As they followed the porters to the train station, Sarah glanced admiringly at the Teutonic pseudo-castle design of the exterior. They walked into the interior with its high domed ceiling decorated with elaborate Turkish inlaid tiling set into the curved ceiling. Large decoratively framed windows cast bright sunlight onto the marble floor. They walked through the interior hall along corridors with grand ceilings held up by stylish arches. They reached their required platform and showed their tickets and travel permits to the attendant. They were in good time. Their train was waiting for them, the engine hissing eagerly to be on its way. They made their way to their carriage. Joshua paid the porters after they carried their cases to their allocated seats.

The train filled with soldiers, merchants, businessman, officials, and a few husbands and wives. Sarah sat quietly waiting for the train to take her away from a year and a half of a wasted life.

Sarah's heart leapt a beat as the train slowly chugged out of the station. As they gradually picked up speed, the last remaining buildings of Constantinople slid behind them. Sarah relaxed for the first time in many weeks. Shedding the urban city that had depressed Sarah so much, the train travelled through a fertile valley. Sarah stared at the blue of the distant Sea

134

of Marmara beyond the brown and green fields. It reminded her of the coastal plain between Zichron and Atlit that she missed so much.

Sarah began to relax and engaged Joshua in small talk. He was an attractive looking man who carried himself with an air of seriousness. He told her he had a young wife called Miriam and a small son waiting for him on his northern kibbutz home. She felt safe and secure in his company. She smiled at him and her own luck. He was the perfect man to have as her escort on their long journey home.

After an hour or so, she brought down a small hamper from the overhead shelf. She opened it and offered Joshua a sandwich she had prepared before leaving her Constantinople home for the final time. They both ate while chatting about the passing countryside which was varied and pleasant. Sarah went back into her hamper and brought out a couple of tasty cakes. They laughed as they both dropped crumbs on their clothes. To crown their lunch together, Sarah dipped once more into her hamper and, imitating a magician, wondrously produced a bottle of wine and two glasses.

"I thought we should celebrate our journey and for me, Joshua, the start of a more meaningful life."

"Thank you, Sarah. I will happily join you in that. There may be many more difficult days ahead." Raising his glass to her, he toasted, "May I wish you the meaningful life you wish for yourself. May it be a long and successful one."

They clinked their glasses and drank the wine.

"Not bad," said Joshua after tasting the wine.

"Not as good as our wines from Zichron Yaakov," laughed Sarah.

"Everything we do is better," Joshua retorted merrily. "Let's have another glass," Sarah suggested.

"Why not?"

They giggled as she poured more wine into their glasses. They both looked around at the other passengers staring at their antics, and they began to laugh hysterically.

Sarah hadn't laughed so freely since before she had left her home in Zichron.

They had to change trains at Izmit. Their train stopped at the large town in the late afternoon. Joshua said it would be best to find a hotel because, he said, there would be no large towns with comfortable accommodation until they reached Bilecik or Bursa much further down the track. Joshua hauled their luggage off the train until a couple of porters came running up to assist them. As Sarah spoke a better Turkish than Joshua she negotiated the price of their porterage and asked them to take them to the nearest hotel to the station. Stopping only to enquire what time the morning train would depart for the next leg of their journey, they followed the porters out of the station and across a cobbled square to a reasonable looking inn where they checked into two rooms. After freshening themselves in their separate rooms they met in the small lobby of the hotel and went out into the town to stroll around and find a restaurant for dinner. Sarah told Joshua that Izmit reminded her of a smaller version of Constantinople. This did not please her. She felt in Izmit that Turkey was still holding on to her soul.

Their train left Izmit late in the morning and crawled its way to the station of Adapazari where they stopped for a good ten minutes to discharge passengers and allow others to embark the train. As the train twisted its way slowly towards Bilecik she gazed out of the left side window and followed the Sakarya River as it flowed between fields and rocky outcrops.

136

Sarah had to admit that the countryside was attractive and varied as they journeyed on.

They debated whether to spend the night in Bilecik or stay on the train until it reached Eskisehir. Sarah wanted to push on as far as they could but Joshua suggested that as they wouldn't reach Eskisehir until the late evening. With the potential difficulty of finding accommodation in the dark of night, they disembarked in Bilecik.

They tipped a couple of peasants to take them to the nearest hotel which turned out to be a small, simple, but clean inn. They decided to go in search of a place to eat in the small town and then have an early night and get back to the station to catch an early train that would take them beyond Eskisahir and on to Kutanya.

There was little by way of cafes in this small wayside town but they found one small hole in the wall that served bitter Turkish coffee and a few homemade bourekas.

The next morning, they were surprised to discover that the passenger service had been suspended for a day due to expected heavy troop movement on the track. They had no choice but to kick their heels in this wastrel of a town. They strolled the few dusty streets. Nothing was far from the railway line and their frustration grew by the hour when no train came through the station until early afternoon. When it did it was not full of soldiers but one of open wagons crammed with sad looking civilians guarded by armed soldiers. The train did not stop in the station but trundled through.

They gazed in silence as the wagons passed them by.

"They must be Armenians being transported somewhere, "Joshua observed.

"So it was true after all," Sarah murmured.

It was a couple of hours later when a long train of carriages packed with soldiers and equipment passed through the station.

The journey between Black and Kutanya was tediously slow. The train seemed to travel at walking pace for several sections. It was already late afternoon when the train crawled into Eskisahir station. Another decision was required and they both erred on the side of caution and disembarked during daylight hours rather than venture into a dark and possibly unfriendly environment. Sarah appreciated that Joshua was being both chivalrous and cautious.

The next day's stage to Kutanya was covered at tortuous pace. Joshua told her that Kutanya was a busy branch line connecting the Turkish train traffic flowing both north and south and also east and west.

"There are bound to be more delays for civilian trains in Kutanya," he said, and he was right. They were held up in Kutanya for a couple of days. Part of the tedium was offset by watching the trains from a sizable café in the town square by the station. They commented as each long procession of wagons and carriages rolled by. Troop trains headed south, each packed with worried looking uniformed men. "They look like conscripts, not volunteers," suggested Sarah. "Yes, they don't look to me like eager warriors," Joshua agreed.

They watched freight trains trundle through the station with many wagons packed with equipment, weapons, heavy guns, and closed wagons that Joshua reckoned contained ammunition and explosives. They saw trains pass by carrying a mixture of men and goods. They guessed these wagons containing food, water, medical equipment for the troops who were gathering in ever growing force at the forward bases in Syria and almost certainly in Palestine.

A train ground to a stop in Kutanya station. Under the flurried harassment of Turkish soldiers, a sorry sight of humanity was forced out of what looked to be cattle wagons. Confused and shabby looking men, women, and children filled the station platform before being herded along the track heading south. Sarah and Joshua watched as, at gunpoint, thousands of dispelled and dirty Armenians were made to march off into the distance. They watched in shocked silence only quietly commenting as the long procession disappeared into the distance.

"This is what I warned you about," Joshua said. "I saw this during my train ride to Constantinople. Here we are a couple of weeks later, and it's still going on. Just think of the number of people that have been misplaced."

Sarah tried to grasp what was occurring in front of their eyes. "This surely cannot be what the Turks intended to do in this war of theirs."

Joshua Haus frowned. "It looks to me as if the government of the Union and Progress Committee is exploiting the war to clean house. I mean, to obliterate factions they don't want in their nation after the war. The Armenian Christians are clearly a part of the population they don't want, so they are getting rid of them."

Sarah looked worried. "What do you mean, get rid of them? Where are they going?"

"They are going to die, Sarah. They are going to die."

Sarah thought of something she had been too afraid to verbalize. She grabbed Joshua's arm.

"What if they intend to do the same to us in Palestine?"

More disappointment greeted them on the third day in Kutanya. The station master told them that all passenger trains had been stopped for the foreseeable future. The line, he said, was being dedicated to the war effort until further instructions. He advised them to head for Afyon-Karahisa by carriage or cart, a distance, he said, of eighty kilometers. There was little to discuss. It was either waiting here indefinitely, or go in search of a cart or carriage driver.

They were fortunate. Apparently, the prolonged train disruption had given rise to a new local trade. Redundant townspeople and poor farmers were plying a new trade in providing stranded travelers passage between Kutanya and Afyon. They found one of the last carriages when they exited the station. It wasn't a comfortable ride once they got out of town and on to the country tracks. Potholes were plenty as they bumped and jerked their way along the uneven earthen paths.

Despite the lateness of the year and the seasonal change from autumn to winter, it was a warm and dusty day. They set out heading south west through an arid plain below a mountain range that towered above them on their right. As they made their way through this flatland they awed at the massive terracing that previous generations had carved out of the mountain to capture the winter and spring rainfall on fertile soil. They remarked that this must be a bountiful place for needy crops to sustain the villagers. With Joshua being a kibbutz farmer back home, they both shared an expert eye on the agricultural aspects of the landscape of their route.

The long and tiresome trek skirted between cultivated fields under the shadow of the mountain and a barren expanse of nothingness on their left.

It was an uncomfortable and long ride. Their driver had told them it could take up to three days and he was right. Jolting and bouncing off rutted holes Sarah, thinking of her destination, began to look on parts of the scenery and made comparisons with Palestine. They compared their observations.

Joshua spoke from his northern perspective while Sarah informed him of the similarity to her coastal environment. They both remarked how much richer the flatlands would look if their collective pioneers were developing the land here. Sarah was homesick but happy. She was traveling through places that looked, in places, like home. She was travelling toward the place she loved.

They made the final long push to Afyon-Karahisar, arriving as night was falling. They asked their cart driver to deposit them at a hotel or inn close to the train station. They had become quite friendly with their driver, whose name was Salim, during the arduous trip. They shook his hand wished him goodbye after he brought them to a medium sized hotel within walking distance of the train station.

They groaned when the innkeeper confided that it was highly unlikely that passenger trains would be stopping in Afyon the next day, but they decided to check for themselves. They both desperately needed to soak in a bath or take a long shower to wash four days of dust and grime from their bodies. They had worn the same clothes for the journey and Sarah offered to take Joshua's filthy clothes and wash them in her bathroom. The innkeeper offered to prepare them a meal and they decided to eat at nine o'clock giving them a couple of hours to clean up. Before their meal, they walked over to the station. It was deserted. Not even the station master was present.

They returned the following morning after breakfast. The station master was in his office. He told them that no civilian train would arrive that day but he expected one to stop in Afyon the next day. He invited them to return in the late afternoon when he hoped to have the time of its arrival.

Frustratingly, they killed yet another wasted day in Afyon by sitting outside a café nursing two cups of thick brown Turkish coffee and staring at a huge black rocky outcrop that towered above the town. The café owner told

141

them that Karahisar Kalesi housed a three-thousand-year old castle on its peak. Its imposing presence had a huge physical presence that hypnotized Sarah. She let her tired mind go blank as she stared endlessly at this force of nature, endlessly, that is, until darkness descended. Joshua had asked her if she wanted to go visit this historic site but nothing motivated Sarah except to make progress toward home. The only benefit to the enforced delay in Afyon was that it allowed their freshly washed clothes to properly dry. Sarah had hung them over the small balcony railings on the tiny veranda outside her hotel room.

The station master told them that their train would arrive at nine thirty in the morning. The platform filled with people. It was hard to fathom where these people emerged from as the remote town was not large and hardly had any hotels of any size. Joshua guessed that they had travelled in by carts during the night. "That must have been an awful ride," Sarah said. The train pulled into the station twenty minutes late. It was quite full as they squeezed aboard, battling the other passengers who were as eager as they to find a seat for the long ride south.

The crowded train tried its best to pick up speed along the vast, flat, plains. Sarah urged its engine to find more power. By mid-day it pulled in to Aksehir station allowing both Sarah and Joshua to find more comfortable seats vacated by departing passengers. They were fortunate to take two window seats facing each other before impatient passengers surged into their carriage to fill up the remaining empty seats for the rest of the journey to Konya. Several had to stand throughout the long journey.

The empty landscape and the rhythmic rattle of the train soon had Sarah drifting into a deep sleep. She experienced a strange dream of being pulled in different directions. Aaron, Chaim, Avshalom, Rivka, her father, Alex, flittered in and out of her reverie. Voices told her, *Return to Constantinople. Go to Atlit. There are dangers! Come home! We need you! I love you, Sarita! Where are you, Sarah? It's not safe here!*

142

"Who said that?" she cried. Then she opened her eyes. Joshua was smiling at her.

"You must have been dreaming."

"I was? How did you know?"

"You shouted out, 'Who said that.'"

"Did I? Sorry," Sarah looked around the carriage in embarrassment, then apologetically said to Joshua, "I had a dream, or a nightmare. Oh, I wish this journey was over."

"Patience, Sarah. We still have a long way to go."

"Has it always been like this?"

"Not that I am an expert. I have only been to Turkey by train once before but, no, it was not as bad as this. The Turks and the Germans are pushing tens of thousands of troops into Syria and Palestine. What with them, their arsenals, their equipment, and, of course, the displaced Armenians adding to the transport system, civilians are left at the back of the queue. They are also extending their train line. The Germans are constructing a line that goes from Berlin to Damascus."

It was getting dark as the train slowed for the approach into Konya. As they peered out of the window through the dim light of the passing landscape they were aghast at the sight before them. Lifeless forms lay on the ground. Skeletons barely covered with rags were being picked by dogs. They were stunned into silence until the scene slid behind them and the train entered the station.

"My God, Joshua, what was that? Where are we? This is hell," Sarah cried.

Joshua didn't have an answer.

As they struggled with their luggage onto the station platform they were surrounded by a crowd of jostling men begging to be their porters. They tried to gather their bearings. A row of leafless trees stood beside a series of low dirty white buildings with brown tiled roofs. The platform was nothing but compacted dusty earth. Although they had left the hellish scene a mile prior to the station they were keen to get away from this place of death. They joined others lining up to discover how quickly they could proceed on their journey away from this hellhole. They were told that because of the war and work on the railway line through the Taurus mountains further down the track there would be no scheduled passenger trains until the mid-morning two days later. The station master blamed it on the war. Utterly dejected, they ordered the porters to take them to a hotel away from the station as quickly as possible.

They asked the hotel manager what had happened here.

"We had the migrants camped here. Some died before they could be transferred further south."

"What do you mean by migrants?" Sarah asked.

"You know, the Armenians. They were getting in the way of our war effort so they got moved."

"But why the bodies?"

The manager gave a shrug. "Some people got sick. There was disease. The authorities had to move people to another location, and some people died. We didn't want to bring the disease into the town, so they got buried there, in the camps."

"But is no one taking care of them?" Sarah asked.

144

"Well, there is the American hospital and the orphanage."

"Who is running it?"

"There is an American woman. I think her name is Cushman."

"Where can we find her?"

The manager gave Sarah directions. Sarah looked at Joshua. "We are stuck here tomorrow. Let's go and visit her in the morning."

The manager asked them if they wanted to eat before they retired to their rooms.

Sarah shook her head. "No, thank you. I lost my appetite coming into Konya."

In the morning, they following the manager's instructions and came across a tall building with a sign announcing 'The Apostolic Institute.' They ventured into the building and were met by a woman who greeted them in Turkish.

"Are you Mrs. Cushman?" Sarah asked.

The woman smiled. "No. Miss Cushman is busy with the children. Can I help you?"

They explained that they were making their way out of Turkey by train and had witnessed the shocking scene.

"What happened here?" Sarah asked.
The woman led them into a barely furnished office and offered them a seat and a glass of water.

"Konya is a detention camp for the unfortunate Armenians who were brought here by train. The camp is in an open field just out of the town. Many hundreds died. They died of hunger. They died of disease. They died of exhaustion. They left many orphans. With the help of the Americans we try our best to care for them, to feed them as much as we are able, to educate them, to give them order and security."

"What of the rest, the adults?"

"They have been moved down the road," the woman said pointing south.

"To what fate?" Sarah asked.

The woman simply shrugged.

Joshua asked, "And who is Miss Cushman?"

The woman smiled again. "She is an angel. An American angel who came here out of nowhere to save the children."

A wisp of a man with a neat goatee beard entered the office. The receptionist introduced them.

"This is Professor Haigazian. Professor Haigazian manages the institute."

The professor shook hands with both Sarah and Joshua. "Welcome to our Institute. Where are you from?"

Sarah answered. "We are on our way back to Palestine. I live a place called Zichron Yaakov?"

"And I also live in Palestine. In the Galilee which is in the north of the district," added Joshua.

"Ah, yes. I have heard of that place from the Bible. I am myself an American and an Armenian, so the Galilee is a place that resounds for me in my faith. You must be Jewish, correct?"

They nodded. The professor sighed.

"We are both punished people," he said enigmatically.

"Can you share with us what happened here?" Sarah asked boldly.

The professor took a moment to gather his thoughts.

"Would like some tea? I am sorry we cannot offer you much else. Aline, would you bring us tea, please?"

The receptionist went to prepare their refreshments.

"There was a church here. An Armenian church. The government demanded that the congregation tear down the bell tower. When they refused, the authorities came and destroyed the church. They presented the Institute with the bill for its destruction. By the time the priest could contact the outside world, the Turks were arresting and deporting the Zeytoun Armenians. When the Americans heard about it they protested to the Germans in the knowledge that they would have influence over the Turks. We are very grateful for the intervention of Ambassador Morgenthau."

"I know Mr. Morgenthau. He visited us once," said Sarah.

A surprised Professor Haigazian asked, "How so?"

"My brother, Aaron, runs an Agricultural Research Station that is funded by American trustees. He collaborates with the American Department of Agriculture. Mr. Morgenthau came to Zichron to see what we are doing in Palestine to develop the land."

147

"Ambassador Morgenthau is indeed a resourceful and powerful man. The Turks do not want to provoke the Americans into joining the war against them but, sadly, they cannot resist persecuting my people. That is why I am here, to attempt to protect the children, to give them hope for a better future."

"How many children do you have here?" Joshua asked.

"We have six hundred orphans, roughly the same number of boys and girls."

"Where do these children come from?" Sarah enquired.

"Really from all over the Ottoman controlled territory. Some were transported down from our Armenian towns in the east to Anatolia in the north west. There has been a total destruction of our people centered in Van."

"But why are they doing it?" Sarah persisted, curious to understand.

The professor shrugged. "They claim they evicted the Armenians to remove them from harm's way, but the real truth is that my people are being ethnically annihilated."

Joshua asked, "I don't doubt you, Professor Haigazian, but what evidence is there to prove what you say?"

Professor Haigazian gave Joshua a rueful smile. "If that was the reason, why didn't they also remove the Muslim Turks? The local Turks remained in the towns and villages and took over the homes and the possessions of the evicted Armenian Christians. This is clearly an ethnic war against my people, Joshua."

Aline retuned with a tray. She was accompanied by a woman who waved at the professor as she entered.

"Ah, this is Emma, Emma Cushman. How are you, my dear?" The professor had risen from his chair and offered the woman an affectionate kiss on her cheek. "This woman is extraordinary," he said as they shook hands.

Miss Cushman was not as Sarah expected. The woman that entered the room was a heavy-set bespectacled American lady in her sixties.

"Emma, our guests are making their way home to Palestine. Aren't they fortunate?"

"They are indeed." Miss Cushman possessed both the demeanor of a spiritual person and the steeliness of someone who had known hard times.

"How are the children today?" Professor Haigazian asked.

"They are a miracle," Emma said with a sad smile. "How they can be so resilient amazes me, considering what they have gone through, what they have witnessed," she added with a frown.

The professor and Aline nodded. The professor drained his cup and rose from his seat. "Well, I must go and teach the children, to give our dear Emma a break." He approached Sarah and Joshua who had also arose from their chairs to take his outstretched hand. "It was my pleasure to meet with you. I hope you have a safe journey home. God bless you both."

Joshua shook hands with the professor. Sarah embraced him.
"God bless you, professor for what you are doing for the children here. I will remember what we have seen. The world needs to understand what is happening here."

"Thank you. That is important to us." And with that, the slight figure of a giant man left the room.

Emma Cushman took them on a tour of the orphanage. They met well behaved and clean children. Sarah engaged a small group in conversation with a smiling Emma looking on. As they strolled through the building, examining the rooms, they chatted about the circumstances that brought an American woman to this place. She told them she was trained as a nurse and later trained other nurses at a hospital in Kansas City. Serving as a foreign missionary she had served in Asia and Africa before coming to Konya to work in the American Hospital alongside two American doctors. When the Ottoman's entered the war they ordered all foreigners to leave. The doctors left, but the redoubtable Miss Cushman remained. She was a large lady and a determined woman. The antagonism of the Turks against the Armenians grew, she told them. The Turks exploited the Armenian men to labor on the rail project in awful and underfed conditions. She began to receive children whose parents had been killed. She converted the Apostolic Institute building into an orphanage that had grown to over six hundred children.

"But where do you get the funds to run this place?" Sarah asked.

"We are well supported by the American Committee for Near East Relief," Emma answered.

"Professor Haigazian told us where the children came from," Sarah said, "but how did they end up here?"

Emma Cushman said sadly, "They were mainly transported here by train after being separated from their parents and family. The Turks unloaded them from the trains but prevented them from entering the town. They were herded into the camp just outside the town where they lived, many without tents and without food except for what we could provide them, but we had far too little resources to help them all." She added, "The sick children we brought to the hospital, but many died of hunger or disease, so we brought the orphan children into our care."

Sarah heard the harrowing story of a freight-load of wagons that arrived in Konya one day filled with children but no adults. The children had been transported without their parents. In most cases, the little children did not know the fate of their mothers and fathers, Miss Cushman explained. When Emma tried to bring the children into her orphanage the local Turks complained to the authorities that she was kidnapping Turkish children and converting them into Christianity. They arrested her and put her under interrogation. Only an appeal to the Governor of Konya got her released.

"It must be dangerous for you to be here," said Sarah, in awe of this courageous woman.

"We are existing here, living under threat, but we have to give the sick and the children as much humanity as we are able. Who else will look after them? Actually, Professor Haigazian is in more danger than I am. I have the protection of my government, unless they join the war against Turkey. But he is an Armenian. This leaves him far more vulnerable to the dangerous whims of the Turks. He left his family in Greece to come here and do what he can for his people. He is a courageous humanitarian, and he has already been arrested and mistreated by the Turks. Armenag was only released after the intervention of the American Embassy rescued him from their cruel hands. He could have escaped to America, but Armenag remains here to help the children and the sick," Emma said of him, referring to the professor by his private name.

As they took their leave, the formidable Miss Emma Cushman made an ominous prediction.

"I hope you have a safe journey. You are certain to see more signs of the Armenian destruction and persecution along your route. Be a witness, "she begged, "and be sure to tell the world about it. I intend to report what is happening here if I survive this war. Those responsible must be brought to justice for the terrible crimes that are being committed here."

Sarah and Joshua walked slowly and silently back to their hotel in somber mood. Both were buried under the grave impressions that scarred their minds and their souls.

I will bear witness to this atrocity, Sarah vowed to herself, and to the persecuted Armenians.

The train to Karaman was scheduled for ten thirty. They were happy to hear that the train would continue to Eregli, a distance of a further eighty-five kilometers. Anything to get them further away from Konya.

There were a number of familiar faces on the Karaman train. It seemed that a few people were suffering the same fateful passage to Syria. Sharing this tortuous journey forced a fleeting acquaintance between fellow passengers. Polite conversation emerged, though talk of war and what they had witnessed remained unspoken. Sarah was sensitive that her fellow travelers were Turkish and would harbor a far different opinion to her.

By two thirty in the afternoon the train arrived at Karaman where it remained at the platform for a good twenty minutes before picking up steam for the eighty-five kilometer ride to Eregli. Joshua noticed they were travelling north east, keeping the Taurus Mountains on the southern side of the train.

Sarah was in a depressed mood by the time they reached Eregli. This was made worse by what she saw on arrival. In Eregli, the poor exiles were encamped in open fields not far from the station. There must have been thousands of them. No protection from the weather had been afforded them. The only tenting that Sarah could see were those that the more fortunate refugees had made out of carpets, course matting, cloaks, or

152

sacking material. There were no sanitary arrangements that she could see. The stench was appalling. She knew that dysentery and typhus must be running rampant among the desperate folk that hung on to life in this pathetic patch of earth.

They were told that this leg of the train route would terminate at Bozanti and, from there, they would have to take whatever mode of transportation was available to take them through the Taurus Mountains to Tarsus where they could connect to Adana for their onward journey. Emma Cushman's dire warnings were apparent in the desperate scene that lay before them at Eregli station. Sarah wanted to get away from the horror as quickly as possible but dreaded what lay ahead.

It was luck of the draw what form of transport was available from the Bozanti. When they emerged from the station they saw passengers haggling for the carts that were lined up to take passengers south through the mountain range. An ox cart tethered to a pair of mules was one of the last wagons. They quickly deliberated whether to chance waiting to see if another more comfortable mode of transport would arrive.

"How do we know it won't be worse," ventured Sarah, "or if another will come at all?"

They thrust a small pile of money into the hands of the driver and threw their luggage into the cart.

The overuse and neglect of the road was evident to Sarah with every bump and shudder of their slow and painful ride through the twisting rough track that snaked its way through the huge rocky outcrops of the towering Taurus mountains. They traversed small, stone bridges over dried out wadis. Joshua remarked that, in another month, these gullies would be impassable with winter's heavy rainfall. As they rose through the mountain range they felt the first chill of winter. It was mid-December. At one small stop to stretch their limbs they opened their cases to take out warmer clothing.

The rocking wagon frequently drew perilously close to the edges of ravines that dropped steeply into deep gullies. Occasionally, they had to move aside to allow faster moving motor vehicles to pass them by. In the rugged heart of the mountain range, as they rounded a sharp bend with yet another steep drop over Sarah's left shoulder, they came across an impressive engineering project. A huge bridge like structure emerged out of a deep chasm. It was being built to support a train line that would emerge from one dark tunnel and disappear into another that was being blasted and mined from the hard rock of the mountain. As their cart navigated around the construction work they were impressed by the magnitude and size of the project but also by the mass of laborers who were carrying out the hard graft that was producing this modern engineering achievement. They looked filthy, ragged, and miserable. It was clear to both of them they were conscripted Armenians likely underpaid, if paid at all, and existing on starvation rations and probably living in primitive conditions. They were being supervised, or more accurately, guarded by uniformed Turks.

Another twist in the road led them to the relative isolation of the mountain. Their mountainous trek suddenly emerged on to a twisting downward trail leading them out of the mountainous region and into the plateau of the southern lowlands. As they approached a bridge straddling a broad river they asked their driver to stop a while so that they could wash the dust and grime from their faces. Sarah washed the trauma off her skin but not out of her mind. As they cleaned themselves in the cold waters, their driver told them the river was called the Berdan, but locals called it the Tarsus River. It flowed through the first lush fertile greenery they had seen for days. They gazed into the flowing waters for several minutes. Sarah luxuriated in the cool breeze that wafted her face. She looked at the green of the trees, grasses, shrubs, and plants. Taking in the scene around her and listening to the gurgling flow of the river, she told Joshua that this place reminded her of the northern parts of the Galilee. Joshua agreed. The yearning urged her back to the wagon to continue her homeward bound odyssey. Refreshed and impatient now, she sat in the cart doggedly staring straight ahead for mile after flat mile searching for the town of Tarsus.

Barony, on the northern Mediterranean coast was once the kingdom of the Cilician Armenians. Although some were mountain herdsmen and farmers, others were artisans, lawyers, academics, successful international tradesman. Their civilization and prosperity had been wiped away by the suspicious and resentful Young Turks who replaced the indolent, benign, Ottoman sultans. By the time Sarah and Joshua passed through their once thriving territory it had been stolen from them by force and cruelty leaving them destitute, homeless, and desperately struggling to stay alive under the brutal regime of the utterly misnamed Committee of Union and Progress.

The Armenian remnants that Sarah saw in the few hours she spent in Tarsus were a sad sight. On the train from Tarsus to Osmania, she stared out of the window at the shocking spectacle of thousands of Armenians being herded south on the paths and rough ground by the side of the train tracks. A fortunate few were being transported on ox carts. Some rode on mules while other had their mules carry their belongings as they walked alongside. But the vast majority were on foot. Sarah noticed that many were walking shoeless.

They were horribly hypnotized by what they were witnessing. They noticed many people lying by the wayside, too exhausted or sick to continue. A steady procession trudged by, barely glancing at the fallen, each consumed with their own fate. Sarah watched as small family groups sat huddled by the side of a prostrate and dying loved one. A father, a grandmother, about to be released from their earthly misery by finding their final release from the barbarity of the inhumane Turks.

The camp at Osmania stretched for miles. It had been used several times by different convoys of Armenians and no attempt at sanitation had been employed either by the Turks nor by the Armenians themselves. The ground was in deplorable condition. The stench beyond description. They could smell it in the train carriages even with the windows tightly closed.

As they pulled into Osmania station they heard shouts and screams. The engine driver blew his horn loudly and repeatedly. There was a commotion at the front of the train. As they descended from the carriage to see what had happened, they were mobbed by crowd of outstretched hands. Women and children were pushed aside by men begging for food, money, anything. They targeted Sarah.

"Hanoun! Have you bread?" "Hanoun. I haven't eaten in three days!" "Hanoun! Please give me food or money so that I can feed my baby."

Joshua tried to forge a passage to escape the desperate crowd. As they reached the front of the train a scene from an inferno of hate and violence greeted them. The railway track was full of prostrate and bleeding people.

Sarah noticed many that were dead. People were shouting that the train had drawn into the open station and the driver had continued beyond the station platform to deliberately drive over people too weak or sick to rise as the train approached. It was a grotesque sight of dead and injured. There was blood everywhere. Police and soldiers tried to force people away. They began shooting, first in the air, and then into the crowd. Looking away, she glanced up into the locomotive engine and saw the sooty face of the train driver. She saw him watching the pandemonium he had caused. He had grin of pleasure on his dirty face at the deadly chaos he had caused. Sarah felt sickened. They returned hurriedly to their carriage.

As the train south proceeded south and entered Syria, the vista gave them little escape from the haunting sight of thousands of hopeless refugees tramping to God knows where. Perhaps death was the only certain outcome. From her carriage window Sarah witnessed some of the worst sights of her terrible journey. She watched as people, walking endlessly, began to give up in the heat of the day. Even in December the sun beat down mercilessly on these miserable souls. Sarah watched people collapse through lack of water. They were literally dying of thirst. She silently wept as her train window slowly passed a couple of teenage girls lying unconscious, approaching death, their once pretty faces bloated from exposure to the sun and the wind.

Sarah was distraught as the train arrived in Aleppo. Joshua tried to assure her that the worst was behind them. They queued at the ticket office to reserve two seats on a train on the Hejaz line through Syria to the junction at Deraa that would split off into Palestine on the line that would end in Haifa. As they discussed their options with the ticket clerk they were informed of a potential delay on their route. Because of troop movements there would likely be a delay in civilian train travel from the junction at Deraa and possibly at the junction at Afula. He advised them to book their tickets on the train leaving Aleppo the next morning as this would almost certainly connect up with a train to Haifa. Armed with the timetables and their tickets they went in search of a hotel. After they checked in, Sarah asked Yitzhak to escort her to the local telegraph office. She wired a message to her brother, Aaron.

"Dear Aaron. Chaim in Germany on business. Decided to spend winter with family. Train expected to arrive Haifa 4 pm Friday, December 16. Send confirmation you will meet us by reply telegram to Aleppo telegram office by Thursday night latest. Love. Sarah."

In the late afternoon Sarah walked with Joshua back to the postal office to enquire if a telegram had arrived for her. The postal clerk searched and handed over an envelope. Inside she found a typed message;

157

"Dearest Sarah. Be at the Zelkind Hotel. Looking forward to seeing you again. Love. Aaron."

Sarah hugged the note to her breast and exhaled a long and happy sigh. Smiling, she said to her protective escort, "Finally, Joshua! I feel we are almost home."

"Yes we are, Sarah. Almost there."

There, in the postal office, ignoring everyone around her, Sarah embraced Joshua.

"I could never have done this journey without you, Joshua. Bless you for being with me all the way."

Joshua smiled. "You are a far stronger woman than you give yourself credit for, Sarah. It's been a harrowing trip and I don't know many women to could have kept their composure as you did."

They spent their last evening in Aleppo sitting at an outside table at a decent restaurant. After ordering their food, Joshua told Sarah that he was so looking forward to returning to his wife and son.

"She has a couple of months to go before giving birth to our second child. Nothing is going to keep me away from her until then," the HaShomer emissary vowed.

They both contemplated their future. Joshua's was one of a happy and growing family. Sarah's future was still unknown.

Sarah stared at the moon. "The best days of my life have been spent alongside Aaron, Alex, Avshalom, and the boys who work in our agricultural projects. I realize now that what we were doing was not just to develop the land but preparing it for our people's future. Things have changed. We will lose our future if the Turks and the Germans win this war."

Joshua nodded but remained silent.

"If the last couple of wasteful years and this journey have taught me anything, Joshua, it is that I now have an expectation of myself to do something meaningful. I think I am going to find out when I get back to Aaron. Whatever it is, I have to do it."

They changed trains at Deraa and their connecting train was almost two hours late arriving at the station. They clambered aboard. Sarah was in an excitable mood. The train travelled south searching for the exit in the high plain that would take them west through the Golan Heights and down into the Jordan Valley. She almost bounced in her seat when the train track curved right and began a descent. Eventually, the barrier of the hills fell revealing the placid waters of the Sea of Galilee.

"Look! Look!" squealed Sarah like a teenage girl. Joshua smiled as he gazed at the serene scene.

The train pulled in to the junction station of Tzemach, just beyond the southern shores of the biblical lake. Their carriage and much of the train emptied as hundreds of Turkish and German soldiers and officers disembarked to catch their troop trains to their garrisons throughout Palestine. A number of officers, men in civilian clothes, and family groups boarded. For the first time in two years, Sarah heard a smattering of Hebrew being spoken in Palestine. She sat back in her seat with a contented look on her face.

The train sped through the Jezreel Valley towards the northern end of the Carmel hills. Sarah searched for the crack in the Carmel range that she knew led through Wadi Milik and to her home in Zichron Yaakov. She wished the train would stop so that she could run all the way home, but she knew that Aaron was waiting for her at the Zelkind Hotel in Haifa.

They skirted the hills heading north before the train line turned westward toward the Mediterranean Sea and one of its important ports in Haifa. Sarah noticed they had managed to make up a bit of the lost time as they pulled in Haifa just an hour and a half later than the scheduled arrival time. She knew that the unflappable Aaron would be waiting patiently, but her heart was racing uncontrollably.

They took a motorized cab for the short ride from the station to the hotel. As she and Joshua helped the taxi driver remove their luggage from the cab she heard a familiar booming voice.

"Sarah!"

She turned and saw the imposing figure of her older brother. She ran and leapt into his outstretched arms. Sarah wrapped herself around him. He swept her off her feet in a circling embrace before putting her down to stare into her beaming face. They kissed and embraced again, hugging each other for a period that Sarah hoped would be forever.

When they unlocked themselves Sarah turned to introduce Joshua to Aaron.

"Aaron. This is Joshua Haus. I could never had made this trip without him. He's been wonderful to me. He protected me through the most awful journey you can possibly imagine."

The two men shook hands.

"Your sister is a remarkable woman."

160

"Yes. I know that. Thank you for protecting her. You must tell me about your journey. I have booked rooms for us for the night. I know you are anxious to return home, Joshua, but you must allow me to repay you for your kindness to my sister by accommodating you tonight and buying you dinner."

It may have been the comforting thought that she was, at last, home, or it could have been that she had not eaten regularly throughout the three-week ordeal of her journey, but Sarah was ravenously hungry after their exhausting trip. As Aaron stared at her over the dinner table he could not fail to notice how gaunt and thin she looked. The black rings around her recessed eyes were witness to the torrid time that had taken a toll on her physical beauty. Yet, for Sarah, being back in the presence of her beloved brother enriched her appetite. Here, in this Haifa hotel, she felt a sense of profound relief.

"How was your journey?" Aaron asked.

"It was a nightmare. A terrible nightmare," Sarah answered. Joshua maintained a stoic silence.

Sarah blurted out the many experiences and the horrible scenes they had witnessed along their route in southern Turkey and into northern Syria.

"What the Turks are doing to the poor Armenians is like the pogroms inflicted on our people. In fact, I think it far worse in the scale and numbers of the slaughter."

Aaron studied Sarah as she told of her harrowing journey. Her experiences had affected her deeply but he noticed there was a steeliness that hadn't seen in her before, a maturity that only coping with suffering could induce in a person. He was upset by the physical wear and tear that

161

her journey had taken out of her, but he was also impressed by the way his sister comported herself. Although her explanation wobbled between dispassionate eye witness testimony and emotional heart-wrenching narration she methodically outlined her traumatic tale in detail. Sarah encouraged Joshua to share their anecdotes with Aaron.

Joshua corroborated Sarah's remarks. "It is systematic, too organized, to be a spontaneous local persecution. The mass expulsion and deportation of defenseless people clearly comes from the top. They deny they are deporting people. They prefer to use the term 'relocation,' but they are leading masses of Armenians to their death by induced starvation and the subsequent disease which goes unattended, except in the rare cases we saw, such as at the Apostolic Mission in Konya."

"It sounds like the Turks are strengthening their national majority at the expense of the Armenian Christian community and using the war as a cover," Aaron suggested.

Sarah leaned over the table. "Aaron. What they are doing to the Christians they can easily do against us. All they need is the slightest pretext and we will be next."

Aaron nodded. Joshua added, "What concerns me is that it began by the Turks depriving the Armenians of the few weapons they had. This left them defenseless. Over here, it's happening to us already. They are banning and confiscating our possession of rifles and weapons. Our HaShomer defense organization is trying to hide as much as we can, but they are conducting searches and punishing those who have not handed them over."

"Yes, I know," Aaron confirmed. "They came to Zichron and demanded we surrender our weapons. Our Gideonites hid them in the threshing house, but after they searched the houses and didn't find anything, they arrested seven of our young men, including Alex, and began beating them to extract information about where the weapons were hidden."

Sarah put a hand to her mouth in shock. "You mean that our Alex was tortured?"

Aaron nodded and placed a soothing hand on Sarah's arm. "Yes, they whipped the underside of his feet with their bastinado canes to try to extract information. Alex said it was painful. His feet bled, but he gave nothing away. Neither did the other men. So the Turks rounded up some of the young girls of the village and told the elders that they would be given to their soldiers if they did not report where their weapons were being stored. They had no choice but to hand them over."

Aaron looked at Sarah. "It's all right. Alex is all right. They released the men and left the village with the weapons."

Sarah said, "The Turks must lose the war, otherwise we are doomed."

Aaron nodded. "I would like both of you to write down everything you saw. We will send a report about the atrocities you two witnessed to our American contacts and have them bring them to the attention of the United States Administration. These Turkish crimes will not go unpunished."

Aaron raised his wine glass and looked over at Joshua.

"Joshua, I want to thank you for escorting and protecting my sister. It was very gallant of you to accompany her along the way. Here's to you!"

Sarah joined him in drinking a toast to Joshua Haus. "No need to thank me, Aaron. Sarah made my journey so much more bearable."

"Now let's get some rest," Aaron ordered. "It looks like you two need it."

After breakfast, Sarah bade Joshua a fond farewell with a hug and an affectionate kiss on his cheek. Aaron pumped the hand of the HaShomer agent, thanking him for his kindness to Sarah. They parted ways, then Aaron carried Sarah's luggage to his Ford Motor car for their ride home to Zichron Yaakov.

On the way they talked. Aaron told Sarah why he had sent Rivka to study in Beirut.

"I wanted her out of Zichron. Things are happening, Sarah, and I wanted little Rivka to be somewhere safe until the war ends."

He glanced over to Sarah. "And Alex has gone to join her." He saw Sarah's raised eyebrows at the shock of this news.

"I wanted Alex to be our person in America and, after his arrest and beating, he's a marked man. He can be useful to us as our contact man in the United States, and he can take care of Rivka there."

"How is papa?"

"He is as stoic as he always has been. You know him, Sarah. He's a tough old bird."

As they drove out of Haifa and approached the fields of Atlit that she loved so much Sarah noticed the bleak barrenness of the landscape.

"Where is all the greenery? What happened here?"

Aaron told her the horror story of the locust plague that had wiped out all the crops throughout Palestine.

"It was a biblical invasion. I make no exaggeration, Sarah. It devastated the whole area. They came in their millions. They blackened the sky, so great were their numbers. When they landed, the earth seemed to move and sway with their movement as they devoured everything. We tried everything we could to fight back but it was an impossible task made worse by the Turks not giving us the gasoline we asked for to kill them and destroy their eggs which hatched in the ground. Now everyone is suffering. The village lost money because of producing no crops and nobody has much food to eat. It's been a very tough year."

Sarah asked hesitantly, "And what of Avsha?"

Aaron glanced over at his sister as he drove. "Sarah. There is something you need to know. I didn't want to talk about it yesterday in the presence of Joshua. Things here are not the same as they were when you left. There is no fighting going on over here, yet. But we are convinced that the British will open up a new front here to defeat the Germans with the Turks on their side. Over the other side of the Jordan River, the Arabs are making deals with the British to drive out the Turks. They are claiming their territory for an Arab kingdom and it looks like the British are helping them. Avshalom has been pushing me very hard to do the same thing over here. I am persuaded that only the British can remove the Turkish yoke from our necks and this will open the way for establishing our own Jewish homeland out of the vacuum left by a Turkish defeat. Our ancient rights to this land are far stronger than any other claim, let alone the Hashemites from Mecca."

Sarah was excited at the thought. Aaron paused long enough to take another, even longer glance at Sarah.

"Consider this. The British will eventually take on the Turks here and they need to do it now before the Turks reinforce their troops and defenses.

165

Their victory is assured if they take the initiative quickly, but they will need help. That is where we come in."

Sarah was curious but remained silent taking in Aaron's every word.

"We have developed a network of resourceful and brave people who are dedicated to the land and to the future of our people. They work tirelessly for our agricultural projects, but these young men and women can also be our secret intelligence gatherers. The British need to know which troops are located where and in what numbers. We can provide them with details of strategic routes, meteorological reports, even give them Turkish military intelligence. In short, we can give the British everything they need to win this war with greater efficiency."

This news surprised Sarah. "What? You mean like spies?"

"Well, I would prefer to call them intelligence investigators."

"But what of Avsha?" Sarah hadn't heard from him, or of him, for months.

"This has everything to do with our intelligence work. You know Avsha. He is so passionate about everything. He wanted to form a fighting group to take on the Turks. Of course, they would easily have been outnumbered, outgunned, and slaughtered, but he persuaded me that we had to do something about the Turks. Only the British can defeat the Turks militarily. Our talents, our network, and our license to operate among the Turks, who are now our enemy, can help bring about a British victory if used intelligently. I told Avsha we can contribute to driving out the Turks not by force but by the intelligent use of our skills and our eyes and ears. We can give the British the vital intelligence that they will need to defeat the Ottomans militarily. I sent Alex to Egypt to speak with the British but he had no success. The Brits can be so unreasonably stubborn. Avshalom begged me to allow him to try his luck, so I sent him down to Egypt and he made an excellent contact with a British naval intelligence officer. Through him we set up a method where a ship would come to Atlit with a list of the information they need and we would provide it. It's quite simple really. He came back on the boat which anchored at night off the coast near our station. They give us instructions of what they want and we give them satchels full of the information that their military intelligence need to prepare their battle plans."

Sarah was excited. She was beginning to understand why her brother had limited his letters to her.

"Then the ship failed to turn up," Aaron continued. "We have no other way to communicate with them and we have intelligence reports piling up with no way to get them to the British. Some of it is critical. That's why Avshalom is on his way back to Egypt. He left a couple of days ago with Joseph. You remember Lishansky don't you, Sarah?

Sarah paused as she realized that with Alex and Rivka in America and Avshalom heading for Egypt, Aaron was alone in bearing the burden of work.

"So, with Alex and Rivka in America, and Avsha and Joseph heading down to Egypt, you are virtually running everything on your own?"

"I guess so. Yes."

"Not any more. I'm here now, ready to get involved."

"Wait..."

"No Aaron. No more waiting. I didn't leave Chaim to be a cook and house clearer. I came to renew myself with our project, no matter what it is."

"This intelligence gathering is dangerous work, Sarah. It is deadly business."

"No matter, Aaron. I left Chaim and Constantinople to dedicate myself to whatever must be done. Nothing will dissuade me otherwise."

Aaron looked over at his sister's haggard but determined face. He found himself looking not at the sister he knew, but at a person with an absolute resolve.

The few villagers who were out on the street that day did a double take as Aaron's car drove by. Sarah waved at familiar faces who were surprised to see her returning to her home.

"Now watch gossip's tongues start wagging," Aaron half joked. Sarah didn't care. She was glad to be back.

As the Ford drove into the compound of their home, a door opened and Ephraim appeared, drawn by the sound of the engine. Sarah leapt out of the vehicle and ran over to her father. They hugged in a prolonged embrace.

"How are you, papa?" she asked.

"All the better for having you back. Welcome home, Sarah."

Sarah looked at her father. His face was more lined than she remembered it to be, but he seemed to be as sturdy as ever. Ephraim studied her with a serious expression on his face. "It looks as if we need to fatten you up a bit. You've lost weight, my girl," he said.

"We'll join you soon, papa, for lunch," Aaron interjected. "Sarah and I have some talking to do. We need to let her know of all the changes that have taken place since she left us."

Sarah kissed her father and smiled. "It's so good to see you again, papa. I really missed you while I was in Constantinople. I thought of you a lot. Let me speak with Aaron. We will have plenty of time to talk."

Aaron filled her in about the terrible locust invasion that had destroyed all the crops and had made life impossible for the villagers of Zichron. This, added to the burden of a Turkish oppression executed in the name of the war effort, had increased the burden of survival immeasurably.

"However, there is bright side," said Aaron. "The locust problem was so serious that I managed to obtain wazira travel passes for most of our team. They now travel around the country with their official documents to research or investigate the effects and locations of the locust plague everywhere, including in military installations and camps."

Sarah was puzzled. "Why is this important?"

Aaron gathered his thoughts. "I told you on our ride home, about using our knowledge and contacts to help the British. I brought our staff to a meeting at Atlit. I gave all our guys the option to continue with their agricultural projects and not become embroiled in what will be dangerous espionage missions for the British. All of them, without exception, wanted to be part of an operation that will drive the Turks out of Palestine. Because of the dangers, they cannot share any information with their loved ones. This has to be covert. Top secret. I spoke with papa. He knows we are planning something but I explained to him that is better if he remains unaware of what we are doing. We are all vowed to utter secrecy."

Sarah was intrigued. She remained silent, waiting for her elder brother to offer more information.

"Somehow the British seem reluctant to take on the Turks. The local committee, the labor unions, even the Zionist groups are staying neutral should war break out against the Turks here. Ben Gurion even volunteered Palestinian Jews to join the Turkish army."

Sarah said, "Yes. I heard about that."

"They claim they don't want to risk the repercussions from the Turks if they discover there is an active sympathy for the British against them. In light of what is happening to the poor Armenians, they may have a point, but we must inform the British that victory here can be made infinitely more likely with our contribution to their military efforts. Most of the British top brass in Cairo seem to have their heads buried in the Egyptian sand but, as I told you, we are beginning to feed them information."

Sarah was aghast and thrilled by what she was hearing. Aaron continued, "It began well. Avshalom came back on the first voyage, and we began to give the British what they wanted."

"How did that work?" Sarah enquired.

"I'll tell you that later. As I told you on the way here, after a few successful trips, the ship stopped coming. We didn't know why. We had no way other way of communicating with them. Avshalom went every night to the beach in case the ship turned up. It didn't, so Avsha volunteered to go back to Egypt and find out what happened. He set out for Egypt just four days before you arrived in Haifa."

Sarah excitedly began to see the affirmation of why she had left Chaim and an empty life. This was the mission that had been calling her. Aaron had offered her nothing, but she knew that now she had a role that would define her life.

"How long will it take Avsha to make contact with the British?"

"Hard to say. I would think a couple of weeks."

"Aaron. You must allow me to join you. I have spent far too long languishing far away from the action. You must let me in."

Aaron studied her. He was hesitant to embrace her into their secret cabal. She was, after all, his loving sister. That was too close to the fire. He didn't want her to get burned. He didn't want to jeopardize her safety.

Sarah noticed his hesitancy. "You have no option but to have me join you. Alex and Rivka are in America. Avsha is on his way to Egypt. What will you do with me? Send me back to Constantinople? Make me a housekeeper? I came here to do something useful, something meaningful, no matter the danger. That is why I left Chaim. I can't sit idly by while the world is going up in flames. I am here. I intend to stay here, and you are going to give me a leading role."

Sarah stared at her brother, an expression of defiance on her face. Aaron knew he was cornered. His workload was impossibly heavy. He was trying valiantly to stay on top of his agronomical endeavors. Above all, he knew, before the British knew, that they had to be enticed into opening a front against the increasing number of Turks and Germans that were pouring into Palestine. There was just so much he could do alone in running such a massive operation. He needed close support from someone he knew and trusted. Sarah's sudden arrival gave him the possibility of having someone share the load. But his sister? Could he put her at such risk, despite her obvious enthusiasm to throw herself at the task? He was surprised by the new Sarah sitting defiantly before him. It was the same strong-willed sister he knew and adored, but it was also a new woman of steel and purpose.

"All right, Sarita," he said. Sarah smiled. This was the first time since her return that her older brother called her by her affectionate nickname. "Let's wait and see what Avsha can achieve with the Brits in Egypt. Meanwhile, we have plenty of work to do. Avshalom sent a one hundred and fifty-page report on the Turkish mistreatment of the Armenians to Henrietta Szold in America. Henrietta is not only one of our trustees, she is also the head of the Hadassah women's Zionist organization, and, as a respected humanitarian, she has the ear of top members of the United States Administration. I want you to write a report on your personal experience of the Armenians suffering and let me have it as soon as you can. Add your eye-witness account to the record of Turkish crimes. The world must learn firsthand what is happening to them. As for now, let's go have lunch with papa."

THE SHIP

Sarah swiftly returned to the routine of helping her brother. The team were delighted to see her back again. She was met with hugs and kisses and introduced to the new members of the Atlit team. The affection they showed her was gratifying to Sarah. They loved to work with her and took her instructions with a happy willingness.

At the end of each day Sarah would ask Aaron, "Any news from Avsha?" He always answered with a silent shake of his head. After a week, a worried Sarah began to rephrase her question. "Any news of Avsha?" Aaron's answers were the same negative shake of the head.

She went about her business with a fevered determination. Save for her nightly question she made no mention of Avshalom Feinberg except to give the same negative answer to the young men and women of the Atlit project that enquired about the fate of their friend and leader.

Then, one day, Joseph Lishansky suddenly showed up in Zichron. He rushed into a meeting with Aaron. Sarah got to hear of his arrival from one of the boys who happened to be working in the rear house. She ran to her brother's office. She found both men in deep and serious conversation. Joseph was amazed when he looked up and saw Sarah. In his surprise he leapt up from his chair and embraced her. "Sarah! You're here!"

"What is it," Sarah demanded to know. "It's about Avsha, isn't it? I know it is."

Aaron answered. "Avshalom has been captured by a Turkish patrol near the no-man's land close to the Suez Canal."

Sarah put a hand to her mouth. "Oh no!" she blurted.

"They brought him to a prison in Beer Sheba," Joseph reported. "I'm sorry, Sarah, but the news gets worse. They have accused him of spying and want to hang him."

Sarah slumped into a chair desperately trying to maintain her composure. Joseph took up the story. "He is in good spirits, Sarah. He is trying to convince the Turks that he was down there doing his job, investigating the locust situation for Djemal Pasha. He is even taunting the Turks to hang him. He is threatening them that they will follow him to the hangman's rope if the Pasha discovered what they had done."

Sarah nodded. That was so like Avsha. The courageous swashbuckler.

"We managed to delay the sentencing by paying bakshish to the prison governor and other officials until we have time to bring a release from Djemal Pasha. I have left Naaman Belkind in charge of things. He knows the people down there and has access into the prison while I came to report to Aaron."

Sarah looked pleadingly at her brother. "What are we to do, Aaron?" she asked. Her brother was decisive. "I'm going immediately to Haifa. I will speak with the governor and the agricultural administrator and demand an urgent meeting with Djemal Pasha. This is a situation that only he can resolve. Sarah, you are now in charge of things here. Joseph, you remain at Atlit until you hear from me. Is that clear? Both Sarah and Joseph responded with nods. They all rose. Aaron went to fetch a suitcase from his bedroom at the back of his house and they followed him out to the compound and his car. As he opened the door to his car, he spoke to Sarah. "I'll be away for a few days. Keep things running smoothly and try not to worry."

Sarah gave Aaron a sisterly kiss and wished him luck as he got into his car. She opened the gate for him and watched as his vehicle disappeared at increasing speed down Founder's Street on a mission to save the life of her past love.

Aaron was granted an audience with the brutal Turkish warlord. He had to take the train from Haifa to Damascus for the meeting. The dictator was busy with war preparations but agreed to spare him a few minutes. Aaron was escorted into a large room that acted as the office of the Turk responsible for everything that moved in Syria and, by implication, Palestine. He was the law.

Aaron had met the stocky, ugly, and bearded Djemal Pasha several times, but it was always an intimidating experience. The Turk, in return, had a grudging respect for the Palestinian Jew that stood before him.

"Salaam, Aaronsohn! How are things with you?"

The Turk greeted his visitor, offering him a seat with the wave of his arm. Aaron knew this greeting was an empty courtesy, the foreplay required before getting down to business in the Levant. Aaron played the game of small talk. He waited as they consumed the customary small cup of thick bitter Turkish coffee made more pleasant by the taste of the sweet treacly baklava delivered to them on an exquisitely carved copper tray by one of the Pasha's lackeys.

The Pasha eventually turned to the matter of crop production. He asked his visitor about the current situation. Aaron was well aware that this was a matter of critical importance to him.

"We can now begin planning the sewing of the new crops that will provide for next season's food production," said Aaron in a businesslike manner. He continued, "But we are worried. We see a potential recurrence of another outbreak of the locust invasion. I sent my man down to the south to investigate and bring back a detailed report on what the situation is."

Djemal Pasha frowned. This was not the news he wanted to hear.

"Prepare me a detailed report immediately."

Aaron hid a smile. "I would have done this a week ago, you Excellency, but the stupid Germans have arrested my chief operator. I sent him down south to investigate the locust situation and they now accuse him of being a spy. They say they intend to hang him." Aaron glared into the Pasha's face. "Hang him for what, your Excellency? For spying on locusts? Only you can save him."

Aaron knew that Djemal had a disrespect for the Germans. He found them arrogant, frequently making disparaging remarks about his Turkish officers. Accusing the Germans of arresting Avshalom was a calculated gamble for Aaron. He knew Djemal would quickly discover it was his Turks that were holding Feinberg.

Djemal Pasha was thinking of his options. Brazenly, Aaron interjected.

"I cannot give you a completed scientific report if they kill the person who is undertaking the research for you. Avshalom Feinberg must be released from custody. He has been wrongfully arrested and prevented from completing his mission."

The two men stared at each other. Aaron looked unblinkingly into the face of Djemal Pasha. The Turk was stressed. The pressure on him was great. The German generals were demanded to know if he could satisfy the food supply to hungry troops without which they could not maintain their war aims in the Middle East. Now he felt this Palestinian Jew making more demands on him.

176

"By Allah, Aaronsohn! I have a good mind to hang you too!"

The Palestinian Jew patted his broad girth before calmly replying, "I doubt, your Excellency, you have gallows that can take my weight, and when your gallows crash and fall they will hear the sound of breaking timber all the way in America."

Djemal Pasha did not depose the Ottoman sultans by mere brutally. It took political cunning. He quickly understood the implications of Aaronsohn's remarks. This man of international repute who sat before him had top connections in the American Administration. The last thing that Djemal Pasha wanted was to intimidate the United States into joining the Great War on the side of the Allies. He hid his anger at Aaronsohn's defiance. Instead, he erupted in an exaggerated guffaw of laughter.

"By Allah, Aaronsohn, you are a formidable Jew!" The bulky Turk rose from his throne of a chair.

"Leave the matter of your agent to me. Prepare your report as soon as you can."

The two men shook hands. Both fully aware that they needed each other at this stressful time.

Two weeks later, Avshalom Feinberg turned up in Zichron Yaakov. He had hardly arrived at the Aaronsohn household when Sarah got word that Avsha was in Aaron's office. She rushed over to Aaron's study, pausing for a moment to attend to her appearance and to compose herself before opening the door to her brother's bureau. She saw the back of a familiar figure who was speaking with Aaron. He looked round as she entered the room. She froze in the doorway as Avshalom turned. A look of sudden surprise came over both their faces. Avshalom hadn't been told that Sarah was back in Zichron. He rose from his chair.

"Sarita? Is it really you?" He came over to her. Her heart was pounding in her breast as he said, "Am I really seeing you, or a I dreaming?"

Sarah looked into his face as he was talking. He had gown a beard in his captivity. It suited him, she thought. It made him look more manly than the youthful Avsha she remembered so fondly.

Any awkwardness was broken when Avshalom suddenly embraced her, swinging her round in a circle of laughter. Sarah allowed herself to surrender to his impulse. She hoped that Avsha could not hear or feel her beating heart. The emotional reunion was brought under control by Aaron.

"Now that we got that out of the way, can we get down to business? As you are here, Sarah, you may as well join us."

Avshalom held out a chair for Sarah before regaining his seat. Aaron hesitated before speaking to Sarah.

"Sarah. Today I received a letter from Chaim, your husband. He wrote to me demanding that I send you back to him. What do you want me to tell him?"

Before Sarah could speak, Avshalom blurted, "Tell him this. I swear to you that you will not see Sarah again for a very long time."

Sarah said, "I'm not going back to him, Aaron. I am staying here."

Aaron considered the matter. "In that case I shall write that he can come here to see you if he wishes but that I have no intentions of sending you back to him. What do you say to that?"
Sarah replied briefly. "I agree."

Aaron turned to Avshalom. "You had bad luck to be caught just a few miles from the British, but this still leaves us out of communication with them." He sat back in his chair before continuing.

"They still need to be fully persuaded about how useful we can be to them. Quite frankly, they have no idea what is happening in Palestine. We've tried the Egyptian route but it seems to me that their General Staff in Cairo are too short-sighted to initiate an offensive here. How can they take us seriously if they haven't realized yet they can win the war by defeating the Turks and the Germans here? We need to adopt a bolder approach."

Avshalom asked, "What are you suggesting?"

"I have been thinking about it for some time. Any decision on what the British do is made in London, not in Cairo. In Egypt, they just follow orders. We need to speak with both their government and their military decision makers. Someone has to persuade the British why they must open a war front over here and that we can be their eyes and ears behind enemy lines to help them win a great victory. That's why I have decided to go to London and knock on doors in Whitehall. The decisions are made there, not in Egypt."

Sarah was thunderstruck by Aaron's proposal. Her brother was always one for bold thinking. It seemed to her to be highly ambitious but there was a logic in what he suggested. If anyone could convince the British it had to be her brother, a man of remarkable achievements and a knowledge that would impress them in the British capital.

Aaron continued, "The Turks must never know that we are offering ourselves to the British. If they ever get wind of it, we are all in peril. And so I have devised a subterfuge for my trip that will deceive the Turks into believing that the British have arrested me on suspicion of being a Turkish spy."

He smiled at Avshalom. "I got this idea when I heard of your arrest. Let them believe that I am rotting in a British jail for the duration of the war because of all I did for the Ottoman Turks in Palestine. In reality, I will be working behind the scenes and we will be providing them with the intelligence they need."

Both Sarah and Avshalom were intrigued.

Avshalom said what was in Sarah's mind. "It's a clever if risky ruse. How are you going to do that?"

"I am still working my way through the details. Believe me that I will leave nothing to chance. Be assured that the Turks will believe I am out of the game, but I will either return or be inside British intelligence and policy making and I will be coordinating things with you through them. With me over there and you over here, we will guide the British forces through Palestine, informing them of the Turkish strengths and weaknesses, and helping them to victory."

Aaron added," I am taking Lova Levy with me. You know Lova from Hadera."

Avshalom nodded but Sarah said, "Not really. I don't think I ever met him."

"He was one of the boys that were arrested with me while you were away," Avshalom told her.

"He's a reliable and loyal sort," Aaron said. "I am taking him with me. He will be based in Berlin. He and Avsha's sister, Tzila, who is a student

180

there, can be our liaison people so that I can send them messages to pass over to you or Avshalom, and you can send messages to me through them. The Turks know we have contacts in Germany with our agricultural research projects so it will raise less suspicions for them."

Turning to his sister, Aaron said, "I have no choice, Sarah, but to put you to the test. You will work with Avshalom. You will help him recruit the right people. Help him train and instruct them in their missions. Nobody can compile records and reports like you, Sarah. I have complete confidence in you."

He reached over and squeezed her hand. "I wouldn't ask you to take the risk but our time has come."

Sarah felt the significance of the moment. "I'm ready," she said.

"Just one thing," said Aaron, looking at them both with a serious frown. "No loose tongues. No frivolity. This is dangerous stuff. Be careful and guarded. Treat anyone not in our team with suspicion. Monitor our people all the time. Make sure there are no slip ups. One slip can be catastrophic. And no swashbuckling adventurism, Avsha. We operate with cautious action, so no overt heroics. With God's help we will change history."

Aaron drove to Haifa to request an urgent meeting with Djemal Pasha. The officials in the port town knew Aaron's reputation. They knew that when Aaron Aaronsohn came asking to meet their Pasha it was a request that could not be bought with a bribe. Aaron was told that the warlord would receive him in Jerusalem. He travelled there with the locust report he had promised Djemal. The report came with a provision that he be allowed to travel to Germany to meet with scientific colleagues on how to defeat locust plagues and to conduct more research on a new strain of corn that contained more oil. He told the Turk that this would be beneficial for both human and animal feed. The Turk merely nodded. He also told the

181

Djemal Pasha that he needed to travel on to America to receive additional information on solving pest and locust problems and to bring back much needed funding for his Station's agricultural projects for the coming year. These were requests that Djemal Pasha could hardly refuse.

With travel permit in hand, Aaron bade farewell to his father. He kissed Sarah, assuring her he had full confidence in her. He hugged her before stepping into the family carriage that would take him to Haifa port on the first leg of his journey to Germany.

Sarah discovered that while she had withered in Constantinople, her brother and Avshalom had created a team of intelligence agents from among their closest and most trusted friends. Their Zichron cousin, Reuven Schwartz, shuttled between their home and Atlit. An old family friend, Menashe Bronstein, who sometimes helped them at Atlit, had been drafted by Aaron. Avshalom recruited his two cousins, Naaman and Eitan Belkind from Rishon le Zion. Naaman had both Jewish and Turkish friends in Beer Sheba that were well placed for both agricultural and espionage duties. Joseph Lishansky from the north, a close friend of Avshalom, had joined the Aaronsohn inner circle. Lishansky had fallen out with the HaShomer group. He thought they were too timid against the Turks after they had been deprived of their weapons and restricted in their movements. Like his friend, Avshalom, he was impatient for the removal of the Ottomans. Avshalom's work with the Aaronsohn group at Atlit gave him hope.

Abu Farid, the Aaronsohn's loyal coachman and messenger, had been brought into their confidence. Abu Farid, they knew, would rather die than betray the Aaronsohns and their team. He was both appreciated and loved by Aaron and Sarah. The same applied to Frida, their Arab cook and housekeeper. She worked mainly at Atlit, but frequently at their Zichron home.

Sarah began recruiting others. An easy choice was her lifelong friend in Zichron, Tova Gelber, a pretty, intelligent and talented young woman who could be entrusted with numerous tasks. Sarah liked her. She had more courage than many of the men in Zichron, Sarah thought.

Slowly the team began to grow, made up of people that Sarah and Avshalom knew intimately. No chance was taken by speaking to strangers, or people unknown to them, unless they were highly recommended by those they trusted. Even then, these people were double and triple checked before being welcomed into the fold.

As they travelled the country, purportedly carrying out their agricultural research, they noted the extension of train lines, new roads being laid, new bridges spanning rivers, garrisons being strengthened, particularly in the south. Supply centers began to appear by key railway stations. But there was little reason to work frenetically on intelligence gathering. They had yet to be informed when the British ship would arrive.

Aaron had set off for London replete with heavy files on topography, weather patterns, the poor state of the agriculture following the locust plague. He knew that the vital information the British needed was becoming outdated before the Brits knew about it, or were even aware that they needed it. As Aaron had said, the British had no idea what was happening in Palestine. All it took was a signal from the British and the team would spring into action. The waiting was so frustrating, especially to Avshalom who was raring to go. Sarah knew she had to calm him down.

"Patience, Avsha. Our time will come."

On a ride together from Zichron to Atlit they discussed intimate things for the first time since Sarah's return.

"It's great to have you back, Sarita. The project has missed you. I have missed you."

"It's good to be back." She paused, then, "It's a pity that Rivka is not here. I miss her."

There was a message in these words. A hint that was not lost on Avshalom who rode on in silence.

What happened after I left? Why didn't you marry Rivka?"

"She wanted to wait," he said. "Then the difficulties and the war happened..."

"But there was plenty of time before the war," pressed Sarah. There was an awkward silence before he answered.

"Everything changed after you left. You left a giant vacuum that Rivka felt she couldn't fill. Everyone missed you, including Rivka...especially me."

"But you gave her your word, your pledge to marry her."

"Yes. I gave her my word and I intended to honor it, but she kept telling me she couldn't take your place. She loved me. I know that, but she knew how we felt for each other and, well, when you left with Chaim she knew that a part of my heart went with you." Another pause, then, "You were always there between us, even in your absence."

They rode on in silence. Sarah knew instinctively that this was not the end of the conversation. She couldn't think of a word to say. Neither looked at each other until Avshalom, lost in his thoughts, said, "Is it me, or is it you

Aaronsohn girls? What is it that makes it impossible for me to cross that chasm to either of you?

He didn't say that directly to her. He was staring ahead with a sad look on his handsome face. He was expressing his inner thoughts, the thoughts of a man in turmoil. He realized the impact that his words may have on Sarah. He turned to her and apologized. "Forgive me. I shouldn't have spoken like that."

Sarah couldn't answer. She felt for him in his emotional confusion, but her own feeling prevented her from offering a reply. She was still married. He, still engaged to her sister. They were both caught in a trap that kept them apart. Despite their closeness, even fondness, there was a chasm, a chasm that she had created. But was this a time where she could begin to bridge that divide? With the world about to explode around them, Sarah felt she didn't have the confidence to lower her defenses, to get closer to the only person she ever truly loved. Any entanglement would surely consume and detract them from the dangerous mission they were embarking on. Yes, life had become a mission. Their future together, had to be put on hold.

As Reuven Schwartz walked out of the yard at Atlit early one morning to start another day in the field his attention was drawn to a white piece of paper fluttering in the gentle morning breeze. Strangely, it was waving at him from the shaft of a plow by the pathway. He wandered over and extracted the paper. It had a jumble of letters that made no sense to him. He was about to throw it away but then decided to show it to Sarah. He found her in the kitchen preparing breakfast for the work crew.

"Is this one of our documents? I found it outside, stuck to the plow."

Sarah examined the paper not understanding what was written. Then it dawned on her. "It must be a coded message. It must be something connected to the British. I have no way of reading it. He never taught me how to decipher their communication. No point really, as the communication was broken some time ago. He'll be here at mid-day. I'll ask him what it is. Thanks Reuven. Leave it with me."

When Avshalom arrived, Sarah was in the Atlit office. She handed him the paper.

"Reuven found this flapping around on the plow outside. It's a coded message. What was it doing out there?"

Avshalom studied it in growing excitement. He asked for a pen and began scribbling words as he deciphered the message. When he finished he let out a loud shriek. He surprised Sarah by giving her a big kiss before staring at the paper saying, "Look at this!" He showed Sarah what he had written. The message on the paper read 'AF. BUSINESS TO RESUME SHORTLY. PLEASE HAVE GOODS READY. W.'

"You know what this means," he said triumphantly waving the paper of his head. "It means we are back in business! It's a message from British naval intelligence. Come. Let's go speak with Reuven."

They ran out into the field and found Reuven working among the rows of a new set of crops.

"Reuven, when was the last time someone worked with the plow?"

"Let me think. Ahmed did some plowing about three days ago, I don't think anyone used it since. Why? Has it anything to do with the paper I found?"

Avshalom surprised Sarah but especially Reuven by planting a kiss on his sweaty face.

"It has indeed, my dear friend," he answered, giving Reuven a hug. "The Brits must have been here a couple of nights ago but no one was here to receive them."

Reuven was puzzled. "It couldn't be. I was sleeping here that night. Wait!" He remembered something. "Two nights ago, Demon, our guard dog, woke me up making a hell of a racket, but after a while he quietened down so I went back to sleep. We weren't expecting anyone, were we? If it was them, why didn't they come into the building?"

Sarah suggested, "Perhaps Demon scared them off. The lights were off. They assumed that no one was here, so they left this message for us."

Avshalom took over. "OK. Here's what we do. Every evening we have two men on the beach and others watching for the arrival of the ship from the roof. We stay alert throughout the night and we keep it going until they arrive."

Sarah added, "I will prepare our reports for them to take back to Cairo." She paused. "They couldn't have come because of Aaron. I doubt he has had time to make contact with people in London, let alone in Egypt." Avshalom agreed. "This message is from the officer I made contact with in Port Said when I was down there. It's signed 'W.' That's Lieutenant Woolley. He's the only one that took us seriously. He provided a ship.

That's how I returned from Egypt. He gave us instructions on what information they needed, a code system, a signaling method. That's when we began gathering military intelligence for him. Aaron also prepared a lot of material that he said was invaluable for their preparations for a campaign here against the Turks and Germans. Then we lost contact with them, or they lost it with us. Either way, the ship stopped coming. We have intelligence that is withering on the vine so to speak. We have a pile of stuff for them, but some of it is now a month old. Now, at last, they've renewed contact with us."

"Could this be a sign that they are beginning to appreciate how much they need our help?" Sarah asked.

"I hope so, Sarita. I really hope so."

In the midafternoon a ship sailed slowly across the horizon. They watched excitedly as it emitted black smoke from its funnel.

"This is it," Avshalom shouted as they viewed from the sea facing balcony on the upper floor of Atlit station. "Let's hold out the white sheet from the window. That shows them we have seen them." They ran and unfurled a large white bed sheet from one of the bedroom windows and continued to watch the ship. It turned west and began to sail out to sea away from them. Sarah looked disappointed but Avshalom and Reuven let out a whoop of victory and hugged each other.

"That's their signal. They know we have seen them and will be ready to receive them tonight. We have work to do. Let's get our reports ready to give them. Reuven, you and I will go to the beach tonight. Sarah, you will stay here with Joseph and Nathan. Maintain darkness. Flash us twice if there is any danger. We will hide if there is a problem here."

"What problem could there be?" Sarah asked.

"In case the Turks saw the ship and put up road blocks while we are on the beach. Or maybe they'll post watchmen on the station. We have to be on high alert ready for any eventuality," Avshalom advised.

Avshalom and Reuven left the Atlit compound at midnight. Avshalom explained the ship usually arrived at one or two of the clock at night. The two ran silently along the avenue between the tall palms. They crouched as they reached the road. They listened and looked for any sign of movement, a Turkish patrol, transport along the highway. When they were confident that nobody was around they dashed across the road and into the wadi that led down to the beach. Before emerging onto the shore they again crouched down and searched the beach for movement. All was quiet. Avshalom searched through the dark for the horizon of the sea. After what seemed more than an hour he thought he saw the outline of a ship on the seaward side of the old Crusader fortress. Another hour passed, then he was sure he saw a single flash of light about two hundred yards into the sea. Reuven saw it also and, from the cover of the wadi, he flashed a signal with his torch in response. The sea was calm. The waves rippled softly on to the beach. They waited a couple of minutes until they glimpsed a row boat approaching the shore. Avshalom hissed at Reuven and the pair began to race to the water's edge. Two men leapt from the small boat that was now in the shallow tide. They carried a couple of packages as they waded ashore. Avshalom recognized one of them. Raphael Abuhazera was the friend who had introduced him to Lieutenant Leonard Woolley, a British naval intelligence officer in Port Said, during his short and successful visit to Egypt. Now his friend had landed at Atlit. They embraced and exchanged whispered greetings.

"It's great to see you again, Rafi," Avshalom said, patting his friend affectionately on his shoulders.

"And you, Avshalom."

"Have you seen Aaron?" Avshalom enquired.

"No."

"He left for London a month ago. He intends to make contact with you when he gets there. He's gone to convince the British in Whitehall why they need to take us more seriously."

"I haven't heard from him. Neither has Woolley. They haven't heard anything about him in Cairo either. They would have told me. Woolley sends his regards. He's on the ship. He wanted to make sure we reconnect with you. He's a fine man. Give him my best wishes. At least he realizes we can be useful to the British. But what happened? Why did the ship not come to us?"

"There's a turf war going on in the General Staff between the army and the navy. Some of their military decision makers don't see the point in being kept updated on the enemy positions in Palestine if there are no orders to move into Palestine. They much prefer sending war chests of money and weapons to the Hashemites in the Hejaz. They changed the signaling system but they forgot to inform us about it. But Woolley made a stink about it and here we are."

"Idiots!" Avshalom was disappointed at this news, but Raphael continued.

"But things are changing. I heard rumors that the Prime Minister is leaning on the War Cabinet in Whitehall for plans to open a new front here, so it will be useful to have Aaron there to apply added pressure. It's just a matter of time before things happen here. Anyway, here are your instructions. We intend to be back in two weeks, so collect as much information as you can. We've also scraped some money for you to keep your operation alive."

He helped lift three waterproofed packages that had been thrown onto the sandy beach on to Avshalom's and Reuven's shoulders.

"Thanks Rafi, and thank goodness for you and Woolley. Tell him we are enlarging our network. You remember Aaron's sister, Sarah, don't you? She is now here and part of our team. If you should make contact or meet with Aaron tell him she is doing good work here."

"I will. Take care, Avshalom. Stay safe."

Avshalom handed Rafi an oilskin-wrapped package that contained the vital information that they had gathered.

"It may be a bit out of date. This stuff was gathered during your absence."

Avshalom and Reuven paused long enough to watch the row boat disappear into the dark of the sea before carrying their weighty packages off the beach and negotiated their silent way through the dark wadi up to the road. After pausing to make sure their way was safe, they raced to the other side of the road and along the avenue to the protection of the station buildings.

Sarah, Joseph and Nathan were waiting for them in the kitchen. They were cold after spending hours in the night air of the seafront, but they buzzed with excitement as they entered the room. Sarah poured them mugs of steaming hot tea as they dumped their packages onto the kitchen table. The team celebrated their relief that this part of the operation had passed successfully with collective hugs and laughter that relieved the tension. Avshalom pushed a heavy satchel across the kitchen table toward Sarah telling her that this was the money provided by the British to cover their expenses. Sarah weighed it in her hands and remarked that it would barely cover their debts. Avshalom opened a second package and began to read through the instructions. He whistled. "They want a ton of military information from us, mainly about what is happening in the south. It looks as if we have to get busy. Rafi said they will be back in two weeks. Boys and girl, we have work to do."

A meeting was called with all the team operators. They gathered at Atlit. Avshalom and Sarah sat at the head of the table. Avshalom kicked off proceedings.

"Friends. As you may have heard, the British seem to be taking us a bit more seriously, and we are back in business." Avshalom was interrupted by loud applause. "It is up to us to give them updated briefings on military movements, strategic locations such as supply dumps, equipment storage facilities, weapon arsenals, the strength of the enemies garrisons, the development of their infrastructure such as roads and rail, communication lines. We even want to get into their signaling systems if we can. We have to give them weather conditions. I guess they need to prepare the way for a large army and its supplies to battle through Palestine once they decide it is in their interest to do so. Actually, we know what is best for the Brits even before they do." This brought a round of laughter. Avshalom raised a hand.

"They have to beat the Turks over here in Palestine to turn the tide of the Great War. We know that don't we?" A gleeful shout of "Yes!" erupted in the kitchen. "The problem is, the Brits don't, but they will - any day now." More laughter erupted at this repeated joke before Avshalom added, "This is true. We have to show them what is good for them because, at the end of the day, what is good for them is good for us. That makes us the best allies they can ever have."

Sarah raised her hand. "Aaron told us that we can help win this war not by rifles but by our eyes and ears. This is our time to play our part not by violence, but by stealth. I want you to use your eyes and ears and bring me any information you think will be useful to the British army. Bring your reports to me. I have to translate them into the new code system we have just received. So there's a lot to do and less than two weeks to gather as much intelligence as we can. Naaman and Eitan, most of what they are asking for involves your sectors around Beer Sheba and the south. Bring me as much useful information as you can find. Think of good people to recruit. We'll discuss it after this meeting ends. Joseph, I'd like you to report on what is happening with the Turkish army in the north particularly in Nazareth and Tiberias, and the movement of their traffic from Syria into Palestine. Give me a list of who is in charge of each unit and where they are based. What is the relationship between the Germans and the Turks? Is it efficient, or is there any internal conflict between them? The British need to know if they are fighting a coordinated enemy, or is it dysfunctional. We need to probe where the enemy's weak spots are, as well as informing the British where they are gathering in strength. If this operation is successful we will be enlarging our network with carefully selected new operators. Remember at all the times that secrecy and discretion is vitally important. No loose tongues. No gossiping to friends or family. Believe me when I say that you, each of you, are going to pave the way to the restoration of our homeland once we have helped the British drive out our enemy."

It was not just Avshalom that was impressed by Sarah's grasp of what was needed by the British General Staff in conducting their war against a mutual enemy. The young men who had worked with her before she had left them for Constantinople were struck by her maturity and command of what was needed to deliver them from the Turks.

One late evening, after a full day of frenetic activity, Sarah and Avshalom sat on the balcony of their agricultural station. They were wrapped in blankets to keep warm against the chill of the night. Their team members were dispersed around the country completing their tasks, or sleeping the deep sleep of hard-working enthusiasts in their beds at home or in the building dormitory.

"The guys love you, Sarah. You know that, surely? You show them an affection that only you can give them, and they love you for it."

"What else can I give them other than an appreciation for what they are doing? We are always behind with their salaries yet they don't complain." She gazed out into the dark. "On some days, I can't even give them a decent meal, and yet they remain dedicated to us. That is the definition of true love. To sacrifice yourself and expect nothing in return."

Avshalom wrapped his hands around his hot cup of coffee before moving the subject of love in a more intimate direction.

"I know you can't marry me, but know this. I still love you. I always have. Always will. I thought you felt the same" He mused, "I think, perhaps, I got close to Rivka because you rejected me, on the rebound, so to speak. I cared for her. I truly did, but not with the intensity I felt for you." He paused for thought. "This may be why she held back from marrying me. She knew I still felt for you, even in your absence. I struggled to understand how you turned me down and yet married Chaim. I guess I was jealous of him."

"It was a mistake," admitted Sarah. "I knew that as soon as I arrived in Constantinople with him. It was the most miserable time of my entire life. So empty, so meaningless, so loveless."

She turned to him. "I didn't think about you much. I suppose I was repressing my feelings for you, but I missed you terribly."

He looked at her and reached out and took her hand. They peered into the emptiness of a dark sky towards an unseen sea, both hoping that their unspoken prayers would be answered.

The ship returned. When Joseph and Reuven got back to the station, they reported that the sea was rough, that the row boat had to remain in deeper waters while two swimmers relayed the packages to them and took their coded reports back to the ship. They were told to prepare for the return of the naval ship in the next ten days to two weeks.

Sarah mapped out the locations where they were short of manpower in their voluntary secret group. Menashe told Sarah that a friend of his had been conscripted into a desk job in the Turkish military headquarters in the Syrian capital and was working in their communications room. She called Menashe and Tova Gelber, two of Sarah's entrusted friends from Zichron Yaakov, to a meeting at her home. Menashe and Tova had recently got engaged to be married. They both worked in her agricultural research projects and were actively engaged in the intelligence side of Atlit activities. Sarah was particularly sensitive to their relationship to each other and had spoken to them about it. They insisted they were both totally committed to whatever task she would give them. Sarah looked on them as her Manya and Israel. She would protect them whenever she could but would send them out on dangerous missions when it became necessary.

In Aaron's study she told them. "You know I love you both and I wouldn't ask you to do this if I didn't think it was important." She paused.

"I want to send you both to Damascus. You will deliver a research report to the Turkish agricultural department there. It's on one of the projects you have been working on so that will give you added cover. I will arrange travel passes for you from the authorities in Haifa. Menashe, get to meet your contact and find out what he can supply us. If it is anything serious, I will post someone up there to liaise with him and arrange with one of you to shuttle up to Damascus to bring his reports back to us. Are you willing to do this?"

"Certainly," Tova replied.

"Absolutely," agreed Menashe.

"All right. When we are ready, tell your families that you may have to go up to Damascus to report on crop production or locust problems."

Material was being gathered in increasing volume. As Sarah coded the messages she appreciated the importance of their reports for the planning section of the British Army in any future campaign. She was frustrated that they were so slow in making that fateful decision. One night, as she worked on the reports, she listened covertly to the BBC on the radio. She was dying to hear they had begun to confront the Turks and had begun their invasion but, sadly, all the news was about the heavy and tragic fighting on the Western Front in Europe. Frustratingly, she closed the radio and got on with her coding in the silence of the night.

THE DEPARTURE

At the end of a busy autumn day at Atlit, Sarah dismissed the last of the farm workers thanking them for their labors and remarking how well they had recovered from the disasters of the previous year caused by the locust invasion that she had heard so much about since her return from Constantinople.

That seemed far away from where they were now. Their crop production had been excellent, better than the fields of the Zichron villagers or their Arab neighbors. Their farming system was more efficient and their experimentation was producing good results. Satisfied, she walked back into the quiet house. No ship was due for another week but Sarah still had a long evening ahead of her compiling coded documents for the next shipment. She headed first to the kitchen to prepare dinner for herself and for Avshalom who was due to arrive with a batch of reports.

He arrived as she was washing the vegetables. He threw a satchel on to the kitchen table came over to her. From behind, he threw his arms around her waist pinning her against the sink. She felt his beard against her neck. It tingled. She fought back the excitement she felt.

"What are you doing?"

"Something I should have done a long time ago."

He kissed her neck and she sighed a weak sound of resistance.

"What are you doing?" she repeated.

"Giving you something you have missed for far too long."
"What is that?" she whispered hoarsely.

"Giving you the unconditional love you need."

"Who says I need it?"

"You know you do."

He swung her around to face him before burying a kiss onto her lips. She attempted to say something but her words remained in her throat unable to escape the thrill of the moment. She wanted to struggle against the vortex of passion that swirled within her. The prolonged kiss hid the conflict that was raging inside her. She wanted him but something was preventing her. Gradually, resistance gave way to surrender and she started to respond to his intimate closeness. She felt a fire she hadn't experienced since she was last in his arms so long ago. She started to weep as she threw herself emotionally into the kiss.

It was a new Sarah that went on the offensive. She hurled herself onto him and they staggered around the kitchen in a half dance, half struggle, of passionate love-making. They broke off when he took her hand and led her up the stairs. Not a word was said as he brought her into the bedroom where their passion reignited as they struggled to deprive each other of their clothing. When they were both almost naked they fell on to the bed in a violent embrace. They attacked each other in a war of love. Wordlessly, bodily, each communicated their innermost feelings for each other. They writhed, they flipped each other over, they explored each other's bodies with their hands, their lips, their mouths. Sarah had missed this moment. For far too long. In her subconscious she had yearned for it. For him. She was ready to respond to passion. He looked into her face with a fire in his eyes. Her eyes closed as she gave a guttural moan. He kissed her beautiful face and they made love with each other. To each other. For each other. For themselves. He wanted her to feel the strength of his love for her. It had been so long. Too long. She never wanted it to end but, gradually, the storm receded as they collapsed in a sweaty embrace, both worn out from the exertions of their spontaneous and wordless passion that had expressed itself far better in silence than in words.

All the team were fully employed. When the ship arrived, the voluminous amount of intelligence they garnered was received by the ship's officers and by Raphael who began to decode and select the most urgent information to be telegraphed back to the British intelligence bureau in Cairo as they steamed away under the darkness of night from the shores of Atlit.

Then, inexplicably, the ship failed to appear yet again. Sarah's only contact was through the naval vessel. Without it, she felt utterly isolated.

This was December, 1916, one year exactly since Sarah had returned from Constantinople so brimming with enthusiasm to free her people from the suffocating shadow of fear. Now she felt totally cut off from her saviors.

Where are they? Where is Aaron?

The team continued to bring in valuable material. Sarah could do nothing but code the data and store it in the hidden alcoves they had constructed both at Atlit and in the hidden basement and passageway that ran underground from Aaron's house to the rear building of their home in Zichron Yaakov. Steps had been taken, a couple of years earlier before Sarah returned from Constantinople, to hide precious documents and weapons from the prying searches of the authorities. Aaron has shown her the secret niches and cubbyholes that defied even the most expert of prying eyes. The files in the threshing mill has been handed over to the local police but Aaron and Alex had stashed away a couple of short-handled pistols and a rifle in case of emergency in secret niches and passageways. Now Sarah used the underground passageways at Atlit to warehouse the gold that had arrived on the ships for distribution to the various settlement committees. She also felt the need to preserve and hide their covert material until such time as the British reappeared.

199

Sarah informed each of the boys about the unexpected non-arrival of the navy ship. The growing sense of frustration was palpable throughout the network. Sarah saw the enthusiasm sink in the body language of her dedicated operatives. After an empty week, she had no choice but to instruct her staffers to return to full duty on the agricultural projects. This too was important, she told them.

Avshalom was becoming agitated. He arrived at Atlit accompanied with his close friend, Joseph. They sat at Sarah's desk as she was compiling sets of accounts. "There is no word from Aaron. We have no idea where he is. Now, the Brits have decided to ignore us. We have no alternative. Joseph and I have been discussing heading down to Egypt to find out what the hell is going on there."

Sarah was shocked. "No. I absolutely forbid it."

Avshalom raised his arms in gesture of frustration. "What alternative do we have, Sarah What? You tell me. The intelligence is piling up, getting out of date with every passing day of their absence. What else can we do? We need to find out what happened to them."

Sarah had no practical alternative solution. She knew he was right. With no word from Aaron and no appearance from the British ship something had happened that she needed to know about. Still, she had lost Aaron. She didn't want to lose Avshalom.

"It's too dangerous. Remember what happened to you just over a year ago? Do you want that to happen to both of you? How can we operate without the two of you? No, I don't agree."

Joseph tried to reason with her. "Sarah. Avshalom was caught by the Bedouin because he dressed in his normal clothes in the Sinai. The authorities down there didn't believe his excuse of researching locusts in no-man's land. We plan to go through this stretch of territory dressed as Bedouin and we'll take with us a Bedouin guide to help us avoid the Turkish positions and patrols. It will be a safer journey, I promise you. "

Sarah was dismissive. "No journey down there is safe. I don't agree. My instincts tell me you shouldn't do it."

As the two men rose to leave Avshalom calmly said," We really don't have any alternative."

For a couple of nights, as Avshalom shared her Atlit bed, he never mentioned the journey to Egypt. By then, they had abandoned the night watch for the ship. Sarah reckoned that if the ship did not make a pass during the afternoon hours it would be highly unlikely that they would appear in the middle of the night. With each delivery of new intelligence, she brooded about the growing waste of what could be invaluable information gathering dust in her cellars.

As they got ready for bed after a wasted day, Avshalom said, "We have no choice, Sarita. We have to go and find out what is happening." Sarah didn't answer. Avshalom didn't continue the conversation. They made love passively before surrendering to sleep.

It took another couple of days before Avshalom pressed Sarah. "Well, have you given it more thought? Do you have an answer, an alternative plan?"

Sarah negatively shook her head. She had racked her brain but there was no alternative she could think of to get to the bottom of why they were being ignored and why they hadn't heard from Aaron. She had seriously considered dropping their espionage mission completely to concentrate on their crop cultivation and research projects. This was far safer than their unappreciated clandestine activities on behalf of the British. But what had happened to Aaron? The trip down to Egypt may, at least, reveal what had become of her brother. She could quite easily maintain the agricultural work until Avshalom and Joseph returned.

"I don't feel good about you going down there again. I wouldn't be able to sleep until you got back and I don't know what I would do with myself if anything happened to you."

Avshalom gave a half smile as he put the palm of his hands around her pretty face. "But you'll let me do it, won't you, my pretty Sarita?"

She looked into his eyes with a frown on her sad face. "I would never let you go, but it seems we have no other choice."

He kissed her. "Don't worry, my love. Everything will be fine. If I get caught again I am sure you'll bail me out."

She hit him with a pillow. He laughed. "I'm joking, Sarita."

"Don't make jokes about that. It's far too serious…" He interrupted her with a kiss. They rolled on the bed as a desperate passion overtook them both.

Days later, they made their farewells in the compound of the Agricultural Research Station at Atlit. Joseph had gone ahead to make arrangements for their journey from Naaman Belkind's home in Rishon leZion. Sarah had prepared provisions for their long trek to the Egyptian border and Avshalom tied them to the saddle of his horse. They kissed openly and passionately. As Avshalom mounted his horse Sarah gave him a package.

"What's this?" he asked.

"They are your favorite dates. I know you love them." He looked at her with love in his eyes. "They are sweet like you. I will not eat them until I reach Egypt. I will keep them here in my jacket, close to my heart," he said patting the inside pocket of his woolen jacket, "where I always keep your sweet love."

Sarah wept a tear as she waved and watched him ride away along the long straight avenue beneath the stately palms.

LOVA

It was the beginning of 1917, and a sad way to begin what was become a dramatic and fateful year.

Avshalom had gone, accompanied by Joseph, and Sarah was left alone to head the Atlit projects. She organized the routine, though there was little routine to the hectic dual life that she and most of the boys were leading. Balancing the two unlikely roles of agricultural experimentation and espionage demanded total dedication and commitment. Sarah had little choice but to keep her willing workers underpaid but happy. Her coffers were depleted due to the difficulty in receiving the regular payments from the American trustees that kept Atlit functioning. How the boys and girls kept their faith in her was a wonder, she thought. They worked so hard for such little pay yet they never complained. She loved them, and they loved her. She mailed her reports to her trustees in America. At least the mail service to America was still functioning as long as America remained neutral in the war. She wondered why Aaron had not communicated to her through one of the trustees, or through Lova, or Avshalom's sister in Germany. She reckoned the reason was that he didn't want to risk being compromised if his correspondence was intercepted by the enemy.

Each night, as she lay alone in her bed, she thought of Avsha. Sarah tried to estimate where he was along his route. She felt consoled by thinking of him from the pillow of her bed. She found tranquility in these intimate, lonely moments before sleep. Fantasizing about him was better for her soul than counting days. She willed her thoughts and silent prayers to reach his soulful spirit so they could reconnect in some mystic form.

Despite her resolve to put aside the intelligence work, her workers continued to bring her interesting and valuable information about the enemy. She fortified her loneliness by throwing herself into the coding of messages, writing reports, keeping records, calculating expenses against a diminishing balance, composing letters to the Americans that generously supported them, and, when she was not in conversation with the staff members who worked at Atlit, or who came to visit her there, she spent what little time she had left, usually at weekends and occasional nights, in conversation at home with Ephraim. As the days turned into weeks, her concerns grew for the two men who carried her life and her love.

On a stormy January day, a figure arrived at the Atlit compound. It was the sudden and unexpected arrival of Lova Levi. He told her of his harrowing experiences since leaving Zichron with Aaron.

Over a hot meal prepared by Sarah, he told that when he and Aaron had arrived in Constantinople after a terrible journey he had been unable to obtain a travel pass even with Aaron's considerable but unsuccessful help. Without a travel pass, Aaron instructed him to remain in Constantinople and become his contact man there. Aaron told him to wait for messages from him via Avshalom's sister, Tzila, who was studying medicine in Berlin. Lova told Sarah that he remained in the Turkish capital, loyally waiting to hear from her brother until he reached the point of penury. He ran out of the money that Aaron had given him. Lova became emaciated with hunger. He sold matches on the street to try and buy scraps of food. Yet he heard nothing from Aaron. Despite this, he waited patiently while living in abject poverty. One day, he said, a man recognized him as he wandered the streets. The man was Doctor Arthur Ruppin who, like Aaron, was a renowned Palestinian agronomist. Ruppin, as with other prominent Palestinian Jews, had been exiled to Constantinople under Djemal Pasha's orders, as he had done with Manya and Israel. Weeks later, said Lova, he knocked on Ruppin's door asking for assistance. By that time, he was begging for food. He did not divulge to Ruppin what he was doing in the capital. The good doctor gave him some clerking work to do. This, and selling matches on the street, gave him a minimal sustenance. Then, one day, Doctor Ruppin asked him a direct question. "Tell me, Lova. Do you favor the British or the Turks in this war?" The poor Lova unhesitatingly said he chose the British. Ruppin smiled and told him to come back in two days. When he did, Lova discovered that Arthur Ruppin had arranged a passage for him to Palestine to accompany a German officer named Klein. Ruppin dressed Lova in an ill-fitting suit and sent him with the unlikely alibi of being a forestry expert with the Atlit Research Station to conduct a forestation survey.

Lova told Sarah that he managed to evade the German in Damascus and boarded a train to Haifa via Afula. From there he had walked the thirty miles to Atlit.

Sarah gazed at Lova as he devoured his meal. Lova was emaciated. Although Dr. Ruppin had provided him with a shirt and suit it was scruffy and stained from his journey. He was a rough diamond, Sarah thought, but there was an attractive quality about him. Lova had displayed a profound level of loyalty to her brother that touched her soul. Despite his poor physical condition, he had shown great strength of character and purpose. He asked to be allowed to sleep the night at Atlit. She made up a bed for him in one of the staff bedrooms. He told her he wanted to head to Hadera early the next morning to reunite with his family.

The following morning Sarah prepared a breakfast for the hungry man. Sarah got Abu Farid to drive him to Hadera in the station's carriage. Lova professed his deep gratitude to Sarah for her kindness and she invited him to come and help at the research station whenever he wanted.

When Reuven, Menashe, and Tova arrived for work, Sarah spoke about the visit of Lova Levi the previous day. Both Reuven and Tova knew the Levi family and vouched for Lova as a capable and loyal person.

Four days later, Lova Levi returned to Atlit. As he entered Sarah's office he produced a piece of paper from his coat pocket and offered it to her.

"Read it," he said. She peered at the writing. Her eyes opening in wide wonder. She recognized the handwriting as that of her lover. It was a poem, and the poem was dedicated *To Lova.*' She was speechless. She stared at the mysterious visitor who said, "I would be grateful for any work or mission you can give me. I pledge to you my loyalty in honor of your brother and my friend, Avshalom. I am here for you. Just tell me what do you want me to do?"

Lova's strong character appealed to Sarah. She liked what she saw in him. She gladly welcomed him as a new member of her team.

THE SHIP RETURNS

Sarah had no inkling that Aaron had arrived in Cairo from London under the nom de plume of William Mack. He was coopted by the British intelligence team of the Arab Bureau. Aaron immediately set about persuading anyone and everyone about the exceptionally courageous and talented network of secret agents at his disposal in Palestine. Most of the senior officers did not want to listen to him. A combination of distrust of Jews and the fact that Palestine was not on their military cards left them indisposed to accept Aaronsohn's recommendation to bring his network into the circle of British intelligence. Aaron was not prepared to take no for an answer.

Aaron struggled to discover why there had been a disconnect between Egypt and Atlit. He was sent to meet with naval intelligence based in Port Said and tried to re-establish the contact with his Atlit station. He went in search of Avshalom's friend, Lieutenant Woolley. He met Captain Lewen Weldon, a gruff Yorkshireman who appreciated Aaron's down to earth honesty. Weldon had also been impressed by Avshalom Feinberg who he had met on Feinberg's initial trip to Egypt. He was the officer that had given him the signal system that they had used between ship and station at Atlit. Aaron found himself, for the first time, in the company of someone in naval intelligence who appreciated the value of what his network could provide to the British. "I have a vested and mutual interest in advancing your cause, captain," Aaron told the naval officer.

Weldon gave Aaron the shocking reason why the ship failed to appear. Woolley's boat had been sunk by a Turkish warship off the coast of Lebanon. The naval intelligence officer and some of his crew had survived the explosion and were now sitting out the war in a Turkish prison camp.

Weldon made the rounds with phone calls and meetings to re-establish naval contact with Aaron's team of espionage agents. He succeeded in requisitioning a replacement ship. They scheduled a sail date. Aaron insisted that he be aboard the ship. The naval intelligence captains, Weldon and Smith, agreed, but with one harsh condition that left Aaron no alternative but to agree. Aaron would not be allowed to leave the naval ship, not even to approach the shore of Atlit in the row boat.

"You're too valuable an asset to lose," Weldon told him.

One of Aaron's first friend in Egypt was Raphael Abulafia, a handsome business man who had, despite his wealth, also been deported from Palestine by the Turks for being Jewish, and was now acting as an agent helping British intelligence. When he learned of Aaron's effort to reconnect to his network Raphael recommended the services of Leib Bernstein. Leib's duties were to be a Hebrew translator would be to rendezvous with Palestinian agents on the shores of Atlit, and to help decode the messages aboard ship. Aaron met Leib and was impressed by him.

Leib Bernstein had fought in the disaster known as Gallipoli. He had fought under the dynamic Zionist leader, Ze'ev Jabotinsky, who had persuaded the British to allow him to organize a volunteer force of donkey-pullers known as the Zion Mule Corps. He, along with hundreds of others, had been selected from among the Jews that were rotting in an Egyptian refugee camp after being deported from Palestine by the Turks. Their job was to bring ammunition and supplies from the beaches of Gallipoli on the backs of pack mules to the fighting men at the front of the Dardanelle battles against the Turks. Following the bloody failure of Gallipoli, Leib returned to Egypt where he had been recruited as a courier by Raphael.

In the middle of a grey day in February, Reuven ran shouting into the Atlit building where Sarah was working.

"Sarah! Sarah! Come up to the balcony." She turned to see Reuven run up the stairs to the sea facing balcony. She chased him up to the balcony in time to see a boat belching black smoke into a cloudy sky. They ran to strip a white sheet from one of the beds and unfurled it out of a window. They watched as the ship turned seaward and disappear over the horizon. They hugged each other in celebration and danced around the room.

"Reuven, who do we have here today?" Sarah's mind was racing.

Reuven gave the roster to Sarah. "We have Menashe, Tova, Yehuda and Lova."

"Menashe and Tova will stay here to guard the station tonight. You, me, Yehuda and Lova will go down to the beach tonight to be taken back to Egypt."

Reuven was surprised. "But Aaron gave you instructions never to go to the beach rendezvous…"

Sarah's excitement was palpable.

"Forget that. I'm here. Aaron isn't. There is no way I am going to miss this rendezvous, even if Aaron steps out of the boat."

The evening brought squally wind and rain. The sea was wild and angry. As they made their preparations, Reuven appealed to Sarah.

"Sarah, in my opinion the weather is too bad for them to make a landing. We are going to get soaked. Let me and Yehuda take the packages down to the shore in case they do come. Lova will help us and then take the boat back to Egypt. We'll give them as long as possible. If they don't land tonight, they'll likely return tomorrow night. Save yourself for their next visit."

Sarah put aside her disappointment and reluctantly agreed with his suggestion.

Reuven was right. The three men ran out into the storm. Sarah anxiously paced the upper floor through the dark and stormy night. She occasionally peered from the balcony but saw nothing, heard nothing except the wind howling through the trees. It was an hour or so before daybreak before they returned. Their oilskins did not save them from receiving a frozen soaking. They were drenched, shivering with cold, and disappointed with an unsuccessful rendezvous as they dragged the deadweight of their wet packages back into the building. Menashe went to get towels and dry clothes. While they showered and dried off, Sarah and Tova prepared hot drinks and sandwiches to revive them.

They organized a lookout the following afternoon. There was a slight improvement in the weather. At two in the afternoon they saw the ship cruising past the Crusader fort. It slowed and belched black smoke. They threw the white blanket out of a bedroom window and kept it there until they saw the ship turn and sail directly away from them.

Sarah wanted to spare Reuven and Yehuda, their new recruit, another uncomfortable night at the beach but they both insisted on completing their mission. Sarah gave Lova an affectionate hug and told him, "Give Aaron my love. Have a safe journey."

Reuven and Yehuda set out from the station with Lova an hour before midnight. They told Sarah they wanted to huddle under a blanket at the end of the wadi until the arrival of the row boat. Sarah waited with Tova and Menashe. Tonight was to be different. Surprisingly different.

It was a stormy night as the ship anchored in the dead of night off the beach of Atlit. Aaron could only watch from the deck of the darkened ship as Leib set out in the small row boat to meet his sister.

211

As the boat neared the coast the sea conditions were strong. The row boat with the Egyptian Abdullah and his two brawny sons, paid recruits in the service of the British navy, pulling at the oars, and carried Leib Bernstein toward the shore. Abdullah shouted at Leib that it was too dangerous to get closer than two hundred yards. He feared they would not be able to pull their boat back out to sea if they got closer. The tide was too strong. Leib saw that it would be impossible to transfer their heavy load of packages and provisions for the covert group waiting for them ashore. A decision had to be made. Leib began to strip off his clothing. He told the Egyptian to wait in calmer waters for a maximum of an hour and a half. He instructed Abdullah to watch out for two flashes of a torch and to send his sons to swim to the shore and help him negotiate the heavy breakers on his return.

Without waiting for an answer, Leib jumped off the row boat into the surging waves that carried him toward the beach. The three from Atlit were surprised to see a naked figure wash up on the beach. A shivering Leib introduced himself. He told them that Aaron was aboard the ship but he had been forbidden to come ashore.

"Aaron wants you to take me to the station to meet Sarah," he told them. "We don't have long," he said. "I have to be back here in an hour." They ran with him to the wadi where they wrapped him in their blanket against the cold. They made their way quickly but cautiously to the road where they waited to make sure it was clear of passing convoys or patrols before racing along the avenue to the station.

Sarah gasped when four men burst in. She stared aghast at the naked man wrapped in a blanket. "What's going on?" she asked. "Who is this?"

"I am Leib Bernstein. I work for your brother. Aaron is on the ship. He is not allowed to come ashore. He sends you his love."

Sarah was in shock, then composed herself. "Tova, make the men cups of tea or coffee, and some sandwiches for them to eat. Menashe, get Leib some dry clothes."

Leib put up a hand. "Thank you, but I only have minutes to tell you what is happening. I have to get back to the ship."

"You can eat and drink while you are talking. I insist. Someone get him a towel."

Sarah looked at the wet packages into the floor.

"Why did you bring the packages back? Where is the dispatch bag from the ship?"

Reuven explained. "The sea was too rough. The boat didn't make it close enough to shore. They wanted to return to the ship, but Leib jumped into the sea to meet you. There won't be an exchange of material on this trip. It's a chance for Lova to get to the ship and work with Aaron. "

"Do you want to join Aaron?" Sarah asked Lova. He said that he would. Loyalty was everything for Lova.

Reuven said, "We only hope that Leib and Lova can get to the ship. The sea is terrible."

"First of all, I want to give you this." Leib opened his fist. In the palm of his hand was a medallion. Sarah put her hand to her mouth to staunch a gasp. She recognized the pendant. "This is Aaron's. He always wears it around his neck."

"He wants you to have it. It's his sign to you that he is alive and well."

Sarah kissed it and began to cry. She quickly regained her composure. "I'm sorry. It is knowing that my brother is so close by and yet we cannot embrace each other. Go on, Leib, tell us what we need to hear."

"Aaron is in Cairo with British military intelligence. He has succeeded in establish contacts with naval intelligence. They will now start delivering their intelligence requirements. You will be sent instructions of what is needed and we will try to rendezvous with you between every ten days to two weeks. If the weather is bad it may stretch to three week visits."

"Fine," said Sarah, "but the ship's visit is too precarious and uncertain. Look at today for example. You are here but you can't take the hoard of material we have for you. Isn't there any other method of communication we can use? This system is too unpredictable."

Leib shook his head. "I'm sorry. This is the best the British can do right now. Both Aaron and his contacts in naval intelligence are having a hard time convincing the General Staff to put more resources at your disposal. Their attention is in other directions, but Aaron wants you to know that things are changing. He sends his love and he wants all of you to know that he's thinking of you and working very hard to change the minds of some stubborn people in Cairo. Now I must get back to the ship. Thanks for the sandwiches."

As Leib and Lova headed for the door, followed by Reuven to escort them through the dark night to the shore, Sarah said, "Wait! Have you seen Avshalom Feinberg?"

"No. Should I have seen him?"

"Yes. He set out for Egypt weeks ago with Joseph Lishansky. Hasn't Aaron met with them?"

"He never mentioned it. I would think he would have given me a message for you had they arrived."

Sarah was silent as the three men ran out of the door and into the dark rainy night.

Where was Avsha?

They got to the shore and Reuven flashed two short bursts of light toward the dark expanse of sea. They waited a minute and heard the oarsmen yell for them to come to them. They saw the two swimmers waiting in the water. Lova stripped out of his clothes and dived into the broiling waves to follow Leib. Reuven and Menashe watched as they battled the rough seas. They heard shouting as Leib disappeared with the two Arab oarsmen. Lova struggled his way back to the beach.

"It's too strong," he gasped. "I couldn't make it. Leib said they will return to pick me up tomorrow night if the sea isn't as rough."

The following night was blustery but dry. Sarah went with Lova down to the beach. They were escorted by Reuven and Menashe. Lova kissed Sarah before wading out into the surf. He was helped to the row boat by Abdullah's sons.

THE ARGUMENT

Aaron Aaronsohn was livid. He was delighted to be reunited with Lova after so long, but he was shocked by the news that Lova gave him after he clambered aboard the ship.

He was stricken to his bones to learn that Sarah was alone in charge of his enterprise, and that both Avshalom and Joseph Lishansky were missing. Both the agricultural and espionage activities now rested on her shoulders. How had that happened? Lova told him that both Avshalom and Joseph had taken off for Egypt but hadn't been heard of since. Now Aaron really had a crisis on his hands. Both his top two men had left his sister in charge of a dangerous mission in order to venture down to Cairo. This was madness. This was the adventurism he had been afraid of. Both of them were missing, and now Sarah was left on her own to handle everything.

A huge row erupted at the Savoy Hotel in Cairo. A meeting had been called by the EMSIB, the Eastern Mediterranean Special Intelligence Bureau.

EMSIB had been formed in February 1915 when MI5's Major Eric Holt-Wilson sailed to Egypt to discuss the creation of a regional intelligence organization with the head of the local director of military intelligence, Colonel G.F. Clayton. Up to then the naval and military intelligence units had collected information without coordination.

Clayton was part of the General Staff. They came up with a plan to coordinate all intelligence, both army and navy, under one umbrella for the Middle East region. EMSIB's Branch included Egypt, the Sudan, Abyssinia, Cyprus, Eritrea, Tripoli, and the Palestinian district of Syria.

Aaron Aaronsohn was ordered to a meeting of a sub-committee of EMSIB. He was angry. Very angry. He was receiving growing complaints from his operatives that Captain Smith, in charge of naval intelligence at Port Said and a frequent sailor aboard the rendezvous ship, had been dismissive of Aaron's network and was treating them with rude arrogance to the point that, on occasions, he had refused to drop the row boat off the coast of Atlit blaming the weather even though the agents felt they could have made their rendezvous and completed their mission. Lova complained to Aaron that Smith's attitude was not only insufferable but that he was endangering the lives of his people on the beach, in fact, the safety of the whole operation.

Aaron found Captain Smith to be obnoxious. He had witnessed Smith's arrogant behavior during his voyage to Atlit. Smith was not only insulting to his team in Palestine, he was also grudging in the amounts of money he reluctantly sent to Atlit to cover the expenses of the operation, demanding a full accounting of every half penny from Sarah. After arguing unsuccessfully with Smith, Aaron raised the matter with Major James Malcolm, deputy head of the Palestine unit, and Captain William Edmonds, with whom he had a good working relationship. The major told Aaron that he would deal with the matter, but matters deteriorated further when Malcolm failed to provide answers or solve the problem.

Aaron had a lunch date with Major Wyndham Deedes who he had met in London and found to be receptive to his background and ideas. Deedes had been transferred to Cairo as a senior intelligence officer and was empathetic to Aaron's dilemma. Aaron poured out his heart to Deedes. He spoke about his personal connection to the young people, headed by his sister, who had the courage to risk sacrificing themselves to help the British.

"It is cruelly wrong that they must suffer from the insulting and dismissive behavior of Smith," he told Deedes. Aaron's lunch resulted in

Wyndham Deedes instructing Malcolm to reinstate a meeting and solve the outstanding problems.

The meeting opened with a shouting match between Aaron and Smith. Smith spoke of Aaron's intelligence group with disdain. Aaron went for the jugular.

"If you were privy, Captain Smith, to the communiques from Whitehall you would know that I and my team know everything the General Staff needs to know about launching a successful military campaign in Palestine."

Smith scoffed loudly.

"Captain Smith. I have the answers to all of your questions relating to how to win a decisive victory over the Turks and Germans in Palestine from an intelligence perspective. I even have the answers to questions you don't yet know what to ask. That's why GS acknowledged my amendments to their handbook. I'll happily give you a copy if you like."

"No thank you," replied Smith snootily.

Malcolm had to restore order, and he did it badly.

"I think there is too much fuss being made on this matter. It has been allowed to blow up out of all proportion."

"Too much fuss? Out of proportion?" Aaron exploded. "This man is playing with the lives of my friends, including my sister, for heaven's sake! They have been providing you people with the most valuable intelligence you will ever get from Palestine."

"Valuable intelligence," Smith snooted. "Your people are frauds. They provide amateur reports and out of date information."

"They wouldn't be out of date if you provided a regular ship service to pick them up. It's because of your incompetence that valuable intelligence is being stored for weeks at Atlit."

"Am I responsible for the weather conditions? Why risk my ship? Their work is worthless. It can be done far more effectively by other people."

"Really," Aaron responded. "In that case you go find these other people. I will not endanger my friends and my family any more for an unappreciative and arrogant intelligence officer." He stood up and pointed at Captain Smith. "If you can't respect the people who are risking everything for you, then I'm out of the game. Put me on the next boat to Atlit. I'll direct them back to my agricultural research projects. At least they won't be tortured and killed by the Turks for that!"

Malcolm and Edmonds tried to calm things down. Eventually, Major Malcolm brought this meeting to a hasty close.

"Either you two gentlemen settle your differences or the situation will be clarified and accepted without depending on the whims of this or that captain or the vagaries of the weather, or we shall exchange our goodbyes. We will discuss this matter, Mr. Aaronsohn, and let you know our decision."

When they left the room, Malcolm took Aaron aside. "I have to tell you, Aaronsohn, that it was out of order for you to go over our heads to Major Deedes. That was most unfortunate."

Aaron said nothing. He knew that Deedes was leaning on them from above, and they didn't like it. *Strange,* he thought, *how unintelligent senior intelligence officers can be.*

Aaron lunched with a friend, Captain Philip Graves, a senior officer in the transport and supplies department of the General Staff. Graves was consulting with Aaron on the types of illnesses and diseases that British troops might experience while fighting their way through Palestine. Aaron had introduced him to Dr. Naftali Weitz, a renowned expert in the field of tropical diseases, particularly those found in both the coastal and hilly reaches of Palestine. Weitz had been born and raised in Zichron Yaakov before leaving to take up his medical studies and his research prior to becoming one of the thousands who had been deported from Palestine. He had been treating people in the refugee camps when Aaron found him on his arrival in Egypt.

They discussed Aaron's research into the locations where malaria had its sources due to the swampy mosquito-laden stagnant pools.

"Keep clear of these cesspools. They carry infections. Use the maps that I provided," advised Aaron. Be careful, Philip, with the unripe barley that could poison the horses. I suggest you wait until late March or early April before you advance in a serious manner into Palestine. That is when the corn will be approaching maturity."

Aaron warned Graves about the dangers of fighting in the heat of a Palestinian summer with the acute shortage of water. He told Graves he knew where water supplies lay hidden underground. He offered to coordinated with the engineering corps of the British army to dig in the locations he had conducted geological studies based on his knowledge of the Bible as being where water aquifers existed under the desert sand.

Their conversation turned to Aaron's problems with Smith and the EMSIB sub-committee. After listening carefully to Aaron's account of the last meeting, Philip Graves smiled sympathetically. "I have serious doubts that Smith has any mysterious alternatives to your people. In my opinion, Aaron, he's bluffing."

Aaron grimaced. "It goes well with his character."

A couple of days later, Edmonds invited Aaron to a quiet meeting. Edmonds acted nonchalantly as if nothing had occurred the previous day but their conversation searched for an alternative to the erratic naval rendezvous with Atlit. Aaron knew that his friend, Captain Graves, had presented an urgent communique to his superiors saying that, from a strategic position, *'every effort must be made to ensure that valued military and tactical intelligence should continue to be received from our reliable Palestinian source at the General Staff from EMSIB, even if we are compelled to abandon other sources.'*

The meaning was abundantly clear. If Major Malcolm and Captain Smith could not sort out their mess Graves was suggesting that Aaron's network would be moved into a branch of the General Staff.

Armed with that information Aaron was not surprised when Edmonds opened their meeting with a question.

"What is the possibility of us making overland contact with your people?" he asked.

"Not advisable," replied Aaron. "It's far too risky. The enemy is there in greater numbers and increasingly jittery. Putting aside our espionage activities for a minute, my advice has always been that you should launch a major sea invasion into Palestine several miles south of Haifa where the coastal defenses are virtually non-existent. You can land a large number of troops without being challenged in any serious manner and, by creating a large bridgehead, cut the Turkish forces in two leaving their southern forces cut off with your armies squeezing them from the north and the south. They are already demoralized and hungry, according to our reports."

"Interesting, Aaronsohn, but let's concentrate on our brief which is intelligence gathering. What alternatives do you suggest?"

"We should work on a covert signaling system that my people can use to communication with your ships. That way removes the danger of interception of our people on the beach."

"It would, however, be vulnerable to signals interception by the enemy which would further endanger your people. It will take quite some time before we come up with a satisfactory technology that would avoid that risk. We need to take a more simplistic approach. How about homing pigeons?"

"Are they safe?" Aaron enquired." After all, they'll be flying from our facilities over the heads of the enemy."

Edmonds smiled reassuringly. "They've been used with great success on the Western Front bringing important information rapidly back to London. I see no reason why they cannot be used by your people after we have trained them properly."

They agreed that this should be tried until a more sophisticated method of communication could be found.

"By the way, Aaronsohn. We just got word that there is a Palestinian lying in the hospital in Alexandria. He was picked up near the border. He's been injured. We think he may be one of your people."

The blood drained from Aaron's face. The thought flashed through his mind, *it must be Avshalom*. "I'll check on that immediately. Permission to leave for Alexandria?"

"Granted. Keep me updated."

Aaron phoned Raphael Abulafia from his office. "What have you heard about an injured Palestinian that was picked up on the border and is in the hospital in Alexandria?"

"Hello, Aaron. Yes, it's Lishansky. I tried to call you but I understand you were in meetings. I intend to go see him today."

A disappointed Aaron responded, "I'm coming with you."

They took the train to the Egyptian port town, and a taxi from the station directly to the hospital. They raced to the reception and asked where they could find Joseph Lishansky.

They found him lying in a bed. It was indeed the missing Lishansky. Above the bedsheet Aaron could see that he was bandaged on his left shoulder.

"What the hell were you thinking?" Aaron stormed. Heads turned in his direction. Raphael gripped his arm as a warning for him to lower his voice. Aaron gritted his teeth.

"Were you insane to leave Sarah on her own?" He put his head close to the patient's ear. "Have you no responsibility?"

Lishansky was stunned to find Aaron Aaronsohn red faced and angry at his bedside.

Raphael touched Aaron's back and leaned closer to Lishansky. He asked, "Joseph. Where is Avshalom?"

Lishansky looked up from the pillow with sad eyes.

"He's dead."

Aaron and Raphael gazed at him in stunned silence.

"We were surrounded by Bedouin. Our guide led us into a trap. They wanted to take us to the Turks and claim a reward. We were not prepared to be captured so we opened fire on them. We tried to escape but Avshalom and I were both hit. I saw him fire at them but he got hit again and fell off his horse. I turned around. He was lying on the ground. The Turks were gathered around his body. I had to escape otherwise I would have been captured or killed. I had no other choice, Aaron."

Aaron was fuming. It was not enough that he now had Lishansky lying in an Egyptian hospital, he had Sarah stranded and alone in charge of his network, and his best friend was dead.

"You're a disgrace."

Aaron stormed out of the ward. Raphael patted Joseph. "Get yourself better."

"We had no other choice. Aaron had disappeared. The ship had disappeared. What were we supposed to do? We had to try to establish contact."

Rafi felt sympathetic, even though his friend was dead. "Leave Aaron to me. I'll try and calm him down."

Rafi found Aaron sitting on a form in the hospital corridor. He sat next to him. They sat in silence for several minutes. Their thoughts on Avshalom's fate. Manly grief did not allow them to speak until Aaron said, "I suppose we'd better get the train back to Cairo."

Malcolm and Edmonds found themselves pounded from another source angry at Smith's behavior. Wyndham Deedes had called a meeting with the three EMSIB officers and laid into them.

He repeated the accusations against Smith. Both Smith and Malcolm, covering each other's backs, went into denial mode. They denied they had ever treated Aaronsohn or his men badly. They denied they had ever said anything derogatory about them. They denied they had suggested they had other sources that could do Aaronsohn's job better.

Deedes diplomatically gave them a metaphorical slap on the wrist. "Get this thing with Aaronsohn sorted out," he demanded, "otherwise, I will bring this dispute to the attention of General HQ."

At the renewed meeting between the MSIP officers and Aaron, when Major Malcolm said, for the record, that Aaronsohn had misunderstood them, Aaron replied by insisting that "Captain Smith must be taught what our aims are and that he should accommodate them to the best of his ability and to treat my people with the proper respect."

The minutes of the meeting were sent to General HQ Intelligence who decided that the Aaron's network was the one reliable source in the area. In a bland summation by a diplomatic Wyndham Deedes, carefully crafted not to ruffle feathers, he wrote, "We considered, at a meeting in Port Said with Captain Smith, the suggestion of closing down some of the agencies along the Mediterranean coast. It was decided we should not be justified in closing them down since, if anything happened to our very reliable Aaronsohn organization, we would have nothing to fall back on."

It took a week before they released Joseph Lishansky from hospital. Aaron arranged for him to convalesce in a hotel in Port Said until he was ready to return to Palestine. Naval intelligence set the date for the next voyage to Atlit. Aaron had pressed to be allowed to sail on the ship. He was ready to defy orders so that he could see Sarah, to hug her, and to give her added strength for her difficult and lonely task. But Aaron was denied permission to sail. Together with Raphael and Lova, he took the train to Port Said the day before Joseph was due to embark. Aaron asked that Lova accompany Joseph back to Atlit, to wait there until the next ship's arrival and report back to him everything that was happening there.

He needed Lova to confirm that Sarah had everything under her control and to send her his love. Aaron decided, under advise from Raphael, to mend fences with Lishansky before sending him back to the network. They picked up Joseph from his hotel and took him to a nice restaurant for dinner.

"Nothing is more important to me in this world than Sarah. You understand that, surely?" It was more a statement than a question. Joseph agreed.

"I want it also to be clearly understood that she is in charge of the operation now, and she needs all the help she can get. Unwavering help. There can be no room for rebellion, or private initiatives without her knowledge and approval. Is that clear?" Again, Joseph agreed.

"The work is clandestine. It has to be carried out with somber reflection and cooperation. There has to be no place for adventurism. One little slip and the game is over. I don't want Sarah, I don't want any of you, to fall into the hands of the Turks because of one ill-considered action. Do I make myself clear?" Joseph answered, "yes."

"I hope the British can devise another safe system of communication, but until that happens we are stuck with the ship. Tell Sarah they are training carrier pigeons. They are not foolproof, but the British say they have working successfully in their European war against the Germans, so we may try them out when they are properly trained. Let's hope the ship's schedule will be more reliable and regular than it has been in the past."

Aaron paused, then continued. "The work will not be the same without Avshalom. You have to be there supporting Sarah. I have thought hard and long about his loss." Another pause. "Listen, Joseph, under no circumstances must you tell anyone that Avshalom is dead. Not his friends, not even his family. You can tell Sarah. She knows how to keep a secret, but not the others. I hope you know how to keep a secret as well. Do you, Joseph?" Joseph replied, "Yes, I can. But why? Why can't they know? They were all so close to him. They worshipped him."

"That's precisely why you can't tell them. The network could fall apart if they know that Avshalom is lost forever. More importantly, if news gets out about how and where he was killed and that you were with him all sorts of rumors will spread and you will have the Turks on your neck. You do understand the implications of that, don't you, Joseph? If the Turks are on your neck, they will be on everyone's necks. We cannot let that happen. You will tell everybody within our circle, those that know you went down to Egypt with him, that Avshalom is here, undergoing training with the British for special missions. If they ask, you don't know the details. They are secret. Is that clear?"

Joseph understood the danger to everyone if word got out about the terrible events that had taken his friend's life.

The following morning, Aaron and Raphael escorted Joseph and Lova to the ship. Aaron spoke to the captain before shaking hands with Joseph.

"Look after her, Joseph. Never leave her side. Give her my love and this." He handed her a brown envelope. "It's my personal letter to Sarah who I love deeply. Make sure she gets it, will you."

He turned to Lova as Joseph made his way to the gangway. "Keep an eye on him and let me know how he is performing his duties."

NEWS

Sarah waited on the upstairs balcony for the return of Reuven, Menashe, and Yehuda. The three had carried the waterproof bags filled with the accumulation of their work for the British. They were expected to return laden with fresh orders, supplies, and, hopefully, money.

Sarah could never concentrate on anything else when the boys were on their precarious job of rendezvousing with the ship and bringing the sacks back to the station. It would always be a tense journey. Sarah didn't know why the balcony was her preferred waiting place. She was exposed to the weather, the cold of night, and rarely caught any sound or sight of them save for Demon's friendly bark as they entered the compound. The dog barked and she ran down the stairs to greet them.

Her jaw dropped as five men stumbled out of the dark and into the building. Reuven, Menashe and Yehuda were accompanied by Lova and Joseph Lishansky.

She stood rooted to the spot, speechless as Joseph came to her and embraced her.

"How are you, Sarita?" He rarely used her affectionate name in company.

"What! How! Where is Avsha?" she stuttered.

Joseph put on a smile that Sarah instinctively felt was disingenuous.

"He's fine. Avsha's in Egypt. The British are preparing him for an important job."

There was something in Joseph's speech that made Sarah uncomfortable. She saw that he glanced at Lova as he mentioned Avshalom. She and Tova made the boys hot drinks as they ate the sandwiches she had prepared for them. Heavy waterproof sacks filled with documents, orders, money, and some supplies were dumped on the floor.

Joseph gossiped about his trek down to Egypt with Avshalom and how they had eventually met up with Aaron. He told her how Aaron was working hard integrating himself into British intelligence circles and making contacts with members of the General Staff, how he was working out of the office of the Arab Bureau located at the Savoy Hotel in Cairo, and how difficult it had been for Aaron to promote their interests with the decision makers but that he was making progress. Sarah heard his voice almost as background noise. She felt herself detached from his conversation. Her mind was somewhere else. Something was wrong with his demeanor. Joseph was overly excitable, ranting a story. She glanced over at Lova. He seemed ill at ease. Eventually, Sarah said, "You boys must be exhausted. Go to bed. Get some sleep. I'm going into the office. I want to get started on the next batch of instructions."

Reuven handed her one of the sacks and kissed her goodnight. Lova had an appealing, almost apologetic look on his face as he mumbled something about it being good to see her again. Sarah turned her back on them and made her way silently to the office.

After about half an hour, Joseph came into the room. He closed the door. She had half expected it. She stared at him from her chair. A feeling of doom swept over her body as she felt, rather than saw, the look on his face. She gripped the arms of her chair.

"Sarita." Joseph paused, struggling for the words. "Avsha is dead. Our friend is dead. He was killed in the desert. We were attacked by a band of Bedouin. Our guide ran to them shouting in Arabic. They wanted to take us to the Turks and claim a reward. Avshalom and I started shooting at them. We tried to escape but they had rifles and I got hit." His hand automatically reached for his left shoulder blade to show her where he had been wounded. "They injured me and shot Avsha. I saw him fall. He fired at them as he fell but they shot him as he lay on the ground. They killed him. There was nothing I could do. I was wounded, so I rode away as fast as I could. I was hit, twice. Somehow they didn't come after me. Later that day I was found by some Australian soldiers and taken to a hospital in Egypt."

Sarah got up and slapped his face.

"It's your fault!" Sarah was angry. "You encouraged him to take this trip. I told you not to do it." She was hitting his chest and face.

"Why didn't you listen to me? Avsha would be alive now if you had listened to me…" She collapsed back into her chair in an outburst of tears. He stood there, embarrassed and ashamed. Eventually, he said, "Sarah. He would have gone anyway. You know that. That's why I went with him, to try and protect him. I failed. I've regretted it ever since. I know how much you were attached to him but he was my best friend also. I have been grieving ever since."

He paused, then he touched Sarah's shoulders and said, "Sarah, listen to me. Aaron insists that nobody must know about Avsha. He told me this explicitly. He said that you should know, but nobody else. Nobody. Not even his family. It would be too risky for us if word got out what happened to him. It will dishearten the team, and his family may make a big scandal about it. If word gets out that he was killed while we were on our way to reach the British we will all be doomed. We cannot risk that. It's an order from Aaron, and he's right. The day will come when people will learn how he died, but not now. Not yet"

Sarah stared ahead, not speaking, not looking at him.

"Do you understand this, Sarah?" She nodded. "There will be a time for grieving, but not now. Is that clear?"

She nodded again, but nothing could prevent her from grief.

"I'm sorry, Sarah. So sorry." Sarah's response was minimal. He stood there awkwardly. There was no response from Sarah. Eventually, he said, "Good night, Sarah. Get some sleep."

He left the room leaving Sarah staring at a darkened window. She tried to summon up Avsha's face. She sobbed silently as she muttered to herself, "Avsha. Avsha. Why did you leave me?"

She sat there for hours, until the first soft light of a new day dimly lit the room. She rose and went up to her empty bed, wrapped a sheet around herself and fell asleep, hoping to dream of Avsha.

In the morning, Sarah hypnotically went from her bed to the balcony. Dark heavy clouds hung low over a gray sea. The black clouds were pregnant with gloom and rain. She felt the chill wind on her face and her aching body as she stood there in her flimsy night clothes. She let the cold embrace her frozen soul until she began to shiver with grief.

The voices of her friends penetrated from the floor below reminding her she had work to do. She had to take Avshalom's enterprise onto her shoulders. *This is why I am here, to continue his legacy - his, and Aaron's.* She smiled sadly to herself. *It's what I was born to do. It's what has led me back here. Nothing is more important than this. It's an expression of my love for them, them and my people. The fate of our people is in our hands. I have to make it work. For Avsha's sake. I love you, Avsha.*

232

She lingered a moment longer. The dark clouds moved inexorably toward her. Still in somber mood, she stared at the incoming clouds. *Are they coming for me, or for the Turks? Or are they coming for both of us?*

The chill caught her. She shivered. *Enough of the melancholy. I have work to do.*

She turned to prepare herself to face her loving team that depended on her now more than ever, a team that was blissfully unaware of the dark black secret that only she, Joseph, Lova, and Aaron so far away, knew.

NILI

When Lova was rowed back to the ship, Aaron was waiting at the top of the ladder as he clambered aboard. They embraced as warmly as they could on a cold and breezy night at sea. Lova found himself buried in the huge chest of his friend and master.

"So tell me. How is my sister?"

Lova smiled. "Very attractive."

"No seriously, how is she?"

"She is seriously attractive, and Aaron, she is fully in command of her team and the situation. She's frustrated about the infrequent visits. She can easily provide more important information if we came more often."

"Come. Let's get you warm. You have to tell me everything about what is happening there."

As they sat in Aaron's cabin. Lova gave Aaron as full a description of the work of the network as he saw it in the limited time he spent at Atlit.

"Sarah's work is impressive, and Joseph is obedient to her every need."

"How did she take the news about Avshalom?"

"I never spoke to her about it but I watched her body language after Joseph had told her. She put on a brave face. She is very stoic, but I saw the sadness in her eyes. I think she will steel herself to her loss."

"Good. I hope so. She has a terrible responsibility to bear and I am still not sure about Lishansky's ability to support her."

"He seems in his element over there," observed Lova. "We can only pray that he doesn't slip up," he said as he idly fingered a small copy of a Bible.

"What's the book?" Aaron asked out of curiosity.

"It's a bible," Lova said, passing it over to Aaron to inspect.

"It was a gift from Avshalom. He gave it to me some years back. See," he said pointing to the opening page, "he inscribed a message to me here. I brought it with me when we heard about his death."

"Maybe your bible can help me," suggested Aaron. "I've been asked for a suitable code name for our group. While we were waiting for you Weldon reminded me to come up with a name for our network, but I'm afraid I can't come up with anything catchy."

Lova scanned the pages. He stopped at a chapter from the Book of Samuel. As he recited the Hebrew text, Aaron's ears pricked up when Lova uttered the words in Hebrew,

"He who is the Glory of Israel will not lie, nor will he change his mind, for He is not human that He should change His mind!"

Aaron was struck by the profundity of the message. "The Glory of Israel will not lie. *Netzach Israel Lo Ishakar*, in Hebrew."
The two men peered into the page of Lova's small bible.

"NILI," said Lova. Aaron looked at him.

"NILI - the initials of *Netzach Israel lo Ishakar.'* That's the name of your network."

"NILI. Yes. I like it. And I like the message it represents. It's profound. It could be our motto. It's perfect. NILI we will be. The glory of Israel will not lie."

They went in search of Captain Weldon. "We have the name of our intelligence group, Captain. It's NILI."

"Nice name for a girl. Who is she?" Weldon asked.

Aaron could only think of Sarah.

JEALOUSIES AND FEARS

Sarah was cautious about the men and women she recruited. Yehuda Zeldin was typical of many of the young men of NILI. Quiet and unassuming, he would take instructions with the nod of his head. He was of medium height, not imposing but strong, both in his physical strength and in his character. Raised on the ambition that the land would, one day, revert to being the Jewish homeland, Yehuda saw that everything he did with NILI and the agricultural project was leading, inevitably, to that goal. He was happy to play his part. Sarah appreciated his understated willingness to accept any job she gave him. He refused no task and executed them well and silently. Yehuda was a welcome and reliable addition to the team selected to receive the ship at night.

The return of the ship meant more instructions, more work. Sarah went in search of new recruits. With the difficulties of local travel, she entrusted Joseph to accompany her on occasional but vital long journeys. They were driven in the carriage to Haifa by Abu Farid. The end of the locust crisis meant an end to their official travel passes. It was back to the bureaucratic procedure of applying for domestic travel passes. Their request for a wazika to go to Jerusalem was turned down. The Turks were dividing the administrative areas of Palestine differently. It required Sarah to take a circuitous route. They wanted to recruit new candidates in the area of Joseph's origins to the west of the Sea of Galilee. It became clear to Sarah that there was a reluctance to help Joseph by his family and friends. Joseph explained that it derived from their unhappiness when he turned his back on the HaShomer group which was particularly strong in the settlements and villages in this area.

In Tiberias, they managed to obtain their passes to travel to Jerusalem, but Sarah was keen to visit Afula on their route to the holy city.

David Sokolov, a distant cousin of Sarah's and a struggling farmer in the Jezreel Valley, was down on his luck and finding it hard to put bread on his table to feed his hungry family. He had come to visit Aaron in Zichron Yaakov when Sarah was away in Turkey. Aaron had given him money to rent a room near the Afula train station and turn it into a tea room. David's wife made the sandwiches, and soup in winter, while David served the travelers waiting for their trains at the station. This was becoming a busy junction with both German and Turkish troops passed through on their way to and from the growing garrisons in central and southern Palestine. Aaron and Avshalom didn't ask for payment. They wanted David to provide them with information on troop movements, including names of the units, their senior officers, and their destinations. In the chatty business of dispensing tea and coffee to passengers, David was provided with rich information that slipped from lips in idle conversation. But, today, Sarah was after a bigger prize.

Sarah went in search of Moshe Neuman. Moshe had been the pharmacist in Zichron Yaakov before qualifying as a doctor. Sarah knew he had been conscripted to serve as a physician at the small military hospital based in Afula near the train station. It was his duty to give all military staff, from simple private up to the generals, a medical checkup for potential contagious diseases. Everyone passed through his stethoscope.

When they reached Afula, she made for the hospital. She asked Joseph to stay with the carriage and she entered the hospital alone. She quickly recognized him. He was surprised to see her. She invited him to have coffee with him at David's café when he was off duty. When he arrived some hours later, they sat at a corner table. David served them with food and coffee. After exchanging pleasantries, Sarah came to the point. Speaking in a whispered voice she said, "Moshe. We need your help."

She explained what they were doing. "You are privy to a lot of vitally important information. Information that will eventually drive the Turks and

238

Germans out of Palestine. I know you from Zichron. I know you share our ambition to get rid of our enemy. I know you have a Hippocratic oath as a doctor, but this is your chance to contribute by helping us." Sarah explained in a whispered voice her connections with the British. "Moshe, you are perfectly placed to be of immense value to us. Will you agree to help?"

The doctor shook his head. "I support what you are doing but don't ask me to do this. I'd like to keep my head on my shoulders."

Sarah gave him a scathing look.

"Look at me, Moshe. Look at me. I am a woman. I am doing it every day throughout Palestine, and my head is still firmly on my shoulders. Are you telling me that you are more of a coward than this simple girl?"

She stared at Moshe, shaming him to say no. Eventually, he nodded his approval. "God help me, but I will help you."

"Bless you, Moshe. I knew I could depend on you. Use David, here at the café. He will bring us your information."

Moshe surprised her. "I'll speak to my brother, Mendel, I think he will act as a courier for us."

"Excellent, Moshe. I look forward to receiving your reports."

Sarah and Joseph headed up to Jerusalem, driven by their loyal Abu Farid. They decided to stay as close to the enemy as they could, taking rooms in the Fast Hotel on Jaffa Road, a short walk from the Old City. Abu Farid went to stay with his Jerusalem family that he had not seen for a long time. Sarah knew she was assured of his total discretion. They would never know that he was more than a simple cart driver for a Jewish family.

The Fast Hotel on Jaffa Road was the preferred watering hole of the enemy. It was where the top German and Turkish officers, diplomats, engineers, and administrators stayed, ate, drank, and slept. It was where Sarah chose to stay for their three-day sojourn in Jerusalem. The casual exchanges between men at bars, she told Joseph, should be enlightening.

"I will concentrate on the Germans. You engage the Turks in conversation," she instructed Joseph as their carriage approached the entrance of the hotel.

They didn't have to lie about who they were. Their credentials of representing Djemal Pasha on the locust problem and crop production were genuine and these topics, added to the amiability of Sarah and Joseph, seduced important people to relax in their convivial company and impart information that should otherwise have remained secret. They even shared a dinner table with a couple of German officers, staffers with General von Kressenstein, who liberally told them of troops movements, the names of unit commanders, their final destinations, and the defensive engineering projects that were being constructed in certain garrison towns and outposts. They gathered so much knowledge as they wined and dined that Sarah had to excuse herself. In the ladies' powder room, she jotted down names and numbers, putting her written notes in her bag before heading back to the restaurant to gather more precious jewels for the British.

During the day they had meetings with new potential agents and made a couple of converts. In the evening, Sarah chatted to a German engineer about transport infrastructure. He divulged where roads were being extended and bridges being built. Joseph propped up the bar, engaging a group of Turkish officers and important administrators in conversation. As they retreated to the safety of their rooms they compared notes before Sarah catalogued the goldmine of intelligence in her note pad.

While in Jerusalem they met Nahum Wilbushevski, a Jewish engineer conscripted by the Turkish military to plan and supervise the construction of bridges and fortifications. He frequently travelled between Jerusalem and Damascus and, as a military engineer, possessed a wazira which allowed him access to sensitive military facilities. They met at an anonymous café in one of the warren of alleyways inside the Old City. He noted on a map the locations of the few fortifications in and around the Jerusalem. Wilbushevski told them that there were only two conceivable escape routes between Jerusalem and Damascus and the top brass would not wait to find themselves besieged inside Jerusalem, but evacuate the city before the British could surround them.

Wilbushevski explained where important strategic bridges that carried the flow of supplies and troops were located. He pinpointed key bridges near Tulkarm and at a place called Delhamiyeh. Before Joseph had left Egypt Aaron had told him to check the bridge at El Jama'a where the railway line from Beit Shean to Tzemach in the Jordan Valley crossed the River Jordan. Joseph discussed this target with Wilbushevski who advised Joseph not to send people with explosives.

"It's a remote and open area. The attackers will be exposed to the enemy. Making a getaway is too high risk. Better to get the British to bomb it from the air," the engineer advised.

The next day, they walked to the Old City as if they were tourists. Armed with Wilbushevski's map they visited and marked the locations mentioned by the engineer who was now providing major military secrets to them.

They had been away from home for a week but they still had a few more important people to see. Leaving Jerusalem, they headed for Rishon le Zion for a meeting with Naaman and Eitan Belkind. Naaman was a close friend of Joseph, but he had been even closer to Avshalom. Although the Belkind brothers gave him valuable intelligence, Naaman was belligerent and anxious to talk about the missing Avshalom.

"It's just not possible that I have not heard from him."

"How can he contact you without compromising you and himself?" Joseph bluffed.

"He would find a way. We were close, very close. He even got me messages when he was sitting in prison in Beer Sheba."

"That's because I bribed his guards," was Joseph's rebuttal.

Sarah hated lying about Avshalom, especially to someone as important to her as Naaman. Despite her conflicted soul, Sarah intervened. "Leave it alone, Naaman. You will learn everything in due course. In the meantime, it's better to leave him where he is. There is nothing to be gained by creating a situation that could compromise and endanger us."

It was difficult for Sarah to lie to the Belkinds. They were trusted partners in the group, but she had little option. Joseph was impressed by Sarah's apparent calmness and confidence. He knew how painful it was for her to talk about Avshalom, let alone lie about him. As for Naaman, he was not convinced by Sarah's and Joseph's explanations. Despite this, the Belkinds were enthusiastically active in both Sarah's agricultural and espionage operations.

Naaman Belkind had recruited a young man who had been unhappily conscripted by the Turks. His name was Amnon Fein and he was providing them with amazing intelligence from within the Turkish military garrison at Beer Sheba.

Eitan was Naaman's younger brother, but he possessed the maturity and coolness to have extracted top secret codes from a German broadcasting center in Damascus. He had befriended another conscripted Jew who worked there as a translator. Eitan persuaded him to give him a copy of the codes. Tova Gelber had met him and smuggled the codes to Sarah on her return from Damascus. They were now in the possession of the British.

On her return to Atlit, among Sarah's dispatches were the following reports;

In the south east of Beer Sheba, the Turks intend to hold temporary defensive lines and in the event of a heavy attack to withdraw to the mountains of Jerusalem and to Hebron which they are fortifying.
German forces in Palestine number 50,000.
German's informed by Bedouin spies that British have an army of 100,000 men in the south but German aerial reconnaissance reduce the number down to 50,000.
Population in Jerusalem is poor, hungry, and dispirited. They want the English to come. Enemy expected to flee Jerusalem in advance of Allied arrival. Defense positions highlighted in attached map.
Map highlighted by key bridges and rail junctions. El Jama rail bridge should be bombed by air.

The HaShomers didn't like to be out of the loop. They also wanted nothing to do with espionage. They saw themselves as the official organization for the welfare and the defense of the Jewish settlements and communities throughout Palestine. They linked themselves to the domestic Zionist organizations to coordinate policies respectful of the Turkish authorities. Even as they hated the increasingly oppressive regime, they determined to remain loyal citizens and wait out the war. What they hated almost as much was the private success of Aaronsohn's organization that attracted capable young men like Avshalom Feinberg, Joseph Lishansky who had been one of their rising stars, and others who were leaving HaShomer for the Aaronsohns. Perhaps what they hated most of all was

243

the sums of money that were being dispensed by the Aaronsohns' people to the settlements and other communities from foreign sources. They hated that their cash-strapped organization had no access to the Aaronsohn trustees and funders. Neither did they like the Aaronson's covert adventures.

It wasn't just jealousy. They were fearful. This fear was real. The shadow of the Armenian fate hung over Palestine. They were worried that the actions of privateers would jeopardize the safety of the people they were protecting. With the Aaronsohn group in mind, they issued a notice to all their members;

Our policy in the present situation is one of absolute civil loyalty. Any action outside these limits must be seen as an attack on the existence of the community.

The HaShomer issued orders to their members to have no contact with the Aaronsohn group. In the unexplained absence of Aaron and Avshalom this increased the gossip and notoriety about Sarah and her team. The pressure on Sarah was growing.

Jealousies and fears grew. The HaShomer men would frequently bump into Sarah's operators. Some were envious of Joseph, seen dressed in fine clothing, often seen riding through the country at the side of the beautiful Sarah on a mission to somewhere.

It didn't end with the HaShomer group. The elders of Zichron

Yaakov, sitting on the small town's committee, tried unsuccessfully to get to the bottom of what the Aaronsohns were up to. Ephraim Aaronsohn, who worked every day in his vineyards, when pressed by the town elders offered no more than they already knew, that they were busy with a national agricultural program which was supported and funded by their overseas donors. He would shake his head as they accused his sons and daughter on conducting surreptitious and dangerous activities. And where were Aaron, Alex and Rivka, anyway? Why was Sarah disappearing so often with Joseph Lishansky in her carriage for long periods? What were they up to? Whatever it was, it must be no good for Zichron Yaakov. This despite the fact that Sarah would come to them with bags of money or gold coin for the village.

They gossiped negatively against the Aaronsohns in general, and Sarah in particular. With the others out of the country, she was the accessible target of their venom. They didn't want to know what she was doing out of fear of being incriminated, but they wanted her to stop as they feared that what she was doing would impact them badly one day. They needed the foreign funds that she occasionally brought them, but were envious of the Aaronsohn's independent access to the donors. The atmosphere in the small town was toxic.

1917

The Spring of 1917 was a tumultuous period. The work at Atlit was frenetic. The British were gearing up for an attack on Gaza. They were in need of as much accurate intelligence as they could obtain about the enemy's troop movements and military emplacements. Their only reliable source was from their new spymaster, Aaron Aaronsohn, and the NILI espionage network run by his younger sister, Sarah.

With the regular arrival of the ship, reports were dispatched from Atlit with increasing detail;

Naaman Belkind reported from the south;

Meeting - Abdel Rahim Pasha, Commander of Turks 20th Army Corp with German staff officers and engineers about construction of trenches and artillery gun emplacements at Gaza. 11 large guns arrived. 8 more being sent down to Gaza. Plans of emplacements attached. Snr German officer named Tiller & all his staff killed in air bombing raid on Gaza.

Moshe Neuman was proving himself to be precise and enthusiastic.

MARCH 20 1917 – Train from Damascus carried one motorcar, 4 canons belonging to the 53rd Division, 2 wagons of benzine, 2 wagons of food, 70 soldiers of the 53rd Division, one complete airplane accompanied by pilot and 2 German mechanics. Plane called Fokker after its inventor. It can attain a very high speed. Armed with a machine gun that can emit 700 bullets a minute. The machine gun can be adjusted to fire in all directions, upward, downward, left and right. It is forbidden to fly the Fokker across enemy lines to prevent any inspection by the enemy if it was brought down. Its purpose is defensive.
MARCH 24, 1917. The 137 Battalion arrived from Lebanon. All the men are weak and hungry. All except one are barefoot.

MARCH 28, 1917. *Toward nightfall 4 Germans came through Afula - General von Lante, Dr Baron von Malten, and 2 officers. They are attached to the military commission sent from Germany at the request of Enver Pasha to inspect the front. Cheered by wine at my home, they told me that the greater part of the army was at Tarsus, Taurus, and as far as Aleppo. Djemal Pasha is leaving Damascus tomorrow for Ma'an and then to Jerusalem. Divisions 3, 16, and 53 are at Beer Sheba. They are bringing up Divisions 4 and 5.*

Sarah sent Reuven to Beirut after reports of submarine sightings. He returned with the following report;

6 subs in Med. 2 large, 4 small. Task of small subs to bring ammunition to large subs. Reuven provided the names of the officers and crew of submarine 63 and a photo of the sub. He included the following important information for British intelligence; Central *ammunition storage for subs in Med is in Constantinople. Local storage for Beirut is at Rayak on Beirut road to Damascus.*

From the north came these reports;

Yarmuk River Bridge in northern Palestine carries main rail line to Damascus. See map.
Bnot Yaakov Bridge north of Sea of Galilee and over River Jordan is on main escape route from Nazareth and Tiberias to Damascus. See map.
Damascus. Officer stealing rations from soldiers. Many desertions.
Nazareth. Ammunition dump in courtyard of Carmelite Convent. See map.
Nazareth to Tiberias road. Poor crop production in fields. Some grain being sown on side road to Sejera.
Haifa. Turkish patrol along coast road but not on beach. Heavy guns facing sea on Mount Carmel hilltop. Navy beware.
From central Palestine came advise for the British air force;

Plane wreck half hour east of Ramle on Jerusalem road. Near wreckage are large and small tents. All empty. This is a decoy target.

247

Shechem. Ammunition dump located in large granary under Mt Gerizim. Should be destroyed by air.

One of Naaman's reports confirmed the information provided earlier by Moshe at Afula;

Rishon le Zion - 53rd division just arrived. Numbers unknown. Camp not yet set up.

He added;

Turkish soldiers just arrived at Nahlat Yehuda (see map). Will provide details later.

To Sarah, immersed in reading and coding the messages, some of the material appeared to be vitally important and urgent while others seems to be trivial. She faithfully worked on every snippet of information, every detail. It was up to the people in Central Intelligence to decide what information should be acted on, and which recorded for reference.

Sarah burned the midnight oil meticulously coding each message. She knew that Aaron would be the first recipient of her reports and that he was fluent in Hebrew and English. Each report, delivered to her by her agents, was written or typed in Hebrew. Sarah spent hours painstakingly rewriting each report in a coded form that she and Aaron had devised. She used English letters to spell out the Hebrew words so that they would appear to be gibberish to any German or Turk not understanding the code. Names of towns were given numbers. Gaza was number 1, Beer Sheba 2, Jerusalem, 3, Afula 4, etc. To the uninitiated, this confusing jumble of letters and numbers would be meaningless. Only Aaron, or someone trained by him, would be able to unlock the coded reports. Sarah knew there was always someone onboard the British ship fluent in Hebrew and English. Once the oilskin packages were delivered to the ship, this agent would glance through her reports, select the most urgent of them, decipher them in English to either Captain Smith or Weldon who would decide if they warranted immediate signaling to naval intelligence in Port Said from the ship. The author of this ingenious code system was Sarah.

When General Murray, pressed by Whitehall, decided to attack Gaza in the middle of April, the Turks and Germans had been allowed sufficient time strengthen their defensive lines and bring a large force into the fortified garrison town of Gaza. Murray was outwitted and outgunned by German General Kress von Kressenstein, the Commander of the combined German and Turkish armies. The Battle of Gaza was an unmitigated disaster for Murray. Some say that Murray lost fourteen thousand men in those two bloody days, but General Sir Archibald Murray put a brave but false face on his report to London.

He cut his casualty figures in half, proudly claiming that *"It was a most successful operation, the fog and waterless nature of the country just saving the enemy from complete disaster."*

His vastly reduced army had retreated, the enemy remained in full control of Gaza, and the days of Sir Archibald Murray as Commander of the British forces in Egypt were numbered.

The joyous Jewish holiday of Passover that celebrates the tale of freedom from slavery and oppression in Egypt was shattered in Palestine with the dreadful news that thousands of Jewish residents of Jaffa and Tel Aviv were being forcibly and suddenly expelled from the towns by the Turks and were being made to march north. Those who had vehicles or carts were fortunate. Those without were forced to walk on foot. Most had been evicted from their homes without time to collect their possessions. In their wake came wholesale looting. Hardly had they left their homes, gangs of local Arabs enter their homes and stores in free and uncontrolled abandon to steal their property. It was a strange fate that, three millennia later after the first exodus, the Jewish people would be losing their liberty at the hands of a new oppressor, here in their ancient land.

The order had been given by Djemal Pasha. The order stated that they could not make their way to Jerusalem. The Jews of Jerusalem took this news as a premonition that a similar fate was being planned for them. The exiles from Jaffa and Tel Aviv were ordered to march north. Many were received in homes, villages and settlements that soon became overcrowded. The less fortunate were ordered to continue marching up into the far north western reaches of Syria beyond Aleppo.

This was eerily familiar to Sarah. She vividly recalled, with startling horror, what she had witnessed there. She knew what happened there. Jews throughout Palestine were experiencing the early stage of a Turkish genocide being practiced against them, following exactly the methods they had executed against the Armenian Christians. Djemal's earlier order to deprive them of their weapons had left them as defenseless as a similar order had done to the poor Armenians. Now came the deportations and the long walk to nowhere for those without food or shelter. The ancient prayer to be delivered from slavery and oppression fell upon them with wicked mockery and pain. Sarah had to let the world know.

The first word that reached Aaron about the plight of his fellow Palestine Jews was received in a graphic report from Sarah just a couple of days after the execution of the sacking of Jaffa and Tel Aviv. Sarah added that a couple of Jews had been hung from a tree in Jaffa.

After he sent the information up the British intelligence ladder and over to the British High Command headquarters, Aaron spent the entire day sending out Sarah's report to everyone of influence that he knew in London and America. This was not something that needed to remain in a covert intelligence file. This was something the world needed to know. The world had to be warned about this heinous crime against his people. He begged his American trustees to bring this outrage to the attention of their friends in government. He got up from his desk and rushed to meet his friend, Major Wyndham Deedes who had friends in high places.

250

The pebbles thrown out by Sarah about the fate of her people began to ripple across the waters of the world.

SARAH IN EGYPT

In Whitehall, people were discussing the future of the Middle East. Decisions were being made by ministers and diplomats, and those who considered themselves experts on the Levant. In London, people, including some in high government circles, were lobbying for the Jewish cause in Palestine. Prominent among them was the Zionist leader, Chaim Weizmann, who had been making inroads with British Cabinet members for the establishment of a national home for the Jewish people in Palestine. Aaron was determined that government ministers and decision makers should hear his Palestinian perspective. After all, nobody knew the land as thoroughly and as scientifically as he. If powerful people in London were deciding the fate of his land, he had to be there to influence their decision. Aaron decided that it was the time to invite Sarah to Egypt.

As she prepared to leave, Sarah asked her team to bring her as much updated material as they could, concentrating on troop movements and Turkish military construction projects in the south. She gathered her team just days before the next naval rendezvous. They met at Atlit in the large entrance room.

"I will be sailing to meet with Aaron on the next ship," she told them. "I will report back to you what is happening at British headquarters. Aaron is not only in contact with their intelligence officers. He is also speaking to important people in London. I will be back as quickly as possible and will tell you everything you need to know. In the meantime, keep things going. I love you all."

Sarah's arrival in Port Said coincided with the second British attack on Gaza. As she walked down the gangway, Aaron was at the dockside to greet her. He was accompanied by Lova.

Aaron was furious to see Joseph Lishansky follow her down the gangway. He tried to keep his anger in check. He kissed Sarah with a stony silence and they headed to a waiting cab.

It was only when they got into the privacy of a hotel room that Aaron let his feelings vent.

"Are you totally insane?" he yelled at Joseph. "Have you no sense of responsibility? Did you learn nothing from your last jaunt to Egypt, and what I told you?"

Joseph made to offer an explanation. Aaron was having none of it. "How dare you again countermand Sarah and leave our network without a leader? In fact, are you a leader, at all?"

Sarah rallied to sooth the situation. "Aaron. Everything is fine. The boys know what to do until I get back. They are disciplined and no ship is calling until we go home."

"He should never have left. Why did you bring him?" Aaron questioned her in an angry voice.

"There will be things you want to tell us that are important for him to hear as well. He is here now so let's get on with things."

Aaron wanted to tell her that there would be nothing he wanted to say to Sarah that he wanted to share with an undisciplined Lishansky. His silence prompted Sarah to add, "I couldn't have done what I did without Joseph's help. I had considered travelling alone dressed as a man but Joseph talked me out of it. There was no way I could have travelled round the country unaccompanied." Sarah saw Aaron raise an eyebrow at that statement. She smiled and gave him a nudge in his ribs. Aaron didn't know if she had been joking.

"Joseph has also recruited some good people to our network. He's a tireless worker. He needs to know everything relevant to our network."

Aaron decided to drop the matter until he had Sarah to himself.

When they were alone, Aaron was still angry. "Lishansky takes too many wrong decisions, too many personal initiatives that risk our operation. He cajoled Avshalom to trek down to Egypt. You surely remember that. Now this. He's a loose cannon."

Sarah disagreed. "He wasn't the one who cajoled Avsha. Avsha couldn't be dissuaded. If Joseph hadn't gone with him, we would never have learned what happened to him."

Aaron had to admit that Sarah had a point.

"He was the one who dealt with the Turks when Avsha was locked up in Beer Sheba. Let's remember that, Aaron."

The next day Aaron had calmed down somewhat, though he still treated Joseph coldly. They took the train from Port Said to Cairo. During their journey the murmured conversation concentrated on how they were operating the network. Aaron plied them with questions and Sarah and Joseph answered in detail. Aaron gazed at his sister as she answered. She had lost weight. She looked exhausted. He could see signs of stress on her face as she spoke about the pressure that the Jewish organizations and the village committee were putting her under.

"They are more of a nuisance than the Turks right now. They are interfering with our operation more than the Turks to be honest. The latest situation with the expulsions will keep them off our backs for a while," said Sarah.

Aaron nodded. "I have made an appeal for foreign funds. Hopefully that will keep them quiet when I can get it to you," he replied.

"That will help," said Sarah. "Some of the refugees were starting to appear in Zichron as I left. It would love to accommodate them at home. We have the space. It would be company for papa, but I can't have them prying into our affairs. It would be too risky for all of us."

Aaron agreed with Sarah. "Quite right. We don't need you worrying about who is poking into all the nooks and crannies of our home and discovering our secrets, especially when you are away..."

"...which is most of the time," Sarah added.

"How is papa?" Aaron enquired, suddenly aware he hadn't seen him for far too long.

"He is fine. He's a tough old bird. He still works daily in his vineyards. He has his friends in the village. Unfortunately, the work keeps me away a lot, but I try to keep him company during the holidays and festivals, as much as I can. I am working over most weekends as well."

They talked intensely about all aspects of life in Palestine. Aaron wanted a full assessment on conditions there. He told them how difficult it was for him to persuade senior members of the General Staff to use new initiatives in conquering Palestine. "I pressed them to invade from the sea when the Turks had far fewer troops and equipment in Palestine. It would have been so easy for them to breach Palestine south of Caesarea and split the country in two. They could have created a beachhead with their initial naval invasion and brought in reinforcements. They missed an opportunity. I think they are still in such shock after their defeat in Gallipoli that they don't want to risk another such invasion again, so they are back fighting the same stale battle tactics of conventional frontal warfare as they are doing so badly in

Europe. They are doing it again in Gaza. Murray is using the same tired tactics of throwing troops against strong defenses. I expect him to be sent home if he loses this battle and then we will have to wait for his replacement That's what I mean by the British lacking any original thinking. They are a stubborn lot. Too set in their ways. It's so frustrating. That's why it is taking so long for them to do what they should have done a year ago. They could have cut through the Turks like a knife through butter. When they eventually get their act together, they will find the enemy far stronger."

"They have to win. Our future depends on it," Joseph said.

"With the right military leader they can still win decisively," Aaron replied, "the problem is their policy and decision making is done in London, not in Cairo. This lot in Cairo cannot see beyond what they are ordered to do by Whitehall. No initiative. They simply carry out orders. That's why I have been developing contacts with people here who have direct contact with the right people in London. We have to bring our case to them. That's why, Sarah, it was so important to have you provide me with the news of what happened to our people in Tel Aviv and Jaffa. It was so critical for us. As they get to read your reports not just in Cairo, but in London and America, this is going to open doors for us."

Aaron had booked rooms for them at the Continental Hotel. Lova had to share his room due to the surprise arrival of Joseph. As they received their keys at the reception desk and the porter placed their luggage on a trolley, Aaron said, "Sarah, get some rest, then put on a nice dress. I'm taking you to dinner tonight."

He turned to Lova and Joseph. "Gentlemen, I assume you don't object to me spending this evening in the company of my sister."

They did. They much preferred to be joining them in being wined and dined at a nice restaurant, but they acceded with good grace. "

Good. Then I'll knock on your door at eight o'clock, Sarah."

256

Aaron took Sarah to a casual diner called Gutti's. "I come here for some of my informal meetings with colleagues, or for coffee alone when I need to relax or gather my thoughts," Aaron explained to her as they entered the restaurant.

A waiter greeted them and escorted them to a small table by the window. Aaron nodded to a number of diners as they followed the waiter through the restaurant to their table. When they were seated, Aaron pointed out, in a whispered voice, some of the people who were dining there. Sarah looked around the room. She noticed that most were men, very few ladies, and the men interrupted their private conversations to gaze at her. When she mentioned this to Aaron he took a quick glance and smiled. "A lot of these men have been posted here to serve in either the General Staff departments or the civil administration. You'll find that these sort of places look like a man's club. There are a few people here I have to work with. These people are looking at you because they have realized who you are. Being with me means you are either my wife, my mistress, or my sister and, as I don't have a wife or mistress, they know who you are because they've read your reports."

They ordered and, while waiting for the first course to arrive, Aaron gave Sarah some surprising news.

"Sarah. I have been thinking deeply about moving to London. It's clear to me, as I mentioned on the train, that London is where decisions and policy is being made about Palestine. The British have to win this war and take charge of it, to be a protectorate if you will, until we are ready to declare our self-determination on the land. This lot here can help rid us of the enemy, but none of them can make the decision to open a new front or decide to replace the Turks with us. That decision lies in London and I have to be there.

Declarations in our favor by British Christians are fine but I need to be there to represent those of us who are laboring and fighting in Palestine.

257

That is one of the reasons I wanted to meet with you. To tell you this personally."

Sarah was intrigued until Aaron added, "Sarah. If I go to London, I want you to stay here and replace me and coordinate between our NILI group and the British command here in Egypt. From London, I can be in contact with you here daily, and you can keep the boys fully informed about developments for our future land." He touched her hand. "And I am concerned for your safety. You have done a brilliant job. I want you to be safe yet still doing the important work we need to do. Let me arrange a place for you here."

"No, Aaron," Sarah answered without hesitation. "My place is there. The boys need me. Without me, they will lose their motivation. Who could replace me over there? You said yesterday that Joseph is not a leader. He is dedicated. He does some amazing things. He is a tireless worker, but the boys will not rally round him like they do for me. I'm not boasting, Aaron. This is the simple truth."

Aaron gazed into Sarah's tired eyes. He wanted her so much to be out of danger, but he knew her assessment was correct. Without Sarah, the structure would crumple and collapse. His mind raced. He feared for her but could think of no other alternative. His thoughts were interrupted by a polite cough. He turned and saw Captain Edmonds standing slightly behind him.

"I'm sorry to intrude into your dinner, Mr. Aaronsohn, but is this your sister, Sarah?"

"It is indeed, captain."

Edmonds shook Sarah's hand.

"I just wanted you to know, Miss Aaronsohn, that we really appreciate and value all that you are doing for us over there."

"Thank you, captain, but please call me Sarah. Most of the credit though should go to my brother," replied Sarah modestly.

Edmonds laughed. "You don't know how right you are, Sarah. Aaron seems to be running GHQ. Congratulations Aaronsohn, on your amendments to our intelligence handbook. They made a terrific impression on everyone at HQ."

Aaronsohn smiled contentedly at the compliment as Edmonds again took Sarah's hand.

"However, all of us who are in the loop are grateful to you, Sarah. I want you to know that should you decide to remain in Cairo I can assure you that we will be pleased to accommodate you here."

"Thank you, captain, but that won't be necessary. My work is over there and I look forward to returning and help my team bring you the information you so badly need to win this war."

Edmonds smiled at the courage of this attractive and exceptionally brave young woman.

"Just know that you are always welcome here whenever you feel the need. It's my honor to meet you and hope we will meet again while you are here. Now please, enjoy your dinner."

Edmonds' intervention had attracted the attention of other diners who were now smiling and nodding at Aaron and Sarah in appreciation of their service.

"Well, that was a surprise," smiled Aaron. "Edmonds is not the sort to gush compliments. You see the impression you make on people, Sarah."

As they gazed around the room people smiled back at them.

Aaron leaned over to Sarah. "It seems you have been initiated into the men's club."

Aaron was busy, though he kept most evenings free for Sarah. During the day, Sarah accompanied Joseph and Lova in sightseeing and shopping trips, or hanging out at open air cafes and observe the Cairo street life.

It was more accurate to say that Joseph and Lova accompanied her. The two men didn't care where they went as long as they were close to Sarah. She was aware of a rivalry developing between them as they vied for her attention. It made her smile. Lova had begun delivering flowers to her room every morning. She was just down the corridor from their room. It intrigued her how Lova managed to order flowers without Joseph knowing about it. The flowers always came with a simple note saying, *'Good morning, sweet Sarah! From Lova,'* or, *'Looking forward to spending time with you today. Lova.'*

For a bit of added fun, she began to interact with them in a coquettish way. She was amused to find that this only made their rivalry even more competitive. Each one fought for who would pay her bill whenever they sat for coffee and cake, or for lunch. Sarah tried to keep their lunch breaks to places that were not too lavish or expensive. She knew they were strapped for funds during this trip. She tested herself as to which of them attracted her most. They had their different charms, but Lova had this animal magnetism. He showed it in his body language, in the way he walked, even in the way he looked at her. In her private curiosity she was drawn to Lova's manliness over Joseph's more traditional manners. It was Lova's raw masculinity that drew her to him over Joseph's temperament.

Sarah enjoyed accompanying Aaron of an evening. They enjoyed a number of fine meals in select restaurants. She could hold her own in the sophisticated circles that Aaron moved during their evenings in Cairo. The elite society life was a far cry from the village life and Bedouin encampments that Lova and Joseph enjoyed at home. They lacked the social graces, and Aaron set up dinner dates and reservations without them. Sarah, however, could glide gracefully between the differing worlds and never be out of place.

When out with Aaron she always attracted the gaze of the other diners. In the presence of the military, intelligence and diplomatic class she had gained a certain celebrity. Their meals and private conversations were frequently interrupted by people who wanted to be introduced to her. It gave them an opportunity to shake her hand and express their gratitude for what she was doing in Palestine. It made her feel that her work did have some resonance, even if she couldn't see any effect for the risks they were taking.

"They keep thanking me," she said to Aaron as they sat in a swanky restaurant one evening, "but when are we going to see them act decisively? It seems to me they are taking our intelligence reports and not using it at all."

"It goes into their planning logs, but you are right, Sarah. Their inaction is tied to their inability to display any initiative. You have to understand, Sarah, that initiative before orders can get you demoted. They are afraid of going out on a limb and, heaven forbid, initiate an unsuccessful mission. They are hampered by lack of leadership and direction. But it is coming. This second defeat at Gaza is going to shake things up. You wait and see."

"How long must we wait? That's the question," asked Sarah, impatiently.

"I want you to stay here, Sarah."

"Aaron, my place is back at home taking care of our team. I'm ready to go back."

"Are you sure you won't stay?" Aaron was still concerned for his sister's safety. "It's important you replace me here?"

"No. Thank you, Aaron. I want to go back. If I stayed here nobody would remain to keep an eye on papa, and the team will fall apart under Joseph's leadership. You know that's true. Why don't you get Alex to come here from America? He'd be the right person to step into your shoes."

Aaron smiled. Sarah had read his thoughts.

"I'm thinking of inviting Alex if you won't sit at my desk here. I could have gotten you a clearance to remain here. Even Edmonds told you he'd welcome you here."

"So bring Alex over. Get a clearance for him, and get us on the next boat to Atlit."

"Maybe I'll do that. It will take some time to set things up. In the meantime, keep sending me letters in the dispatches letting me know how you are."

"I will."

The group met in the lobby of the Continental Hotel. Aaron had the date for the next sailing. Lishansky was looking nervous and depressed.

"The next ship sails on May 13," Aaron informed them.

"I'm not going. I am staying here." Joseph's statement shocked them. They all looked aghast.

"What are you saying?" Aaron demanded to know.

"I'm staying here, in Egypt. You can find me a position here."

"What has gotten into you?" Aaron was trying to control his anger.

"I'm not appreciated. I should be treated like a leader not like a schoolboy."

"Then act like a leader," Aaron fumed. "Oh, this is impossible. I'm off to the bar." As he went to the find the bar, he turned to Joseph. "If you want to be treated like a leader, then damn well act like one."

Lova did not help by blurting out, "Nobody is more important to Joseph Lishansky than Joseph Lishansky." He got up and followed Aaron to the hotel bar.

It was left to Sarah to deal with Joseph's tantrum.

"Joseph, look at me. I could have stayed here, but I didn't. I told Aaron I have to go back. The team needs me. The team needs us." Joseph looked up from the floor as Sarah said, "I have to go back, but I can't do what I need to do without you. I need you. The team needs you. God help us, the British need you. They need you there with me. Will you do it? For me?"

Sarah carried a sympathetic expression on her face. She knew the cause of his sulking. It was a combination of Aaron's anger and misplaced disappointment in him and a fear of what awaited them as the flames of war erupted back home. He returned his gaze to the floor.

"I'm going to bed, Joseph. Think about what I said. Good night, Joseph."

She got up and left the lounge. She detoured to the bar to kiss her brother goodnight, whispering in his ear, "Joseph will be fine in the morning."

She glanced at Lova whose face was, as usual, fixated on her. "Don't upset him tonight, Lova. Let him rest without disturbing his emotions. Can you do that for me?"

Lova nodded like a friendly puppy. Sarah smiled and made for her bedroom.

By breakfast the next morning Joseph had agreed to sail with Sarah. Aaron and Lova rewarded his response with hearty congratulations and back-slapping. Later that morning they were told that the departure of the ship had been delayed by three days due to bad weather along the coast.

Prior to departure, Aaron pulled them together for a final briefing.

"Sarah raised a question about Avshalom. How do we explain his disappearance?"

Sarah spoke up. "When we get back everyone will be asking us about Avshalom." Feeling a lump in her throat and glancing at Joseph, she continued, "They are all going to ask about him. I don't like it but I have to agree with Aaron. We have no choice for now but to continue to cover it up for everybody's safety. They think he is here. What do we tell them?"

Aaron replied without hesitation. "Tell them that you didn't meet with him because he has been transferred to England to train to be a pilot in their air force. Tell them that he wants to be the first Palestinian Jew in the skies over our land."

The story was as flimsy as a British spotter plane, but Sarah loved the image of her Avsha flying in the skies above her beloved land.

In Cairo and London, Sarah's information about the plight of the exiled Jews from Jaffa and Tel Aviv had created a stir. Mark Sykes, the British diplomat, had wired Sir Ronald Graham, the Assistant Under-Secretary of State at the Foreign Office on April 29 that, '*Aaron Aaronsohn asks me inform you that Tel Aviv has been sacked. 10,000 Palestine Jews are now without home or food. The whole of the Jewish communities in Palestine is threatened with destruction. Djemal Pasha's publicly stated Armenian policy will now be applied to Jews.*'

On May 8, the Assistant War Secretary and Aaron's friend, William Ormsby Gore, advised Sykes, '*I think we ought to use the pogroms in Palestine as propaganda. Any spicy tales of atrocity would be eagerly welcomed, and Aaronsohn could send us some lurid stores for the Jewish papers.*'

Aaron understood the value of this crudely worded communique. Large funding would be needed for the newly destitute Jews and for the communities that were receiving them. Stories of suffering would open the purse strings of the wealthy in Britain and America. The plight of the unfortunate Palestine Jews would also be added proof of the need for the rapid development of the land and the new settlements to house the refugees and sympathy from the British would soon come to their rescue. Aaron asked Sarah to continue to furnish him with detail and facts that would light a flame in support of Jewish claims to the land based on the inadmissibility of the Turks to retain control of the land due to their hostility and humanitarian crimes and inevitable defeat.

SARAH'S RETURN

On May 16, Sarah and Joseph boarded the *Managam*, but not until Sarah and Aaron had exchanged a tearful farewell. Sarah may have hidden her fears, but Aaron was fully conscious that he may not see his sister again if things went terribly wrong.

By noon the next day, Sarah could see Zichron Yaakov perched on top of the Carmel but, by the time they reached the Atlit bay, the sea was too rough for a landing. Frustratingly, the captain told them they must return to Egypt. Sarah stared at the receding Atlit and felt a yearning for her young men and women who must be watching as her ship disappeared from view over the horizon.

In Egypt, they had to wait another two weeks for permission to sail. Sarah's frustration and boredom unsettled her.

Sarah returned to the hotel after spending an evening with Aaron. She found Lova sitting in the lobby nursing a drink.

"Where's Joseph?" she asked.

"He went to spend the evening with Raphael."

"Didn't you go with him?"

"No. I told him I wanted to relax in the hotel. I got bored and came down for a drink. Now you are here."

"Well, I'm going up to my room. That's enough for one day."

"I'll come with you."

Sarah thought Lova meant that he was heading to his room. When the elevator doors closed, Lova reached over and, pressing her to the wall, kissed her, first tenderly, then passionately. His masculinity, his animal magnetism that had wandered in and out of Sarah's consciousness during their days in Egypt, lit a flame within her. She exploded with a feeling that had been pent up within her for so long. She threw her arms around his neck and responded to his kiss. They groaned as they forced themselves on each other, breaking apart only when the elevator stopped and the doors opened. Hand in hand, no word spoken, they headed down the corridor to Sarah's room. She inserted the key. The door opened. She turned to embrace Lova who slammed the door shut with the heel of his shoe. They grappled their way to her bed clutching at each other's clothes, eagerly stripping them off to explore what lay waiting impatiently underneath. Before they were completely naked, they looked at each other. Sarah hesitated. He kissed her neck until she squirmed with pleasure. He ventured down to her breasts which he cupped in his hand. He kissed them tenderly. She groaned as he kissed her neck. His hand glided down her soft stomach toward her thighs. She groaned with her conflicted soul. She wanted him so much. She didn't want to lose him as she had lost Avsha. She was ripe but time was not. She was ready, but it had to wait. He noticed her hesitancy. He glared at her with passion in his eyes.

"No, Lova."

"Why?"

"Not now. Not yet." Her words echoed a memory of words said to Avsha so long ago.

"When?"
"One day. When our work has finished. When the war is over."

267

"I will come to you." Lova was looking at her beautiful face with a fiery intensity. "I will come to you and be with you. For eternity."

Sarah smiled at Lova. No man had been as loyal since Avsha. But Avsha was dead. Gone from her forever. Now she was alone, had to be alone, until her job was done. Then, maybe then, she could contemplate a life of love with Lova as part of her destiny. She stared into the face of the man who desired her. *Yes. It could be you, Lova,* she thought to herself.

They lay together, wet from the cauldron of spent emotion. They looked at each other, wordlessly questioning each other with their eyes. They kissed, and kissed again. Eventually, Lova rose. He grabbed his clothes and headed for the bathroom. He emerged dressed. He came over to the bed and kissed Sarah tenderly. They spent a moment staring at each other. Then Lova smiled, kissed Sarah one last time, say "Goodnight, sweet Sarah. I will come to you when all this is over."

He quietly opened the door, examined the corridor and, finding it empty, headed to his room.

Sarah was surprised, even shocked, at herself. She lay on her pillow staring up at the ceiling. *What just happened? As I still searching for Avsha? Am I reaching out to Lova to love me? Not now. When this awful time has ended, then I may find time to surrender myself to him. I cannot allow myself to become distracted. First my people. Then myself.*

She closed her eyes thinking of what just happened, what she had experienced, until exhaustion seduced her into the depths of a fitful sleep.

THE MISSION

They sailed with a full complement. Sarah and Joseph were accompanied by both Lova and Leib. Sarah and Lova kept a covert silence on their intimate hotel rendezvous, but Joseph was sensitive to the flirting smiles between the two of them.

Lieutenant Kane was the new captain of the Managam. The doughty Captain Lewen Weldon was on board to supervise their rendezvous, make certain they got ashore safely at Atlit, collect the material waiting for him from the NILI agents, and to telegraph any urgent intelligence straight to intelligence HQ in Egypt. Aaron was forced to remain in Egypt.

Kane, new to the area, needed the help of Weldon, Sarah, Leib, and Lova to pinpoint the approach to Atlit by positioning the naval craft to the east of the Crusader fort. They emitted their smoke signal and waited for a response through Weldon's binoculars. They jumped excitedly when he reported seeing a white sheet unfurl from an upstairs window. The Managam turned seaward to spend the hours until dark over the horizon.

On this trip, the Managam deployed two wooden boats. In the first, rowed by Abdullah's two sons, were Joseph and Leib. They were the advance party to make sure the coast was clear of the enemy and the NILI agents were there to greet them. Sarah sat in the second boat. Lova held her hand. They were rowed to their holding position by two British sailors. They waited silently off shore for the signal to approach. In Sarah's craft were several weighty oilskin bags containing gold coins for the relief of the refugees. Another bag held money for the maintenance of the research projects from their American trustees, and the British budget for the expenses of NILI's operations for which Captain Smith expected a full and detailed accounting from Sarah. There was also a satchel full of instructions from British intelligence.

269

A double flash of a torch signaled Sarah's boat to come ashore. Joseph and Lova were waiting for her in the low tide. Lova and Joseph helped Sarah step out of her boat and wade ashore through the shallow water. Reuven, Yehuda, and Lova's brother, Mendel, were waiting for them on the beach. Lova embraced his brother and shook hands with the others before they returned to the boats to hectically carry the heavy bags to the beach. Lova and Leib both hugged Sarah before wading back to the row boats. Lova's embrace was prolonged. They kissed. Lova whispered, "Wait for me," before he broke away from her and ran through the shallow waves to his waiting boat. Sarah watched as the two small boats disappeared into the dark.

The bags were heavy, but Sarah did her part in carrying one of the bags through the sand to the wadi. They rested for a while before the powerful Yehuda and Reuven led the way with their weighty satchels over their shoulders. By the time they reached the road Sarah was panting. She felt the sweat on her face and body. One after the other they raced across the road to the palm-tree lined avenue that led them to the shelter of their station. Smelling their scent, Demon gave a welcoming bark.

It was an emotional and traumatic reunion. Sarah and Joseph had been missing for much longer than expected. This had caused concerns and doubts in many of the NILI team and their agents. Reuven told Sarah that the team had become demoralized by their prolonged absence. Some thought they intended to stay in Egypt until after the war. After all, hadn't Aaron, Alex and Rivka fled? He told her that the villagers of Zichron had noticed that, yet again, Sarah had gone missing. They were speculating where she could be, and what she was doing. It was the gossip of the town, even as Zichron Yaakov was busy absorbing a thousand refugees from Jaffa and Tel Aviv. Reuven told her of the desperate families that were being accommodated in the homes, barns and stables, of the villagers. Some were even being temporarily sheltered in the cellars of the winery. Reuven told her that some were complaining that, while this was going on, the wealthy

Aaronsohn spread was empty, with only the father living in their three house compound. According to Reuven, Ephraim had been closed lipped when interrogated by the village elders to explain why his daughter had disappeared again.

"The rumors are so widespread, they must have reached the Turks," Reuven warned. "Even this money will not satisfy them," he added, pointing to the bags. "They are sure we are spying for the British. How else could we receive gold coin?"

Sarah realized that even the good deed of smuggling much needed money to the communities only added to the pressure, and the risk, of their operation.

"Some of our helpers thought," Reuven continued, "that it would be better if you and Joseph left the country immediately. Don't misunderstand me. We here are loyal to you, but your long disappearance has caused tongues to wag, especially by people who are envious and jealous."

This was not what she expected on her return. "Sarah. You don't know who are your enemies and who are your friends any more in the town."

To make matters worse, Avshalom's name came up. Everyone wanted to know how he was. Joseph was quick to provide the practiced answer, that they hadn't met him because he had gone to England to learn to fly planes.

"You know how Avshalom was," Joseph said. "He wants to be the first Palestinian to fly over our land and drop bombs on our enemy." To Joseph, it sounded convincing. It was received with unease and a few raised eyebrows.

Sarah had to take command of the situation. She changed the subject and got back to NILI matters. "Joseph and Mendel. I want you two to go and negotiate with Meir Dizengoff and the Refugee Committee. I'll tell you how much we have for him. He's bound to know it came through Aaron and the British but you have to insist that he keeps his mouth shut about it. I will deal with the Zichron Committee later."

The Avshalom storm was not over. The main problem was when Naaman arrived to greet them and discover what had become of his closest friend. He listened to their explanation with a jaundiced ear.

"He didn't write anything all the time he was in Cairo? Avshalom, the writer? Avshalom, the poet? Avshalom, the dreamer, who always poured out his soul and his thoughts onto the page? Yet, nothing? Not even a letter to you, Sarah? Not even to me, his best friend?" he asked unbelievingly, pointing to himself. "Not to his family?"

"I want you to believe this," said Sarah quietly. She felt guilty, soiled by having to lie to someone who loved him as much as she did.

"You want me to believe it, but I don't. I don't believe he was there at all." Naaman was angry now. He glared at Joseph. "I think Joseph knows everything. Joseph goes down to Egypt with Avshalom, and comes back on your arm. Something is not right. Something isn't right," he repeated.

"Let it rest, Naaman. Let it rest."

Sarah had little else to offer him.

"Why don't you tell them the truth?" Ephraim said after yet another visit to their home from the busybody town committee who wanted to know what Sarah was up to.

Sarah was sitting next to her father as he sat in his armchair.

"I'm sorry, papa. I wish I could, but it would endanger us all. Do they pester you so much?"

"Don't concern yourself, my dear. It takes more than these villagers to break me."

Ephraim Aaronsohn had always been a man of strong convictions and few words. She kissed his forehead sympathetically. She regretted how circumstances had left her father so lonely and so isolated in a village he had helped create yet was putting herself and her father under so much pressure. Sarah had just undergone another unpleasant meeting with the two council heads.

Sarah met with the two Alberts. Albert Alter was Reuven's uncle. He sat on Zichron's town council under Albert Lederman who was known as 'the Mukhtar' by the villagers. They used the Arabic name, *Mukhtar,* meaning tribal chief, to describe Lederman. It was patently well deserved in Lederman's case. Lederman was a born politician. By force of his wily personality, he had maneuvered himself into being voted as chairman of the village committee. That was many years ago and, like a lot of canny politicians, he never relinquished that position. As Zichron Yaakov grew, he became the head of the town council. He played the card of power well. He ingratiated himself as a member of his people's national Central Council by offering the loyalty of his town to their national policies and policies and planning.

The villagers treated him with the level of respect and deference that he felt he deserved, with the notable exception of the Aaronsohns who plowed an independent path. Unlike most of the villagers, they never came to the council begging for help or assistance. On the contrary, they were the only family that came to the cash-strapped council with occasional gifts of money from their American sources. The Aaronsohns, with the exception of Ephraim, worked away from Zichron on their agricultural projects funded by their wealthy donors from abroad. Many rich and famous foreign visitors came to Zichron Yaakov. Some of them passed through the town on their tourist journeys between their ship in Haifa or Jaffa to visit Jerusalem and the other holy places, or to examine the burgeoning results of the Zionist enterprise. Those that stayed overnight usually staying in the one major hostelry in the town, the Graf Hotel. And some of the special dignitaries came to the small town specifically to visit the Aaronson's home to meet with Aaron or, in his absence, with Sarah.

Lederman had cajoled Aaron into having the council involved in the management of his project, a proposal that Aaron had forcefully rejected. That was when the mukhtar began complaining about the Aaronsohns' lack of transparency and arrogance. That was how the schism began between the council and the Aaronsohns.

Now the two Alberts met with Sarah. They wanted to know what all the disappearances were about. Sarah told them it was none of their business. They told her that the village found her comings and goings, accompanied by Joseph Lishansky, scandalous. Lederman reminded her that she was a married woman. Sarah told him she was insulted by his implications, that there was no dalliance with Joseph who worked for her project in a senior position due to the absence of her brother, and that their trips were strictly business. Alter accepted her answer with a slight nod. Lederman simply glared at her.

"We know you are involved in activities which jeopardize not only the people of our village but the whole of our national program. It has to stop."

"My work is for the benefit of our people," Sarah responded. "Everything we have done is for our people.'

"Who gave you the right to act in an independent manner that risk lives, that endangers our lives? It has to stop!" he repeated.

"If it stopped I would not be able to get you the money that has helped our people here in Zichron and in the other settlements. Yes, I have been away from Zichron. Yes, I have returned with money to help the refugees. I have returned with money for our people here in Zichron. You should be grateful for what we are doing and support us. Instead, you are mean-spirited and envious. It is clouding your judgment, Mr. Lederman."

"Your adventurism is clouding your judgment, Mrs. Abraham. No matter how we feel about the Turks, they are the authority here and, for our safety, we have to remain loyal to them."

Sarah laughed. "Did this loyalty save our people in Jaffa and Tel Aviv? Will you come with me to ask them, those that are sheltering in fear in the cellars of our winery, or the homeless families who are living in our barns? Shall we ask then what they think of the price of loyalty?"

"At least they have their heads!" erupted Lederman.

Sarah looked him and shook her head. "And you pretend to be the example of a proud Jew. Shame on you, Albert."

"Enough!" Albert Lederman was fuming. Nobody had ever spoken to him with such defiance. "You will close your business both here and at Atlit!"

"And if I don't?"

"If you don't, we will come to Atlit and close it for you."

Sarah laughed. "Really? Have you forgotten that the research station is an American project, paid for by many of the influence people you have seen coming to visit us in this town. The same people who have donated the money I have brought for our people here in Zichron. Is that what you want to do?"

Lederman realized she had a point. "Very well, I will go back to the council and tell them you are not ready to cooperate."

"No," said Sarah restoring calm. "You don't have to do that. You can give them the money I brought for them and tell them that I will continue to operate our activities from our Atlit station and not here in Zichron."

Albert Alter spoke up for the first and only time. "That sounds reasonable, doesn't it, Albert," he said to Lederman who huffed and mumbled, "We will discuss it and will let you have our decision. Good day, Mrs. Abraham."

The last thing that Sarah needed was the burden of committees breathing down her neck. She was fully engaged in answering British demands for specific intelligence. She reckoned her appeasement to the local committee to confine her work to Atlit would hold them at bay and allow her to continue her covert operation.

During her Saturday home visits, one or two of her childhood girlfriends, now, like her, vivacious young women, would come to chat with her. They, at least, made no demands on her. They were gossipy young women but discreetly knew their boundaries and did not probe her too much about her secret life, despite their obvious curiosity. They, at least, were not judgmental. They had always admired her free spirit and independence, and enjoyed the rare moments they shared in her company. They did, however, inform Sarah that certain women of the village were stirring up scandals about her. They whispered four names - crazy Pearl, the bossy Tzipora, nasty little Adele, and the ring leader, Gita. These were Sarah's local troublemakers. Added to the town council, Sarah became acquainted with the individuals that were causing her problems within her community. Her

276

family's isolation and covert activities were creating an atmosphere of suspicion and jealousy.

Joseph, back in familiar territory, quickly reasserted his authority over the network, liaising with the agents about British requirements, and bringing their new findings back to Sarah for coding. Sarah appreciated his help in relieving her of this important work. It freed her to concentrate on the documentation and preparation of the accumulating reports and maps prior to their transfer to the next ship.

She always made herself available to staff members who wanted a moment with Sarah to discuss their private needs and problems. It was important for them to know that Sarah's door was always open to them. Without asking for it, she regained their confidence and trust. Whenever any of them came to her she would quietly tell them, "I want you to know that I am here for you. I am not going anywhere."

With each arrival of the ship came ever increasing and specific demands for information. Sarah's reports were making their way up the chain of command at General Headquarters and into the hands of those responsible for the British war planning in Cairo.

At the beginning of July, Sarah received an urgent request for the following information;

'Send details of Turkish 125 mm cannons, Turkish ammunition dumps, food, fodder, storage, train movements. What is the volume of military traffic? Roads, where are they being built or projected for construction, routes? Train extension lines? Bridges? Accuracy of British aerial bombing. Changes in German-Turkish personnel. Do Turks have flame throwers or poison gas? What do Turks know or believe about British battle plans? Are they planning any form of deception tactics?'

Sarah replied with details of Turkish army movements to bolster the defenses of Gaza. She reported that the Turkish army had drained down the number of troops from the garrison at Beer Sheba and sent them to Gaza, though they were digging defensive lines of trenches to the south, north and east of Beer Sheba, and that they were placing explosives around the existing water wells. They were also preparing artillery gun emplacements to defend the first two lines of infantry trenches.

The incomparable Moshe Neumann was transferred from Afula to Ramle hospital at the start of July. Sarah scrambled to find someone to replace him as her operator in Afula, as the troop movement through this town was of vital important to British intelligence. Moshe, in his new location, began to send her new and accurate news from Ramle which included information about a German airfield which he had visited in his capacity as a doctor. He also located a Turkish radio station, ammunition dumps, the hospital, and their military HQ, which he accurately marked on a hand-drawn map.

Within a week of the delivery of more money for the refugees, Sarah received a visit from a representative of the Central Committee to her home. She was surprised by the news he brought, but it came with a sting in the tail. "Mrs. Abraham. The committee has sent me to thank you for facilitating the payment of funds for the refugees. I have been asked to tell you that the committee has decided to cooperate with NILI, but on one condition."

"What is that condition?"

"That Lishansky leaves your organization, or continues in your employment, but out of Palestine. If he is to continue his spying business let him do it there with your brother in Egypt, but not here."

He must have spotted her involuntary reaction.

278

"Yes, Mrs. Abraham. We are not without our contacts in Cairo. We know your brother is there. How else could the transfer of the money have been made?"

Sarah was suspicious of his proposal. She needed to think this through. On the one hand, this would relieve her of the stress of having the committee on her back. But would it?

"Thank you, but you appreciate that I have to consult with my brother. I'll get back to you as soon as he reaches his decision."

"Please do, Mrs. Abraham."

Alone in Aaron's office, Sarah played with a paper knife as she mulled over the proposal and what was really behind it. It was obvious to her that people from the HaShomer group had inveigled themselves in to the central committee and were targeting Joseph Lishansky who they hated. Sarah reckoned that, once they succeeded in removing Joseph, they would replace him with one of their own, likely a lackey from the HaShomer group loyal to hierarchy of the Central Committee and not to the Aaronsohns. It was a power play, and not such a subtle one at that. Once they had inserted their person into NILI, its days would be numbered. They could degrade it or destroy it, because they had no intention of improving or enlarging it. That would go against their policy of appeasing the Turks.

That was it, thought Sarah. *They want to turn NILI into a shell to gain access and influence to the money source in America. If I accept their terms they could claim that they had been allowed into the echelon by me. It's a pure power play to divide and rule. They think they can hoodwink me,* she thought, *because I'm a woman.*

Sarah prepared a summary of her meeting with the central Relief Committee representative for Aaron. She wrote that she had decided to reject their proposal, advising him that if they were to make any direct approach to him he should support her decision. She was sure that Aaron would back her in not allowing them to insert any of their proxies into NILI without her approval.

Rumors were still spreading about her. Her girlfriends confided to her that the village gossips were saying that Sarah and Joseph were having an affair. The gossips were sniping at Sarah for riding out of her courtyard in her stylish dresses, the ones she had copied from a French fashion magazine, accompanied by a smartly dressed Lishansky in suit and tie, and disappearing for weeks. The slander mongers had a field day concocting all sorts of fictions about Sarah flaunting her affairs in public.

Sarah's persistence in leaping to Lishansky's defense whenever the town council wanted to throw Joseph to the dogs only added to the flame. In truth, Sarah knew she couldn't run NILI without having Joseph take up the brunt of the travel and coordination with her staff spread around Palestine and Syria.

Joseph did have an attraction to Sarah. That was clear, but he also had a wife and child. He had been irked by Lova's behavior in Egypt. There, he wanted to be close to Sarah to protect her from the distractions of Lova's charm offensive. Joseph was aware that, in return for his loyalty to her, Sarah would stand up for him. His attraction to Sarah was passionate but platonic. Sarah knew she was in no position to staunch the rumors. They were too immersed in their work to be distracted by the tittle tattle, no matter how damaging and hurtful it was to them. As Sarah admitted in a letter to Aaron,

'All these distractions interfere with my work and doesn't leave me with a clear head to think and plan. All this at a time of great urgency.'

In response to Aaron's written plea for her to return to Egypt, she wrote,

'As for leaving this place, I cannot contemplate that. If there are problems here, what would they be like in my absence?'

Another ship arrived laden with money, satchels full of instructions and requirements, and wooden frames to be assembled into pigeon coops. They also sent two crates of cooing carrier pigeons to relay urgent messages to Cairo.

Abdullah's two sons, Leib Bernstein, and Lova came ashore carrying their cargo while Abdullah and a couple of sailors kept the rowing boat steady in calmer waters. Reuven had been joined by the powerful Yehuda and Nissan Rutman to collect the delivery. After embracing the men from the small boat they realized they needed a fourth man to help them lug the equipment and heavy bags back to the station. Lova was quick to volunteer.

"Leib, wait here until I get back. If there's a problem on the beach, head out to sea and wait there until you get the signal that it's safe to come and get me."

The silence of their cautious trek through the wadi was broken only by the occasion grunt of pain from Reuven and Nissan lugging their uncomfortable load, and from the cooing of the excited pigeons. Nissan swore at the birds, muttering, "If they don't pipe down before we get to the road I'm going to break their necks. Better a bunch of dead birds than a bunch of dead NILI members."

It was as if the birds understood his threat. As they reached the edge of the road, the birds went silent until they were disturbed by Demon's barking as they reached the station compound. This was the signal for Sarah to open the door to let them in.

Sarah didn't know what surprised her most, the arrival of the birds or the arrival of Lova. After a few rapid words of welcome, Sarah ushered everybody into the building, including the pigeons.

"We'll leave them in here tonight," Sarah said. "We'll erect the pigeon coop tomorrow morning."

Lova said, "Sarah, I've got to go. They are waiting for me by the boat."

She walked with Lova along the avenue. As they reached the road they exchanged a long and passionate kiss. She found it hard to let him go. As he pulled himself away he whispered his hotel appeal to her, "Wait for me."

"I will," she replied. He kissed her and was gone. Pausing only to check the road, he looked back, blew her one last kiss, and disappeared into the dark of the gully and out of her life.

The satchels from Egypt to Sarah always contained personal notes and letters from Aaron. One such letter in late July resonated with unusual excitement. Aaron wrote;

I met with the new British Commander. General Allenby has replaced Murray. He is an imposing figure. Strong of character and a no-nonsense officer. He means to shake things up. I like him. We got on very well. He is keen to adopt my knowledge of Palestine. There is a new air of expectancy here.

He asked me questions about the topography, the terrain, and asked my advice about the preferred routes for his army to take against key locations. He particularly mentioned Jerusalem. I told him that the malarial infested swamps of the coastal approaches to the hills leading up to Jerusalem had prevented Richard the Lionheart from taking Jerusalem. Allenby is a bit of a military Bible buff and he was intrigued to learn that Richard's army had come along the coastal plain in September when the mosquitos are most vicious and deadly, and his army was decimated by fever. I am sure Allenby took this into his thinking.

Allenby has heard about my research into the sources of water his army will need and he asked me to provide him with my scientific evidence. You will find them in our archives. Please send me urgently the boxes containing rock formation samples, photographs, and

282

the files with details of the locations of the samples and my estimates of the drilling depths to reach water.

In fact, he wants to know everything about the Turkish Army. It seems, Sarita, that our life's work is leading to this moment. Pray God that it may liberate our land from our accused enemy.'

Sarah and her team were desperate to get the British everything they needed to help them launch their attack against the enemy. To an impatient Sarah, the British seemed to be too hesitant, too heavy in their deliberations.

Aaron has been pressing the British to launch a massive naval invasion on the coast to the south of Haifa and create a bridgehead for the landing of troops. He assured British intelligence that the Turkish coastal defenses were almost nonexistent in Palestine and their patrols were comprised of a handful of middle-aged men and under-aged conscripts. The fit Turks and conscripts had been drafted into the 4th and 5th armies. Controlling the narrow coastal strip to the foothills leading to Jerusalem would have the advantage of splitting Palestine in two. It would cut off supplies to the enemy's army in the south. Aaron's advice was that, from this position, it would be possible either to lay siege to the enemy's southern army, caught between Allied troops in to their north and south, until they surrendered, or to attack them with artillery until they were sufficiently weakened and traumatized to surrender to their siege.

Aaron pressed his case even though he appreciated that shell-shocked Britain was still feeling the ignoble defeat and huge loss of life of their last naval invasion at Gallipoli. Winston Churchill had been forced to resign as First Lord of the Admiralty and the wounds were still too raw for them to contemplate taking on the Turks with another naval exercise.

When Aaron saw that this approach would not be accepted he urged General Allenby to ignore Gaza and, instead, attack Beer Sheba.

"Why should I choose Beer Sheba?" Allenby demanded to know.

"Because that is where the water is," answered Aaron." Whoever controls the water controls southern Palestine. You cannot possibly win the Palestine campaign with hundreds of thousands of men, tens of thousands of horses and camels, and your motorized vehicles without adequate water. Take Beer Sheba and you take southern Palestine."

"But where is this water?" the general asked.

"Under the desert sand lying in aquifers. I know where they are."
The General liked the idea. Pouring over his maps, Allenby saw that a victory at Beer Sheba would have the additional advantage of allowing his troops to pincer round to the north side of Gaza and isolate the Turkish garrison from the rest of Palestine.

"Excellent! Excellent!" Allenby was impressed.

Naaman Belkind was still brooding about his missing friend Avshalom, but he still provided Sarah with the best intelligence from the south. He had a man, Ronya, who served as a radio operator at Turkish military headquarters in Beer Sheba. Ronya was a reluctant conscripted Jew who felt uncomfortable working for the enemy. The last thing that Ronya wanted was for the Turks to win this war. He provided Naaman with startling reports that Naaman rushed to Sarah, usually through Joseph, for urgent transfer to the British. One of Ronya's reports offered the transcript of a conversation by German General Kress von Kressenstein complaining that too many Turkish officers were deserting. The general also complained that no more than 30,000 Turkish soldiers were fit for battle on the Beer Sheba-Gaza frontline, and that more reserves were urgently needed. This was intelligence gold to the British. Included in Ronya's report was the information that the Turks were holding temporary defense lines between locations indicated on his maps at Shelal and Sharia and that they planned to withdraw to Jerusalem and Hebron should a successful attack take place in the south. This vital information would be pivotal in Allenby's decision to attack Beer Sheba.

But Naaman still harbored a serious problem. He personally came up to Atlit with his latest crop of reports. This was a rare visit as activities in the south were frenetic. He closed the door to Sarah's office. "Sarah. Have you heard from Avshalom?"

"No, Naaman. Nothing has been received from him."

"Of course you wouldn't, because he's dead."

She looked up in alarm.

"What are you talking about?" Sarah was temporarily confused. Had someone spoken to him?

"I'm sure that Lishansky killed him."

"What? Are you crazy? Why would he do that?"

"He was jealous of Avshalom's love for you. He wanted Avshalom out of the way so that he could take his place alongside you. That is exactly what has happened, hasn't it?"

Sarah was shocked by his outburst. "I don't know what to say, Naaman. This is nonsense."

"Is it? Or is it nonsense that Avsha is learning to fly? Avshalom would never have reached Egypt, met Aaron, gone to England, without writing to me. He would have given you a letter for me." He stared into her face. "Tell me I'm not telling the truth."

Sarah's mind raced. "You know what, write me a letter for him. Do it right now. I will send it to him via Aaron. Would you be satisfied with a reply from Avshalom?"

This was a delaying tactic. Sarah was playing for time. She knew she wouldn't get an answer. Even had Avsha been alive, she could blame the delay on the British who everybody knew were unreliable with their naval rendezvous. She would ask Aaron to write a letter in Avshalom's florid style and sign it. She hated to deceive him, but Naaman was leaving her little choice.

"I don't understand why you picked Joseph over me. Why is he your main person while I am the one bringing you your best intelligence? Why him? Why not me?"

Now Sarah understood that Naaman's concern for his friend was tinged with jealously.

"Who said I picked him over you? This is nonsense, Naaman. You know I value everything you do."

"Avshalom would have picked me over him."

The hard-pressed Sarah had no patience for Naaman's childish jealousies and suspicions but had little choice but to humor him.

"Believe me, Naaman, nobody can bring us the material that you bring us. There is nobody that I trust more than you to recruit people. You have seen how I accept your people without question. I don't do that with anyone else. I ask you to treat me with the same trust. Intelligence gathering at source, Naaman, is more important than message delivery. You do see that, surely?"

In Egypt, Aaron pursued his goal of being sent to London to advance the cause of his people. In one of the satchels, Sarah found a sealed envelope from Aaron. Inside was a triumphant letter from her brother;

'Sarita. Today I had a meeting with Sir Reginald Wingate, the British High Commissioner. We discussed the reasons for my request to transfer to London. His approval seems assured. In his words, he told me to go to London to see what he called 'the great ones' and to tell them what we know, but what they don't know.

From today and onward, my dear sister, we have the right to look on our activities with confidence. Up until now we were just a few isolated dreamers who endangered ourselves. Now, at last, when the highest authorities have given their official approval of our work, no one can doubt the rightness of our vision and of our action.

Be proud, dear Sarita, for you have been the cornerstone of this achievement. But now it is time for you to come to Egypt and replace me here. Please reconsider and agree to take up my role as the link between NILI and the British. With me based in London, and you here, we can strengthen our cause together.'

Sarah knew that Aaron's prime concern was for her safety. She wrote a short reply to his letter.

'I appreciate your offer, Aaron, but I want to be together with our people in a place of danger at a time of danger. I cannot leave them at the time when the greatest difficulties lie ahead of us. God speed, my brother. I have faith in your ability to advance our cause. Your loving sister, Sarah.'

Then, and for the rest of August and into September, the ship stopped coming.

THE ARREST

The same day that Aaron flew to London on September 13, Sarah received news that Naaman Belkind had been arrested.

The disappearance of his closest friend had weighed too heavily on Naaman. Love and jealousy swirled and festered in Naaman's mind. A growing distrust of Joseph had gathered strength leading him to a suspicion that Lishansky had something to do with Avshalom's death that nothing, not even Sarah, could assuage. Naaman hadn't been embarrassed in accusing Lishansky of murder. He fantasized a scene of his friend being shot in the back by Lishansky as they approached British lines, then claiming that they had been attacked by the Turks, or Bedouin. His muddled thoughts would not let him rest and he had set out on his own to discover the truth somewhere in Egypt with Aaron's help. He knew that Aaron had scant respect for Lishansky. In Aaron Aaronsohn he expected to find an ally in his resolve to uncover the truth about his missing friend.

On his way through the Sinai, he and his Bedouin guide were attacked and robbed. His guide was allowed to escape but they recognized Belkind as a Jew. He was taken by his Bedouin attackers to the Turkish authorities where they hoped to receive a small reward for his capture.

Naaman was arrested and accused of being a spy. General von Kressenstein wanted him hanged as an example to others in Palestine, but Belkind was allowed to fester in a Beer Sheba jail where the Turks tortured him in an attempt to extract information before his execution.

Joseph heard about his arrest from Naaman's family. He raced up to Atlit to meet with Sarah. A distressed Sarah gave Joseph five hundred Turkish lira as bribe money to try and get Naaman released or, at least, a stay of execution. Naaman may have accused Joseph of duplicity, but it was Joseph who raced up and down Palestine to raise the money in an attempt to rescue him.

Joseph returned to the Naaman family home late the same night, exhausted and dirty from a full days fast riding.

He found that the family had managed to raise two hundred liras and were short of three hundred which Joseph gladly gave them.

Together with Eitan, Naaman's younger brother, Joseph gathered a few of Naaman's southern friends and NILI members. They began to plan an attack to rescue him. They discussed ways of gaining armed access to the prison to grab him and fight their way out. Someone suggested bribing the prison governor to discover where they would be taking Naaman for sentencing and then attack his guard escort along the route and rescue him. Joseph said, it was vital to find out if Naaman had surrendered anyone's names to his torturers.

The town committee called Sarah to a meeting.

"We have warned you in the past. Your work is putting the whole of Zichron Yaakov in danger. God knows that our lives are impossible with the famine and the additional thousand mouths we are trying to feed, but your work puts us in jeopardy with the Turks. Do you want us to go the same way as Jaffa and Tel Aviv?"

A weary Sarah listened in silence.

"We demand that you, a daughter of Zichron Yaakov, immediately stop your activities. You are not only risking our lives, you are risking the lives of everyone in all our settlements and communities. If suspicion falls on you, it will also fall on us. You know the vengeance of Djemal Pasha. Do you want us to all share the fate of those who have fallen under his shadow?"

I speak to you in the name of all the other committees who live in fear," said an angry Lederman.

Sarah struggled to remain composed.

"You do not represent other committees. Speak with Meir Dizengoff. His committee is prepared to work with us."
Her words put the chairman off balance. She pressed her advantage.

"Surely you know that he sent a representative to meet with me?"

Lederman changed his tack.

"I speak in the name of this committee and we represent the people of Zichron."

The chairman continued. "We asked you to work from Atlit but we find that we are at grave risk as a result of your work there. If, despite our warnings, you want to continue your dangerous work, remove yourself from Zichron Yaakov. Go and join your brother in Egypt."

Sarah realized she was trapped. She needed time.

"I hear what you have to say. You know I run an extensive agricultural project. I have workers I am responsible for, who need to be paid. I have partners, not just here but in America, who must be informed. They need to help me find a solution. I will consult with them and inform you of their solution."

"Another delay?"

"No. I am employed by them. We operate with their help and assistance. They must make the decision what to do with their research station."

"How long will that take?"

"A month, maybe."

"A month!" Lederman did not like such a lengthy delay but showing his committee that he could command a situation caused him to listen to the views of his committee members. Several of them had raised their hands.

"Wait outside. We will tell you of our decision."

Minutes later, Sarah was ushered back into the committee chamber.

Lederman glared at her. "All right. One month, but then you close down."

With Naaman's arrest and torture, the demands from the elders of Zichron, and the pressure from the Central Zionists, an exhausted Sarah wrote a private letter to her brother and placed the envelope into one of the communications bags for the next ship assignment as Sarah agonized over an impending fate and the non-arrival of the British ship. The pressure and the loneliness of her responsibility was getting to her. Her weary words read;

If the establishment decides to rise up and oppose us, they can certainly stop our work. And if the people don't want to understand the value of our work, why should we go out of our way to do it? If people are afraid to risk themselves, can we really force them to do it? And if, God forbid, with all our caution, we still fail, it will not only be ten or twenty heads that will roll. No, the entire community will be tried. The revenge will be terrible and the people will point to us and say, 'look what your work has done to us!'

Is it worthwhile continuing to endanger ourselves, and to continue until we are caught? Or should we stop at least until their fury has passed us over?

Our situation is grim. We have no money left to operate our network. The money needed to rescue Naaman has left my coffers empty. What happens if the ship never comes? What do we do? Send someone down to Egypt, following in the footsteps of Avshalom, and Naaman?

We do not know what tomorrow will bring. Do I stop the operation, or keep it going?

The time has come to allow those of our friends and their families to leave the danger they are under.

Please send a ship to rescue them.

Your loving sister, Sarita.'

Sarah also composed a letter to Lova.

'Dear Lova,

I am writing to Aaron but I want you to know what is happening here. It seems we must suspend our work, pay all the workers. But how? We have no money to pay them.

We no longer have the resources to continue. We have no money and precious little food. Naaman is in jail undergoing all sorts of tortures. The Turks must know of our activities. Is it possible we have been abandoned by the British? Where are they? Will they ever come? What is stopping them? Must they wait until the Turks and the Germans strength is so great that they will lose far greater numbers of brave soldiers? Even the village children ask me what is stopping their army from coming to save us.

We go down to the shore to spend every night shivering and return empty handed. My dedicated team are, yet again, talking about the lack of British resolve. It has been almost a month. Nothing.

Naaman may not be the final sacrifice. The ship must come, or we are doomed.

Sarah.'

GATHERING CLOUDS

Sarah got a response from a pigeon. She had sent one of the birds to Cairo demanding to know what had happened to the ship. The bird returned with details of the ship's arrival tied to its leg. She sent her letters with the large batch of intelligence reports.

Sarah's letter failed to reach Aaron by a day. Her brother left Egypt the day before its arrival. He flew on a new De Havilland aircraft to Paris for a reunion with his old benefactor, Baron Edmond James de Rothschild, before heading for London and the corridors of British power in Whitehall.

Unbeknown to Sarah, Alexander had arrived from America to replace him in the job that Aaron had desperately wanted her to fill. Aaron hastily introduced Alex to the officers with whom he would be working, then departed for Europe and England.

It was Alexander that opened Sarah's letter to Aaron. He was traumatized by her words. New to his job, he set about galvanizing his contacts in British intelligence and Aaron's influential friends on the General Staff to send a ship laden with specially minted coins and French francs for the relief of the Palestinian refugees, and to rescue his sister and her team that were serving the British so selflessly.

The ship left Port Said with the heavy sacks of gold coins. It was escorted by another craft to pick up the NILI members and bring them to safety in Egypt.

By the time the ships arrived off Atlit beach, Sarah had regained her composure. She had found a renewed strength of purpose. She had rekindled in her soul the reason she had dedicated herself for her cause. Her adversaries in the community were wrong. They may oppose what she was doing, but this was partly because they didn't know, couldn't know, the depth of involvement she had with a British military intelligence that would soon lead the inevitable Allied invasion of Palestine, if only it would begin. Sarah, however, had gathered her main operatives to tell them that she had requested a ship to take them and their families to safety.

Reuven asked her, "And what of you, Sarah? Are you coming with us?"

"No Reuven. I will stay here."

"Then I will stay with you," Reuven told her.

At that fateful meeting all of her loyal friends decided to stay with her, save one, a young woman operator. With no shame or disgrace, the others embraced the one and wished her God speed.

When the ships moored they found the beach empty of fleeing NILI agents, save for the three, a close friend of Sarah and her parents, that were waiting for them. Sarah was one of those waiting that night on the beach to see them safely board the ship.

Lova and Leib were on the row boat and waded ashore. They embraced Sarah before hastily dragging the heavy waterproof bags ashore.

"What is with Naaman?" Lova asked.

"We don't know. He is still in prison. God knows what he must be suffering, but we have not seen any actions from the Turks. We don't know if he has divulged our names."

"So let's go. Where is everyone?"

"We're not coming, Lova. Not yet. Please ask Aaron to send the boat to pick up the team in a couple of weeks unless you hear from us that we need it earlier. I will send a pigeon with the message."

Lova broke the news. "Aaron is in England now. Alex has taken his place."

Leib interjected. "We must leave, Lova. Let's go."

Lova gave Sarah a hug and a kiss. "Stay safe, my love. Stay safe and make sure you leave when you can. I will be waiting for you."

"Give Alex my love and tell him to send the ship on October 2nd to take us away if sea conditions permit."

Sarah could feel the net tightening.

Sarah's team continued to provide valuable information thick and fast. The most pressing intelligence she coded and attached to the legs of her homing pigeons. She enjoyed releasing them into the sky and watch them beat their wings and disappear on their southern flight to her brother in Egypt.

Sarah was busy, and she was exhausted. Her workload and the tensions from Naaman's arrest and from the pressure she was under from both the village committee and from the central council were constantly on her mind but she felt content, satisfied that she was doing dangerous but purposeful work that would reach its conclusion in a matter of days.

One way or another, it will all be over in a couple of weeks, she thought.

Joseph was spending most of his time dashing between Atlit and Naaman's family in the settlement of Rishon le Zion, or with Naaman's friends in Beer Sheba. They told him that Naaman's last message had said he was in bad shape but that he had divulged nothing to his captors. Joseph wondered if that was true. The only good sign was that the Turks had not come banging on the family door. Neither had they arrested Naaman's worried agents with whom Joseph met to collect their reports. He and Sarah discussed the team's evacuation and Sarah instructed Joseph to have them to be ready to be at Atlit on October the first to be taken out of Palestine. Sarah was in awe of their courage that kept them at their post. *If only*, she thought, *the British truly appreciated their bravery*.

Sarah released a batch of four birds from the pigeon coop, watching them soar into an early morning September sky.

She returned to her office to prepare reports on their agricultural work. Despite everything, the research and development of the land continued. She had her loyal Arab agricultural workers to pay and to take care of.

By the afternoon, and after a quick lunch, she went into the courtyard to clean out the bird house. She was surprised to find one of the pigeons standing on top of the coop cooing to be let in. This bird had one of her messages attached to its leg. It was one of the birds she had released earlier in the day.

"Silly bird," she said, lifting the reluctant pigeon off the roof of the wooden structure. "We all have our work to do, now go do yours." Sarah threw the bird into the air and watched it reluctantly disappear flying low toward the south.

A couple of days later, Reuven Schwartz came running into Sarah's office.

"They caught one of our pigeons!"

Sarah looked up and saw the alarm on Reuven's face.

"Nissan's informant told him that one of our pigeons came down in in the yard of Ahmed Bek in Caesarea. It couldn't have landed in a worse place," Reuven said.

Sarah could sense the panic in his voice. Ahmed Bek was the Emniyet Amiri, the local Turkish police chief at the headquarters in the old Roman garrison at Caesarea. Bek controlled law and order in the Palestinian district south of Haifa, and Bek had one hobby. Pigeon breeding. Sarah was shocked to her core by this cruel twist of fate as Reuven told her, "He wouldn't have noticed, except this pigeon had one of our coded messages attached to its leg. It landed in his yard, Sarah. It landed in his yard! He's now started searching for spies in Hadera."

Instantly, she remembered the reluctant bird. It had tried to tell her it didn't want to make the journey. She had forced it to do something it didn't want to do. She fought to quell the sickness she felt in the pit of her stomach. She knew that Ahmed Bek would extend his search and come to Zichron Yaakov and Atlit.

"Get Yehuda and Menashe. They're working in the field. Kill the birds. Bury them. Destroy the pigeon coop. Make sure there is no trace that we ever had them."

She slumped in her chair as Reuven raced out of the building.

Now this? On top of everything else, now this?

She felt the world was conspiring against her. Her body was shaking. She struggled to stop herself from crying.

Ahmed Bek possessed an overlarge moustache which dominated his brutal looking face. He requisitioned the Lang's house as his local headquarters when he brought his investigation to Zichron Yaakov and the surrounding area in his ongoing search for spies. Hadera had brought him nothing except the name of Avshalom Feinberg who had gone missing earlier in the year. Bek was looking for Feinberg's accomplice, a man named Joseph Lishansky.

The Langs, Michael and Neta, were a wealthy English couple who had built themselves an expensive mansion in the town. It was their way of expressing their passion for the Jewish endeavor in what had once been the land of Israel. Now it lay empty. As British citizens, the Lange's had sensibly returned to London even before war was declared. For them, Zichron Yaakov was a lovely concept, but not a place to risk your life over. Now, without their knowledge or approval, their deserted house was being used by the occupying power against their beloved neighbors.

Ahmed Bek called the council members to a meeting in the Lang's house located on the far side of the town square.

Councilmen Lederman, Blumenthal, Epstein, Alter, Arison, Epstein, Appelbaum, Lerner, Goldstein and Leitner made their worried way to meet the police chief.

The bulky Ahmed Bek glared at them. "We are searching for spies. I can assure you that your God will not help you if we find that you have traitors in your village. I want the names of anyone who has pigeons."

He looked at each of them. They all had blank expressions of their faces.

Bek whipped a cloth from a cage. The councilmen stared at the cooing bird inside.

Bek shouted, "There is are spies in your village. They are sending messages through these birds to our enemy in the south. We will not be satisfied until we have apprehended the traitors. Do I make myself clear?"

They nodded.

"We are looking for Joseph Lishansky." Ahmed Bek stared at them. He detected a reaction.

"Don't pretend you don't know who he is. You will find him. The consequences for you will be dire if you do not. If you fail to bring him to me or fail to give me information that will lead to his arrest within twenty-four hours my men will round up the prettiest young girls and feed them to our soldiers. I think you know what this means. Now go!" He dismissed them with a wave of his hand.

The men were panicked. They knew Lishansky all right. They split up into small groups and called on their neighbors to help in their search for anyone giving Lishansky shelter. They send a couple of farmers to search the fields on horseback. They divided up groups of villagers to work their way up the street, house by house. The main vigilante headed for the Aaronsohn's house and hammered on the door. Ephraim answered their loud knocking.

"Where is Lishansky? Where is your daughter?"

Ephraim told them, "Lishansky hasn't been here for days. Sarah has been working at Atlit, but you know that. You sent her to work there."

"We want to search your house. We think he may be hiding here."

Ephraim was angry. "How dare you doubt my word! If I tell you that Lishansky is not here, he's not here. Look at you! You are doing the enemies bidding. You should be ashamed of yourselves. Now go away!" Ephraim slammed his door in their faces.

Their search continued. Pearl Baum was sitting on the porch of her house at the end of Founder's Street. Her house did not need an inspection. Her husband was one of the council vigilante out on the street as part of the search. By now the searchers were followed by a gaggle of nosy women. As they reached Baum's porch, Pearl made a gesture with her head toward the next door house. It was the home of Tova Gelber. They burst into the house as Tova opened her front door. Others ran to the rear of her building to search the outhouses in her back yard. They found Nissan Rutman inside the house hiding under Tova's bed. They dragged him out. They had no compunction about handing him over to the Turks. Rutman was not a native Zichronite. He lived in nearby Hadera where that other rascal, Avshalom Feinberg, came from. He was courting Tova and, in the eyes of some, he was one of those who contaminated her with his dangerous ideas and actions. If they couldn't find Lishansky at least they would show Ahmed Bek that they had tried. Rutman would be their trophy victim.

They hauled him out and held him while a couple of them ran to bring the police.

As Nissan was marched down Founder's Street, three women ran up to him. In a public display of venom, Marta Blum slapped him in the face while Adele Gold spat at him and hit him with her shoe. They were urged on by a cursing Gita Feld. Pearl Baum was no longer sitting on her balcony chair. Her handiwork done, she had retired into her darkened house and peered at the scene with satisfaction from behind the closed slats of her shuttered window.

They hoped by handing Rutman over to Ahmed Bek, he would go easy on the village. They were wrong.

Chaim Schwartz was a deeply religious man. Every year, He set off on an annual pilgrimage from the Carmel village to pray at the ancient Wailing Wall of the Temple Mount in the Old City of Jerusalem. Seventy miles as the crow flies, but far more when taking the snaking roads and pathways leading up to the holy city.

300

He was also a farmer in Zichron who lived at the southern end of Founder's Street just before the cemetery. Chaim was also the father of Reuven Schwartz. Chaim needed all the strength that a lifetime of faith and prayer had given him when he was dragged out of his house to be taken to the ominous grey torture house at the other end of the street. They only wanted one thing from him, the whereabouts of his son. The beatings were an expression of the anger and frustration of the torturers. Chaim would not have told them, even if he knew where his son was hiding.

The Ribniker's house was as far as one could go on Founder's Street. The road ended a few strides after their grey house. Anyone travelling further needed to negotiate the sharply descending sandy lane that led to Wadi Milik, the gorge that divided Zichron Yaakov from the Arab village of Faradis.

In the autumn of 1916, the Ribniker's were not at home. They had been rudely evicted by the Turkish commissioner who wanted their house for interrogation and torture. The house had been carefully selected due to the extremity of its location. Fewer people would be disturbed by the screams of those undergoing questioning. Treason and espionage demanded nothing less than the required harsh interrogation. Furthermore, it would not do to spill blood on the floor of the exquisite Lang residence.

The gloomy building matched the heavy atmosphere within its grey walls.

They came for Albert Alter, Reuven's uncle. Being a member of the council did not save him from the beating as they led him led down the main street. He cried out Reuven's name as the blows hit his head and body. "Reuven, come! In God's name, come!"

Reuven was hiding, not too far from the village. Word reached him that his father and uncle were being tortured at the cruel hands of the Turkish police chief. Reuven couldn't let his family take the punishment for his absence.

Knowing that his fate would be dreadful, Reuven walked into the village and gave himself up to the vengeful Turks. They took him to the Ribniker's place.

As he reached the terrible house of interrogation he saw Menashe, Tova, and Nissan. He saw his father's bloody feet from the bastinado torture and his uncle's bleeding nose. He pleaded with the uniformed police that they be released. They beat him senseless. They only had one question which they repeated over and over again with each blow. "Where is Joseph Lishansky?" His answer was true. He had no idea where Joseph had escaped to, or where he was hiding. This did nothing to stop the rain of blows that left his shirt and face sodden with his blood.

Then they came for the Aaronsohns.

Sarah had managed to sneak back to her home the evening before from Atlit where she had spent more than a day destroying all traces of evidence of their espionage work. She had glanced from the balcony to see if the ship approached. The sea was calm and empty. When her work was completed, she made her cautious way through Ephraim's vineyards and steered her faithful horse silently to the rear of their house undetected. They had posted soldiers outside the front gate. Maybe they were sleeping, but they did not see or hear her quietly enter the house in the dark.

In the morning, an officer, accompanied by two uniformed policemen, hammered on their door. Ephraim answered. Sarah was standing beside him.

"Ephraim Aaronsohn. Sarah Aaronsohn, also known as Sarah Abraham. You are both under arrest on charges of espionage against the Turkish government."

The policemen cuffed their wrists and tied chains around their necks. They were led out of their home and down the main street. *Like cattle*, Sarah thought, *to the slaughter.* The road was eerily empty and silent. Sarah saw the eyes of the villagers peering at them though semi-closed shutters and the cracks of curtains.

They could hear screams as they approached the Ribniker's house. Sarah led her father up the six steps and into the place of pain. They were led to a large side room. This was clearly a holding area prior to interrogation. As they passed a room on their left Sarah saw the slumped figures of Reuven and Nissan. Their faces were swollen and bloody as they looked up at her through distressed eyes. She gave them a reassuring smile.

In the holding room, Sarah came across Tova, who was crying, and Yehuda. Tova whispered to Sarah that she hadn't yet been beaten but they had given Menashe, Reuven, and Nissan, a hard time. Despite the pain inflicted on their bodies they had given the Turks no information. Despite his size, Yehuda looked fearful. Sarah held their hands. She looked into their eyes. They noticed the determined look on her face.

"Don't be afraid. I am going to tell them that I acted alone. That I am the only one they can accuse. That all of you only worked on our agricultural projects and knew nothing about what I was doing. This has to be your story."

She looked at them for a response. They nodded.

"But what about Joseph? They keep asking about Joseph?" Tova asked.

"I will tell them that he was my escort when I had to go to meet people but that he thought my trips were to do with the station business. It's flimsy, but that is what I will tell them."

"Do you think they caught us because of information they got out of Naaman?" Yehuda asked.

"I don't know," Sarah answered. "I don't know if it was that, or the pigeon, or if someone snitched on us."

"Who would do that?" asked Tova.

"We had so many people who were jealous or afraid of us. Who knows? It may have been people in the village."

Sarah sat back against the crumbling grey plaster of the wall and tried to collect her thoughts. *It couldn't have been from the pigeon. There were no names in the message on the pigeon's leg. Only indecipherable code. How did they have names? Perhaps it was from Naaman's confession...*

Her thoughts were interrupted by a couple of uniformed Turks who entered the room and dragged her father to his feet.

"Be brave, papa..."

Ephraim turned to her, as he started to be dragged out of the room. He had a defiant look on his face.

"My daughter is telling me to be brave? Let me show you how it is done, my daughter..."

They took him to the small room directly opposite Sarah's. She saw them order him to remove his shoes and stockings. They hit him because he was

304

doing it too slowly. When he was bare-footed they turned him around and made him kneel on the chair, his front to the back of the chair. Ephraim stared across the corridor directly into Sarah's face. They tied his hands to the frame of the chair and wedged a rifle through the back of his bent knees before tying his bent legs to the chair. Then Sarah saw a soldier approach him from behind with a cane whip. After a couple of practice swipes, he targeted the bare soles of her father's feet and brought the cane down with a fast whip of his wrist. Ephraim exploded in shock and pain. The executioner repeated the blows with increasing rapidity. Sarah saw the agony on her father's face as, through closed eyes and clenched fists, he screamed. "No! No! God! God!" with each blow. Sarah wept.

After ten blows, an officer faced her father, obscuring Sarah's view. She heard him ask, "Where is Joseph Lishansky?" She heard him reply, "I don't know." She saw the officer nod to the torturer. As he stepped aside

She saw the whip coming down again, again, and again on her father's now bloody soles.

"Shema Israel!" Ephraim cried to God to hear his agony.

"Enough!" Sarah was screaming. "Enough! He knows nothing. It is me you want. Only me."

The beating stopped in the other room as the torturer looked at the officer for instruction. He raised his hand and, with a twitch of his finger, they began to release Ephraim from his painful cramped position. The old man found it hard to walk so they dragged him back to the room. Sarah noticed the trail of blood across the floor from his bleeding wounds.

With another twitch of his finger two soldiers marched into the room, grabbed Sarah, and escorted her across the corridor into his interrogation room. They sat her in the chair on which her father had been abused.

"So. It is you we want. Is that correct?"

"Yes. Me. Nobody else."

"I see. Why should it be you?"

"Because I am the only one involved."

"Involved in what?"

"Involved in hating you. Involved in wanting to see you gone."

The officer smashed a fist across Sarah's cheek. The blow threw her from the chair and on to the floor.

"Get up!" he ordered. Sarah staggered to her feet.

"Sit, Miss Aaronsohn, Mrs. Abraham, or whatever you call yourself."

When she was seated the officer put his face next to hers. She could smell his pungent breath. "Where is Joseph Lishansky?"

"I don't know."

A blow hit her head knocking the chair sideways and backwards. Sarah was skewered out of the chair and back onto the floor. Her face was stinging. She involuntarily put her cuffed hand to her cheek and felt blood.

The officer was smiling. He gave an order in Turkish. She understood what he said. Two soldiers picked her off the floor and dragged her back into the holding room. They disappeared and returned pulling a reluctant Reuven with them. They tied him to the chair and, without asking him questions or speaking to him, the torturer approached his with an implement while the two soldiers held his left hand firm on the chairs arm rest. He began to extract one of Reuven's fingernails. Reuven screamed in agony.

"Stop!" yelled Sarah. "I told you they don't know anything. It's me you want. Only me."

She saw the officer look at his watch. He paced the room, considering his options before going into another room. Sarah could not see him but she heard him making a phone call. The conversation was too distant to hear what he was saying or to whom but, a few minutes later, he re-emerged, spoke quietly to the soldiers, and disappeared again.

After a few minutes, soldiers came into their room and grabbed Sarah, Ephraim, and Tova. They tied ropes to their necks before leaving the torture house to escort them back to their homes. As they reached Tova's house, Sarah shouted to her not to worry, that she would take the responsibility on her shoulders. One of the soldiers, who had participated in what had been inflicted on her, delivered a blow to her head that made her stagger and fall. He kicked her as she tried to stand with hand-cuffed wrists. Ephraim bent down to help her. He whispered, "Be brave, Sarita. Be brave," as he helped her to her feet.

The walk up Founders Road was agony, particularly for Ephraim. As they got into their house, father and daughter collapsed into each other's arms.

"I'm so sorry, papa. So sorry…"

"Ssshhh!" Ephraim stroked his daughter's hair. "Never apologize for what you did. Not to me. Not to them. Keep your courage, my daughter."

"But you, papa. You are innocent of everything."

"So are you, Sarita. So are you."

"What do you mean, papa?"

The father pulled away slightly and looked tenderly into his daughter's tearful face.

"Do you think you committed a crime?"

"No, papa. Of course not."

"Do you think you have done your people wrong? Do you think that what you did was for the future of our people?"

"Of course it was for the future of our people, papa. There was never any other reason. The Turks are our enemy. They have to be defeated."

"Then you are innocent, my child. Innocent. They are the guilty ones."

"But you, papa. I cannot stand what they are doing to you, and to our friends who gave so much."

Ephraim tutted and softly kissed Sarah's bruised face.

"I am with you, my Joan of Arc. To the end, Sarita. To the end. I would take all the blows on me to stop them falling on you, my child."

Sarah began to sob uncontrollably. Her father had reminded her of memories of her teenage years, reading about Joan of Arc, her girlhood heroine. Learning about the fate of her people and the Spanish Inquisition. *How could they have withstood their suffering with so much faith and courage,* she had puzzled.

She realized her moment had come. She was about to find out.

"Be strong, Sarita. Whatever they do to us, stay strong."

She thought to herself, W*as there such a thing as destiny?*

Sarah spent an anguished night of little sleep. She fleetingly considered escaping from the guarded house but quickly dismissed the thought. She could never succeed escaping with her father. The effort would be futile. No. She was determined to face her destiny as Jeanne d'Arc had done, as her people had done too many times in their terrible past, with sublime faith and the love of a just cause.

They came for them the next morning. As they were led from the house, four black-dressed women hovered silently on the other side of the street to witness the spectacle, like vultures inspecting their prey.

Sarah stared at them with contempt as she and her father were led in chains down an empty street. Ephraim limped. His injured feet tender to each tread of the road. She looked over at her father's dogged face knowing he was hiding the pain. Sarah glanced at the windows and shutters of the houses she passed knowing they were being watched. As she walked slowly to the dreaded house, she began to visualize her childhood fantasy of the fate of Joan of Arc, and the women who were among those put to the rack and the flame in mediaeval Spain, all suffering for their faith and their beliefs. She had wondered, as a girl, what it had taken for these brave women to stand up to their oppressors. She realized that was a dedication to their core beliefs that transcended pain and suffering. It was a deeply embedded sense of indescribable love and devotion.

As they approached the corner of Benefactor Street, a small group of her childhood friends ran out from the shade of the synagogue building. They tried to get close to Sarah so that they could embrace her but the guards butted them away with their rifles.

"Sarah, be brave!" "Sarah, be strong." "Sarah, we love you." They walked with her despite the harrying of the soldiers. Sarah put on a brave smile, but the girls were distressed and began to cry. Sarah felt a lump in her throat and tried, unsuccessfully, to stop the tears from flowing.

"Sarita! Courage," Ephraim shouted to her and Sarah nodded as they walked down to the Ribniker's house.

A small crowd had gathered on the other side of the road. Knowing the Sarah was coming. They broke into excited whispers as Sarah and Ephraim approached the building then quietly watched as they made their slow progress up the slab steps and through the front door.

When they entered the place of pain Sarah saw Menashe and Yehuda sprawled on the floor. Tova was standing. All looked unharmed.

"Where are the others?" she asked them.

"Reuven and Nisan are downstairs in the cellar," answered Tova.

"What are they doing there?" Sarah was afraid to ask.

"They are waiting to be taken to Damascus for further interrogation and sentencing," replied Menashe.

"Silence!" Two uniformed men burst to and began to discipline them with body blows from their rifles.

When the men stepped back, Sarah said rapidly, "You have nothing to fear. It's me they want, not you."

Her message was met with another rifle butt that made her stagger against the wall.

Later that morning, Sarah and Ephraim were pushed into the room that served as an office for Ahmed Bek. He was sitting at his desk writing a report. He left them standing until he had completed his work. Then he looked up.

"Ah, Miss Aaronsohn. I have heard so much about you. Your stupid treason has now resulted in the sorry fate of your friends, your family, your village. Aren't you proud of yourself, silly girl?" he said with a cynical smile on his ugly mustachioed face.

"Yes. Yes, I am proud," Sarah said defiantly. "but what I did had nothing to do with the others. It was me, and me alone."

"We will see about that, but I doubt it." He smiled again, and said, "We will spend the day finding out the truth. I will see you later, Miss Aaronsohn." He nodded to his men and returned to his paperwork. They were taken to the holding room and thrown onto the floor. They sat waiting for the inevitable. Ephraim was quietly praying, but Sarah was listening for voices from the other room, words that would help her understand her predicament.

Then a delegation arrived. A burly man in an impressive uniform marched in escorted by a couple of soldiers and a couple of officials in civilian dress.

They glanced into Sarah's holding room as they passed. She recognized him as the Kaymakam, the provincial governor, who had come down from Haifa to check on what was happening in Zichron Yaakov. Sarah knew that his visit was to receive an update that would enable him to send a progress report to Djemal Pasha in Damascus. She also knew that the overlord would bring down harsh judgment on anyone who the local authorities chose to transfer to the Syrian capital of Palestine.

Sarah strained her ears to eavesdrop on the conversation between the Kaymakam and Ahmed Bek. Sarah was fluent in Turkish but the distance allowed her to hear only a smattering of words. She heard Naaman's name mentioned but couldn't make out the context. Then Joseph's name was followed by a brief exchange between the two men. Her heart stopped when she heard the Kaymakam ask about the woman in the other room. They were talking about her. Sarah heard Bek mention the names Baum, Feld, and Blum. Sarah could not hear all the conversation but she was sure that Bek was telling the Kaymakam that it was the women of the village who had betrayed her, and not Naaman. She waited until the meeting ended. There was little else to hear. Her fate had been sealed. As the Kaymakam passed her room he paused, looked down on Sarah and, with a shake of his head, strode out of the gray building to his waiting car.

She held her father's hand as they sat on the stone floor. She felt as fragile as she had when she was a little girl, innocent of where her life was leading her. She had always felt safe in her father's house. Safe to explore a world in books, exploring other worlds, other lives. Fascinated by tales of suffering and heroism. Wondering and marveling about the courage of people who faced enemies with superhuman resolve and courage. It had been a world in which she was led by a charismatic and remarkable brother who showed her a world of nature and a land waiting to be nurtured for a people yet to come. She had always known that he was leading her to her life's purpose, her destiny. He had led her to Avsha, the beautiful personification of a cause greater than any one person. She had loved him with her body but she had embraced the cause more than any one person. She loved that cause with her soul, practicing it in secret even in the face of the enemy, just like the Anusim Jews of Spain. And when caught, they stayed true to their cause, faithful despite the pain. Not surrendering, despite the threat of the ultimate sacrifice.

She had known her life was leading her to a moment of triumph. This is what she had tried to express to Avsha, the love of her physical life. Now she had to defend her friends. Those who had followed her along that dangerous path to this moment. On her shoulders rested the responsibility for their lives. Sarah prayed for the strength to resist what was to come.

They came for her. She tried to kiss her father one last time but they dragged her from him before they could embrace.

"I love you, papa."

"Stay strong my daughter. I love you."

Papa had rarely spoken of his love for her though she knew he cared for her with a stoic passion.

She was hauled into the now familiar room of pain. They positioned her in a chair that was also familiar to her from her father's and her own suffering. They were going to start with the bastinado. She mentally steeled herself for what was to come.
Ahmed Bek walked into the room.

"Perhaps we can save you the pain. Just tell us about your criminal activities and you can save yourself and your friends a lot of pain."

"My friends did nothing criminal. They worked on our agricultural projects."

"We know you spied for the British. We know you worked with Lishansky and Belkind. We know they reported to you. We have Schwartz, Rutman, and others."

"They can tell you nothing."

"Then we will have to see what you tell us, won't we?"

Sarah's mind raced as she braced herself for the crack of the cane against the exposed soles of her feet. Bek had mentioned a few names but he had said nothing about any of their activities. Maybe her boys were holding up against their interrogators.

Crack! Sarah yelled in pain. Her mind now concentrating in preparing itself for the next blow.

Crack! Sarah took a sharp intake of breath.

Crack! The shock of the blows. The sharp pain tightened every sinew in her body. She screamed as she felt the sharp cane slash her feet.

Ahmed Bek signaled his men to stop. They sat her down in the chair facing the police chief.

"Now. What can you tell us about your activities? How did you pass your messages over to the British?"

"By pigeons." Sarah knew that Bek had caught one of her errant birds.

"How did you come to be in possession of homing pigeons?"

"They were sent to me?"

"How? By who?"

"By ship. I met a ship one night. They brought me a cage of pigeons and told me what to do."

"Just you?"

"Yes. Nobody else."

314

"And who was your contact?"

"My brother." Sarah knew she could play that card. Aaron had been missing so long and the Turks had been told he had been arrested by the British. Maybe they would assume that he had been tortured as they were torturing her. It would also strengthen her story that she had acted alone.

"Your brother! Interesting. Who else?"

"No one else."

"Really? Not even Joseph Lishansky?"

"Joseph sometimes came with me to meetings with our project managers and your officials. But you must know that already."

"And he had nothing to do with your spying?"

"No."

"You're lying."

"If you think I am lying go search my house. Send your men to Atlit. All you will find is records and samples of our agricultural work. That's all."

"You said you sent information to your brother who is acting for the British. That makes you a traitor, Miss Aaronsohn. What information did you send him, and who else helped you?"

"Nobody helped me. I did it on my own."

"What information, Miss Aaronsohn? Information about what?"

Sarah realized that whatever information she gave him would implicate someone in her organization. She remained silent.

"I am waiting, Miss Aaronsohn. Don't let me apply pressure on you."

Sarah glared at him defiantly.

"Do you like eggs, Miss Aaronsohn?"

She failed to understand his question until he nodded to one of his uniformed henchmen who left the room and returned with a pan of boiling water.

Ahmed Bek nodded to two of his men who ripped the top of Sarah's dress. With her handcuffed hands, she involuntarily tried to stop the dress revealing her breasts. The police chief smiled.

"Don't worry about them. We'll get to them later."

He nodded to the man with the pan who took a steaming hot boiled egg and, carrying it with a spoon, inserted it under her armpit that had been raised by one of the men that was holding her in her chair.

Sarah screamed at the burning sensation.

"Tell us, Miss Aaronsohn, everything you know."

Sarah shook her head. Bek nodded again and the man extracted another steaming egg which was applied under her other armpit. She screamed as she was prevented from raising her arm to avoid the burning pain.

Ahmed Bek moved his hairy face close to her.

"We have only just begun." He stared down at her half exposed breasts and then returned his gaze into her wet eyes. He lit a cigar and asked one of the men to bring him a cup of coffee. He waited until the man returned with a finjan from which he poured thick steaming liquid into a small cup.

Ahmed Bek drew on his thick cigar and emitted the smoke into her face. He was smiling as he picked up the coffee cup and drank it in one gulp. The man poured him a second cup which he carried over to Sarah.

"Would you like some hot coffee?"

Before she could answer he poured the scalding contents over the top of her breasts and watched the hot brown stain trickle down her white skin. Bek took a deep suck on his cigar until Sarah could see the tip emit a bright red flame. Ahmed Bek took the cigar from his mouth, blew out the acrid smoke, and stubbed the burning end onto her soft breast. Sarah screamed as she smelt her flesh burn.

"Bastard! Your cowardly bastard! First you kill Christian women and children. Now you pick on another woman. You are a coward, a sick animal!"

Sarah was flung from her chair by the blow of Bek's hand, the one holding the cigar which became entangled in her hair as she fell. She heard and smelled the singeing of her hair as two soldiers hauled her arms and threw her back into the chair.

Ahmed Bek was angry that she had ruined a quality smoke, so he hit her again. The explosion of the blow toppled her back onto the floor. She felt blood spurt out of the side of her mouth where his ringed finger had struck her. Again, she was dragged back into the chair.

Bek moved close to her and began to speak. "Are you..." Sarah spat into his ugly face. She saw her blood mingle with her spittle embed itself into his messy beard.

Ahmed Bek pointed to the wall. The two guards lifted Sarah from her seat and marched her to the wall. They took her handcuffed wrists and connected them to an iron ring high on the wall above her head. As she faced the wall, Ahmed Bek came behind her squeezing into her back and bottom as he whispered into her ear, "Don't make me do this. Tell me what I need to know, and save yourself the suffering."

"Go to hell!" Sarah's face was pushed into the wall by an angry Bek. She saw stars as her nose hit the hard surface and blood trickled out of her nostril.

She felt Ahmed Bek rip her dress off her shoulders and it dropped to her waist, exposing a bare back to her tormentors. She heard the woosh of a whip a split second before it ripped into her skin. Then immediately after, the sound of a cane that hit her back with excruciating pain.

"Harder!" commanded Bek. "Woosh!" Then, "Whish!"

"Faster!" commanded Bek. "Woosh!" "Whish!"
Sarah screamed and screamed at every blow. She felt as if they were ripping the skin off her back, slowly peeling her alive.

Her cries were so loud that the men in the basement, and her father, winced at the sound. Her screams were so piercing that the small crowd of villagers out on the street froze as they felt her pain.

They beat her until her body collapsed and she was hanging limply from the hook on the wall. Ahmed Bek ordered one of his men to throw a bucket of water over her to revive her.

She hung there shivering feverishly.

"Do you have anything to tell me?"

"Go to hell," she whimpered.

With the flick of his finger, Ahmed Bek ordered his men to take her off the wall. He grabbed her by her hair as she began to fall and dragged her back to the chair.

"You will tell me what you know."

Through the pain she stared at her tormentor. "You torture innocent men and women. You are evil! You have lost. I have opened the gates of hell for you. They are coming to push you there..."

She attempted to spit at him again but he lashed out at her during her final words and sent her sprawling one more.

"I have no patience for you anymore. You deserve what you are going to get."
Two soldiers brought up a table and held her hands firmly on the wooden top. The man who had brought the boiling eggs approached the table. He had pliers in his hand.

Ahmed Bek peered at her fingers. "Nice fingernails, Miss Aaronsohn. May I keep one as a souvenir?" He nodded to the man with the pliers and stepped back. Sarah couldn't bear to look. She turned away as she felt him grip a fingernail, then pulled. She screamed as she felt her nail resist and then tear. He pulled again, and a third time, before the nail ripped from her finger. Sarah felt she was about to vomit. Her body lurched with pain and shock.

"Let's try another one," Bek ordered. The torturer picked her middle finger and applied the tongues again as Sarah tried to prepare herself for the inevitable trauma.

It came. Sarah's shriek was cut short by her vomit and a collapse into delirium.

They didn't try to revive her. They left her there, gently moaning, barely conscious. Sarah didn't know how long she was alone. She struggled in the hazy netherworld between excruciating agony and reality. She realized she was close to breaking point. Her resistance was failing her.

Ahmed Bek returned with his henchmen.

"I've done with you, Miss Aaronsohn. You will be transported to Damascus where they are waiting for you. You will discover that I have been gentle with you. There, they have other, more brutal ways, of extracting information. I can assure you, Miss Aaronsohn, that for you, it will be a one-way journey."

Sarah's mind was racing. They both knew that she would not be able to resist the Damascus torturers.

"Then prove to me you are not a total beast. Do not send me there looking like this." She gestured to her torn clothes. "Allow a woman to go home and change."

She tried to put an appealing expression on her painful bloody face. Ahmed Bek considered her request. He looked at her. He felt a strange respect for this woman. She was an enemy, a traitor. He had failed to force her to reveal what she had done but now, as they faced each other, he was drawn to her courage. Her fate, he knew, was sealed. What harm could come from one small gesture to this woman. Why not? She had put up a gallant fight that would shame no man.

Ahmed Bek nodded. He ordered two of his men to escort her to her home and allow her to clean up, and then bring her back for transportation.

"Hurry!" he ordered them. "I want all the prisoners transported out of here before nightfall."

The small crowd were shocked as the door opened and Sarah was led barefoot down the steps of the Ribniker house. They murmured at the apparition. It wasn't the bold, beautiful, independent, confident, Sarah Aaronsohn they saw. Instead, they were greeted by a bleeding, battered, semi-conscious rag of a woman they barely recognized.

The soldiers pulled the chained Sarah slowly up the road. The crowd followed behind as if following a body to burial. They were silent, apart from one or two gossips speculating what was happening to her.

Sarah was woozy from the punishment, but her fuddled brain was working to a plan. Each painful step reminded her what bad shape she was in. She felt the racking pain of her broken body. Her spirit had almost been extinguished. Each stride was agony. Each tiny stone, each grain of dirt, shot a spike of pain through the tender soles of her naked wounded feet. Her head was dizzy from the blows she had absorbed. Her fingers were bloody and raw.

As they reached the town square, her childhood friends rushed out from the shade of the trees onto the road. They paused. One girl put a hand to her mouth. They walked alongside weeping as the soldiers watched them. Sarah looked at them and gave a watery smile. The girls didn't know what to say. "Poor Sarah," was no comfort for their girlhood friend.
"Are they releasing you? Miriam asked.

Sarah gestured negatively.

"What are they going to do to you?" another asked.

Sarah didn't say anything. She just looked at them.

Each step of the walk was agony for Sarah. She remembered the times she had run up this road to her house as a schoolgirl. It had taken her only moments to arrive home barely out of breath. Now she measured and felt each agonizing step up Founder's Street to her house.

Sarah looked at Miriam. Miriam had always been her most reliable school friend.

"Miriam. When it's over, take this dress."

"I don't know what you mean, Sarah. Take it where?"

Sarah glared at her and repeated, "When it's over, take this dress..."

The soldiers stopped their conversation. As the girls accompanied her up the street she saw Gita Feld hurriedly lead Pearl Baum into her house. When they reached the gate of the Aaronsohn compound Sarah turned to the girls.

"I love you girls. I hope you will remember me kindly."

They wanted to rush to her, to kiss her, to embrace her, but the soldiers barred their way with the guns.

"Don't forget the dress, Miriam," Sarah said as she was led through the gate of her home and into the compound. She pointed to latticed portico entrance to Aaron's house. One of the soldiers opened the door and closed it after Sarah and the other soldier entered. She led the soldier through the house to the rear bedroom. She gestured to the soldier to release her from her handcuffs and chains before closing and locking the door for her privacy.

Sarah picked up a piece of paper and a pen from the desk by the bed and began to compose her thoughts to paper;

'Give the families of Reuven, Menashe, Nisan, and Yehuda, 105 francs each. Give Abu Farid, or his family if he does not survive, 105 francs. We do not know the fate of our Arab workers. Let them share from the food store at Atlit, and give them 30 francs a month until they find work.

From what I heard, we were betrayed by women of the village.

I do not believe we shall survive having been betrayed. Tell them about our sacrifice and make them understand why we did it. The news of victory will come and let them know that Sarah willingly spilled her blood to drive our accursed and cruel enemy out of our land.'

She rubbed her bleeding tortured fingers before continuing.

'They said they will take me for more depravity to Damascus. They will beat me and then hang me. Believe me that I have no more strength to endure. I prefer to end it here rather than let them torture me again with their bloodstained hands. I will not allow them to force our secrets out of me.'

She read through the letter. The page had become smeared with her own bloodstained hands. Then she wrote;

'I am sorry to have seen my father and my friends suffer as they have. I love them dearly.

They tried all their tortures on us but we did not speak. Remember us not as traitors but as heroes, for we served our people and kept our silence.

Those that judged us badly will be judged. We have died as brave warriors and did not surrender. Let the wicked gossipers, Pearl and Gita, know the truth, I know we have paved the way for the defeat of our enemy and the hope of a better future.

I have striven for my people and, if this is my fate, so be it.'.

Sarah's thoughts were interrupted by a loud banging on the door and the soldier shouting, "What are you doing I there. Come out immediately!"

She hastily scribbled, *'They have come. I can write no more.'*

"Just a minute," she shouted. She folded the paper and put it in the pocket of her dress. She patted it as she hobbled over to the door. Instead of opening it she pressed a wooden panel in the doorframe. It lifted to reveal a crevice. It was one of Aaron's carefully crafted hiding places. She reached inside and extracted a short barreled pistol, one that Aaron had hidden away from the Turks before he had left for England.

Sarah walked into the bathroom. She hesitated. The soldier hammered against the door. He was trying the door handle. Sarah placed the gun into her mouth with trembling hands. She heard the soldier try to burst open the door, calling for his comrade as he did so. She pressed the trigger.

The soldiers smashed the door and ran into the bathroom. They found Sarah lying on the floor. Blood was oozing out of her mouth. One of the soldiers ran out of the house. He called to Sarah's friends who were standing on the other side of the road.

"Fetch a doctor!" he shouted at them. The girls reacted with shock. They were rooted to the spot.

"Go get a doctor! Fast!" The girls looked at each other, then Miriam began to run down the street. The other tried to enter the house but the soldier kept them outside.

"What happened?" they cried. The soldier refused to answer.

"Where is Sarah? What have you done to her?" Panic was beginning to take over the scene. Others began to assemble on the street. A couple said they had heard a gunshot. Others wanted to know what had happened.

After twenty minutes Miriam returned with Doctor Joffe.

As the soldiers admitted the doctor into the house, Miriam boldly accompanied him. She screamed as they reached the bathroom. Sarah was lying unconscious on the floor. Her blood was oozing onto the tiles. Miriam stood aside as the doctor examined Sarah. Her pulse was faint. He searched in his medical bag and brought out a syringe. He inserted a caffeine solution into the syringe and inserted it into Sarah's arm. They waited. The doctor looked anxiously at Miriam who was handling the situation with a rare maturity.

"You'll make a good nurse," he said to her.

"Will she live?"

"Too early to say." The doctor did not want to give her his dire prognosis. He knew this was a desperately bad case. "Run and tell my nurse to come here immediately."

While Miriam went to bring the nurse Sarah regained consciousness with a groan. She opened her eyes, saw the soldiers peering over her and the doctor, who she recognized.

In a fearful voice she painfully croaked, "Doctor Joffe, for God's sake, end my life."

The doctor held her hand and tutted. "Don't fret, Sarah. Relax."

"No. doctor. I beg of you," she gasped as blood seeped from her lips, "kill me. Allow me to die."

"Ssshhh! Let me examine you. Can you move your arms?"

He waited for a response there was none. "Come, Sarah try to move you left arm." There was no response. "Your right arm?" Nothing. "Let me try your legs. Try moving your left leg, Sarah." He felt her leg. There was no response. Sarah simply groaned. "Now your right leg. Try lifting it." There was no reaction. Doctor Joffe asked the two soldiers to help him lift Sarah off the floor.

"Gently now!" They slowly moved her inert body to the bed. Sarah was unconscious by the time they rested her on top of the bedsheets.

Miriam arrived with the nurse.

"Sarah is paralyzed," the doctor said to the nurse. "She shot herself in the mouth and the bullet has lodged in her spine. The best we can do is try to stabilize her and get her to a hospital."

"Oh my God," cried Miriam. "Will she live?" she repeated.

"It's touch and go. I can only administer painkillers and try to revive her with occasional injections. Nurse, take her temperature. Make sure she doesn't choke on her blood. She had internal bleeding."

A groan came from Sarah's throat. Her head moved ever so slightly. She half opened her eyes. "Doctor Joffe, please let me die." The doctor shook his head. Sarah struggled to mouth the words, "You don't understand. I cannot let them know what I know." Doctor Joffe understood. As he examined her injuries he could see she had been tortured by Ahmed Bek. She was scared of blurting out names in a fit of delirium. "They tortured me," Sarah gurgled painfully from her damaged throat. "I told them nothing. They must not know. For the sake of the others, help me. Please!" she pleaded, the effort of talking exhausting what little strength she had.

Doctor Joffe knew he had been put in a professional quandary. He was unable to give her a clear answer. His code required him to save her life, whatever was left of it. Yet, he knew some of the people who may become victim to a similar fate should Sarah begin to rant in a fit of semi-consciousness. He held her hand. "Sarah, Don't worry. Either I will be here or a nurse. We will take care of you. Now rest."

Sarah's head was still but she moved her eyes to her friend.

"Miriam!"

"Yes, Sarah."

"My dress. Pocket. Take it."

Miriam searched in Sarah's clothes, found the pocket and took out the piece of paper. Sarah tried a painful smile.

"Keep it until you can give it to someone from my work."

Miriam nodded. "I love you Sarah."

Sarah soundlessly mouthed the words, "I love you, Miriam." Then she closed her eyes.

The nurse sat at Sarah's bedside through the night. The doctor demanded to see Ahmed Bek. In the privacy of their meeting, he lambasted the policeman for causing Sarah's condition.

"I am not responsible for this woman shooting herself," Bek protested.

"I saw her other injuries. Any person would choose to end their life rather than undergo such inhumane treatment. Any person, Officer Bek, let alone a young woman."

"She is a traitor and a spy."

"Then put her on trial, if you have the evidence. Put the others on trial if you can prove their guilt. But what have you gained by the torture you inflicted on that poor defenseless girl? You should be ashamed of yourself. She is now crippled and not likely to survive her injuries. I demand that you remove the guard on her home and let her rest in peace. I demand that you reconsider the way you treat the people of my village. Good day to you, officer Bek."

Ahmed Bek reported Sarah's injuries to his superiors. The following day an ambulance arrived at the Aaronsohn home. A Turkish army doctor and two nurses came from Nazareth. They examined Sarah in the presence of Doctor Joffe.

The local nurse reported to them that Sarah's temperature had been erratic throughout the night and that she had suffered bouts of delirium. A physical examination showed that she had a slight movement in one of her feet, but she was completely paralyzed in both her arms and her left leg. The army surgeon wanted to take her in the ambulance for hospital care in

Nazareth but, after a discussion with Doctor Joffe, they decided to keep her in her own bed until she became more stabilized. They both knew professionally that Sarah's condition was still extremely critical.

As they spoke together, Sarah cried out. She had an expression of panic on her distressed face. "Please, let me die. Let me die!"

"Don't worry, Sarah. Ahmed Bek and the military will not subject you to torture again," said Doctor Joffe. The army doctor nodded in agreement.

"You don't understand. I must die!" Sarah protested.

Joffe told the Turkish doctor this was part of her delirium. He preferred to keep the army surgeon uninformed of what she had said and what she meant. The Nazareth surgeon gave Joffe a supply of morphine injections for Sarah. He also ordered the two nurses to remain and assist Joffe administer the patient until she would be able to be transferred for hospital treatment.

Throughout the day, Sarah's friends stopped by. Most of the time Sarah was unaware of their presence. Some prayed by her bedside as she lay in a world of pain, anguish, and unconsciousness. Sarah had rare moments of lucidity. She received her visitors with silent grace, preferring to keep her agonized speech limited to those she knew and trusted. Even with these people she said nothing about those she was protecting, only giving evidence, in few words, to the immense cruelty of Ahmed Bek and his henchmen. She asked her close friends to stay by her and make sure she did not divulge anything that would endanger others. They agreed that one of them would always be with her, day and night, to protect her and administer any help she needed.

On the third day, she asked her friends if she had been hallucinating. They told her she had said nothing that could harm anyone. Her temperature had been very high, and Miriam told her that the doctor had been brought to visit her three times in the night. Sarah croakingly told them that she felt she was losing her mind. She told them, repeatedly, that she wanted to die. They held her hands and cried.

Despite the injections, despite the efforts of Doctor Joffe and the nurses, by the fourth day Sarah's condition worsened. She was weak, terribly weak. She could barely speak. She asked to say goodbye to her father. She was told that her father was not at home. She asked everyone who came to see her to look after her papa. She told her friends, "I am dying. Please make sure I do not say anything that will be bad for our friends." In a moment of lucidity, she asked Doctor Joffe to plead with Ahmed Bek to release her father.

As evening approached, Doctor Joffe told Sarah's friends to wait outside the house. He, and the two nurses from Nazareth, watched over Sarah as she lost touch with them for the final time.

She lapsed into a troubled sleep and, at eight thirty in the evening, Sarah surrendered her soul peacefully, having protected the secrets of her loyal friends.

SARAH'S LAST JOURNEY

That night, Ahmed Bek received a delegation of the village committee. They requested that he lift his curfew and allow them to take Sarah's body, according to tradition, to her final resting place in their cemetery in the morning. With some reluctance he agreed.

A large crowd gathered on the road outside the Aaronsohn home. Young men and women who operated the research stations, those that had not been arrested and tortured, risked penalty and arrest to accompany their beloved Sarah on her last journey. They were joined by many of the Arab workers and fellahin from the surrounding villages who came to pay their last respects to the woman they had known and considered their friend. Even the villagers who had threatened and taunted her were there, standing silently, perhaps guiltily, in the background.

Sarah's body was carried out of the family house. She was wrapped in a thin shroud made from the mosquito meshing around her bed. They carried Sarah's body to her final resting place under gray somber skies. Her immediate family were missing. They were abroad, unaware of her death. Her beloved papa was on his way to a Damascus jail.

She was borne on her last journey by the young men who loved her, those that were not on the run or captured. The cortege made its way slowly up the incline of Founder's Street and through the stone archway that marked the exit of the little town. Just beyond and to the right was the town's cemetery. They were escorted by a guard of Turkish soldiers.

The procession entered the cemetery led by a rabbi who chanted prayers to God to welcome Sarah's soul into His protective care. They brought Sarah to lie next to her mother. Sarah's grave had not been dug. Turkish restrictions had not allowed them to prepare her grave in advance of receiving her body. It took over an hour for the grave diggers to cut through the rocky ground.

Someone muttered that this precious earth was reluctant to receive the body of so young and precious a soul.

As they dug, the grey skies opened and it began to rain. It was as if the angels were weeping over Sarah's painful exit from her life on earth. Perhaps some of the tears from heaven fell from the eyes of those who perished in Spain, and in the pogroms. Perhaps the Armenians, and even Sarah's girlhood heroine, Joan of Arc, wept in solidarity with Sarah.

As the large drops of rain fell on the assembled crowd, and on Sarah's shroud, her face emerged through the sodden and transparent linen. People stared at her. She looked serene. Some said she was almost smiling. Everyone remarked how beautiful she looked as they lowered her body into the earth she so loved.

The earth to which she had dedicated her life now enveloped her as the men she loved solemnly shoveled the soil over her shattered body. Some wept.

As they laid her to rest, the first heavy rains of winter began to pour down on the mournful crowd. Rain that would eventually help wash away the pain, though not the memory, of all those present. Rain that would replenish the earth and give them sustenance for a better future.

EPILOGUE ONE – AARON

Aaron did not hear of the fate of his beloved sister until three months after her death when he was in America on a mission for the Zionist Organization. He was stoic as he received the news but, after weeping in the privacy of his hotel room, he wrote in his diary,

"The sacrifice has been made. The heroism of Sarah and how she rose above such great difficulties is almost impossible to bear. It is impossible to know where she found the courage, or to imagine how much she suffered. I shudder when I attempt to think how you took the responsibility and the sacrifice on your shoulders - alone. Such bravery. Such dignity. I am proud of you, Sarita."

EPILOGUE TWO - EPHRAIM

Ephraim was taken to a Damascus jail where further torture and sentencing was imposed on the Jews of Palestine who had resisted the oppressive reign of the Young Turks.

Unlike the other prisoners, Ephraim was not harmed, although he had to endure the suffering of Sarah's friends. It took a year before he was released and returned home. The men had been transported to Syria before learning about Sarah's fate. They had been kept isolated from the outside world behind the cruel walls of a Turkish prison. As he limped into Zichron Yaakov he was told, for the first time, of Sarah's sacrifice.

Rather than enter his house, he slowly walked up the street to the cemetery. He stopped at the white marble slab that carried one word – Sarah. She lay alongside the grave if her mother, Ephraim's departed wife.

Ephraim painfully sat on the ground by the two graves and did something he hadn't done for many years. He cried.

EPILOGUE THREE – JOSEPH

Joseph Lishansky was on the run. He decided to head north. He walked by night and hid by day. When he reached the homes of people he knew and trusted, he begged shelter and food. A few protected him for a short while, then asked him to leave. Others slammed the door in his face.

As he walked by the side of a road one dark evening he heard a carriage approaching. He hid beside some bushes as it slowly went by. He peered at the two men driving the carriage and recognized them as being two of his former comrades from the HaShomer group. He rushed out of the dark shadows and ran alongside the carriage. The men reined in the horses when they realized the stranger in the night was Lishansky.

"For God's sake, give me a ride north," begged Joseph.

They looked at each other and told him to climb into the carriage. They knew there was a reward for his recapture. When they reached the farm settlement of Tel Adashim, they offered him a room and a change of clothing. They told him they were going to deliver the contents of their wagon and would return to prepare a meal for him. They reported their find to their superiors who insisted they get him away from Tel Adashim as soon as possible. They wanted no connection with Lishansky, they said, as this would bring the Turks down on their heads.

The two HaShomer members returned to Lishansky's room and told him they had to continue north that night as it was not safe to stay where they were. As they rode, Lishansky was told they were heading to Metulla near the border with Lebanon. Before reaching Metulla, they were intercepted by two riders. In their conversation, Lishansky understood that these were outriders from the HaShomer group who had been instructed to meet up with the men escorting Lishansky. As the men discussed what to do with

Lishansky, Joseph wandered over to a spot that overlooked a steep ravine. As he peered down into the abyss a shot rang out. Lishansky felt a searing pain in his shoulder. The impact forced him to fall into the ravine. He rolled and bounced into the pit. Although in pain, he pretended to be dead as he saw the three men peer down into the dark ravine at him. He closed his eyes waiting for the next bullet. Instead, he listened to them talk about reporting his death to the Turks and bringing them to Lishansky's body. Joseph heard one of them say they should say they had killed Lishansky and wanted to claim the reward being offered for bringing him to the Turks, dead or alive.

Joseph waited motionless for some time to make sure they had gone before painfully finding his feet. He staggered his way through the wadi of the ravine and away from the scene. Fortunately, the upper Galilee close to the Lebanese border was thick with bush and shrub. Once he had distanced himself from the scene of his shooting, he found a hollow to hide until the following evening. He headed east and spent a couple of days cautiously transiting over to a family member's home in a small farming settlement to the west of the Sea of Galilee. The family was disturbed by his desperate knocking on their door around midnight. They were surprised and scared to find a wounded Joseph. They allowed him in and dressed his wound.

"Joseph. You need a doctor or a hospital," they told him.

"No matter," he replied. "I have to get to safety. I will try to get to Atlit and see if the navy will somehow come by. They said they would come. I don't know if they will," he rambled. "If not, I will head south and try and reach the British."

"Joseph. There is a manhunt out for you, and not only by the Turks."

"I know that. Can you take me over the Carmel range so that I can get close to Atlit?"

"Joseph. We love you, but we cannot do that. It will be too dangerous for us. You can take one of our horses, if you are able to ride."

"Thank you," Joseph said in pain. "I will do that. I don't want to get you into any trouble."

"Here. Take this food with you and a fresh dressing for your wound. Come, let me get the horse saddled up so you can get away while it is still dark."

Instead of heading to Atlit, Joseph struck south to Petah Tikva to the home of Pascal Peretz who he had met when in Cairo with Sarah and Aaron. Pascal had been deported to Egypt by the Turks, but his wife and two daughters remained to maintain their family assets until he would be allowed to return. Days later, when Pascal's wife, Miriam, saw Joseph's condition, they bathed his injury, fed him, and took him to the outhouse to sleep. Joseph was so exhausted and weak that he slept through the night and through the next day. They fed him again that evening but, when they walked him into the main house, he noticed that his horse was missing.

"Miriam. I have to go. Somebody has stolen my horse, or maybe they reported it to the Turks. I don't want to cause you any danger, you and your daughters. I had better leave tonight. Tell nobody that I was here."

Joseph walked by night and hid by day. Gradually, he worked his way down beyond the Jewish towns and settlements and into Bedouin territory. He knew it would take far too long, and he would be exposed if he walked south across a desert, barren, landscape. He spotted a Bedouin encampment in the distance. He saw they had a herd of camels. He hunkered down in a wadi and waited for night to fall. In the dark of evening he slowly approached the camp, stopping ever few strides to listen out for movement, or a dog's bark. He didn't want to risk being found because of a dog's warning, but no noise greeted his approach. He slowly untied one of the camels and gradually made off into the darkness and the desert before mounting it and trotting south.

His camel theft had been spotted by a young boy who, unseen by Joseph, had been sleeping under the stars between the camp and the camels. Joseph's activity had disturbed him. The boy has been too frightened to move as Joseph made off with the camel, but he ran into his father's tent after Joseph had left. The father woke the sheikh and, together with three other men, rode off in pursuit. They soon reached Lishansky as dawn broke. Joseph knew that escape was impossible. As before, with his travail with Avshalom, and with Naaman's failed journey, he was so near, and yet so far, from safety.

Once again, his misfortune was a Bedouin reward. The Turks couldn't be bothered torturing him in Palestine. It brought them enough glory to know they had captured the infamous Joseph Lishansky. Let the higher authorities in Damascus deal with him. Joseph was transported under heavy armed guard all the way to the Khan al Basha prison in the Syrian capital.

The authorities did not need to torture Joseph. They had rolled back the NILI spy ring. They had enough evidence to sentence and convict him. Even if the evidence would not stand in a proper court of law it was sufficient to satisfy a Turkish court who needed to show their public, and send a message to their subjects in Palestine, that they meant business.

Joseph was thrown into a cell. He found his cellmate was Naaman Belkind. Naaman had endured a rough time. The Turks had taken out their anger on him. This showed on his swollen face and broken fingers.

"I didn't expose Sarah," insisted Naaman. "I didn't."

"Is she not here?" asked Joseph.

"No," answered Naaman.

"Then where is she?"

This was a mystery they would take to their graves.

There was a mass sentencing. It was as if the Turks wanted to get the trials over as quickly as possible. After all, they had a war to fight.

Naaman Belkind and Joseph Lishansky were sentenced to be executed.

Eitan, who was in another cell, tried to bribe the guard to allow him to say goodbye to his brother, but the guard was too frightened to permit it, despite the fact that he could have done with the money.

Eitan banged on the door of his cell but to no avail. Early the next morning, he heard a disturbance of clanging doors and voices. He rushed to the grill of his iron cell door. Naaman was being escorted along the corridor. He begged his guards to allow him one minute outside his brother's cell. He tried to reach Eitan's small window to kiss his brother but the guards prevented any physical contact.

Naaman smiled at Eitan. "I'm glad it's me and not you who is going to the gallows, Eitan."

"I love you brother." The brave Eitan was crying.

"Give my love to our family. Tell them I died bravely. If it's possible, try to bring my remains home to Rishon. Bye, brother!"

"Bye, Naaman. I love you, brother."

Then Naaman was gone.

Moments later, the opening of another cell door. The sound of chains and voices heralded the last march of Joseph Lishansky.

As he was being escorted to his execution Joseph shouted, "Goodbye, my friends. Know that I died bravely for our people, for our beloved homeland."

From every cell, the prisoners clapped, banged on their cell doors, and made as much noise as they could to give Joseph the courage to meet his end.

The execution was in the public square not far from the prison. Hand written notices of who they were and their crimes of treachery were hung around their necks as they were paraded through jeering crowds. They had to wait by the corner of the square as the finishing touches were being put to the gallows of their execution. Joseph mocked the crowd and their executioners.

"See," he shouted. "You can't even put up gallows in time. You people are lost. You are doomed."

In Arabic, he shouted to the crowd. "We are not traitors. How is it possible to be a traitor to the ones you love? A lover can never betray the one he truly loves. But he can never love the homeland of his torturers, the homeland of his executioners. We hate those who torture and kill our loved ones. We have not betrayed our people, or those butchered by you. You may kill us today, but we have been digging your grave. Now others are coming to liberate our land. While you are preparing to hang us, your gallows are being built. Prepare to lose your empire for the world hates you. It is we who will inherit our ancient homeland."

Naaman joined Joseph as they were led up the wooden steps to the platform. He shouted, "Our deaths cannot prevent our victory. We go to a better place, faithful to our people. You are doomed."

The only other person to die was Reuven Schwartz. He had endured repeated and cruel torture. He didn't know who had given the Turks the information that, as a neighbor to Sarah and a close friend and partner, he was one of the top NILI leaders, but they went after him with a vengeance.

When they threw his shattered body into his cell one evening he could not face another day of pain-racked abuse. In the night, he made a hangman's noose from a torn bedsheet, tied one end to the iron bars of his cell window and hanged himself.

Tova was sentenced to six months' imprisonment. Moshe Neuman, Yizchak Halperin, Yehuda Zeldin, Menashe Bronstein, received prison sentences of twelve months each. Tova's fiancée, Nissan Rutman was sentenced to two years in jail. Despite his family connection, Naaman's brother, Eitan, escaped with only a twelve months' sentence due to his youth.

EPILOGUE FOUR - AVSHALOM

During the Six Day War, the Israeli army was chasing the invading Egyptian army back across the Sinai Peninsula toward the Suez Canal. An Israeli army unit camped out in the desert for the night by a Bedouin encampment. The officers were invited to drink coffee by the chief of this desert Bedouin tribe.

As they sat cordially chatting about life in the desert around a fire that kept the fin Jan hot, the mukhtar told them of a palm tree near their encampment which he called 'the Jew's tree.' The officers were intrigued. The sheikh spoke of two Turkish officers who had sat where they were sitting during the previous great war, fifty years earlier, when a member of his tribe rode in to report seeing two foreigners dressed as Bedouin riding through the desert. The Turks went in pursuit of the foreigners and came across them not far from the camp. There was an exchange of gunfire and one of the strangers fell dead. The other managed to flee. The tribal chief told the Israeli soldiers that the Turks had told him that they reckoned the men had been Jewish spies. They ordered him to bury the body in the desert.

Years later, a strange thing happened. A palm tree began to grow out of the ground exactly where they had buried the Jew. The inquisitive Israeli soldiers asked the chief to take them to see this mysterious tree in the morning's first light.

In early dawn, before the sun rose, the chief sent two of his sons to ride in their armored car through the desert to what he called '*kabir yahud*,' the Jew's grave. They drove across the flatland, around a couple of sand hills and through a small wadi until, out of the arid barrenness of the Sinai Desert, their vehicle approached a sprouting palm tree surrounded by a cactus field. They scratched their heads as they walked around the tree. One of the officers took a couple of pictures for posterity. Another suggested that the tale of a dead Jew was a desert fantasy, a fata morgana, with no substance. One of the officers joked they were looking at a mirage. The tree was real, but the story was hokum, said another cynically, but one soldier, Shlomo Ben Elkana, suggested that it could be the burial place of Avshalom Feinberg. Elkana, a police detective when he wasn't in army uniform, had heard the tales of the NILI spies, once led by a man called Feinberg who had disappeared, reportedly killed, in the desert.

The war ended with the Israeli army on the Egyptian side of the Suez Canal.

Detective Shlomo Ben Elkana was a man with an exceptional sense of curiosity. After the war, he researched the history of Avshalom Feinberg. He met Feinberg's family, including his aging sister, Tzila.

With Tzila's approval and with a special permit from the IDF, Shlomo Ben Elkana ventured back into the desert in search of the elderly chief called Youssef Abu Safra of the Rameilt tribe. He was accompanied by two pathologists from the Israeli police force. He was well received by the old man who remembered him. With the sheikh's help, he returned to the tree. It stood tall in a clearing beyond a cactus field. They dug around the roots of the wild palm tree until they came across a skeleton. It could be anybody. They needed forensics to identify the remains and someone to verify the DNA. Avshalom's sister, Tzila, was thrilled by the potential discovery of her long lost brother. They carefully exhumed the bones and transported the remains back to the police laboratory for forensic examination.

The skeleton was given as the same height of Avshalom. The hand of the skeleton had a broken finger. The same finger, Tzila told them, that had been fractured on Avshalom's hand by the discharge of a rifle in his youth. The skeleton had a broken tooth. The same one that Tzila claimed had been chipped by Avshalom as he crunched one day on a nut shell. The gap

343

between the skeleton's front teeth were identical to that of Avshalom's sister. The body that lay in the desert for fifty years was that of Sarah's Avsha. But why under a palm tree?

The last item that Sarah had given her beloved Avshalom, before their final kiss, was a bag of dates, the dates that he had sworn not to eat until he got to Egypt.

The dates lay in Avsha's coat pocket, close to his heart, for decades, slowly fertilized as his decomposing body fed and gave life to the seeds, until they sprouted from the dry desert earth as a green palm tree reaching up to the heavens as the green palms of Atlit had done so long ago when they were so much in love.

Made in the USA
Middletown, DE
08 November 2022

14398082R10195